Series

Paranormal

Moons of Mystery
Sara's Moon (MF)
Charline's Solstice (MF)
Diana's Eclipse (MF)

War on Darkness
Darkness Defined (MM)
Order of Light (MM)
Knights of Nyx (MM)

Kisin Novels
Courting Death (MM)
Death, Love, & Tacos (MM)

True Mates
Truth in Exile (MM)
The Inescapable Truth (MM)
Truth in Lies (MM)

Lycan Detective Duet
Hart's Betrayal (MM)
Hart's Redemption (MM)

Contemporary

Ulwich Preparatory Academy
Our Last Fall (MM)
Our Secret Winter (MM)
Our Epic Spring (MM)

Oak Haven Romance
One Brave Thing (Enby/M)
All the Hype (MM)
The Bright Side (MM)

Hart's Betrayal

S Bolanos

Chaotic Neutral Press LLC

Copyright © 2026 by Chaotic Neutral Press LLC

All rights reserved.

No part of this publication may be reproduced, distributed, or transmitted in any form or by any means, including photocopying, recording, or other electronic or mechanical methods, without the prior written permission of the publisher, except as permitted by U.S. copyright law. For permission requests, email contact@sbolanos.com.

NO AI TRAINING: Without in any way limiting the author's [and publisher's] exclusive rights under copyright, any use of this publication to "train" generative artificial intelligence (AI) technologies to generate text is expressly prohibited.

The story, all names, characters, and incidents portrayed in this production are fictitious. No identification with actual persons (living or deceased), places, buildings, and products is intended or should be inferred.

Cover Design by Yellow Butterfly Editing and Design Services

Contents

Chapter 1	1
Chapter 2	8
Chapter 3	21
Chapter 4	28
Chapter 5	34
Chapter 6	43
Chapter 7	54
Chapter 8	67
Chapter 9	81
Chapter 10	90
Chapter 11	102
Chapter 12	110
Chapter 13	122
Chapter 14	133

Chapter 15	144
Chapter 16	154
Chapter 17	168
Chapter 18	182
Chapter 19	190
Chapter 20	197
Chapter 21	211
Chapter 22	224
Chapter 23	232
Chapter 24	243
Chapter 25	259
Chapter 26	268
Chapter 27	280
Chapter 28	290
Chapter 29	301
Chapter 30	309
Chapter 31	318
Chapter 32	327
Chapter 33	337
Chapter 34	347
Chapter 35	358

Chapter 36	366
Chapter 37	375
Chapter 38	386
Chapter 39	398
Chapter 40	406
Chapter 41	415
About the Author	425

Chapter 1

Joshua

Oil disaster averted by water demons in coordination with the North-Western Coven.

Coalition of Supernaturals and United Federation of Humans sign latest treaty regarding...

I FLIPPED THE CHANNEL from the national news, unwilling to hear so much as another syllable about the damned CoS. The godforsaken organization had developed ten years after hundreds of Shadow Demons lost to time had spilled back into reality, a reality that had moved on without them. Thirty years later, all supernaturals were out and proud... and threatening the status quo. Humans were no longer the apex predators, but who knew how long it would take for them to actually figure that out.

> In local news, a lycanthrope from the Klamath pack saves a child from drowning.

"Atlas, turn off the news," I growled out in barely intelligible words. The AI promptly complied, plunging the room into silence. I unclenched my teeth before I ground them all the way down. "Atlas, play playlist Delta." A bing registered the command, then music filled the space. The nearly too loud alternative punk rock song had an edge to it that reflected how I felt perfectly. I rolled my shoulders and tried to let go of the sudden tension that had taken hold of me.

Some days it really was too much. How humans could glorify monsters like vampires and demons was beyond me, and their idolization of lycans bordered on hero worship. I still remembered when regular mortals had flocked to the creatures with the sole goal of becoming one of them. A snicker escaped me as I recalled the panic that had ensued when the desperate supplicants had promptly realized that being bitten wasn't a guarantee of turning. Sure, some of them got their wish, but countless others had died horrific deaths before they even saw their first full moon. That had certainly stemmed the tide of volunteers.

There was a small beep in my ear, signaling an incoming call. I pressed my middle finger into the heel of my left palm, just under my thumb, to accept it.

"Hart speaking."

"Good, you're awake," a harsh and demanding feminine voice said in lieu of an actual greeting.

"Good morning to you too, mother," I replied as I made a throwing gesture at the wall with the same hand I'd answered the missive. Instantly, it converted to a video call.

"Don't patronize me, Joshua."

The woman who stared back at me had long dark hair, not unlike mine. But where she pulled hers into a severe bun, I kept mine cropped close at the sides and only a little longer up top. That's where the similarity ended. I couldn't imagine anyone ever considering the prickly woman beautiful. Sharp cheekbones and hollow cheeks framed a long, straight nose that resembled a bird of prey's beak. Her brown eyes were as cold and calculating as they had been my entire life. She looked significantly older than her fifty-eight years would suggest. Not something she would ever admit, though a natural toll in our family business. That she'd lived long enough to berate me for my attitude was surprising.

Only years of keeping a straight face prevented me from rolling my eyes. "Was there something you needed?" I asked blithely.

Her lips pursed, betraying just how fed up she was with the interaction already. We rarely spoke at length, often with substantial intervals in between. An arrangement I preferred, and I was positive she did as well.

"Are you ready?" At the curt question, the eye roll I'd restrained slipped free. "Joshua Har—"

"This is my job. Remember, Mother? This is also not my first mission."

"We can't afford to mess this up. The community is on the brink of acceptance. You know what that could mean."

I consciously had to unclench my teeth. "Who's patronizing now? I know what I'm doing. I've only trained my whole life. Does my track record mean nothing to you?" I added without hope of an answer. I knew it didn't.

Her lips pursed once more, and the muscle lining her jaw ticked. I wasn't the only one who ground their teeth when they got pissed. "I brought you into this world, and I can take you out."

I raised an eyebrow at the familiar threat. "I know what to do."

The video suddenly blipped out of existence without so much as a half-hearted farewell or good luck, not that I expected one. Some things never change.

I shook my head and finished packing my bag, careful of the box that rested at the bottom of my luggage. The bronze plate gleamed up at me arrogantly proclaiming our family name. I quickly covered it with several layers of clothing and activated an aversion spell to make sure portal security didn't look too closely or develop an interest in the simple box or its contents. The days of proudly displaying our heritage were long gone.

I checked myself in the mirror before leaving the room, finding my father's hunter green eyes staring back at me. Eyes my mother resented. There was no honor in what we did, only necessity.

Elijah

I uncrossed my ankles, but kept my feet propped on the table in front of me and tried to contain my groan. This meeting would never end. My lip curled as I glanced over at the whelp sitting three chairs down. It was because of him that this whole meeting was being held. A sixteen-year-old had no business interfering in pack politics. Of course, at thirty, neither did I. This whole council was a joke and shouldn't exist at all. Democracy had no place in lycan society, yet here we were, all thanks to the Coalition of Supernaturals.

"It's a good idea. The pack needs better press. We can't continue to hold ourselves off from humanity," the youth insisted. The poor pup tried to hide the telling crack in his voice.

I shook my head. A late bloomer whose voice still hadn't settled. This is what we've been reduced to. Children, where there should only have been the Alpha and Beta. Maybe a handful of elders, I mentally added. Some changes could be good. Contrary to what I thought of this ridiculous council, I believed lycan society desperately needed change. Just not the change humans were determined to foist on us.

Conrad, the supposed Alpha of our modest pack, fumed at the interruption. "Sit your tail down, Kale. Or so help me..."

My gaze darted between our Alpha and the scrap who'd been bold enough to interrupt him. Only now, the blood was draining from the youth's face. This council may exist because of the CoS, but that didn't change the sway a real Alpha had. A sway that Conrad was in danger of losing at this rate.

Once we'd been a proud pack–the Portland Pack. Twenty years ago, our borders had stretched across Oregon into southern Washington and as far south as Eureka, California. Now, our territory comprised a mere fifty acres in Klamath County, Oregon, and existed at the whims of our human counterparts.

Much as I hated to admit it, the old days were gone. They hadn't been perfect by any stretch, but they'd certainly been simpler. Kale was right; we couldn't hide forever. No one could. Not since the demons had shown up and ruined everything. Unsurprisingly, humans had panicked, though it was nothing compared to the panic that had engulfed the supernatural world. A panic that had only gotten worse once the human governments got involved. Our particular pack had opted to keep to themselves in isolation. That decision–Conrad's decision–was now coming back to bite our tails. Ingratiating ourselves with the humans we'd scorned wouldn't be a simple task, and Conrad was only making it harder.

I shifted in my seat and wondered if my tail would be as numb as my ass even after I changed.

Kale's gaze darted around the table for support he wasn't likely to find.

The groan I'd been holding back finally escaped. I dropped my feet to the ground and sat forward. "He's right, Conrad."

Several pairs of surprised eyes turned to face me.

"Is that so, Elijah?" Nikolai, our Beta and an immigrant from a Russian pack nearly fifty years ago, asked with an obvious edge to the question.

I sighed, but didn't back down. "We can either choose to participate in the world outside pack territory or be made to. Either way, isolationism is off the table. Which would you rather have?"

Nikolai's eyes narrowed, and Conrad looked as though he was trying to strangle me with his gaze alone. "Humans do not dictate the pack," Conrad said in a flat tone.

I barely held back a bark of laughter. He couldn't be serious. What would it take for him to realize the old ways were gone?

Kale chose that moment back in. "See, even Red agrees."

I shot him a glare that I was sure a few others saw. Sadly, not him.

"This is not a debate," Conrad began.

"Except it is," I cut him off.

His angry glare switched back to me in a heartbeat.

Great, now I'm doing stupid shit too.

"The CoS has left us alone for the most part, but that won't last. With packs like Stone Lake and Yosemite integrating with humans without being asked, others have followed their lead. Hell, even Texas is friendlier than we are."

Conrad's bitter expression turned into a scowl. No one had forgotten the chaos that had befallen Texas a hundred years ago or the precedent they'd set. Now they were one of the strongest collections of packs out there, certainly in the States.

"And you think this... this..." He stumbled over the unusual word.

"Bacchanal," I supplied before Kale could speak up and finally get himself killed.

"That." Conrad waved his hand. "Even *you* must admit the concept is ludicrous."

"Oh, I don't know," I began as I looked around at the host of lycans around the table. Everything from elders to young pups like Kale was in attendance. While our views differed greatly, there was one thing in all their eyes—fear. "I think all of us could benefit from a night of drunken revelry."

A smile bloomed on Kale's face, and I had to check my own. Goddess knew I needed a night to let loose.

"It will give our curious neighbors a safe way to get to know us and us them. Change is painful, we all know that." Nods of agreement rippled around the odd collection of tables and chairs. "But from change, we are stronger," I finished.

The scowl on Conrad's face deepened, but he didn't argue. Instead, he turned back to the group at large and asked, "How do we pull off this hair-brained scheme?"

I finally let my smile loose. "May I make a suggestion?"

Chapter 2

Joshua

I COULD KISS WHOEVER'S idea it had been to make the Klamath Pack Bacchanal a masque. Now I wouldn't have to sneak onto pack lands, *and* there was a chance I could have some fun for a change. Just not as myself.

The glamour fell into place the moment I finished securing the sleek, black silk mask on my face. In a ripple of magic, my appearance altered. My legs didn't seem quite so long, my hair less dark, my eyes not as green, even my face became more rounded, effectively hiding my identifiable high cheekbones. In fact, everything about me became just a little... less. It wasn't much, but it was enough.

I smiled at reflection, pleased with the subtle transformation. I was still handsome, to be sure, but no one could ever identify me without the mask. Of course, the glamour wasn't the only trick I had up my sleeve. I popped the cork on a tiny vial of subtly orange liquid and drank the contents in one go. Lycanthropes didn't have to *see* you to recognize you. All precautions had to be taken. The unpleasant conversation with my mother came back to mind, spoiling my features. My jaw ticked as my teeth ground together yet again. At this rate, I'd have to see a witch about restoring them.

I quickly did an inventory to make sure I had everything and double-checked the two minuscule syringes spirited up my sleeve. I only needed one, but it never hurt to have a backup. Confident they were secure, I tugged the sleeve straight and swept my hands over the ensemble I'd chosen for the night. A violet button-down that would appear nearly black at night hugged a frame widened by the glamour to disappear into charcoal silk slacks. That, combined with the dark dress shoes, and I barely recognized myself. It wasn't my usual, that was for sure, but it was no less expensive. Even with moderate looks, it should be sure to catch someone's eye.

I flashed myself another wicked smile and patted my hair, though it didn't need it. Besides, it wasn't like anyone could see my real hair, anyway. With that, I made my way out of the room, being sure to secure it by key and spell. Security wards were a dime a dozen, and most establishments offered at least the base model, but the best ones were priceless. This one hadn't come cheap, but as long as it did its job, it'd be worth every penny.

Elijah

Music thumped loudly all around me as I wove through the ever-growing crowd amassing in the warehouse. Aside from the borderline offensive sound, the night was going off without a hitch. Humans, witches, and all other manner of creatures near and far had traveled to take part in the ancient, obscene festival, which really only amounted to an excuse to get drunk and fuck anything in sight. Two things I was personally eager to partake in. It probably shouldn't have surprised me that the humans seemed to feel safer, more comfortable, taking part in the festivities behind the false anonymity of a mask. To each their own.

I walked past a couple grinding on what had become the dance floor and instantly picked out the local baker's scent and one of my packmates. As I strode by them, my packmate, Tommy, winked at me before returning to his dry humping of the baker. I shook my head and couldn't help but wonder how his dance partner's husband would feel about the situation. Suppose it didn't really matter. Humans would use any excuse to break decorum.

Someone bumped into my shoulder as they moved in the opposite direction. I turned and caught a flash of green eyes behind a black mask. My gaze quickly traveled down the man's form, taking in the dark button-down and well-fitting slacks. By the time my eyes made it back to his obscured face, he was wearing a small, devilish grin. He glanced off to the side where the large doors hung open to the wilderness outside and promptly returned his gaze to me.

The wolf inside me uncurled, eagerly taking notice of the hungry look in the man's eyes. A grin spread across my face, feral and intrigued. Thanks to my gray mask, that was pretty much all the man could see. His smile ticked up slightly, then he turned and made his way out of the building, never once looking back. Part of me resented his blatant expectation that I would follow, but the wolf was already salivating and urging me forward.

High above, the gibbous moon shone down, adding light to the revelry below. The pack had carefully scheduled the event outside of both the full and new moon. It was another of the many precautions taken to make sure our human and other supernatural guests felt welcome.

My quarry paused at the edge of the tree line as if waiting for me to catch up. He stood framed against the backdrop of the dark forest, looking wilder than his attire suggested and infinitely out of place. Without the pulsing strobe lights to interfere, I could clearly see that the shirt and pants that I'd mistaken as black inside, were in fact an intriguing shade of purple and a deep gray. I took a step towards him.

"Come here often?" His voice was deeper than I would have expected and felt a tad off, as if it shouldn't match its owner.

"You could say that," I answered honestly. Was it possible that he didn't realize I was one of the pack? Or was he simply playing coy?

His teeth flashed white in the moonlight, and he stepped back into the trees.

I followed without hesitation.

Joshua

While I hadn't intended to snag someone straight off the dance floor, I was hard-pressed to dismiss the lycan now tailing me. We were of a height and seemed to be of an age. The lycan's previously unextraordinary brown eyes now shone a bright amber as they soaked up the minuscule light of the waxing gibbous moon. His green button-down was undoubtedly cotton and affected a more casual effect than my own, an impression further emphasized by how he'd rolled up the sleeves to expose his forearms.

Despite the masks hiding everyone's truth, there had still been a million things that had given him away as what he really was. The way his eyes occasionally gleamed yellow as they caught the light. The confidence with which he strode across the room. The way he tilted his head ever so slightly to pick up each new sound as it came to him. Perhaps most telling was the shocking gray hair that didn't match his apparent youth.

There were, of course, also the muscles so clearly defined beneath his humble shirt, displaying a fitness that would never come from a gym or a modification spell. He was all-natural, and all *were*. Heat coiled in my belly in anticipation as I led him deeper into the woods. This wasn't a chase, though, so I didn't bother attempting stealth or gaining a lead. I wanted him to stay interested. Wanted him next to me. I wanted a lot of things, and at the top of that list was the lycan stepping up to walk beside me.

He veered slightly right, silently slipping between two large hemlocks. Unconcerned about the detour, I followed suit. I'd spent hours memorizing the layout of the pack's territory and was confident I could find my way out wherever he led us.

We walked in silence with only the increasingly distant sound of revelry and the typical sounds of a healthy forest to break the night. Eventually, we stopped at a place that seemed appropriately secluded. I casually strode past him, intent on the thick trunk on the opposite side of the intimate clearing, a move that clearly surprised him. By the time I turned back to face him, I could feel the blood in my veins heating.

I took a steady breath to quiet the gradual roaring in my ears, then cocked my head to the side and drank in the specimen before me. Even in the dappled light that made it through the canopy, he was something to behold.

In my line of work, there were certain expectations, rules that were followed unconditionally. At the top of a very long list of don'ts was "don't get involved with the lycans". Naturally, the first thing I'd done the second I'd had even a modicum of freedom had been to go out and fuck the first wolf I could find. I'd quickly became addicted to the sheer animal passion that a lycan's embrace offered. And now, I was staring at my latest hit.

"What?" he asked, his voice a low timbre that had my insides threatening to turn to jelly.

"Just appreciating the view," I answered leisurely.

His chuckle was practically a growl.

The tight rein I was keeping on my reactions slipped ever so slightly.

Elijah

Everything about the man before me, from the relaxed set of his shoulders to the way he held himself, screamed confidence. I was more than a little intrigued by the easy bravado. Humans weren't typically so bold, and he was undoubtedly human. As far as I could tell, he'd walked out here without telling anyone where he was going or with whom. Which either made him incredibly brave or incredibly stupid. Thus far though, he'd shown no hesitation and seemed perfectly at home in the middle of an unknown forest. It certainly didn't hurt that he was an absolute snack.

"What brings you here?" I couldn't help myself.

That same devilish smile made a reappearance, and my blood rushed south. My breathing came a little faster as I waited for him to answer.

His gaze swept unabashedly up and down my body, leaving an almost uncomfortable burn in its wake. "I imagine the same as you." The response held the faintest note of teasing. Then, his tongue flicked out to taste his bottom lip.

The animal inside surged forward, taking me with it. I wanted to taste too. Despite the sudden rush of movement, he never so much as flinched. I was a mere step away when his words pulled me up short.

"What are you doing?" There was no fear in the question. No alarm. Just mild curiosity.

Who is this guy?

I lifted my gaze from his slightly parted lips to meet his completely unconcerned gaze. The shadows seemed to make his eyes greener. I gave him a crooked half-smile, not fooled by his games. "Don't tell me you're one of those guys who's against kissing." I'd never understood it personally. Kissing was nearly half the fun.

His lips curled up in what could only be a smirk. "Suppose that depends."

"On what?" I asked, taking the bait.

His eyes flashed a challenge. "On if you're any good at it."

It was all the encouragement I needed. Between one blink and another, I closed the remaining distance between us and mashed my mouth down on his. The force of my momentum carried us back a pace until he pressed into the tree at his back. I curled a hand around the back of his neck to keep his mouth where I wanted it and used my other to grip his hip hard enough to bruise.

Rather than yelp in surprise or try to pull away from the sudden ferocity, he surprised me yet again and instantly opened up. I gladly accepted his invitation, groaning into him as he arched against me. At the feel of his excitement pressing into me, I gave a low growl.

He let out a small gasp, and surprisingly strong fingers dug into my forearms. I'd expected him to try pushing me away, anxious at the sound, but he seemed to urge me closer, encouraging me to delve deeper. I happily obliged. My inner wolf and I were of the same mind and desperate to taste every inch of this man who had lured me into the woods like some Pied Piper. But in order to do that, I'd have to get rid of the several obstacles between us.

My hands greedily ventured lower. He thrust his hips forward to aid in my efforts, and he swallowed my resulting groan. Fuck if I'd ever met a human that had acted like this. I tugged his shirt free and made quick work of his buckle. Suddenly, he pulled away just enough to break apart our mouths.

"Easy, cowboy."

"Not a cowboy," I growled, closing my mouth over his in another savage kiss. He was panting by the time I released him.

"Werewolf," he amended, with a wicked gleam in his eye.

It'd been a long time since I'd heard that particular moniker. Thanks to the CoS and their insistence on politically correct labels for everything, the common vernacular had been replaced by the more "accurate" scientific one, whether the rest of us liked it or not. For the record, we didn't. That he'd casually thrown it out as a tease convinced me further that there was something unique about the man currently pinned between me and the tree. It also meant that he knew exactly what I was, which made his behavior all the more remarkable.

"Human," I fired back.

"You sure?" he taunted.

I leaned forward to bury my nose in the side of his neck and inhaled deeply, eager to find traces of what made this incredible man who he was. To my infinite pleasure, he wore no cologne or perfume to mask his scent. However, there also didn't seem to be much of one to be found. If ever a smell could be said to be bland, this was it. The wolf inside was every bit as confused as I was. There was simply no way such a man wouldn't possess equally remarkable nuances to his scent.

Rather than give voice to my alarming discovery, I gave him a different answer. "You don't smell like sulfur, so you can't be a demon."

His low laugh had his chest vibrating against mine.

"Nor a witch."

"What makes you so sure?"

I licked the side of his neck, and he jolted at the contact. "You don't smell like magic," I practically hummed. It was true, albeit a deflection. People with inherent magical abilities had an almost electric scent. It sparkled and felt like getting champagne bubbles up your nose.

"Smells can be deceiving." The husky statement slithered inside of me and snapped what little remained of my restraint.

Instinct took over, and I laid my weight against him, pressing him harder into the tree and claiming his mouth without mercy. He writhed against me, his fingers carding through my hair so they could scratch at my scalp. Every movement sent me closer to the edge I was already teetering on. I needed to touch more of him, to taste all of him. I got as far as his top two buttons before, once again, he stalled me.

It took him two tries to get his words out. "No. C-Clothes stay on," he panted.

Through sheer force of will alone, I held back a frustrated huff. "That's not really how this works," I said between kisses as my hand slipped past the band of his pants to grab his ass.

He let out a guttural groan that instantly had me wanting to see what other sounds I could pull from his lips. As soon as the sound died, he mashed his mouth back against mine with shocking fierceness. All too soon, his lips were abandoning mine yet again.

"Some of us still have other things to do tonight. And for that, I can't have shredded clothes." His tongue darted out once more to taste kiss-swollen lips. "Unless you'd rather I'd prick someone else?" His fist tightened almost painfully in my hair.

Like hell I was gonna let someone else touch him after I'd barely gotten a taste. "More clothes don't mean less fun," I finally responded.

The triumphant smile that flashed across his face was worth the concession. Now if only I could actually see his entire face.

My fingers seemed to move on their own and had just brushed the edge of what proved to be a silk mask when his hand gently closed over them.

"Kind of defeats the point of anonymity, don't you think?" he asked evenly.

"Fair," I admitted. After all, the damn things *had* been my idea. I tugged his pants down a little further, and he made to turn around. "Nope," I said, holding him in place even as I fished a packet of lube and a condom from my back pocket.

The fire in his eyes was equal parts intrigue and untamed lust.

"Anything else I should know?" I asked as I palmed his erection. He ground into my hand a moment before responding.

"No teeth."

I couldn't hold back a laugh. "Not interested in turning?" I taunted, though I had no interest in turning anyone. The liability was just too great, not to mention the legal hassle.

That sexy grin was back in all its smugness. "Not everyone turns."

Joshua

I gasped again as the *were* I'd found thrust hard and sent another wave of pleasure zipping up my spine. That he'd effortlessly lifted and held me in the compromising position braced between him and the tree with my legs, along with the pants still on them, resting on his shoulders didn't surprise me. I'd never been bent nearly in half like this before, but at this rate, I was eager to test it out again. I grabbed a low-hanging branch of the sturdy maple at my back for support as the wolf continued to rail me like there was no tomorrow. Even as I found purchase, heat mixed with electricity in my stomach. I dropped my head back and moaned into the night, totally lost in the sensation.

Mindlessly, my free hand gripped and released first his shirt and then his hair until at last it came to his mask. I could feel my body racing towards the pinnacle of release, a release too quick in coming. I clung to sanity with a white-knuckle grip.

Just like that, I was shoving his mask up, practically tearing it off his face. I had to see what he really looked like; had to know. I raised my head and caught the barest hint of a defined brow and squared features before he caught me in another savage kiss.

"*Seven hells*," I gasped, then promptly groaned. Nothing in this world compared to sex with a werewolf. Literally nothing. Despite everything that was wrong with it, I knew I'd never give it up. Especially since my latest hit was currently completely undoing me. I cried out again as the night burst with sudden spots of color, and I finally lost my struggle to hold back my orgasm. My companion was quick to follow, his heavy breathing hot against my exposed neck.

For a minute we stayed there, sagging into each other. While my position was precarious, to say the least, I had little concern about being dropped. Even exhausted, lycan strength was impressive, and I doubted he was anywhere near it. Lycan stamina was legendary. I idly carded my fingers through his silky hair, setting free the mask I'd knocked askew.

"A little hypocritical, don't you think?" he asked as the thin material drifted to the ground.

I smiled, but didn't bother to lift my head. "The implication was that the anonymity was for me, not necessarily you," I countered.

His low chuckle sparked the embers of the fire he'd unleashed in me. Then he slowly lowered me to the ground and huffed a laugh. "So much for staying put together." His low rumble, with its edge of humor, had me aching for an encore. Sadly, there simply wasn't time for that. I still had a job to do.

I absentmindedly fingered my cuff to ensure my cargo was intact and secure. Reassured, I looked down to see his meaning. Ah, of course. The cum decorating my shirt seemed to glow white in the faint light. "Not a problem." Using my opposite sleeve, I wiped the mess away. It fell without issue to the forest floor, and I promptly scuffed dirt over it.

"How the hell..."

"Repulsion spell," I answered the unfinished question.

His gaze rose to meet mine with something akin to wonder. "That's expensive magic."

I quirked a smile. "Yes, it is."

"Who are you?"

"Your very hot, very satisfied hookup, who just so happens to be in possession of a very expensive spell," I responded smoothly. I finished resituating my clothes and stepped forward to steal a final languid kiss. For a moment, I simply gazed at his face before pulling away.

Definitely not this one.

I made it three steps before his strong fingers wrapped around my upper arm. I barely repressed the shiver of excitement that threatened to rush through me and turned back to face him.

"At least tell me your name."

My smile broadened, and I shook my head.

He gave me another one of those gorgeous, crooked grins. "Let's see—designer silk you won't take off, insistence on anonymity, refusing to give me even a fake name, and access to powerful, expensive magic. Did I miss anything?"

My grin got wider with each item listed. I was tempted to add that I was also likely the hottest fuck he'd ever had, but seeing as how I was currently disguised beneath the intense glamour, there was no way he could know that.

When I failed to answer, he asked another question. "Did I just fuck myself some kind of rich playboy?"

I barked out a laugh, caught off guard by his surprisingly astute conclusion. "You could say that."

"Well, fuck me."

"I did," I responded wickedly, then turned on my heel and walked out of the clearing.

The path back to the main event was fairly straightforward, but I didn't take it. Instead, I wove a circuitous route through the trees just in case the sexy lycan followed until I could hear the sounds of revelry once more. In a matter of moments, a body stumbled through the brush, holding a half-empty cup. He staggered a few paces and looked up at me, his eyes glinting yellow. I caught the subtle flare of nostrils as he no doubt dragged in the heady scent of sex that clung to my skin. It was all the verification I needed.

I stalked towards him, simultaneously freeing one of the tiny syringes, which I caught between my fingers as it fell. The lycanthrope's eyes widened in surprise. Without warning, I smacked the side of his neck and spun him around. Before he could get his bearings, I was already walking off to the exit and pocketing the now empty syringe. Behind me, I heard another voice join him and couldn't help but wonder if my hookup would survive this night.

Chapter 3

Elijah

The persistent beeping in my ear gradually grew louder. I groaned and rolled over, hoping to trick the alarm into thinking I was awake. It never worked, and yet I still tried. Somehow I must have rolled just right, because suddenly a familiar voice boomed in my ear.

"Get your lazy ass up." Nikolai's gruff voice still held traces of his Russian origins even after all the years, and was *not* what I wanted to hear first thing in the morning.

"Niko, seriously? For moon's sake, it's only..." I squinted to see the time embedded in my wrist. The faint green glow said it was barely after six. "Come on, the sun's not even up."

His growl rolled menacingly through the line. "I don't give a witch's twitch what time it is. You will come when called."

I barely repressed a responding growl and rolled into a sitting position. Somewhere in my sleep-addled brain, I recognized that the only reason the Beta would call at such an unholy hour was if it was important. Really important. I rocketed the rest of the way awake.

"What is it? Has something happened?"

"Just get your tail to the east slope as soon as possible," he said before the line cut out.

East slope? There was nothing but forest out that way. What could possibly be of interest on the east slope? Officially concerned about what was going on, I quickly dressed and slipped out into a fog-shrouded morning. I gave a frustrated growl that was absorbed by the mist and debated the logic of changing instead of driving. With a defeated sigh, I admitted that even with the reduced visibility, taking a land skimmer would be faster. The pack had several, and hopefully there were still a couple remaining. Now with a much quicker stride, I made my way around the sprawling pack house.

The mid-century modern home that constituted the heart of the Klamath Pack was a masterpiece. Though referring to it as mid-century was a bit of a misnomer, as we were in an entirely different century than when it had been constructed. The unusual layout and impressive angles were indicative of a Frank Lloyd Wright, and while there was speculation that it had actually been commissioned in secret straight from the man himself, no one had ever confirmed such a rumor. Either way, the house was stunning with floor-to-ceiling windows that opened onto a forest of deep greens and rich life. It didn't matter if the day was sunny or like this one and severely overcast. The wilderness felt as if it were part of the home.

As I wandered around the garage where they kept the skimmers, I marveled yet again at how, despite years of additions, the house had somehow maintained its architectural identity. Even the latest wing, where I had opted to bunk for the night, had the characteristic angular roof and jutted out over a fall in the land.

Below it, a small stream wound down the craggy landscape, the same small stream that also wound through the house.

I glanced up at one of the many balconies to see if any other poor souls had been roused from slumber and found none. This was becoming cruel and unfair. What? Everyone else got to sleep in after the party of the decade, but I had to roll out and report for duty? Even as I thought it, fear curled inside me. The anxiety I fought to repress made my skin itch, and I quickened my pace.

Fortunately, there were still two skimmers remaining when I arrived. I eyed the quasi-motorcycle dubiously and once again considered changing anyway. I'd never been fond of the things, but the anti-gravity propulsion *would* be substantially faster than running. I just wished to the moon and back that it didn't also make me feel like every cell in my body was being pulled in different directions.

Finally, I let out a put-upon huff and swung a leg over the nearest skimmer. There was a barely perceptible whine as it flared to life; a sound no human could ever hear. Not that there were any around. Humans weren't permitted at the pack house. And as far as I knew, none had ever seen it in the hundred and ninety years we'd been here. It was one of the few secrets we insisted on keeping.

As expected, the journey was smooth, swift, and all-around unpleasant. I silently congratulated myself for being too distracted to eat before heading out. The unnatural pull on my stomach first thing in the morning undoubtedly would have stolen whatever breakfast I might have eaten.

Twenty minutes later, I pulled up to a cluster of pack members standing outside one of the pack's unused cabins.

"Alright, I'm here," I said, turning off the engine and swinging off the skimmer. "Now, what is going on?"

No one answered, though several pairs of eyes were already on me, having heard my approach. Instead, they stepped aside to make way as I walked closer to whatever held their rapt attention. A dozen strides in, I finally understood Nikolai's blunt urgency.

Amidst a circle of lycans was Tommy. Covered in blood.

Joshua

The screen embedded in the wall flashed a bright red headline of *Breaking News*. I quickly turned up the volume with an absent gesture to hear the story.

"Local woman found dead this morning, a victim of a brutal assault. Police found the body of Tina Carr, thirty-five-year-old owner of Sweet Escape, beloved baker and member of the community, at five o'clock this morning. A young vampire couple discovered the grisly scene while out for a stroll." The screen briefly flashed to the said couple consoling each other. But for anyone who knew what to look for, it was clear their bloodshot eyes had nothing to do with stumbling across a crime scene. Just as quickly, the camera was back on the anchor. "Police have refused to comment and are denying all speculation, saying only that justice will be served and all measures taken to assure the town of its safety. Here's what Tina Carr's husband had to say."

The screen filled with the image of an obviously distraught man. His thinning hair and pallid features were highlighted by the intense fury in his eyes. He was pointing angrily at the screen and appeared to be shouting. At last, his voice and hostile words came through. "They can say it's speculation all they like. We all know who did this! I saw the body! I saw—" I leaned forward, eager to hear the rest of his statement, only to have his voice cut out and replaced by the anchor's.

"Unfortunately, due to the sensitive nature of the case, we are unable to share more of Mr. Carr's interview." In the scene still being shown, Mr. Carr was being actively restrained as he continued to shout what appeared to be all manner of vitriolic slurs at the police. It wasn't until an officer with a white band around her arm approached and blew what looked like glitter into the man's face that he stopped. Instantly, he sagged into the arms of his captors, reduced to half-hearted sobs.

The screen flashed once more, and the image of the local police chief dominated the camera.

I made a fist at the screen, and the man's voice vanished. I had no desire to hear the empty platitudes he was offering the community. I could only hope that the brief snippet of Mr. Carr's outrage would be enough to incite a reaction from the locals.

I walked over to the dresser where I'd discarded my mask from the night before. The silk between my fingers reminded me of the absolutely delicious start to the evening I'd enjoyed. While it had been tempting to let him see the real me, the odds of my seeing him again were too great, and I couldn't afford someone making the connection that I'd been there.

I tossed the item into the closet, where it seemed to vanish. The aversion spell on my private luggage case was still in full effect, and even *my* eyes struggled to make out the small, black mask resting on the chestnut box. The argument could be made that I was being paranoid, but being overly cautious was how I'd made it this far. There was still so much work to be done.

Right on cue, my phone chirped an incoming call in my ear. I didn't need to check the ID to know who the call was from. I was more surprised it had taken so long.

"Hart," I answered.

"Excellent. I hope I haven't caught you at a bad time, Detective."

"Not at all, Agent Smalls. How can I help you?"

"A little birdie told me you were on the West Coast."

"Family business," I said, not actually answering the implied question regarding my whereabouts.

"Upstate Washington, right?"

"That is where my family's ancestral home is," I confirmed.

"Then, if you're still in the area, that makes you the closest."

"Oh?" I feigned surprise. "Closest for what?"

"There seems to be a bit of a misunderstanding in a small town in Oregon."

"Smalls, you know I rarely do small-scale," I side-stepped.

"You'll want this one. It's the Portland Pack. I mean, the Klamath Pack. Fuck, why is that still so hard to get used to?"

I grinned at Small's obvious frustration. "What seems to be the situation?" I prompted.

"Murder of a human without obvious provocation. All signs point to lycan, but the pack is closing ranks and insisting they aren't involved."

"Mmm," I hummed appreciatively. "That *does* sound like something I might want."

"Thought so. How soon can you be there?"

I paused for a few moments to give the illusion of considering. "You're in luck. I recently finished an assignment and was just about to step out. I could be there in, say…twenty minutes."

"I'll let the locals know. They'll escort you to the fringe of pack territory and handle introductions."

"Understood." I ended the call and rechecked my weapons.

The unobtrusive daggers nestled in the harness at my back were firmly in place and no less deadly for their thinness. A lethal dose of wolfsbane tipped each one, and they could slice through bone without breaking. I finished strapping the holster of my firearm onto my thigh and confirmed that a spelled silver bullet was already in the chamber before sliding the firearm home. Guns may not have been my preference, but when your prey was something that could easily overpower the strongest of men, it paid to be prepared.

I straightened my vest and admired my reflection in the mirror. With only a fifth of the weapons the outfit could hold currently on me, I was packing light. There was no real reason to have everything for an initial visit and consultation. As far as the outfit overall, assuming it was pure vanity was a mistake; every thread was of the highest tactical caliber. If it happened to fit like a glove, all the better.

Chapter 4

Elijah

I TRIED TO KEEP my anger at bay, but it kept bunching up my shoulders, and I had zero doubts that I was wearing a scowl that could curdle milk. An hour ago, I'd gotten the unlucky order that I was to be the pack liaison with local law enforcement. As if that wasn't bad enough, a specialist had been called. It wasn't surprising, given the gruesome nature of the attack and all the finger-pointing that was going on, but it didn't make me any more comfortable.

The man literally had a license to kill—to kill lycanthropes, to be exact. Humans always wanted to meddle in things they had no business meddling with, and Lycan Detectives were the government's compromised result. There were ten of them in the world, three of which covered the North American continent, likely because of the historic levels of lycan-human violence.

I rolled my shoulders, feeling them tense up again. This assignment was absolutely retribution for speaking out against Conrad the other day. One moon, I would learn to keep my damn mouth shut. Finally, I got a signal from one of the officers who'd been eyeing me suspiciously ever since I'd arrived.

"About fucking time," I growled as I vacated my seat and made my way to the meeting space.

The small strip of land, all of twenty feet across, that separated the predominantly human town and the Klamath pack territory was considered neutral ground. I waited impatiently for the man who effectively held the power of judge, jury, and executioner. I'd never met a Lycan Detective before or even seen one on the news, so I had no idea what to expect. There'd never been much of a reason for one to venture anywhere near our pack before now, and I hated the circumstances that had brought this one here.

Just when we were finally trying for progress...

The gaggle of officers in blue parted to allow the long-awaited guest of honor to saunter through. Whatever I'd been expecting, this hadn't been it. Almost immediately, all the moisture in my mouth dried up. The man was fucking gorgeous. Dark hair cropped close at the sides fell just shy of his eyes, which were an intense forest green that seemed to perfectly match the Douglas fir he was confidently striding past. High cheekbones and a pouty mouth that was any man's wet dream made him look like he belonged more in a fashion advert than with a gun strapped to his thigh.

I struggled to swallow with no liquid in my mouth as my gaze continued to devour the man getting closer to me with each step. He had an easy grace, and his clothes seemed to be painted on, revealing hints of well-defined muscle on his lithe frame. To top it all off, he had legs for days, legs that were currently being hugged by a pair of skin-tight, knee-high boots.

My mind rebelliously imagined what it would be like to have such fantastic limbs wrapped around me. I quickly recoiled from the fantasy, and the wolf inside whimpered at the sudden backlash.

This man was not here for fun. He was here to find whoever he thought was responsible for Tina Carr's murder and put them down like a rabid dog. I flashed to an image of young Tommy shaking uncontrollably while three of his packmates held him down and his younger brother Kale clung to their mother as he sobbed into her shoulder. The Lycan Detective would likely see Tommy dead whether he'd actually committed the crime or not. The reminder of this man's true purpose was enough to put my libido in check.

I squared my shoulders and stepped forward to meet him.

Joshua

My mouth watered as I took in the delicious creature before me. I'd figured I'd run into the *were* again, but hadn't anticipated that of all the members in the Klamath Pack, he'd be my liaison. He looked even more edible than he had the night before. The gray of his hair, indicative of the timber wolf he was, shone vibrantly in the early morning light and hung in relaxed waves to his jawline. A square jaw that was well-defined with hints of stubble that hadn't been there before. I couldn't help but wonder if he only shaved on special occasions or if he simply hadn't had a chance to.

I repressed a smile and resisted the urge to admire his physique, which I knew by my own hands was impressive. Instead, I focused on his amber eyes that were riveted on my approach. A muscle twitched in his cheek, and I could practically see him clenching his jaw. It was difficult not to laugh out loud and ruin the image of composure. Oh, he was *so* not happy that

I was here. Not that I could blame him, I was all but a signed warrant for arrest.

I gave a discreet cough, and the officer who'd been openly staring at me gave a small jump. It happened frequently, but it didn't make it any less tiring.

"Oh, um..." She scrambled to find her words and whatever was left of her dignity. Finally, she pulled herself together and raised her chin defiantly. "Detective, this is Elijah Bennett. He'll be your liaison to the Klamath pack. Mr. Bennett, this is Detective Joshua Hart." She stepped back to allow us room to meet properly.

I extended a hand as dictated by etiquette. For a solid second, it didn't look like he would take it, instead staring down at it as if it were a live adder. Then, his exceedingly warm fingers wrapped around mine in a cautious handshake. I diligently ignored the memory of where else that hot touch had been and squeezed. He made as if to remove his hand, and I tightened my grip.

"So, Bennett as in Jane Austen-Pride and Prejudice-Bennett?" I inquired with raised eyebrows.

His scowl deepened, darkening his face, and I could practically hear him grinding his teeth. "No. Like Tony. But everyone just calls me Red."

My brow climbed even higher, impressed at the reference to the iconic American crooner. "Whatever you say, Bennett."

"Red," he insisted with a hint of a growl. "This isn't some buddy-cop comedy. None of that last name shit." He pulled his hand free, and I almost chuckled at the blatant fury in his eyes.

Elijah

I didn't care if he looked like sex on a stick. Detective Joshua Hart got under my skin in all the worst ways. He was here to make sure one of my own was caught and sentenced, and apparently, to make my life a living hell. I could curse Conrad for doing this to me. That was absolutely the last time I took part in pack politics.

"I don't typically use the nicknames lycans give themselves. I'm assuming that's what 'Red' is..." His gaze flicked up to my decidedly not red hair and back down to catch my eyes. "Bennett."

I ground my teeth. Fine, two could play that game. "Isn't there a job you're supposed to be doing, *Hart*?" I snapped, intentionally dropping his professional title. The moment his name left my lips, I wished to the moon I could take it back.

Too late. The detective's lip curled up in a smug smile that bordered on a sneer. "Yeah, most people give up saying it pretty quickly. Apparently, it's uncomfortably close to a term of endearment."

I didn't even realize I was growling until the insipid officer, whose eyes had practically fallen out of her head earlier at seeing the detective, stepped up.

Joshua Hart held up a hand without ever breaking eye contact. "I've got it."

He continued to hold my gaze, unblinking until I swallowed my growl. The last thing our pack needed was me attacking the Lycan Detective. I stepped away from him, at some point having leaned in closer. "Whatever you say, Josh."

Anger flashed in his eyes, and I didn't even bother to temper my near-feral smile. He turned his head, finally breaking the hypnotic spell I'd apparently been under, and barked at the poor, unsuspecting officer beside him.

"Daniels, if you could escort us to the crime scene." It was almost a request, but came out more like an irritated demand. "Today," he snapped impatiently when she didn't respond right away.

I almost felt bad for the young cadet as she floundered to gather her wits while her fellow officers looked on and snickered. Then I remembered the hungry way she'd looked at the detective, and any sympathy I had for her vanished.

"Yes, of course, right away, sir," she stammered. "If you'll just follow me." She immediately did an about-face and marched toward town.

The detective shot me a look with a raised eyebrow, as if suggesting I should go first. Predator rule number one: Never let another hostile predator at your back.

I smiled innocuously at him. "After you... Josh."

Chapter 5

Joshua

By the time we made it to where Tina Carr's body had been found, I was seriously questioning the wisdom of sparing Elijah "Red" Bennett. The man may have been hotter than fuck, but he was an insufferable ass as well.

"You were supposed to stay behind the line," I whispered harshly under my breath, knowing full well that he could hear me. *Were* aptitude aside, the beast was practically on top of me. "You're a civilian," I added slightly louder in the hopes that one of the abundance of officers would take note. They didn't.

Bennett gave me a toothy grin, obviously recognizing the ploy, then gave an exaggerated look around at the boys in blue. "They don't seem to mind," he practically purred.

I mentally gnashed my teeth. I'd worked with plenty of pack liaisons over the years, but none had ever been quite so infuriating as Bennett was proving to be. Truth be told, they'd been a little afraid of me. A fear Bennett did not seem to share.

"I do not need a babysitter," I bit out.

"Apparently, you do," he whispered right by my ear. If I hadn't already been so enraged, then the feel of his warm breath caressing the outer shell of my ear might have sent an excited shiver through me. As it was, I turned a furious gaze on him and had to restrain myself from punching him in the throat. He smiled back as if he were fully aware of the effect he was having on me.

The unmitigated gall. "Don't contaminate the scene. Put on the shoe covers. And Don't. Touch. Anything," I hissed.

"You're not wearing any." The way his gaze lazily tracked down my body to my shoes, which in fact did not have protective covers, had me wondering if he was trying to flirt or get another rise out of me. Either way, I didn't have time for this game.

I spun on my heel without dignifying him with a response and marched towards the center of the scene. "What have we got?" I demanded to know as I came to a stop.

The yuppie in charge startled at the sound of my voice and turned to face me with wide eyes. Was all they had working on this police force recently graduated rookies?

The young man paled noticeably as I stared down at him, then seemed to remember what his job actually entailed. He cleared his throat and straightened up. Admittedly, I was a little impressed with his tenacity. Countless others had withered beneath that same glare.

"Victim, one Tina Carr, was found by bystanders at o-five hundred-twenty-three. Apparent wounds indicative of mauling. Her right shoulder appeared dislocated, and there were several marks that might have been elongated nails..."

"Claws," I interrupted.

The young man blinked and looked at me. "Sorry, sir?"

"The proper terminology is claws."

"I-I thought we weren't supposed to make assumptions about the potential assailant," he stammered.

His innocence was almost precious, and I couldn't help but soften my harsh tone. "Officer..." I paused and searched his uniform for a name.

"Mack."

"Officer Mack, do you know what my job is?" I asked gently.

He swallowed hard. "You're a Lycan Detective."

I nodded and made a special effort not to be condescending. "Do you know why I was called?"

Pink suffused his cheeks. "Because there's a lycan involved?" he hazarded.

I nodded again and cracked a small smile. "Or at least they think there is," I said with a wink.

The anxiety that had been dominating him seemed to drain away. He gave me a tentative smile as I clasped a hand on his shoulder. "Yeah, okay."

"Cause of death?" I asked and released him.

"Preliminary report states cause of death as a ten-inch laceration to the victim's left thigh, severing the femoral artery."

"Thank you, Mack. Any other evidence I should be aware of at the scene?"

"Unfortunately not, sir. Place seems to be clean, or at the very least nothing out of the ordinary for the area."

"Excellent, and the body?" I queried.

"Already with the coroner at the local morgue. I can take you there if you like," the young man offered.

I glanced over my shoulder at Bennett, who somehow felt more like an armed guard than the insignificant nuisance he was. "I'd like to look around first, then yes, I would appreciate you giving us a lift."

"Us?" Officer Mack echoed, tilting his head to the side in confusion.

I gestured absently behind me, where Bennett had thankfully not moved.

"Oh. Right. Of course. Um...isn't he supposed to be behind the tape?"

I glanced at the perceptive officer out of the corner of my eye. He'd go far. "Yes," I responded evenly.

He gave me a knowing smile. "Red has always done things his own way. My ma says when he was younger, he was always getting into mischief and getting dragged before the Klamath Alpha. Suppose that's why they gave him a seat on the council."

I raised an eyebrow and spared Elijah Bennett another look. "The council, eh?"

"Yeah, guess they figured it'd settle him down. But if he's here with you, then he's probably in trouble again. Can't imagine any lycan that would willingly sign up for that job."

"No, I suspect you're right," I responded absently as I found myself once again intrigued by the werewolf behind me.

Elijah

As much as I wanted to disregard Detective Hart's insistence that I wear the ridiculous footwear and remain on the sidelines, he had a point. Interfering in the actual investigation would not help Tommy and bore a genuine risk of putting me in danger as well. Special license aside, it didn't take a genius to recognize that you did not want to be in Detective Hart's crosshairs.

I smiled to myself as I relived the minor victory of discovering how much he loathed being called Josh. Naturally, I'd used it as many times as possible between the neutral ground and here. He'd finally caved and demanded no less than three times that I stop calling him that.

I crossed my arms and watched the prickly detective make his way over to the team cataloging the scene. He barked at one of them, and they seemed to leap right out of their skins. It was obvious that Joshua Hart liked to be in charge and in control. Distantly, I wondered if he'd be as bossy in the bedroom. I quickly squashed the renegade thought. My inner wolf was having none of it, though, and stubbornly tried to force the image of what the detective would look like at our complete mercy. Would he fight it? Would he love it?

I growled to myself, startling a few nearby nosy onlookers. They quickly backed away, and I shook my head. *He is off limits,* I reminded the wolf and myself.

Determined to do what I was actually here for, I refocused my attention on what was being said. Unfortunately, there was a silence spell in place that prevented me from picking up so much as a whisper. So instead of hearing whatever he was saying to the cute officer that made him relax from one heartbeat to the next, I had to settle for guessing. So far, my guesses weren't going in a good direction, and I was in danger of growling out loud again when Josh glanced over his shoulder at me. Our eyes met only for a moment, but it was enough to settle me.

His gaze quickly returned to the officer, and then he was combing through the scene himself while the officer made comments from where he stood. Before I knew it, the detective was stalking past me.

I hopped after him, struggling to toss aside the clingy booties. "Where are we going?"

"The morgue," he said as he climbed into a marked hovercar that belonged to the young officer he'd been speaking with earlier.

"The what?"

He caught my gaze in the rearview mirror. "What's the matter, Bennett, never seen a dead body?"

The morgue. I absolutely hated the morgue. I'd been there all of twice in my life, and neither time had endeared me to the place. Once, when I'd been eight and my mother had died in a tragic bus accident along with five other people. Then again, nearly fifteen years later, when I'd been called in to identify my father's body. I still remembered the terrible gashes on his body. The sharp tang of chilled blood in the air. The stomach-curdling scent of formaldehyde.

"Bennett." Josh's sharp voice brought me out of the horrible memory. I scowled back at him as he made to exit the patrol vehicle. "Come on. Don't tell me the Big Bad Wolf is afraid of a little blood."

I bristled at the dig, then realized that he was shrugging into a red leather jacket. Like everything else he wore, the material was of the highest quality and fit like a second skin. There was no way that was going to go without comment. However, I had to wait until he opened the door for me since I was sitting in the back seat like a common criminal—a detail that did not elude me.

Since the backseat was not made for someone built like me, I had to practically peel myself out of the car as the detective watched with a smug expression. I finished straightening to my full height, which put us almost nose to nose. "Whatever you say, Little Red Riding Hood."

His self-satisfied smirk dissolved into a deceptively neutral expression. "Places where the dead are kept tend to be cold, and I dislike being cold."

I took another step closer, invading his personal space. Unsurprisingly, he didn't back down, nor did his scent betray even a modicum of anxiety at my sudden proximity. I pitched my voice nice and low so Officer Mack wouldn't overhear. "Nothing hotter than a werewolf to keep you warm."

Something flashed in Joshua's eyes, but was gone before I could place it. "You going to melt my cold, cold heart while you're at it?" he quipped. My snappy retort to "fly me to the moon" vanished when the young officer spoke.

"Right, so the coroner is ready for us. Here's the autopsy report, Detective Hart." He held out a slim data pad that would likely flood with graphs and notes the moment it registered Joshua's bio-signature.

Except he didn't take it. In fact, he never looked away. We stayed locked in a semi-battle of wills. His forest-green eyes, intense and unblinking. With each passing second, the electric charge between us increased until I was positive we'd each get zapped if we so much as breathed too hard.

"Um... is there something I should know?" Officer Mack asked.

Joshua blinked first and turned to face him. "Not at all. Thank you, Mack," he said and offered a dazzling smile as he accepted the sheet of tech.

I had to clench my teeth so hard they ached in order to hold back the savage growl that was desperately trying to slip free. What had Officer Mack done to elicit such a genuine reaction?

Joshua

I literally had no idea what had possessed me to provoke Bennett or to compound the situation by evoking a stare-off. One minute I'd been fully prepared to tell him to eat his own tail. The next I'd been staring into amber eyes that seemed smoother than the finest caramel. What I did know was that I was already enjoying the challenge of his presence far too much, and that was a problem. I had a job to do, and the mission couldn't afford the distraction. Officer Mack's interruption had been timely, and I'd snatched at the chance to regain my bearings.

I accepted the proffered report, though I didn't need the coroner's findings to tell me what I already knew. As I turned to make my way into the room, I could feel Bennett's eyes on my back like a physical touch. I resisted the urge to engage in more verbal sparring, as it would only drag out the day even further. I still had my report to give.

"Show me," I demanded, catching the coroner's eye.

She was a stout woman with bronze skin and a distinct no-nonsense air about her. I respected that, and even more, the clear detail included in her report. Few coroners, especially those dealing with a Lycan Detective, bothered to exert so much effort. It spoke to her professionalism, and it occurred to me that the town was lucky to have someone of her caliber. I glanced back down at the report to gather her name.

"Dr. Swann," I added.

She gave a sharp nod and pulled the sheet back to reveal the pallid remains of what once had been Tina Carr. As detailed as Dr. Swann's notes were, nothing could compare to the sheer brutality laid before us. Bruises and punctures covered nearly every inch of her body, the sickly purples and yellows standing out in sharp contrast to her sallow skin. The fatal laceration on her thigh was in fact one of three that reached from her groin to her knee.

The wound, drained of blood, hung open like some grotesque, gaping maw. Farther up her tortured torso, her right arm hung oddly disjointed from the rest of her body. Across her shoulder were not one, but four blatant bite marks. Not the subtle puncture of vampire fangs. No, these were large, animalistic bites that tore out whole chunks of flesh.

I noted that the coroner had preserved most of the desiccated flesh in the condition it had likely been found. Perhaps the doctor had a few necromantic tricks in her bag. I glanced out of the corner of my eye to see that Officer Mack was resolutely trying and subsequently failing to maintain his composure. Bennett, however, was remarkably unfazed. He gazed down at the savaged body with a level of detachment I could relate to. That was until his eyes touched on the evidence of mauling. There was a barely perceptible flinch before he turned away.

I spent the next hour scouring the report and conferring with Dr. Swann while inspecting the body myself. It was obvious what species the culprit was, but it also wouldn't be the first time someone had intentionally fabricated a mauling to frame the local lycan population.

When I was done, I encouraged Officer Mack to drive Bennett to the border. There had been a few mild protests, mostly from Bennett, which I hadn't bothered to hear. It wasn't until I promised to meet him at the neutral ground in the morning that he finally allowed himself to be escorted away. I shook my head and trudged out of the office. Long as my day had been, it still wasn't over.

Chapter 6

Joshua

"You're his type, by the way," Officer Mack said out of nowhere.

I looked at him over the file I was reading. "Whose?"

"Red. You're definitely his type."

Well, this was certainly an unexpected turn in the otherwise dull conversation. "And what makes you say that?" I asked, somehow keeping the smirk from my voice. If history was anything to go by, I was pretty much everybody's type.

He shrugged, and his gaze flicked briefly to mine. "You're pretty."

There was no stopping my eyebrow from arching high up my forehead. Officer Mack was full of surprises. Perhaps I had misjudged him.

A slight pink tinged his cheeks as he stammered to unsay what was already out there. "I mean, that's not, well, you, and... oh sweet heavens, I cannot believe I said that out loud."

I let out a small chuckle at the poor kid's struggle. "Be easy, Mack. I'm aware of what I look like."

He shot me another nervous look. "Anyway, you're definitely his type. If that's something you were interested in knowing," he added belatedly.

I had to hand it to him; the kid had balls. I was hard-pressed to think of a time when one of the local officers had ever had the brass to delve into my personal life, not to mention who I may or may not be interested in taking home.

"In my experience, people attracted to pretty things usually want them dumb as well."

Mack snorted. "Not Red. He's one of the smartest guys I know. Honestly, if it weren't for what happened to his da, he probably would have become some fancy professor at a prestigious university."

Now, this was intriguing. "That so?"

Mack nodded absently while he continued to type up his latest report at the adjacent desk. Now that I was here, he was free to work on other cases. Even in a sleepy town, crime didn't vanish. "Probably has something to do with his name."

"Elijah?"

"Bennett. Like in Jane Austen."

So he'd lied to me. I almost had to give it to the *were*. That took courage. "You surprise me," I said to Mack.

Pink tinged his cheeks again, and he avoided eye contact. "I may live in a backwater town in the middle of nowhere, but I'm still familiar with the classics."

I couldn't hold my smile any longer. "Like Tony?"

He finally looked up at me with a quizzical expression. "Who?"

I shook my head. "Never mind. What happened to Bennett's father?"

Sadness swept over Mack. The town at large may struggle to accept the lycans in their midst, but he obviously had no such qualms. "During the Restructure, things got pretty rough around here."

I refrained from asking if he was even old enough to remember a time before supernaturals were integrated everywhere.

"His da was one of the first lycans to die. Some vigilantes thought they could sneak onto pack property... They were wrong."

"I imagine they were." People encroaching on pack territory would have triggered natural defensive behavior, as they did everything in their power to protect their young, much like any animal.

Mack nodded and continued. "The pack heard them coming a mile away and was ready for them. A lot of people died that day, including Red's da. He came home from college to identify the body. He didn't go back."

Well, well, well, Bennett was proving to be quite the interesting treasure trove. Brains *and* beauty, a rare combo in a lycan. Perhaps he deserved another look beyond that gruff exterior. It would be nice to actually be able to hold a conversation with a hookup for once. I dismissed the ridiculous notion for what it was. Once was all I could have; anything more risked exposure.

Mack cleared his throat, and I wondered if I'd incidentally become lost in thought. "But yeah, anyway. Definitely his type."

"Officer Mack, are you offering these nuggets of wisdom because of said werewolf's behavior the other day?" His face went blank, and it took me a minute to realize why. I really was getting distracted if I was using terms like "werewolf" in mixed company.

To redirect, I added as much to myself as to Mack, "He's not mine." And he never would be. There were no such things as connections in my line of work, and certainly not with a lycan.

"Oh."

"Don't get me wrong, he's attractive enough."

A knowing glint entered Officer Mack's eye. "Lycan Detectives can't lie, right? It's to make sure the cases you work on get an honest outcome."

I nodded, exceptionally impressed. Someone had done their homework. "True."

"But it's not just your work life. It covers off the job too."

"The spell cast on me when I took my oath weaves into all aspects of my life."

"How do you do it? I mean, surely there are times when even a little white lie would be better than the truth. Take, for instance, my Granny Ruth's famous casserole. Stuff is awful. It's not famous because it's good. But I can't exactly tell *her* that."

I chuckled and straightened in my chair. "You get very good at telling the truth."

He shook his head disbelievingly. "So…"

"So," I echoed.

"What is your type?"

I barked out a laugh. Officer Mack was persistent, if nothing else. "Asking for yourself or someone else?"

To his credit, no pink suffused his face this time. "My cousin is single. I could get you his data if you're interested."

"I appreciate the offer, but I try to avoid local entanglements when I'm on a job." And Bacchanal notwithstanding, I was doing a superb job of failing miserably.

"Fair."

We fell once more into silence. His fingers flurried away over a holographic keyboard, which provided haptic feedback, while I continued to peruse yet another cold case file. Not that I was expecting to find anything, but if it was at all possible that there were other lycan-human crimes on the books, it was my sworn duty to resolve them while I was here.

Interestingly enough, the Klamath pack seemed to mostly consist of upstanding citizens. There was occasional mischief by some pups being pups, but there was nothing of genuine note.

The preset clicks of typing dissipated, and I glanced up to see if Mack had finished for the day. He seemed to be lost in thought as he stared at a half-filled screen, then without warning or even a glance towards me, he asked quietly, "Does the spell get removed when you retire?"

"This isn't exactly the kind of job you voluntarily retire from."

Mack paled as the meaning of my words sank in. "But, I mean...in theory, right?"

I considered the young officer for a moment before answering. The crude truth was that we'd never been made any promises, not even our lives. The government was sticky that way. "The impression given was that when our work was done, we'd be allowed to live in peace." I let that sit a moment, then added, "Though I don't know of anyone who's ever had the chance to verify that."

Mack swallowed hard, and I thought that would be the end. I should have known better. "Did it hurt? When you took your oath?" he asked softly.

There was no gentle way to tell him what he was asking, so I opted for a literal definition of what had been done. He could deduce the rest. "The oath is administered using Fae magic. It was cast into my bones to ensure that from that moment forward, I would never be able to tell a lie. To be bound to the truth, much like the Fae themselves."

Even as I gave the blandest definition possible, the memory of that night came back to me. The searing pain felt as if the flesh was being flayed from my body. The horrid stench of burning spirit. The magic may have been embedded in my bones, but it reached to my soul. All because Fae didn't trust humans and humans didn't trust Fae. The first wave of Lycan Detectives hadn't survived the process. The second lasted a year. It wasn't until the third that they seemed to perfect the art... and the torture.

I suppressed an involuntary shiver. The memory of that night fourteen years ago, when my mother gave me the official papers, was seared into my memory for eternity. No amount of magical opiates would ever dull the agony I'd undergone not an hour later.

"Aren't the Fae notorious equivocators?" Mack's sudden speech snatched me out of the hole I was rapidly descending.

I smiled malevolently. "Yes, they are."

He blinked a few times as he absorbed the ramifications of what that really meant regarding me. Finally, he opened his mouth, undoubtedly to ask another uncomfortably astute question.

I quickly cut him off before it proved to be one that was not so easily skirted. "You seem to have a rather keen interest in what I do. May I ask why?"

The younger officer instantly bucked up, proudly puffing his chest, and responded with very little self-doubt, "I was considering becoming a Lycan Detective as a career option."

I smiled and barely contained a laugh. The air in his sails instantly deflated.

"What? You don't think I could do it?"

"I have no doubt that you'd make a fine detective." The mild praise seemed to bolster some of his waning confidence. "But this...job...what I do, it requires sacrifice. Your personal life will take a toll. While being solo isn't a requirement, connections are difficult. This is not a job for people who thrive in social settings.

Also, you're not really the right age to be getting into this line of work."

He instantly looked affronted. "How old do you think I am? I'm not much younger than you and Red."

"And how old do you think that is?" I countered. I neglected to point out that that was precisely the issue. To do this job properly required a lifetime of training, and he was well past recruiting age by a good five years.

"Thirty-three," he answered as if it were a challenge.

"Is *that* how old Bennett is?" I asked despite my prior conviction not to delve any deeper into the enigma that was proving to be my liaison.

"Yeah."

I was beyond impressed. Not only had the young officer accurately guessed my age, but Bennett and I weren't just *of*-an-age, we were exactly the same age.

"This town is fortunate to have someone as dedicated as you."

Mack's eyes glinted deviously. "So what you're saying-not-saying is that being a Lycan Detective is lonely and you would hate for me to miss out on the full life I could have in a small town like Adler Springs." Damn kid was like a dog with a bone.

I blinked back at him with a neutral expression, fully aware that whatever I told him would only reaffirm his observations.

"Sure you don't want my cousin's info? Consensus says he's pretty cute," Mack offered again.

I laughed, unable to help myself. "You're alright, kid."

"That wasn't a no," he fired over his shoulder as he left to file his finished reports.

Elijah

I shoved my hands deep into my pockets and tried to follow the conversation. So far, it had been on a long track to nowhere.

"Perhaps next time, we'll be a little more inclined to listen when I say something is a bad idea." The Alpha glared at the council gathered, not bothering to spare anyone, including those who'd supported him. "The Baccha-whatever it was, was a mistake from the start. Humans have no place on pack territory."

It took a concerted effort not to roll my eyes. Conrad had been on the same track for the better part of three hours. Everyone was over it. But as much as I wanted to interject that his blind insistence that "pack business was pack business," nothing would change the fact that a human was dead, most likely at lycan hands. Tommy's hands, to be exact. That he'd apparently been having an affair with the murder victim was not helping anything.

I couldn't help but wonder how long it would take Detective Hart to dig up *that* truth. Already he'd settled three territory disputes, shut down an illegal distillery, and gotten two young wolves acquitted of a car theft they didn't commit. That last had surprised pretty much everyone. When asked about it, Josh had said simply that it was his sworn duty to resolve lycan-human disputes.

"Elijah," Nikolai snapped.

"Yes?" I responded, studiously ignoring his impatience. He'd undoubtedly been trying to get my attention while I'd been preoccupied with thoughts of Joshua Hart, something that seemed to occur frequently since the man had arrived to destroy all our lives.

"You will answer when your Alpha asks you a question," Nikolai ground out in his heavy accent.

I rolled my shoulders and straightened up from my perch on the wall. "Forgiveness Alpha, what can I do for you?"

Conrad's eyes narrowed dangerously, but he didn't call out any perceived slight. "The Lycan Detective, how is he looking?"

Hotter than a midsummer night, with lips fuller than the moon, and an ass that makes you wanna howl. I shook my head to clear the traitorously persistent thoughts. Not only was that not what Conrad meant, they were dangerous things to be thinking about. Josh was off-limits for any number of reasons. His legal right to euthanize my friend and packmate, currently topping the list.

"It's not what you want to hear, but he's doing his job and doing it well. I did a little digging, and it turns out that he's basically the best. I'm not talking about an inflated reputation he gave himself either. He has literally closed more cases, settled twice as many disputes in half the time, and don't get me started on his kill count."

An uneasy ripple went through the council. While Conrad remained visibly unaffected by the information, Nikolai winced sharply.

"We won't be able to keep the truth from him for very long. He'll find out that we're hiding Tommy, and then all of us will be accessories."

"We don't even know if Tommy did it!" Kale shouted, smacking the table in front of him so hard it cracked down the middle.

I looked calmly at the young wolf. My heart ached for him and his family, but there was no denying that Tommy had been involved. Even if he hadn't committed the murder, he at the very least was a witness. "You saw him just like I did," I said sympathetically.

Kale's shoulders fell inward, and he seemed to crumble before my eyes. He sank into his chair and mumbled quietly, "He's not well."

That much was undeniably true. Tommy had been an incoherent, sobbing disaster when he'd been found covered in blood the next morning. It had taken days for him to level out enough to actually put words into a sentence, but every time someone asked about Tina, he dissolved back into a gibbering mess. So far, the most we'd been able to gather had been the news about the affair.

A heavy silence descended on the group, then, to my infinite surprise, Conrad said, "We've called Sabrina Landon. She should be here in a week."

I uncrossed my arms and stood up straighter. "I thought she was doing an internship with Dr. Wilson. That's an opportunity of a lifetime. If she leaves suddenly, she might not be able to go back."

Conrad turned a gaze that could freeze fire on me. "Some lycans still remember that their duty is to their pack. Hopefully, with what she's learned from this... *demon*-doctor, she can deduce what is wrong with Tommy." His distaste for her mentor was apparent; it was a wonder he'd ever let her go study with him. I suspected it had actually been my insistence at the time and the acclaim of Dr. Alec Wilson that had convinced Conrad to even consider the idea.

"Moon help us, she can come up with something," Nikolai added.

Conrad spared him the briefest glance before zeroing back in on me. "It's up to you to keep this detective occupied and out of the way."

I opened my mouth to protest, but was quickly silenced.

"You will do your duty to this pack and keep tabs on Detective Hart, Elijah Bennett. You will inform this pack of every move he makes. If he so much as sneezes, I want to know about it. You will stay glued to his side every moonforsaken minute."

What did he expect me to do to accomplish such an impossible task? Sleep with Josh? If I were being honest, there were definitely worse things. Those moon-blessed legs. *I wonder how tightly he could squeeze them...* I immediately squashed the renegade thought and focused on the rest of the outrageous demands the Alpha was laying at my feet.

"—if he even considers coming anywhere near pack territory, you will do everything in your power to deter him. Is that understood?" Conrad's eyes flashed an angry gray that was more like the storm clouds brewing overhead than their usual steel.

My jaw ticked as I fought the impulse to argue about what a ridiculous scheme this was. Hiding Tommy would only endanger the rest of the pack. Bringing him forward and insisting on a fair trial would at least give us an opportunity to find out what had really happened and, more optimistically, what had happened *to Tommy* to reduce him to such a state.

Several pairs of eyes turned in solemn silence to stare at me. No one said a word, waiting for my response. Tension thickened around me. One wrong word, and everything my father had fought and died for would go up in smoke. There was only one choice. The same choice there always was in order to maintain the peace.

"Yes, Alpha."

Chapter 7

Joshua

THE NIGHT CLOSED AROUND me like a cloak, a near-perfect darkness found beneath the dense foliage. Heavy mist floated low above the ground, adding a chill to the air, a subtle reminder of the storm that had rocked the town the last two nights. Between that, my near-silent tread, and the all-black attire I was currently sporting, I was practically a shadow demon myself. Of course, all the stealth in the world was absolutely useless if someone from the pack scented me before I even got close. That was where the potion had come in. The potent concoction absorbed and neutralized my scent to the point where not even a gifted tracker could pick it out amidst the overwhelming forest.

I'd taken it at the edge of the territory, then ventured another half mile east before finally crossing the border. In truth, it was the same potion I always employed for such missions. It was effective and had a predictable timeline. It was also the same one I'd taken the night of the Bacchanal. A subtle shiver raced through my body that had nothing to do with the pervasive cold. Being forced to work in such continuous proximity to the sexy Elijah Bennett was wreaking havoc on my denied libido.

The lycan had taken to practically stalking me. He was often at the precinct before I was–a feat worth noting–and insisted on staying well past expectations. There had even been a few times I was fairly positive he would have followed me home. I didn't want to think about how close I'd come to letting him. The thought of spending even just one more night lost in the lycan's embrace had been far too tempting. Thankfully, I'd come to my senses, but at that point I'd had to employ some creative maneuvers to lose him. Even then, sleep had been a long time coming.

I shook my head. Thoughts of Elijah were a distraction I couldn't afford this deep into the heart of Klamath Pack territory. One slip is all it would take for everything to be over. Suddenly, a streak of silver flashing through the trees caught my attention. I froze, making an effort to take long, slow breaths, and waited. My patience was rewarded with three pure voices arching up into the night. Rain might not keep the lycans from running, but a storm certainly would. Naturally, they would have ventured out as soon as possible, not caring that the full moon was still weeks away.

As abruptly as it had appeared, the sound stopped. The last shrill note hung for a moment, then faded away. I continued my careful tread, confident I was on the right track. A quick glance around a particularly impressive pine revealed flashes of gray fur between distant trunks, the color a stark contrast to their nearly black surroundings. I followed the three's aimless trail well into the night until at last they paused in a small clearing, presumably to play.

While I got situated, I stole glances at my prey to ensure they hadn't moved on. As I watched the three canines roughhouse in the faint light of the quarter moon, I couldn't help but admit there was a certain purity to their antics, an almost kind of innocence. Then again, animals often were innocent... until they weren't.

The long silver flute I'd tucked into my boot earlier in the evening pulled free without so much as a whisper. I softly blew on the hole-less instrument, and runes briefly flared to life, activating the magic within. Now, whatever was inserted into the tube would be imbued with absolute silence, for a time at least. Long enough to do what needed to be done. I glanced up once more to ascertain who to target first.

The largest of the three was circling around and making a grand show of himself. He had to be at least a hundred and twenty-five kilograms, if not more. Even by lycan standards, he was of notable size. He also seemed to be the most dominant in the group.

He'll do nicely.

I reached down to my belt and cautiously withdrew two large black feathers. The sleek objects were almost heavy between my fingers and seemed to absorb the very night. Hawk feathers may have been better suited for this purpose as they would have been lighter and faster, but after careful observation of the area, the raven feathers I was holding felt more appropriate. Surprisingly, hawks didn't frequent this area, and there was a level of poeticism to using the omen of death.

I slipped the first feather into the tube with steady hands and lifted to take aim. Ten heartbeats went by before I got my opening. I took a deep breath and expelled it through the blowgun.

The raven spread out its glossy wings and departed like hope.

HART'S BETRAYAL

The feather shot out in perfect silence, its calamus unnaturally sharp and filled with a unique toxin. The streak of black death flew true, and my target gave a loud yip as it met its mark.

And quoth the Raven, "Nevermore."

He immediately snapped at his companion, no doubt suspecting foul play in their game. Quickly, I loaded the next feather and fired it shortly after into the companion's haunch.

The soft down of another feather tickled my fingers where they rested on the edge of the pouch. I didn't set up another shot, though. I needed to see how the first two played out. Every lycan would have a slightly different reaction to the serum, and I dared not risk tipping my hand by loosing another. Raven feathers may be unremarkable in this area, but three large ones clustered together could draw attention.

The two targeted wolves circled each other once, twice. Wariness was etched in every line of their bodies. Even from my substantial distance, I could make out the twitch of muscles and flick of ears as their unnatural bodies tried to fight what was happening to them.

Between one blink and the next, the standoff broke.

The smaller of the two lunged at the behemoth. Crimson sprayed into the night, and a howl of pain echoed through the trees as his teeth sank into the skin around his opponent's neck. Despite his speed and surprise, he was no match for the larger *were*. With a savage roar, the largest lycan flung the other wolf free of his body, sacrificing a chunk of his ruff. More red stained the night, but he didn't slow, treating the wound as more of a graze than the deep puncture it was. He lunged, snarling after his attacker, who didn't have the sense to run. There was a sickening crunch as the two came together with enough force to liquefy a normal mortal.

The sheer violence that blossomed before my eyes could have made a grown man's stomach heave. Yet it was no more than could be expected from animals; it was simply their nature. They were too far for me to see much detail, but I didn't need to see it in order to know that the smaller one was raking his back claws on the underbelly of the larger. That blood was seeping red and metallic into the ground with abandon. Skin and muscle were splitting open at the slightest touch of fangs. But it didn't matter how gruesome that battle raged, neither backed off. Every time one fell, they rose again, dripping more red and sporting more grievous wounds than before, to mindlessly renew the assault.

At last, the slightly smaller wolf twitched its last and stopped moving. Through it all, the third and smallest wolf had remained frozen, staring on, no doubt in horror as his friends tore each other to pieces. Still bleeding and high from the kill, the largest wolf turned on his packmate with a growl that could turn blood to ice. Finally, some sense of preservation seeped into the animal's brain. No equal to the substantially larger wolf, he turned and bolted.

Rule number one when facing a predator: *Don't run*.

The enraged wolf streaked after without so much as a second glance at his shredded former companion and packmate. I slipped out from my cover and slunk my way closer, intent on following them. I skirted the edge of the clearing, as the center was a veritable bloodbath and, potion or no, there'd be no hiding that scent if I got it on me.

The path of the two wolves was less haphazard than before, and it only took me half a mile to realize that the creature was making a beeline for home—the heart of Klamath territory. I allowed myself an indulgent grin. Having the large lycanthrope tear apart their very base was an even better turn of events than I could have hoped for.

Satisfied with the night's work and the inevitable chaos that would ensue, I began the arduous process of walking back to town. Unfortunately, I'd ventured deeper into the territory than I'd originally anticipated, and the journey took most of what remained of the night.

By the time I finally made it back unnoticed to the apartment, there were only a few meager hours left before the early light of dawn would beckon me back to work at the precinct, where undoubtedly Elijah would already be waiting for me. I was too tired to suppress the faint smile that followed me into slumber at the thought.

Elijah

Joshua Hart was late. While his not working was probably a good thing, not knowing where he was, was not. Despite my best efforts, it had proven impossible to find out where the damn detective was staying. Portals weren't exactly abundant in Adler Springs. The nearest center being in Portland, and only special commissions ventured nearer. Which meant he had to be staying in town. Right? It made logical sense. But where? It wasn't that big a town, and yet no one seemed to have a clue. That line brought me right back to my original frustration: where was Josh *now*?

I drummed my fingers on his desk, or at least the desk he'd commandeered when he'd arrived, in a loud pattern that was in danger of making permanent imprints if the nervous glances Officer Mack had been casting my way were anything to go by. I spared him a forced grin, and he looked away. Officially fed up with waiting, I surged to my feet with a loud scrape of metal, fully intent on tracking him down myself.

An equally offensive sound pierced the room as the main door flung open and rebounded off the wall, accompanied by a muttered curse. "Fucking hell."

I turned and faced the man striding his way into the room like he owned the damn place. I crossed my arms over my chest and growled, "You're late."

He shot me a withering look. "And you don't actually work here."

"But I do work with you, which I can't do if I don't know where you are," I countered, refusing to budge out of his way so he could get to the chair. He'd either have to physically move me or walk around.

His jaw tightened as he stood there, glaring at me. It gave me an opportunity to notice the gray highlighting his eyes and how they didn't seem as green as usual, almost as if they were missing their usual glow. At a glance, he was as put together as always, but minor details stuck out that spoke otherwise. The man looked bone-weary and ready to pass out.

Before I could move out of his way, he stepped around and dropped into the chair I'd been occupying. He gave a nearly inaudible sigh as he sank into what was likely still a very warm cushion. While the weather was nowhere near as harsh as winters in Hanover, there was still a notable chill in the air thanks to the rain that had soaked the town the past few days. And Joshua Hart hated to be cold.

I propped myself on the desk beside him and noted with pleasure that he shifted slightly to be closer to the natural heat I was emanating. Though I doubted even he was aware of his actions in his current zombie state.

"So where were you?" I asked once he'd settled into a false sense of security.

He gave no physical reaction that betrayed whether he'd been doing something he shouldn't have been without his designated liaison. Rather, he looked up at me out of the corner of his eye and reached around to grab a data tab of reports that I was practically sitting on top of. His challenging look never wavered as he extricated the file without once touching me.

He may not have had any sort of reaction, but I was suddenly and immensely glad there weren't any other lycans in the precinct. The last thing I needed was word of my outrageous attraction to literally the only person I shouldn't be getting back to Conrad.

"Can I get you anything?" Officer Mack asked warily, his voice sounding almost small amidst the tension steadily thickening. I spared a glance at the young man, but his attention remained focused solely on Josh. I narrowed my eyes and somehow contained a muted growl at his interruption of our stalemate.

"Caffeine," Josh supplied in a perfect monotone.

Mack didn't ask how he wanted his requested item, just turned on his heel and vanished to retrieve it. If I had to guess, though, I suspected Josh would take his coffee like his soul–*black*.

"Grab a chair." Josh's demand instantly got my ruff up.

"I'm comfortable here," I responded smoothly. His hand briefly tightened into a fist on the table, then he relaxed and drew the data tab closer. Truth be told, a chair would have been nice, but I was rather enjoying the effect my proximity was having on the unflappable detective. If I was being even more honest with myself, I also just wanted to stay close.

"Suit yourself. But remember, I offered."

"Noted." I stared down at him and refused to cave.

He seemed to visibly restrain himself from rolling his eyes. To cover his blatant disapproval of my decision, he focused his attention on the datapad. At his touch, it flared to life with streams of information. He appeared to pluck one at random, then said without looking up, "Elijah Maurice Bennett."

My shoulders instantly stiffened. The list of people who knew my full legal name was drastically small. Josh officially had my attention.

Still looking down, he asked casually, "Where were you the night of Friday, March 15th?"

I honestly couldn't tell if he was being facetious or not. "That was the night of the Bacchanalia."

"I didn't ask *what* it was. I asked, *where* you were." He finally looked up at me through those obscenely long eyelashes he had. There wasn't a trace of emotion to be found on his face.

"All right. Fine. I'll bite."

Something wicked flashed in his eyes, and the corner of his mouth twitched up ever so slightly. "Please don't. Just answer the question. Unless, of course, you're hiding something?" The hint of a question was more than enough to raise my hackles. Either he truly believed I was involved in the murder of Tina Carr, or he knew about Tommy and the fact that the pack, including myself, was hiding him. Either way, it wasn't good.

For a split second, I seriously considered spilling. I already didn't think spiriting Tommy away was the right thing to do. Josh was obviously good enough at his job to figure it out anyway, and he was practically alluding to already knowing. But almost more than any of that, I just... wanted to. I fought down the impulse to be traitorously honest.

More of my weight settled on the desk, which had the unintended effect of bringing my leg that much closer to him as I shifted my stance not to slide right onto the ground. He held out for a solid five seconds before withdrawing his hand and placing it in his lap, where it was far away from me.

"I was at said Bacchanal, as was all the pack."

He glanced down at the datapad, though he didn't seem to be reading it. "What makes you so confident that 'all the pack' was present?"

"Because attendance was mandatory."

He leaned back in his chair and steepled his fingers as he eyed me. "Even mandatory doesn't mean everyone was there," he finally said.

This time I rolled my eyes. "Alpha's orders. You, of all people, should know what that means."

He quirked one eyebrow and leaned forward under the guise of grabbing a fresh file. The wolf inside howled with denied fury as I fought to keep us both in check. Whether Josh realized the effect he had on me or not, I was one accidental touch away from dragging him out of that squeak-riddled chair and forcing him to straddle me right here in the middle of the precinct.

"Something tells me your Alpha doesn't have quite the control he once did." His green eyes caught the cost-effective lights and shone a bright jade. "So where were you, Bennett?" he crooned in a low voice.

It took an active force of will to stay focused on the question and not fall prey to those depths of green. "Enjoying the festivities as much as everyone else."

"As much?" he challenged.

I flashed him my teeth in a wolfish grin. "Maybe more." At the admission, my memory supplied ample reminders as to just how much fun I'd been having. The silky black mask, the blood-burning sounds he'd made, the way his green eyes had danced in the moonlight. Green eyes, not so unlike Josh's, though they had been nowhere near the spellbinding color that was currently boring into me. I was so enraptured with them, in fact, I almost missed the follow-up question.

"And did she have a good time?"

"He," I corrected without thinking. If anyone had asked me later, I would have sworn to the moon and back that he'd smirked at the comment, but in truth his face remained perfectly neutral and professional.

"And how long were you in each other's company?"

I didn't even bother to hold my smug grin. "A while." If Joshua Hart needed lessons in werewolf stamina, I'd be happy to give them to him.

"Lucky guy," he practically purred.

We both were, I mentally responded. I was still having incredibly vivid dreams about the masked stranger. Dreams that were bound to cost me a fortune in laundry. It didn't even matter that I hadn't gotten any of his clothes actually off him. My body still ached to feel his touch again, desperately pulling me closer, deeper....

"And can he account for your whereabouts?"

Too late, I recognized the trap Josh had easily walked me into. "It was a masquerade."

"How terribly... convenient."

"The masks made people more confident in partaking in the festivities. Especially humans. Which he was. Human, that is." I would have expected another form of mild surprise or at least judgment from Josh at the admission, but he did neither.

"Was he?"

Something about the question tickled my memory. Suddenly it occurred to me I'd never really smelled Josh, nor had I ever sought to locate his scent. Which was odder than I had words to express. It was instinctive werewolf nature to seek everyone's unique smell. My brow furrowed in confusion. Why had I never smelled Josh? Now that I was aware of the failing, I was eager to correct the oversight. He was already so close, and I didn't give a new moon if he filed a harassment report. I leaned closer, prepared to grab his collar and steal the scent if I had to.

Per his usual nature, he stayed firmly rooted. Everything in his body language exuded confidence. There wasn't a bone in Joshua Hart's body that was afraid of me or what I could do to him. Logically, it had to be because we were surrounded by law enforcement that would have me bleeding out on the ground before I could so much as shift a hand, but deep down I knew that wasn't it. Josh genuinely just wasn't afraid. Was it even possible that my masked billionaire and the Lycan Detective were one and the same?

My heart beat heavily in my chest as I continued to close the distance. I'd never met anyone so defiantly unafraid, not even another *were*. It was hotter than a bonfire on the Summer Solstice. My gaze caught on his plump lips that seemed to be perpetually begging for a kiss. Perhaps I'd steal more than just his scent. Maybe find the answers to more than one question...

"Finally got that coffee for you," Officer Mack's voice intruded on my eerie sense of determination.

I froze in my advance and glanced at the young officer, who seemed completely oblivious to what he'd stumbled upon.

"Sorry it took so long. HoT D Coffee was contending with a school board order. Anyway, there you go. Dark mocha with two extra shots of espresso and a caramel chaser." Officer Mack reached across the desk to place the cup in front of Josh and looked up. Uncertainty immediately clouded his features. "Uh... am I interrupting something?"

His question snapped whatever insanity I'd fallen under. I recoiled from the backlash of it, and the desk made a metallic screech against the floor as I swiftly pulled away from the mere inches I'd been from Josh. Officer Mack's gaze darted between Josh's stoically impassive face and my obvious heavy breathing.

Josh blinked once at me and then turned his attention to the officer. He wrapped a hand around the steaming cup and brought it to his face, where he took an appreciative sip. "Mm, Midnight Run with a sweet end. Thank you, Mack," he said with a genuine smile before leaning back in his chair. I hadn't realized that he'd been leaning forward as well. "To answer your question, I was merely querying Bennett here about his whereabouts on the night in question."

Officer Mack snorted rudely. "He was at the party. I already told you. All the wolves were. Masks are great and all, but the Klamath pack is pretty hard to miss for anyone who knows them," he added, pointing to my distinctive gray hair.

"Why, Mack, were you perchance at this eventful soiree?" Josh asked evenly.

Instantly, the young man's cheeks turned a rather impressive and alarming shade of red. "I... that's not... I mean... all the lycans... You know, I just realized I left donuts in the squad car." With that, Mack made a beeline back out the way he'd come.

"There aren't any donuts," I stated to regain my composure and hopefully my footing.

"I know," Josh replied from behind his cup.

Chapter 8

Joshua

Local Boys and Girls Club receives sponsorship from Portland Vampire Clan

Click.

Radiation studies confirm portals not a threat

Click.

Jewelry store on Elm and Main robbed by what police believe to be two sprites

Click.

Fire demons of Klamath provide warmth and shelter for the homeless

Mute.

Un-fucking believable. How was this happening? Where was the carnage? The horror?

"Where are the goddamn bodies?" I growled aloud.

It simply wasn't possible. Not even so much as a mention that a single member of the pack had died–brutally or otherwise. I tightened my hold on the small control device before sending it flying across the room to crack into the wall.

"I saw it with my own eyes. Even *one* should have created enough chaos to leave a trail of blood. And nothing!" I shouted as I waved emphatically at the muted screen, which was still scrolling positive headline after positive headline. My teeth ground together in bated fury while I stood there and seethed.

On cue, a call came in. The specialized ding alerted me to the call's origin and its encryption.

"What?" I snapped upon answering.

"You mind your tone of voice with me, Joshua. They may believe you're some hotshot out there, but we both know the truth. You're a failure just like your father." My mother's waspish voice stung in a million ways. Insult to injury. Nothing new there, but her timing could have been better. Today was *not* the day to test me.

"What do you want?" I repeated.

"Your progress report is overdue. But I can see from national news feeds that, as expected, you have been unsuccessful. I warned you that your ridiculous scheme would never work. Nature is no match for steel."

"The delivery system worked perfectly. I saw it myself. Besides which, how many times do I have to remind you that a trail of syringes would only spark suspicion?"

She huffed but didn't respond. "If it worked so well, then where are the results? Where are the bodies of slaughtered *weres*?"

"I don't know," I ground out. "I've exhausted the town's backlog of lycan-related cases and dallied as long as I dare. The territory itself is next. They must be hiding the infected *weres*. It's the only explanation I can think of." What I couldn't fathom was how they'd done so and still kept the bloodshed quiet. There was at the very least one gruesome death on pack lands, and yet the news was infuriatingly lacking from any major sources. It was a mystery, one I was determined to crack. "I'll figure it out," I said more to myself.

"Get it done, Joshua. I'm losing patience." True to form, the call simply died.

I roared my frustration into the silent room. The woman was an evil shrew and wouldn't know a well laid out plan if it bit her on the nose. The feathers had been a stroke of genius, and they'd worked better than expected. But if that was true, where were my results? Where were my devastated wolves? Where was all the goddamn blood?!

My fingers clenched into painful fists to prevent them from destroying more of the room than I already had.

"I need a drink."

It was something I rarely did. The added complication of reduced inhibitors on top of the magic embedded in my bones made getting drunk a dangerous endeavor, but at that moment, I couldn't have cared less. The day was shaping up to be epically disastrous. Literally the only thing working in my favor was the mere fact that my vile excuse for a mother hadn't said a word about it being my birthday. Yes, a drink was definitely in order.

I buttoned up my vest with its host of poisoned blades firmly nestled on my back and shrugged on a heavy coat. Within the last two days, a cold snap had come and plummeted the temperature to a staggering negative two degrees Celsius. But not even the freezing cold could keep me in my room like some kind of caged animal.

The brandy burned its way down my throat, fighting off the cold that had seeped past my coat. Within minutes, the suffocating heat of the space mixed with the alcohol had me discarding the coat and unbuttoning my vest to get cooler air on my skin. I even rolled up my sleeves to no avail.

A thin bead of sweat snaked its way past my collar. Why couldn't bars find a balance between the cold outside and the heat inside? I rapidly undid my top two buttons, and finally a breath of air found its way to my rapidly thawing body.

I took another drink and set down the empty glass, which was promptly replaced by the bartender. The man was good, I'd give him that, even if he wasn't much to look at. Perhaps he'd be more interesting to talk to. I'd never indulged in the stereotypical act of conversing with a barkeep, though today certainly warranted breaking the norm.

"Do you know who I am?" I asked.

The man whisked away the empty glass, effectively maintaining his spotless bar top. "Couldn't tell you from some random in the street."

I gave him a knowing look. "I wouldn't recommend lying to me."

His mouth twisted at my words, and I internally berated myself. My blunt manner was just one of the many reasons I often found myself alone.

"Don't suppose there's anyone in here worth talking to?" I tried instead.

He gestured with his head towards the entrance. "Suspect that gentleman might be inclined to keep you company," he offered.

My brow furrowed in confusion, but before I could press the man, he'd made his escape. I sneered at his retreating form and turned to see what the devil he was talking about. When my eyes fell on the six foot three man with broad shoulders, thick trunk, well-muscled thighs, and remarkably steely hair walking towards me, I could have cursed out loud.

Elijah Bennett. Did this day have no reprieve?

I spun back to the bar and took a large swallow from the fresh glass. Fire coursed through my veins and only burned brighter when the sexy *were* pulled up next to me.

He leaned on the counter and considered me for a moment before saying, "You weren't at the precinct."

"I took the day," I replied without meeting his studying gaze.

"I wasn't aware Lycan Detectives got days off."

"You're not aware of a lot of things," I fired back and downed the rest of my glass.

"Bad day?" When I failed to answer, he tried a different approach. "Your glass is empty."

"No shit."

"You should let me buy you another one."

Finally, I glanced at him. "Do I look like the kind of guy who needs someone to buy them drinks?" I hated how the small smile that teased Elijah's lips and shone in his eyes only added to the heat growing in my belly.

"Then *you* can buy *me* a drink," he stated as he made himself comfortable on the stool beside me.

I gave him an incredulous look. He couldn't possibly be serious. "I don't generally make a habit of drinking with werewolves."

"Then don't drink. You can sit there and stare at your glass while I drink," he responded, completely unfazed.

I huffed a laugh despite myself and raised two fingers to the surly bartender. The drinks arrived promptly, and someone spirited away my empty glass again. I stared down into the colored liquid as Elijah took a sip.

"Hmm, can't say that I've had all that much brandy, but this is pretty good. Sweeter than I would have expected, with a touch of oakiness."

"Cognac."

"Is that what it is?"

"Your eyes." I held up my glass and considered its amber contents. "They're the color of cognac. I thought honey before, but it didn't feel quite right. This does," I finished and took a more moderate sip than my last few drinks. When I set the glass back down and turned to look at him, he was staring right back. "What?"

"You know, you're not as awful as you'd like everyone to believe."

I snorted. "Don't be deceived."

"Oh, don't mistake me. I'm still very aware of how dangerous you are and the threat you pose to my pack. But there's more to you than you let others see."

I couldn't help but wonder if he realized how commanding he sounded when he spoke about his pack, as if it was his duty to defend them and not someone else's. "One could make the same argument about you."

He gave me a toothy grin and shifted to be more comfortable on his seat. A move that only highlighted how powerful his legs were. I swallowed and averted my gaze to the dance floor, where several sweaty bodies were gyrating with what I supposed was an attempt at rhythm. It really just looked like a mass orgy with clothes. I wasn't particularly fond of orgies. I much preferred one-on-one, where all my focus could be dedicated to pulling out gasps of pleasure, indulging every sweet sensation, and relishing the decadence of hot fingers trailing over my body...

That train of thought wasn't helping my situation any better, so I refocused my attention on my thankfully still full glass. Or had someone replaced it again? Fuck, I needed to keep better count. Drinking was dangerous enough for me without the added difficulty of doing so with a man that I desperately wanted to make every birthday wish I'd ever had come true, right here on the bar.

I shook my head and intentionally took a small sip. At least the music was pleasant.

"Must be a theme night," Elijah said, pulling me out of the seductive beat.

"Hm?" I hummed, glancing at him out of the corner of my eye. Seriously, why did he have to be the perfect embodiment of my deepest desires? It just wasn't fair.

He rested his arms on the counter in a move I wasn't sure he intended to be as distracting as it was. I remembered exactly how easily he'd manhandled me at the Bacchanal to get into the exact position he wanted. "The music. This bar isn't known for playing pop divas. And certainly not anything that isn't from this century. Not that I'm complaining."

I hummed again as I took another sip. That certainly explained why I enjoyed the music. I'd always had a bit of a soft spot for late twentieth and early twenty-first century divas. Though I'd die before admitting it.

"You have a nice singing voice, by the way."

I swiveled so fast to look at him it was a wonder I didn't fall off the stool. "Excuse me?"

"You're singing bits of the song. Though I suspect you didn't intend for anyone to notice since you were doing it under your breath." He gave me a warm smile that did as much damage as the alcohol, maybe more. "At any rate, it's nice," he added before taking another swallow of his drink.

I watched his Adam's apple bob with rapt attention while his words slowly sank in. When they finally did, I ripped my attention away from him with an irritated grunt. Damn werewolf super-hearing. And damn Toni Braxton's seductive music and inconveniently apt lyrics. And damn my mother, the godforsaken government, and alcohol too, while I was at it.

"So... any updates on the case?" he pushed.

I shook my head and cringed inwardly. While Elijah was technically fulfilling the obligations of his role as pack liaison, there was no way I was diving into that nest of snakes while I was inebriated. "I don't want to talk about the case."

He gave me a considering look. "What would you rather talk about?"

I noticed his glass had recently been refreshed and tightened my grip on mine so the overly-attentive barkeep couldn't give mine the same treatment. "Tell me about your studies at Dartmouth. That's not exactly an easy place to get into." What I didn't add was that it was even harder when you were a supernatural. Prejudices still ran pretty deep in some places, one of the oldest higher learning institutions notwithstanding.

Elijah's eyebrows rose in unconcealed shock. "Found out about that, did you?"

I shot him a look, and he laughed again. A rich sound that made me think of rivers running through a forest.

"Touché. I studied late twentieth-century history. A little early twenty-first as well. Mostly American social studies, though I had a few courses that delved into more ancient times."

Fuck me. Why did I not know that? And why were the Tonys ganging up on me? "That explains your comment."

"Which one?"

"The Tony Bennett reference. Though Mack sold you out. I know the truth now."

I'd expected Elijah to have something to say about that. Instead, he smiled, a smile that continued to grow until it dominated his face.

"What?" I asked, increasingly perturbed by his reaction.

"You seem quite familiar with the man yourself."

"What makes you say that?"

"You're humming 'Fly Me to the Moon'."

Fuck. Did I normally sing this much, and no one was ever around to tell me?

I hastily took another drink to hide my discomfort and instantly regretted it. I relinquished my hold on the glass before I could try to down it. Another decision I would come to regret as the bartender magically manifested more of the expensive liquor in my glass. So that's how he was doing it. Man was a godforsaken conjurer. I could have groaned with frustration. This was so not going well.

"This is why I don't drink in mixed company," I commiserated aloud.

"And why exactly is that?" Elijah asked, somehow closer than he'd been mere moments before.

"I tend to make questionable life choices."

He laughed again, a sound I was coming to enjoy hearing.

I glared down at my still half-full glass. Just how much *have* I had to drink?

"Like what?" he purred, the implied invitation rolling through his words. Or maybe it wasn't. Maybe I was already three sheets to the wind and none the wiser.

"Like saying things I shouldn't," I responded honestly.

"Oh? There state secrets that the rest of us aren't privy to?" he teased.

I gave him a lopsided grin. "Bennett, there are a plethora of things I shouldn't tell you." Like what really brought me to Adler Springs, the truth about who I was, how badly I wanted him to drop pretense and just fuck me over the bar.

I drew in a shaky breath and let my gaze fall to the counter, where it instantly became riveted on his fingers mere inches from my exposed arm. My breathing turned shallow while my internal temperature ratcheted up several more degrees as I remembered just how hot that touch was and how good it could feel to have his hands on me.

I swallowed thickly and shifted my attention to look back out at the dance floor. There was no squashing my envy of the dancers' ability to touch each other, the warmth they would find at the end of the night in someone else's arms, the sheer freedom they had to do whatever they wanted with whomever they wanted.

"You should dance," Elijah said in a low baritone right in my ear.

Chills instantly erupted across my body. Chills, I prayed he didn't notice. "What makes you think I want to dance?" I asked to buy time.

"Because you keep glancing over at the dance floor."

I shook my head, though I was grateful he didn't mention the singing again.

"Come on, Josh, those legs were made for dancing." His gaze raked over me, dragging a flush of pleasure in its wake.

I leaned forward, invading his space as much as he'd invaded mine. "These legs were made for a lot more than just dancing." The moment the last word left my tongue, I wished I'd kept the comment to myself.

Elijah's eyes dilated, and their stunning cognac darkened to a deeper amber.

Great, now both of us are thinking about my legs wrapped around him. Or at least one of us is.

Fuck, if that wouldn't be a great way to end this miserable day.

I shot the thought down before it could manifest into yet another ill-conceived come-on.

Stop flirting with the werewolf. Keep it in your damn pants.

Except my pants were already unbearably uncomfortable. Major downside with skin-tight clothing–zero room for an erection.

Enough, I scolded myself and pushed the glass away even though there were still at least another two good swallows in it. I cleared my throat.

"Yeah, dancing is probably not a good idea at the moment." A bead of sweat streaked its way down my back between my shoulder blades. Fuck, it was hot in here, and a werewolf standing practically on top of me was not helping.

"Poor life choices?"

"Something like that," I evaded, though it did little to diminish the knowing look in his eyes.

"You wouldn't have to dance by yourself, if that's what you're worried about," he added.

It took absolutely no imagination to recognize that it would take all of point-five seconds of pretending to have sex to music, to me dragging his furry ass out back and making it a reality. There wasn't a demon's chance in heaven that I'd survive him placing so much as a finger on my hip.

"Fresh air might actually be preferable," I said instead of arguing and shifted to follow my own advice. The stool wobbled alarmingly as I attempted to extricate myself.

Elijah's hand shot out to steady me, but I caught myself on the bar first and held up a free hand to stop him. Heaven and hell help me if he actually touched me in my current state.

"I'm good."

"You sure? I'll come with you," he insisted.

The double entendre had my already weak legs threatening to buckle. "No. I'll be fine. Just need to get out of this stifling heat." On cue, yet another bead of sweat slid freely down my torso.

Out of the corner of my eye, I saw Elijah's nostrils flare subtly. Extra fuck. The potion I'd taken earlier in the day was nearing its end, and actively sweating was only speeding up the process. It wouldn't take much longer, given the circumstances, for my real scent to become public knowledge and enlighten Elijah to a whole slew of things I didn't need him to know.

"Actually, come to think of it, it might actually be best if I just head to bed for the night."

"I'll walk you home," Elijah said completely undeterred as he held out my coat.

For a split second, I was actually afraid to take it from him. I didn't trust myself anymore, certainly not where Elijah was concerned. I conquered the trepidation and took the heavy peat coat from him, somehow avoiding contact and not snatching it.

"Nice try, but where a Lycan Detective stays while they're on the job is typically classified and for good reason."

He gave me a smile that suggested that while he knew what I was saying was the truth, he also recognized the evasion. If that was the case, then I was a special kind of fucked.

"Then I'll see you tomorrow."

I nodded and began the arduous process of leaving without stumbling into anything.

"Enjoy your evening, Josh," Elijah said just loud enough to travel, but with a husky undercurrent that had my entire body aching to turn around.

It took every ounce of training I had to stride out the door without looking back.

Once outside, the sharp, frigid air surged through my lungs, jolting me somewhat closer and painfully to sober. Though nowhere near enough to dismiss the way I'd imagined Elijah's eyes lingering on me as I left. As it was, I was still far too tempted to turn around and plunge back into the warmth of the bar and his unnaturally hot embrace.

I shook myself as if it could shake the persistent delirium free, which allowed more of the bitter air to snake its way past my layers of protection. Just like that, my discomfort at being too warm was a distant memory. Unlike the memory of Elijah's warm gaze and even warmer touch, that was still absurdly fresh and actively burning away my resolve.

I raced back to the apartment, barely having the wherewithal to conceal my route. Once safely inside, I tossed my still unbuttoned vest aside and undid my trousers enough to free my aching cock. I didn't bother removing the rest of my clothes before working myself through the frenzy I'd been in for the last two hours. I fisted my dick, leveraging the copious precum leaking out of me to smooth the glide, while thoughts of my epic night with Elijah at the Bacchanal fueled my frantic efforts.

His savage kisses, his moist breath on my neck, the inescapable heat of him inside of me. I groaned at the vivid memory, and my strokes became more erratic, desperate.

A gasp escaped me as I rode the fantasy, even twisting it so that there was no mask, no glamour. Just me and him in those woods, at the bar, the precinct... I didn't even fucking care where, as long as he knew it was me who'd given him such an incredible night, that *I* was the one who had brought him to such heights.

No lycan in their right mind would ever give me what I wanted from them if they knew who I really was. But I wanted Elijah to, wanted it so badly, just as I'd wanted him to bend me over the bar and take me right there, other people be damned. His heat pressed against me, sliding deeper, claiming me...

My back arched and my head slammed into the wall as I came hard with Bennett's name on my lips. I sagged where I was, panting for breath, until I finally mustered up enough energy to drag my drunk ass to the bathroom and clean up.

I stared at myself in the rapidly fogging mirror with the rain shower falling behind me. Where was the confident man in charge of every situation? The man who made lycans shrink in fear? How had I let it come to this? Practically brought begging to my knees from a brief interaction and a few drinks. I needed to wrap this mission up and get the fuck out of Adler Springs before things with Elijah got anymore out of control.

I swiped violently at the mirror and turned to wash away the evidence of my weakness.

Chapter 9

Elijah

When I walked into the precinct first thing in the morning, it was immediately apparent that something was off. My brow furrowed as I caught Officer Mack's borderline panicked expression from across the room. I quickly sought Josh, suddenly anxious that something might have happened to him. When my gaze landed on his back where he stood by his usual desk, I let out a sigh of relief, then focused on figuring out why the officer was so out of sorts.

At first glance, nothing seemed amiss. He was rifling through reports, a typical pastime for the detective at the start of the day, with his trademark coffee from Hair of the Dog next to his elbow. I did a double take. There were not one, but *three* extra-large to-go cups clustered within easy reach. Even as I noted the troubling distinction, he absently reached down and plucked what I imagined was the only full one left and took a sizable sip.

Concern instantly replaced my excitement to see Josh again after our unusual evening. He'd said he didn't drink often. Was it possible that something had happened after he'd left? I knew I should have insisted on seeing him safely back to his place. He'd put on a good show sauntering out on semi-steady legs into the freezing night, but clearly that's all it had been.

I walked towards him, determined to figure out what was wrong. My fingers hovered inches from the small of his back when he danced to the side and out of reach, all without so much as a glance over his shoulder.

"Josh—"

"Sit down and don't interfere," he barked, indicating a chair pulled up at the far corner of the desk. Order delivered, he immediately went back to what he was doing as if I wasn't there at all.

I stared dumbly at his back for a moment, thrown by the blatant dismissal, then moved to take my assigned seat. My mind reeled with confusion at the stark contrast between his behavior last night and the cold shoulder I was getting this morning. Had I done something wrong? Sure, he was a hard ass most of the time, but this was way past that. Where was the witty banter and snarky comebacks? He hadn't even baited me yet. I sat heavily in my seat, and it groaned in protest.

Officer Mack used the excuse of placing a cup of steaming tea in front of me to whisper, "He's on a warpath. Was already neck-deep in reports by the time I got here." He paused and gave me a pointed look before adding, "At five."

My gaze shot back to the three cups, then to Josh mindlessly combing through reports, his foot tapping relentlessly and his fingers never holding still longer than a second. I knew how strong he took his coffee and suspected that what was in those cups could put a golem into cardiac arrest. And he'd been here since before five in the morning? We hadn't even parted ways until well after midnight. Fuck, had he even slept?

I looked closer and saw the confirmation I didn't want to find. There was a tightness at the edge of his eyes, a hollowness that hadn't been there before, along with something much darker. Worry tightened my chest, and I couldn't have stopped the words if I had tried.

"Did something happen after you left last night?"

It was probably just my imagination, but I could have sworn he winced at the question. Imagination or not though, he didn't deign to respond.

"Josh, answer me," I demanded, my concern growing. "You said you were fine." He'd said it plainly, so it had to be true; everyone knew Lycan Detectives couldn't lie.

Before he could respond, Officer Mack interjected. "You two were together last night?" His face was a mix of surprise and confusion.

"No," Josh clipped at the same time I said, "Yes."

I stared at him, interested to know on what grounds he could give such a definitive declaration, given his unique restrictions.

He glared at me, his normally plush mouth pressed into a thin line, his green eyes dark with barely checked anger. A muscle in his cheek twitched as if he were grinding his teeth to prevent himself from saying something. Finally, he blinked and turned his attention to the visibly distraught officer.

"I was at Salvation's Edge last night."

"You two went to a bar without me?" young Mack asked, obviously upset about being left out.

Josh gave him a very direct look and emphasized, "*I* was at the bar. Bennett showed up and refused to leave."

My ruff was officially up. "I don't recall you ever asking me to."

Fury blazed in his eyes. His mouth opened, no doubt to bite out some scathing retort, but then he seemed to think better of it and closed it without uttering a word. He refocused his attention almost violently on the reports spread out before him. Officer Mack and I shared a look, but we both wisely kept our mouths shut.

Thirty minutes of the tensest silence I'd ever been part of dragged by uninterrupted. My second cup of tea grew cold. Mack ran out of things to pretend to type. Officers passing by were giving us strange looks. Then, without warning, Josh shot up from his chair.

I jolted in my seat, and Officer Mack spilled whatever he'd been attempting to drink. I caught a muffled oath that sounded suspiciously like "Mother of Pearl."

My humor at his choice of curse, however, was short-lived. Josh made a sweeping gesture from his data tab towards the one sitting near the struggling officer. It instantly lit up with the received information.

"I'll be going to these coordinates today," Josh said without even the slightest inflection. Then didn't bother to wait for a reply, merely scooped the three apparently empty cups into the compost collector and turned to leave.

Mack shot me an anxious look, still dusting the once scalding liquid from his uniform, and called after Josh's retreating form. "But this last one is—"

Josh stopped mid-stride and spun on his heel to face the young man. "I'm well aware of what I gave you. Despite what everyone seems to believe, I am still the lead detective on this case and have a job to do. Now, are you coming?" he lashed out with one eyebrow quirked, a move that instantly reminded me of my hookup from the Bacchanal.

Is it really possible?

HART'S BETRAYAL

While I tried to reconcile that the two men might be one and the same, Officer Mack scurried from behind his desk, only just remembering to grab the remote for the squad car and vanished after Josh. Suddenly, I found myself still sitting, completely flabbergasted at what had just happened. I glanced around the eerily quiet room as the reality of my situation painfully reasserted itself.

By the time I made it outside, they'd already disengaged the hovercar from its charging station and were angling out of the lot. Josh shot me a look of challenge through the passenger-side window, but didn't have Mack stop.

Furious, I rounded on the nearest cluster of officers. "One of you, tell me where that car is heading right now," I growled.

The group was a mix of supernatural and human, but all of them looked shaken. The bravest, or the dumbest depending on how you looked at it, stepped forward. She swallowed hard and eked out, "Sorry sir, we can't do that. I'm sure if you just wait inside—"

"I am the Klamath pack liaison and Lycan Detective Joshua Hart was in that patrol car. You *will* tell me where it is going."

The poor soul turned pale, even for a vampire. "Y-yes, sir. I'll find out right away," she stammered. She promptly pulled out an identical data tab as the one Josh had sent the coordinates to not minutes before.

I clenched and unclenched my fists while I waited for an answer. Every second it took was another second Josh had to get farther away and possibly closer to the truth. Keeping him away from Tommy was my job, and somehow I'd let a pair of pretty legs and bright eyes distract me from that. It was honestly a toss-up of who I was angrier with: the duplicitous detective that had given me the slip or myself for being too selfish to do what was expected of me.

Finally, the woman held up the device so I could see exactly where the source of all my frustration had whisked off to. "Looks like they're headed to—"

"The crime scene," I finished for her.

"Yes, sir."

"Fuck," I hissed, causing the group to jump. What on earth could he need from a crime scene that was over a week old and he'd already looked at? Nothing good, that's what. I turned my angry gaze to the cluster trying desperately to make a hasty departure. "Now, which one of you is going to take me there?"

No one looked eager to volunteer.

Two minutes into the drive, my anger dissipated. Nothing about Josh's behavior was unexpected. I was the one who'd been lured in by a false sense of—what? Nothing could happen between us. Wishing otherwise was a pipe dream at best. I had a better chance of sprouting wings on the next full moon than I did of getting a man like Joshua Hart to give up all his secrets. And still, I couldn't let it go.

Something had happened at that bar. Something I was missing. He'd seemed more than open to my advances. Or maybe I'd read him wrong. I'd only ever spent time with him in the context of work. He could be a completely different person when he wasn't hunting down werewolves to prosecute.

Fuck that, I wanted a proper explanation. For moon's sake, the man liked early-millennium pop divas. And he sang... *well*. There had to be more to Joshua Hart than his job, and I refused to believe otherwise.

The car slowed to a stop, and I looked out the window to find that Josh and Officer Mack were already making their way back to their vehicle. I muttered a thank you to the poor woman I'd basically held hostage and launched out of the car to intercept them.

Josh cast a disinterested glance in my direction at the sound of the door slamming shut, then continued on his way. Officer Mack raced up to me, all the while casting anxious glances at the detective. I didn't have time for his platitudes. Josh was practically at the patrol car.

"I tried to tell him..." Mack's words followed me as I stalked past him, intent on the object of my renewed anger.

I was all set to grab Josh by his collar and yank him back to demand some answers when he spun around to face me.

Fire burned fiercely in his eyes as he cracked out, "You lay so much as a finger on me and so help me God, I will have you on your back before you can sprout fur."

For one brief, insane moment, I wanted to call his bluff. Then logic reasserted itself. Joshua Hart had the legal right to kill any lycanthrope he deemed a danger, and that included me.

I dropped my hand, but not my anger. "You left me at the precinct. You can't do that."

His eyes narrowed, and his jaw ticked. "I don't need some pup dogging my every move."

"Some pup?" I echoed in disbelief. "We're the same damn age!"

"Lycanthropes live longer than humans. Averaging what? A hundred and sixty? Comparatively speaking, you're actually several years younger than even Mack."

"I'll have you know my grandmother died at the ripe old age of two hundred. And while we're being technical, humans are easily living to be a hundred and twenty these days, if not longer. Check your math."

He barked a sardonic laugh. "Fine then, you're Mack's age. You're still too young to be nipping at my heels like some kind of retainer."

Mack gave an indignant squawk behind us, which we both ignored.

"It doesn't work that way, and you know it," I growled, stepping closer. "*Weres* hit puberty at the same time as humans. We just get to enjoy the perks longer." I took another step, placing myself firmly in his personal bubble. Close enough to tell that despite my proximity and threatening demeanor, he remained stoically unafraid.

"Back. Up," he warned with a low growl. "Now," he added when I didn't move.

A tiny movement at the corner of my eye caught my attention, and I glanced down to see his hand hovering over the unclipped firearm strapped to his thigh. I took in the blatant promise of violence and brought a level glare up to meet his unflinching, forest-green gaze. "Make me."

For a long minute, neither of us moved. Then he let out a hiss and spun away, now going in the opposite direction of the patrol car. He was going at a good clip, and I had to jog to catch up.

"Where do you think you're going?" I asked.

"To do my job."

I almost laughed at his fierce statement, then I saw where he was going with such determination. My eyes widened with alarm, and I quickened my pace to insert myself between him and his destination.

"Get out of my way, Bennett."

"No. You can't just walk onto pack territory," I countered.

"It is my right and my job. Now move." He stepped forward again, but I held my ground, refusing to budge even an inch.

If I stepped onto pack land while escorting a Lycan Detective, it was tantamount to an invitation, one I couldn't afford to give. When it was clear he'd either have to physically remove me from his path or bowl me over, he stopped.

"I have a right," he tried once more.

"Not without a warrant, you don't."

Sheer animal fury radiated from him. "Are you fucking serious?" he hissed.

"Deadly."

He took one heavy breath followed by another, then glared at me with such animosity I almost stepped back anyway. "Fine. I'll get your damnable warrant, and then you *will* escort me to any part of that godforsaken territory that I want to go to. Understood?"

"Get the warrant," I repeated.

Anger and violence warred on his face as he visibly tried to bring himself under control. My concern from earlier returned with a vengeance. This wasn't the Josh I knew. He could be surly, but he could also be witty and flirtatious. Whatever had happened after he left the bar was bad.

"Josh," I said softly. I didn't even realize I was reaching out to him until his words brought me up short.

"I swear, if you touch me... There will be more than one dead *were* in Klamath." He spun sharply on his heel and immediately began stalking back towards town.

"His name is Tommy. You don't even know if he did it," I called after him. "He's just a kid, Josh."

Josh stopped for a second at my words, then continued his angry march.

Chapter 10

Elijah

I STARED UP AT the ceiling and tried to figure out yet again what had happened and what to do. I missed the Josh I'd gotten to know that night. The one who laughed and relaxed and apparently could sing. The one I'd seen stare longingly out at a dance floor filled with people. The one that had gotten my ruff up in more ways than one. If surly Detective Joshua Hart was an undeniable walking sex symbol, drunk Josh was a moonforsaken incubus. Except *that* Josh was gone, nowhere to be found. In his place was someone who may have looked like Joshua Hart, but had all the warmth of a frozen rock.

I could have and would have spent hours dwelling on every word, every movement, every look either of us had shared since he got here, but I had far more pressing concerns. While Josh had gone back to whatever hole he was hiding away in, I'd gone to the pack house to warn everyone. Conrad had been out on a hunt, however, which left me waiting and obsessing until morning. Time I feared we didn't have. It wouldn't take Josh long to force through a warrant. Moon knew he had enough circumstantial evidence at this point to at least merit a cursory visit, then we'd all be in trouble.

I glanced at the time embedded in my wrist. *How much longer is Conrad going to be? What part of important says take your moonforsaken time?* No sooner did I have the thought than the door opened on the guest room and Sylvan popped his head in.

"Alpha will meet you in the living room. He says not to dawdle," he said, then promptly exited.

I growled at the closed door as I rolled out of bed. This whole thing was a power play, a way to remind me of my place. The pack could not afford these juvenile tantrums; there was simply too much at stake. Once again, I debated just turning Tommy over myself and demanding a fair trial. And just like all the other times, I quickly dismissed the idea. As much as I wanted things to be done differently, going behind Conrad's back would be the end of the life I knew.

The curious eyes of my packmates filled the upstairs hallway as I made my way downstairs to the formal living room. Enough time had passed that pretty much everyone in the pack had heard that I'd basically demanded an audience with Conrad. Doubtless some of them were expecting news of an entirely different nature than I had to give. I let out a sigh and absently pulled my hair back into a tail. The band snapped firmly into place as I rounded the last corner and came face to face with Conrad and Nikolai.

"About time," Conrad grumbled.

I chose the high ground and refused to take the bait. I continued walking until I was in the center of the room. When he didn't encourage me to sit, I remained standing and held my wrists behind my back. "Thank you for meeting with me, Alpha," I said formally.

Conrad nodded at the show of respect and gestured for me to relax, but not to sit. My jaw tightened at the obvious ploy, but again I didn't comment. His treatment of me was not the issue at the moment. Someday it would be, but moon help me, that day was a long time coming.

"You said you had important news," Nikolai said to get things started.

"I do."

"If it was so urgent, why not send a message so we could take action?" he countered.

I diligently contained my sigh at their lack of foresight. This was an argument I had expected, but had vainly hoped I wouldn't encounter. "It seemed more prudent to convey the news in person. Detective Hart has substantial resources at his disposal, and I wouldn't put it past him to tap or otherwise intercept any communications."

Alarm blossomed on several faces watching on in silence. Conrad maintained his glower, but Nikolai's faltered.

"Surely he cannot do such a thing without a warrant of some kind," Nikolai argued.

"That's the thing..."

"He has a warrant?" Conrad interrupted. Gasps cascaded down from the balcony and echoed around the glass-filled room.

I winced at his blunt delivery. There was no help for it. This was the way Conrad had always been. Once that had been a boon that had helped him earn the trust and support needed for his battle and subsequent ascension to Alpha, but times had changed.

"No," I began. Relief whooshed around me in a collective sigh. "But he's getting one."

Fury sharpened Conrad's gaze, and he advanced on me. It was a disorienting sight with the forest looming dark behind him and the antique cream couch beside him. "You are supposed to be keeping him out of pack business."

I held my ground and looked him dead in the eye. "He is a Lycan Detective. His job *is* pack business. You asked me to report on what he does. That's what I'm doing. He would have walked right onto pack lands yesterday if I hadn't stopped him."

Rage crystallized in Conrad's eyes. Some of my packmates withered against the wall, while others squared their shoulders as if in anticipation of a fight. "And why am I just now hearing about this?!"

"I apologize, Alpha. I should have been more diligent in monitoring him and foreseen his actions ahead of time. Thankfully, not even he can manifest a warrant out of nowhere. I just hope it is enough time to allow us to take appropriate precautions." I almost gagged as I swallowed my pride and effectively tucked my tail between my legs.

Conrad's eyes softened ever so slightly. "Well done, Red. We will move Tommy to a more secure location that your detective cannot reach."

I didn't bother to correct Conrad. Josh wasn't *my* detective, even if I did secretly want him to be. I shoved that thought further down. It had no place in these precarious proceedings. "Where will you take him, Alpha?"

Conrad eyed me for a long moment before answering. "I don't think I will tell you."

I barely bit back a growl at the backhanded insinuation that I couldn't be trusted. A similar energy rippled around the room as if my anger at being slighted was catching.

"Plausible deniability," Conrad added, completely unfazed by what was happening around him.

"Can you at least give me a heading?" The look Conrad shot me had me quickly adding, "So that I can ensure we don't accidentally stumble on where Tommy is being moved."

"You need not concern yourself with that, but if you are so desperate for guidance, keep him on the east slopes." Conrad turned away, a blatant dismissal.

I wanted to demand a better explanation. To know what was going on with Tommy. If we'd heard from Sabrina yet. If anyone knew where Keith was, or Levi for that matter. Or what the hell was wrong with Zeke. And above it all, if Conrad was out of his fucking mind having me take Josh to the very place we'd been holding Tommy this whole time.

I voiced none of them. "Yes, Alpha."

Joshua

I couldn't believe he was actually going to make me get a warrant to enter pack territory. My teeth ground together hard enough that I actually heard it. Definitely needed to see a witch about that. I angrily closed the latest report. Now all that remained was to wait. One would have thought that an actual Lycan Detective requesting a warrant would have motivated the local brass to do something faster than a slug's crawl, but apparently not even homicide could get gears turning faster in a small town.

I dropped my head heavily into my hands, where I began massaging my temples. My mind rebelliously thought about how much more effective the pressure would be if it was done by someone else's strong fingers, their natural heat loosening the tense muscles. A sigh escaped me as I fell all too easily into the fantasy.

God, my behavior the other day had been deplorable. I'd done everything I could think of to keep Elijah at a distance, but the stubborn *were* had pushed past all of my defenses and refused to be set aside. I still wasn't sure what was worse: half the awful things I'd said or how much I'd wanted him to call me on my shit.

Warmth suffused the back of my neck as massaging fingers that weren't my own worked to relieve the kinks that had taken up residence. They could have been magical, given how amazing the fingers felt as they worked their way up to the base of my skull. But that kind of magic was not only frivolous but pricey as well. A small groan fell out of me at the instant relief that flowed in their wake.

I didn't want to turn around just yet. Didn't want it to stop. I certainly didn't want to leap into yet another verbal sparring that would end in us nearly coming to blows. His fingers just felt so good. For a few seconds longer, I just wanted to enjoy the feel of Elijah's touch on my skin. It couldn't last, but another minute wouldn't hurt.

However, the massage gradually slowed and then stopped altogether, taking the choice out of my hands. I slowly lifted my head and turned to confront my demons. To my infinite shock, it was not Elijah standing behind me, but someone I didn't recognize. The man was certainly not dressed for police work, with vibrant, striped long sleeves, nor had I ever seen him at the precinct before.

"What do you think you're doing?" I asked as calmly as I could, doing my best to mask my disappointment.

He gave what I assumed was supposed to be a charming smile and extended one hand down in greeting. The other remained firmly placed on my shoulder, which was gradually tightening back up again. The man didn't even have the decency to look abashed. "Name's Jason Mack. I'm Joel's cousin."

I reluctantly accepted the handshake, though I still wasn't pleased that he'd had the gall to place his hands on me like that, forget the fact that I'd been perfectly okay with it a minute ago when I'd believed it was Elijah. "I'll ask again. What do you think you're doing?" I repeated.

The slight blush that tinged his cheeks was reminiscent of the ones I'd seen on Officer Mack's face in the past. At the recognition of the familial resemblance, who he was finally sunk in. Of course, he was Mack's cousin. I'd add not knowing Officer Mack's first name to my list of failings.

Jason snatched his hands back. "Oh, I'm sorry. I just... Joel asked me to check on you. I can see why. You're super stressed. I studied to be a chakra masseuse, and I, uh... thought I could help," he finally finished, his embarrassment now firmly set in. "Oh God, please tell me you're Detective Hart. Biscuits! This always happens to me. Why can't I think before I do?"

I gave the man currently freaking out a subtle once-over. Mack had been right. His cousin was cute, not my type at all, but then Officer Mack also didn't know my type trended furrier. My cheek twitched as I bit back the impulse to lash out. It wasn't his fault he wasn't Elijah. He was just a good person. It was a harsh reality of my life that I didn't come across too many of those. First Mack, now his cousin. It would seem his whole family comprised genuinely decent people.

Confronted with the poor man's awkwardness, I had no choice but to admit that most of it was my fault. If I hadn't been so absorbed in my fantasy, then I would have been aware of someone walking up behind me before they ever laid a finger on me.

"Thank you," I finally said, pushing my chair back to stand.

"Yeah, no problem. It's just, Joel said you were cute. He failed to mention you were freaking gorgeous," he babbled.

I raised an eyebrow but kept any comments to myself.

Soon enough, Jason realized his mouth had run away again and scrambled to catch it. "Oh God, I'm doing it again." He covered his face in mortification, and I had to check my responding smile from emerging. One thing that was definitely going for Jason Mack was that he was adorably awkward.

I placed a firm hand on his shoulder, and he peeked at me from behind his fingers. "Deep breath, Jason. Thank you again for the massage. It helped," I reassured him. It was the truth, even if it hadn't helped in the way the young man had intended.

"Yeah?" he asked tentatively.

"Yes."

His shoulders sagged in relief, and I relinquished my hold on his shoulder.

"Was there anything else?" I asked as gently as I could. It was abundantly clear that whatever chemistry Officer Mack had hoped for between me and his cousin was definitely not there.

"Joel was right. You're a little intimidating at first, but you're actually kind of nice."

I blinked back at him and kept my surprise to myself. That was now twice in less than a week that someone had told me I was nice. Clearly, I was losing my edge.

He smiled openly, then leaned a little closer. For one insane moment, I thought it had all been a ploy, and he was actually leaning in to kiss me, then he whispered conspiratorially, "Also, you're kind of scaring other people around the office."

I glanced to the side to see a cluster of rookies eyeing us like they were waiting for a bomb to go off. A sigh escaped me. "I'll try to work on that."

He gave a small laugh and shook his head. "But seriously, on a professional note, I recommend making peace with whatever has you in such knots before it eats you up."

"Regrettably, it's not quite as easy as all that," I admitted. I neglected to mention that I was pretty sure it was already too late for that.

"Perhaps. But nothing worth having ever is," he said with a wink as if he somehow knew what, or more appropriately who, the actual source of my tension was. With his unexpected wisdom imparted, he turned and sauntered out, regaining confidence with each step he took.

I looked across the table, interested to see what the intuitive Mack had to say about the interaction and maybe ask why the hell he hadn't warned me. My gaze fell on the empty chair that hadn't seen an occupant all day, and I remembered he had the day off.

"Guess that means I'm walking," I said to myself. It might have been easier to ask a rookie, but I suspected the walk would do me good. If only to help eliminate the illusion of Elijah's touch. I gave an involuntary shiver and made my way out into the brisk spring day.

Outside, the pervasive cold was gradually warming to something more tolerable. All around me, the innocuous town of Adler Springs teemed with life and purpose. As I walked down the sidewalk, I envied the parents walking hand in hand with their young child, occasionally stopping to swing the small being above the ground. The child squealed with delight, and I couldn't help but smile. That was certainly not something I had as a child and not likely anything I could ever do myself. I'd be dead long before I could entertain anything as frivolous as having a family. I let out a huff and quickened my step.

The journey to the bakery was shorter than I would have liked. All too soon, I slipped into a sugary-scented warmth. Rather than leap right to questioning the employees, I opted to purchase a decadent sweet first. The decaf accompaniment to the pastry was less than ideal, but after my near overdose of caffeine the other day, it seemed wiser to avoid anything stronger.

I took a seat by the window, which was ideal for observing both the patrons and any passersby. Overall, Adler Springs was proving to be a genuinely congenial place, which made some of the town's apparent hatred for the neighboring pack even more perplexing. Officer Mack certainly didn't harbor any ill will toward his lycan neighbors, nor did most of the populace. Except, I knew from experience working in both larger cities and equally quaint towns, it only took a few stubborn holdouts to make living a peaceful life impossible for everyone.

Oddly enough, it would seem that the pack Alpha himself was on that particular list. It was part of what had made the Klamath pack such an easy target. Unlike their brethren, the Klamath pack seemed to have no intention of integrating with the rest of society, human or supernatural. The bacchanal had been their first endeavor in over ten years to ingratiate themselves with the townsfolk. Whoever had come up with that gem obviously recognized that the pack could not remain aloof forever.

Deep down, I suspected Elijah had something to do with the attempt. He clearly held other views about how the pack should be run. It was a wonder he hadn't done something about it already. But then, Elijah was an educated man who favored words over physical violence, not a trait often found in Alphas, even in this day and age.

I let the thoughts about Elijah go before they could completely consume me. While the *were* was absolutely a puzzle worth solving, I had a job to do. And as the numerous messages from my mother liked to remind me, I was not currently doing it. Of course, it would have helped if *any* of what I'd orchestrated had played out the way I'd intended. I gave a heavy sigh and finished my minor indulgence, then set about asking my questions.

"You mentioned before that Tina had seen the boy before," I said, continuing the line of questioning I'd had with virtually everyone who worked at Devil's Delight.

The woman's gray curls bobbed in agreement. Where Elijah's hair was preternaturally gray, hers was honestly come by, as she was somewhere in her eighties. Despite the age and color, however, she was remarkably spry and gave no indication that she'd be retiring from the bakery anytime soon.

"Oh yes, Tommy was in here all the time. Tina's husband wasn't too fond of that, mind you, but that may have more to do with... you know," she said, giving me a dubious look.

I raised an eyebrow at the blatant speciesism I was being confronted with. "Twenty-two?" I suggested as a more acceptable explanation.

"Well, yes, the lad was definitely too young to be chasing after someone of Tina's age, but I meant the other thing. You know...what he is." Once again, she failed to elaborate.

"Please enlighten me."

The woman finally lost her patience with me. "Now, see here, young man. We both know who you are and what your job entails—"

"I'm very aware of the specifics of my position," I interrupted.

Her face soured as if she'd swallowed a lemon whole, an expression that ruined whatever magical cosmetic surgery she'd had done to preserve her ideal of beauty. I didn't give her any leeway, though. If you were going to hate someone so much on the grounds of something they had no control over, then the least you could do was say it outright.

"You are a very rude young man. Did no one ever teach you any manners?"

"I was taught many things. Now, if you could please answer the question. Was there any particular reason Ashton Carr would dislike Tommy Grant visiting his wife's bakery?"

The woman glared daggers at me. "Ash doesn't like the idea of lycanthropes in his shop."

"Interesting," I said as I made a note in my datapad. I already knew that while Ashton Carr may dislike lycans, the real reason he didn't want the young man in his wife's bakery was because they were having an affair and had been for some time. Something he himself was not any more innocent of. Though it was amusing that the older woman seemed to be clueless about that tidbit.

"What?" she asked indignantly.

I looked back up and met her gaze without flinching. "I was under the impression that Tina Carr was the sole owner of this shop and that someone other than Mr. Carr stood to inherit."

Her jaw dropped and continued to hang open as I pocketed the data tab and made my way to the exit.

"Thank you again for your assistance."

Chapter 11

Elijah

I'D GOTTEN WORD THAT Conrad was moving Tommy a few hours before and was to stall as long as possible. Not that they'd included any clues about where they planned to relocate the kid. All I could do was hope that Conrad wasn't dumb enough to put him at the House. Though knowing Conrad, I might as well wish that the change didn't hurt, and the moon was made of cheese.

I sighed and returned to my task of basically being glued to Joshua Hart. Which should have felt more like a burden than it did. My gaze traveled up his long, toned legs to his equally lengthy torso and arms. Like every other day, his clothes looked painted on. The wolf inside urged me to reach out and push up his long sleeves to reveal the pale skin beneath, to nuzzle his neck, and taste his skin. I struggled to keep the instinct in check, not an easy task considering how much I wanted to lean forward and run my hand along the angles of his body or sink my weight into him.

I shifted in my seat, becoming increasingly uncomfortable as my dick swelled behind my zipper. So far, today had been much the same as the day before, albeit Josh was less violently angry.

"If your chair is so unbearable, then perhaps you should find another," Josh said as he continued to rifle through reports. The latest batch seemed to center on property and taxes. I dared not ask if any had to do with pack land. Adding a boundary dispute to murder was the last thing we needed.

"Am I bothering you?"

His jaw tightened, and he frowned before responding sharply, "You're a distraction."

I leaned forward, giving in to the impulse just a little. He tensed, then seemed to force himself to relax. *What is he afraid I'll do? Especially here, surrounded by witnesses?* Besides, literally none of the things I wanted to do to Josh involved anyone else besides the two of us. "The chair is fine," I finally said.

"Then stop moving around so much."

I kept my snicker to myself. Ruffling Josh's fur was more fun than it should be. I leaned back in the chair and crossed my arms. "I'm surprised."

"About what? That I have ears that work? Every time you move, that damnable chair squeaks," he fired back, still not deigning to look at me.

"You're talking to me today. Unless, of course, you're planning to stop."

He ceased what he was doing and turned to face me, arms crossed defensively over his chest. I diligently dragged my gaze away from his pouty mouth, which was currently set in a frown, to meet his intense green eyes. "Suppose that depends," he said.

I instantly flashed to the last time someone had made a similar statement. My gaze rebelliously flicked down to his mouth again, and I had to drag it back to somewhere less likely to get me in trouble. "On what?"

"On whether you intend to be particularly obnoxious today."

I smothered my grin even as my determination to prove that Joshua Hart and the masked man from the Bacchanal were the same strengthened. "I'll do my best," I replied smoothly.

He rolled his eyes and returned to his perusal of plot distinctions.

Joshua

I gazed out the window in stubborn silence as Mack drove us to Ashton Carr's residence. Elijah sitting in the back seat was a presence I couldn't ignore, though I was doing my damnedest to try. He'd been his usual self all day yesterday and seemed well on track to be the same today. It was driving me crazy. I didn't want his witty banter, or cheeky smile and seductive eyes. Yet, I couldn't seem to stop myself from provoking conversation or seeking his warm cognac gaze that sent waves of heat rolling through my core every time it landed on me.

"What about some music?" Officer Mack suggested out of the blue. He was probably desperate for anything to disrupt the obvious tension between me and my pack liaison. "Any requests?"

Elijah caught my gaze in the rearview mirror, and I gave an involuntary shudder. "Turn it to Time Capsule," he suggested.

Mack cast me a wary look. When I didn't dispute the selection, he shrugged and tuned in the station. Instantly, a peppy beat from the late twentieth century poured through the sound system, accompanied by a female singer belting out catchy lyrics.

I glared absolute murder at Elijah in the mirror. The man had the audacity to smile back.

"I thought you'd appreciate listening to something you know the words to." Elijah's casual proclamation crawled under my skin. How I had ever been dumb enough to let slip the love of such music baffled me.

You were drunk and way too into the man next to you. That's how. I brutally reminded myself.

On cue, Mack swiveled his head to look at me in shock. "You sing?"

I could barely contain my groan. Great, now the officer knew. Fuck my life. *Fuck all of my life.* "Loophole," I ground out.

Elijah miraculously kept his laughter to himself as he hummed along with the pop diva about getting her man. It was too much.

"Maybe silence would be best," I snapped.

Mack withered and adjusted the station to quieter renditions of modern acoustic melodies.

I sagged in my seat and stubbornly ignored Elijah's eyes on the back of my head, even though the gaze felt like a physical touch. I pinched the bridge of my nose and fought off the impending headache. My mind unhelpfully reminded me of my fantasy from the other day and how much more possible it was with Elijah sitting less than two feet behind me. I violently shut down the daydream before it could take hold. If having the insufferable lycan in such proximity was going to be this difficult, I was going to need to find him a different ride.

Elijah

Josh damn near launched himself out of the hovercar the second we stopped in front of Tina Carr's house. I shared a look with Officer Mack, who seemed equally bemused by the detective's behavior. Perhaps suggesting the station had been pushing things a bit too far. Still, the look on Josh's face as the award-winning singer had launched into a chorus of determination and endless love had been absolutely priceless. And there wasn't any doubt in my mind that he knew every single line.

By the time Officer Mack and I caught up, Josh was already at the main door being let inside by a decidedly sour-looking Ashton Carr. The man glared at me with unfettered hatred as I tried to cross the threshold into his house.

"Animals stay outside," he snarled.

In the blink of an eye, Josh was by Ash's side. His green eyes blazed with an anger I'd previously thought exclusively reserved for me. Then, to my amazement, he said in clipped words, "Elijah Bennett is the Klamath pack liaison, and you will show him the respect he deserves. To do any less would insult and demean my position. Step. Aside. Mr. Carr."

Ashton paled at the ferocity of Josh's command. Without further argument, he took a step away from the entrance and allowed me unhindered passage.

"Where are the records I called about?" Josh asked in a suspiciously neutral tone.

Ashton silently led the way to a formal dining room. Boxes filled to the brim with old-fashioned paper and binders of receipts cluttered the table. A couple of datatabs seemed to be stuffed into the mix, but the overall assortment was a disorganized accumulation of history.

I waited until Ashton left the room and Officer Mack absorbed himself in bringing order to the chaos of a box at the far end of the table before I leaned over and purred into Josh's ear, "So you do care."

His gaze whipped around to confront me, his eyes burning with that familiar flame of green. "Do not mistake my professionalism for caring," he snapped.

We stood practically toe to toe while he silently seethed and I struggled not to pull him close. The urge to kiss that stubborn frown into a smile, or even better, a gasping moan, was almost unbearable. If he were my masked stranger, would he feel the same as he had that night? How flushed would he get as pleasure rushed through his body? What differences would there be without a mask to hide behind? My hands itched to find out. To shove the boxes aside and claim him right here, the way he so clearly needed to be claimed. Pure, feral desire battered at my control. It was through sheer force of will alone that I kept my hands by my side.

Josh's gaze narrowed, then he turned away. "Make yourself useful."

I shook my head both at his demeanor and at my stubborn insistence on putting us in potentially compromising positions. As much as I wanted to prove Joshua Hart was my mysterious, sexy playboy, it was possible I was going about it the wrong way. I followed his lead and zeroed in on a collection of my own.

We each emptied a box and began the arduous process of putting everything in some semblance of order. While my hands were busy shuffling yellowed pages, my mind searched for clues that could link the two men. Already, some of Josh's words and mannerisms had reminded me of the silk-shrouded hookup, but it was equally plausible that it was pure coincidence. I needed something more definitive, something unique. Then it hit me.

"You've read Dante's Inferno." I said out of nowhere and glanced up to see what kind of reaction the assumptive statement would garner.

Mack stared blankly back at me, no doubt oblivious to the timeless piece, while Josh responded with a vague, "Yes."

I fought the urge to leer as he stretched his lithe form across the table to retrieve a wayward page.

Officer Mack's brow furrowed as he tried and failed to understand the pertinence of bringing up the nearly nine-hundred-year-old poem. "Why?"

I shrugged as if the answer were irrelevant. "No reason. Remind me, how many levels are there?"

"Nine," Josh confirmed without turning away from his current sheaf of papers. He held one of them up to the light and squinted at the nearly illegible writing scrawled across it, then compared it to the info streaming across his data tab.

"Ah, that's right," I began in mock surprise. "First there's limbo with its wandering philosophers and pagans, then lust and gluttony. You know, I always found the jousting bit with the fourth circle odd. How does that have any relevance to greed? Now, anger fighting it out for all eternity while drowning in the River Styx seems exceptionally poetic." I gave Josh the opportunity to comment, but he remained stoically absorbed in his pursuit. Officer Mack appeared to be equal parts confused and horrified.

When neither of them ventured any opinion, I continued on with my list. "Heresy is an arguably confusing level," I stated cavalierly, bringing me at last to my ultimate destination for the wayward conversation. "Then, of course, there's the seventh hell. Home to violence."

"And sodomy," Josh interjected absently. When I refrained from going on, he turned to me. "If you don't believe me, you're welcome to look it up."

I covered my triumphant grin by saying, "Oh, I'm not disputing it. Most people aren't aware of that distinction." I knew it. I fucking knew it. Josh was intentional about everything, even his curses.

He scowled and crossed his arms, an air of challenge and annoyance practically radiating off him. "And the last two rings are Fraud and Treachery, respectively. If you're trying to gauge the extent of my education, I can assure you, it was extensive."

"Of that, I have no doubt. I was simply thinking how going through this," I gestured widely to the sheer chaos of paper around us, "is a bit like its own special circle of hell." The smooth response gave no indication as to my true motive and clearly didn't sit well with Josh. I could have howled with satisfaction. It may not have been the dead ringer I'd been hoping for, but, fuck if it wasn't adding to the list.

His gaze narrowed as he eyed me circumspectly. "You're playing at something," he accused.

"I don't play at anything." I leaned into his personal space and reached past him under the guise of acquiring a new stack. "Unless someone asks me to," I purred. The hefty pile lifted easily, and I caught his eye as I shifted to straighten up. Unsurprisingly, he had refused to budge at the invasion of his bubble and stood glaring back at me with unreadable eyes and an equally unreadable scent.

Once I was clear, he turned back to his perusal of ancient bakery receipts. "Get back to work."

"Yes, sir," I responded smartly.

He rolled his eyes, but didn't engage. Poor Officer Mack stood all but forgotten amidst his towers of flimsy paper, looking more perplexed than ever. Finally, I let my grin slip free. It didn't matter that I'd basically been dismissed or that the surly detective was elbow-deep in focusing on anything *but* me. One vindicated thought kept circling around and around: *I'm on to you, Joshua Hart.*

Chapter 12

Joshua

Elijah blinked at me, shock plastered on his handsome face. "You *don't* want to go to the House?"

I scowled at him and barely didn't roll my shoulders. It had taken three days to get the damn warrant that would allow me to step foot onto pack property without inciting an all-out war. Which was exactly three days longer than it should have taken. Now, I was grossly behind schedule, and I didn't have time to listen to Elijah repeat everything I said. Though admittedly, even Officer Mack seemed to be a little unsure of my trajectory.

"When I need to go to the House, I'll tell you. As for the rest, I don't particularly appreciate your questioning my methods. Are you going to take me where I want to go, or do I need to request a new liaison?"

His cheek twitched slightly at the threat, and he immediately held up his hands as if warding me off. "No. If you don't want to go to the house, then we won't go to the house. But, um...where exactly *do* you want to go?"

I crossed my arms and stared at him. If he expected me to lay out all of my tactics like some monologuing villain, he was going to be sorely disappointed. Besides which, I'd already wasted enough time catering to his distraction techniques.

His lip curled, and a slight growl rumbled out of him. Thankfully, too low to be heard by Officer Mack standing ten feet away, but it was still sexy as hell. I cocked my head to the side and wondered for probably the thousandth time if Elijah had any idea how much he behaved like an Alpha.

"What'll it be?" I prompted.

The growl died, and he seemed to pull himself back together with an astonishing force of will. "If you're gonna be vague about it, then we can start by hitting the east slopes."

"Perfect," I said and walked past him. And it was. East was exactly where I needed to go. It had the densest forestation and complex terrain. And somewhere out there, I hoped to find the renegade wolves that hadn't caused nearly enough destruction.

Elijah

I glanced at the swiftly darkening sky and back at Josh's receding form. The man was stubborn to a fault and hell-bent on going wherever he had his sights set. It had taken over an hour of meticulously combing through the forest for me to realize that he was looking for signs of Tommy's passage. And it was at that exact moment of realization that a fork of light ripped across the sky. The storm brewing was too distant for the subsequent peal of thunder to be heard by my companions, but that wouldn't last. It was coming and coming fast.

I licked my lips nervously as the static charge built. Storms in the area had become more frequent and less predictable in the last twenty years, and this one was promising to be the worst one yet of the season.

"We should head back!" I shouted after Josh.

He ignored me, stepping around his landskimmer to investigate something I couldn't see. That didn't bode well either.

Another silent flash of light streaked across the sky. I stomped towards Josh, determined to make him see reason. I understood he was frustrated and impatient to get to the bottom of the murder—I was too—but there was no need to risk all our lives in his pursuit. Each passing moment had every animal instinct I had screaming louder to seek refuge.

I pulled to a stop a good three feet away from him. "We need to head back," I tried again.

"You've stalled me long enough. This investigation is going forward whether you like it or not. Go back if you want, but I'm pushing on, storm or no storm."

I took another step forward, arm extended, fully prepared to drag his stubborn ass back to town if I had to.

He casually stepped out of reach at the last second in that eerie way he had and cast me a withering look. "I told you not to touch me."

My jaw ticked as I silently gnashed my teeth at the rebuke. "This is insane, Josh. It's not safe," I insisted. Already the wind was picking up, the subtle whistle between branches well on its way to becoming a howl.

"I'm not an idiot, Bennett. Tell me you're not stalling," he challenged.

I floundered for half a second too long.

"That's what I thought," he scoffed and turned away again, methodically scanning the ground.

"It's not safe," I argued. "You'll get yourself killed out here. These woods aren't as safe as you think. The storm... You don't know what you're up against."

He gave a derisive snort. "Go back if you're so worried."

I restrained a frustrated growl and went for broke. If I couldn't drag his crazy ass back, I'd have to reason with it instead. "What about Officer Mack? Are you willing to risk *his* life?"

At the mention of his name, the young man dropped his gaze from the increasingly ominous sky to look at each of us askance. He was obviously anxious, though it was a toss-up whether it was due to our incessant bickering or the pending weather disaster.

Josh seemed to mull over the predicament for a moment, then sauntered over to his land skimmer. "Do what you want," he said nonchalantly and swung a leg over the vehicle, which promptly hummed to life.

My growl became audible. "Absolutely insufferable, pig-headed..."

The pitch of the engine altered ever so slightly, a subtle distinction that even my enhanced hearing barely picked up. It was the only warning before he took off, heading due east.

"Damn it!" I shouted even as he slipped almost silently into the dense trees. The foliage itself may have been sparse, but there were still plenty of trunks and lush evergreens to obscure his escape.

"Um... Can he do that?" Officer Mack asked from behind me.

"He just did."

"What are we going to do?" His question had merit. *What* were *we going to do?*

I let out an aggrieved sigh. "He may be willing to risk your life, but I'm not. You should head back while you still can." I pointed to my left. "If you go straight that way, in about twenty minutes, you'll pop out on a county road that should lead you to Smithfield."

"What about you?" Officer Mack asked in return, raising his voice slightly to be heard over the gradually increasing wind.

I glanced to where the impetuous and infuriating detective had vanished, heading unerringly towards the cabin that had previously held Tommy. Now I knew why he was looking over all the title documents and land specs. Somehow, he'd found the nearly abandoned rental. I really needed to pay more attention to *what* he was looking at rather than looking *at* him. I gave another resigned sigh and turned to Mack.

"I can't let him wander around without an escort." Least of all in the number one place he's likely to find something truly condemning, I silently added. I cast another glance up as a peal of thunder, loud enough for even the officer to hear, rolled overhead. "You should hurry. Sounds like it's moving fast."

He didn't argue, just walked over to his skimmer and fired it up. With one last concerned glance at me, he sped off at a nearly perfect ninety degrees from the direction Josh had gone. Hopefully, he'd make it back without incident. Meanwhile, Joshua Freaking Hart was gaining more ground by the second.

I was still growling to myself when I straddled the skimmer and powered it up. My stomach lurched as I launched after him. With any luck, the quickly degrading weather had slowed him down and he hadn't gotten too far ahead, though I wasn't optimistic. The man was on a mission.

I twisted the throttle and gained more speed, to the discomfort of literally every cell in my body. I really fucking hated anti-gravity bikes.

Joshua

Elijah was right. Curse the man. The morning's weather report had indicated that a sudden cold front might create a pop-up storm. However, it failed to mention that it would bring hail on top of everything.

I gritted my teeth and squeezed my thighs around the landskimmer that offered zero protection against the golf ball-sized chunks of ice I was now dodging. Elijah's cautions about the dangers of the storm rang in my ears. Perhaps I should have conceded and ventured out another day, but damn if I'd let the miserable wolf delay me any further.

A heavy branch overhead broke under the strain of the increasing wind. I heard the telltale crack just in time to veer clear.

If I weren't so preoccupied with my lycan liaison, I could have done what needed to be done, cinched up the entire case, and been well on my way a week ago.

A gale-force gust nearly toppled the skimmer. I stayed upright by the skin of my teeth and pushed the vehicle harder to no avail. I was already careening across the ground at top speed, and still no refuge in sight. The only hope now was to get to the godforsaken cabin. I'd only found the damned thing by accident. It had been a mere footnote in the property details. That, combined with the unusual receipts mixed in with the typical bakery expenses, pointed a clear arrow to the place as Tina and Tommy's hideaway. I just had to get there in one piece.

"Josh!"

I ignored the call and drifted hard to avoid wind-whipped branches. The detour was enough for the wolf to make a precious gain.

"Josh!" Elijah shouted again, more earnest, though he was nearly impossible to hear over the noise.

I couldn't afford to look away from the treacherous ground, so I didn't. Just because the anti-gravity propulsion kept me a good foot above the forest floor didn't mean that an unexpected dip couldn't send me crashing into the nearest hemlock. "I'm not stopping," I hollered back.

"Then at least slow down! You're going to break your neck driving like that!" The now hurricane-force winds nearly swallowed his warning.

Determined not to lose my seat, I hunkered down, mentally berating myself. I was smarter than this. Why had I ever let myself be pushed to make such a reckless decision? And where the fuck was that damn cabin?

"Josh!" Elijah's cry held an edge of panic that miraculously cut through the noise.

Too late, I realized I'd never dodge the massive pine coming down practically on top of me. No sooner had my imminent demise registered than something solid knocked into me from behind. The force of impact sent me flying free of the skimmer.

Air rushed out of my lungs in a pained burst as I slammed chest first into the unforgiving earth. A small crunch I felt more than heard echoed in my ears. I quickly levered myself up and forced oxygen into my abused lungs. Then, I carefully touched the damp patch on my chest. A cold that had nothing to do with the plummeting temperature seeped through me.

Fuck. The last two syringes.

I glanced behind me at where the deadly pine had laid waste to my unfortunate transportation. A quick look around revealed no sign of the other skimmer. My heart leapt into my throat as I lurched to my feet. I stood frozen in horror as the truth of my inexplicable well-being sank into a mind quickly going numb.

Elijah.

"Are you out of your fucking mind!?" An iron grip on my arm accompanied the angry yell. Heat seeped through my clothes like a brand.

My fogged gaze snapped to my captor, who turned out to be a very bedraggled, very pissed, very *alive*, Elijah. Before I could register anything else, I was being forcefully dragged away.

"Get your hands off of me!" I shouted at him. Despite the sudden, loud crack of thunder overhead and the roaring mix of wind and rain, I knew he heard me. A fact betrayed by the sharp look he shot me.

I growled and ripped my arm free just in time to be shoved through a door that hadn't been there a minute ago. Rage and adrenaline rioted through me. Without thinking, I tore off the contaminated vest and threw it onto a convenient table. My firearm, which somehow still clung to my thigh, quickly joined it. Bare of anything lethal but my hands, I turned to confront him.

"I warned you what would happen if you touched me," I snarled, struggling and failing to rein in my temper.

He shot me a glare over his shoulder as he fought to force the door shut. A task that was proving exceptionally difficult even with werewolf-enhanced strength. He was soaked by the time it finally shut with a hollow thud. Hail continued to pelt the thin barrier while another crack of thunder shook the building, a not so subtle reminder of the chaos and inevitable death that awaited anyone dumb enough to be caught out in the open.

He shook off the water, appearing every inch the canine he truly was. Several of the drops flew across the space to hit me along with everything else in the vicinity, while several more streaked in rivulets to pool at his feet.

"Animal," I spat.

Elijah stopped trying to wring the wet out of his clothes and brought his gaze up. His cognac eyes flashed in the lights that had automatically turned on when we'd stumbled into the cabin, lending them a predatory cast. "You want a piece of me, *Detective*?"

The way he emphasized the title had my lip instantly curling. "You know, for someone in danger of losing their status with the pack, you sure have a high opinion of yourself."

His chest swelled with a rage reflected in his eyes. "And for someone who hates werewolves so much, you sure act like one," he fired back.

Fury swept through me, coloring the room and everything in it red. I couldn't tell lies, and I abhorred having lies told about me. "Take. That. Back," I said in a low warning.

He narrowed his eyes in challenge. "Make me."

I snarled as I launched myself at him. He moved to grab me, and I slipped aside, easily avoiding his grasp. I spun around, planting my elbow in his gut. He grunted, but didn't back down. I immediately popped out his arm with a well-placed open-hand hit to his cubital fossa and followed the move with a kick to his instep. As expected, he flailed wildly and staggered. Both attacks had landed with enough force to break human bones, but they barely fazed Elijah.

My hand was already in route to take out his other arm when a familiar vice-like grip caught me and used my momentum against me. I hit the ground with a thud and quickly rolled into a crouch. Using my right leg, I swept his feet from under him, and he tumbled to the ground with a sharp smack accompanied by a vicious growl. I snickered as I straightened.

"You're a cheeky bastard," he gritted as he found his feet.

"Confident."

He jerked forward, the promise of violence in his eyes. "We'll see about that."

Once again, I didn't bother staying out of reach. Instead, I danced inside his defenses to land an open, double-handed hit square on his chest, framing his sternum. Despite the force, he barely wheezed at the impact. He growled again, and I chuckled as I easily danced out of reach.

"You're enjoying this," he accused.

"Maybe," I responded with an admittedly cheeky grin. Truthfully, I didn't get to do much hand to hand combat. By now, most of my opponents were usually dead.

I expected Elijah to lunge again. He was frustrated, he was angry, and he wasn't a fighter. I was *not* expecting him to grab the small table by the door and hurl it at me.

There was no telling how much the artificially ornate piece weighed as it sailed towards my chest. I instinctively rotated on the balls of my feet and felt the air stir as it passed within an inch of hitting me. At the same time, the sixth sense of movement coming up on my now exposed flank warned me of another impending threat.

I ducked just in time to avoid Elijah's wide swing. Having lost the advantage, I pursued distance. The fabric couch scratched my palm as I vaulted over the back. Suddenly, the ground was coming up substantially sooner than anticipated. I sprawled on the ironic faux-fur rug in an ungainly collection of limbs. A quick glance revealed Elijah had toppled the couch over while I'd been mid-vault. I growled and pushed myself up.

I'd barely gotten my feet back under me when a body of solid muscle slammed into my shoulder. I ignored the pain in my side and swiveled to meet the attack head-on. No sooner had I turned than my back smacked painfully into the wall, an echo of the pain still in my chest from my rude introduction to the ground.

Typically, when I fought in close quarters, I was fine. I trained for this. There were also usually a lot more teeth and at least one deadly weapon at hand. This situation had none of those. Elijah wasn't really my enemy, and the repercussions of actually hurting him were more than I cared to consider. That reality limited how much I could counter his persistent attempts to get hold of me. He, however, faced no such restrictions.

I fought in vain to regain the upper hand without causing too much damage. But, as the close quarters gradually stole the advantage I'd enjoyed in the open space, it replaced it with something else. My previously even breathing became labored and erratic as I now fought my body and Elijah's. Blood roared in my ears, pumping with more than raw, rage-fueled adrenaline. Each deflection became another place where Elijah's touch burned into my already fevered skin. I was sweating profusely with the dual effort of keeping myself in check and him at bay. It was a battle I was painfully aware I was losing.

Soon enough, Elijah had me caged against the wall, each of his hands encircling one of my wrists and holding them a foot away from either side of my head. There was still ample room to react, to get free, but the hundred ways that came to mind would have either killed or seriously injured Elijah. Neither of which I was interested in doing. There was also the added complication that I didn't actually *want* to be free. A desire I stubbornly tried to exorcise.

I struggled futilely against his hold, and he tightened his grip. "Let me go," I ordered.

"Not so cocky now, are you? No matter how good you are, you're still no match for werewolf strength."

I pulled again and even managed a few inches of separation from the wall before he slammed me back again. I curled my lip, showing teeth. "I'm not afraid of you."

His nostrils twitched. "But you are afraid of something," he countered, then he blinked as if suddenly realizing what he'd said and how he knew it. Confusion passed behind his eyes at the same time his nostrils flared again. His chest expanded with lungfuls of air, and his pupils widened.

Fuck. Fuck. Fuck.

I squirmed in his grasp, but it was useless. Elijah was right. Even on my best day, I was no match for werewolf strength. I wasn't going anywhere unless he let me or I killed him. This was it. Between the rain, the sweating, and time, my potion was gone, all of my defenses stripped away.

Elijah leaned forward to bury his nose in the hollow of my neck, where he promptly inhaled the scent that was no longer obscured—the real me—and the truth.

Chapter 13

Elijah

"*Fuuuck*," I moaned as I drank in Josh's scent. It was everything it should have been—harsh, edgy, with a hint of sweet earthiness. There was also a slight undercurrent of fear, but overriding it all was pure, unchecked desire. The intoxicating smell of unadulterated *want* pouring off of him was mind-blowing. He tried once again to pull free with the same result. "How the hell have you hidden this from me?" I whispered in his ear, greedily drinking in his scent.

"Let me go," he repeated in a growl.

"No."

He jerked as I slid my tongue up his neck, stealing the liquid essence of his scent from his burning skin. His breathing was so out of control, he was practically panting. Even his heart was hammering hard enough that I could make out its frantic rhythm.

"You smell incredible," I hummed, nuzzling the crook where his shoulder met his neck once again. Fuck, I wanted to roll in it.

"Thought it was rude for *weres* to talk about each other's smell."

I pulled away enough to see the fire burning in his eyes, equal parts rage and what I now recognized as barely contained lust. "You're not a *were*."

"You are," he fired back.

"That a problem?" I countered.

His intense gaze bored into me while his smell continued to betray him as he considered me for a long second. "Yes," he finally responded, then shocked me by leaning forward to capture my mouth. The savage kiss blazed through me, scorching everything in its wake. His plush lips were hard and demanding, ripping everything out of me I'd tried for weeks to ignore. The fierceness of the possession rocked me to the core, taking no prisoners and offering no mercy. So like Josh. So, *so* like Josh. Abruptly, he pulled back with a gasp.

I let out a primitive growl I didn't even recognize and promptly recaptured his luscious mouth. He didn't resist the renewed contact, but he did moan into me, his back arching off the wall as if seeking more contact. I obliged him by stepping closer, eager to press the rest of my body against his.

Before I could even contemplate releasing him, his weight shifted, and my hold on his wrists became the only thing keeping him up. Josh then used the anchor of my hands to lift his bottom half in a perfect deadlift. His weight resettled when his insanely long legs wrapped around my waist.

I kissed him harder, groaning. How many times had I fantasized about this? Having Josh willingly at my complete mercy? Aching for more? But this wasn't a fantasy; it was reality. A dangerous reality. He was a Lycan Detective. I was a lycan. This couldn't happen.

The thoughts tumbled over each other, but despite their logic, I couldn't let him go. The truth was out now. Josh wanted me every bit as much as I wanted him, consequences be damned. He squeezed out any lingering reservations I had as he tightened his legs around my waist. I leaned into him and repositioned my hands, releasing him so that I could lift him higher.

The moment he was free, he twined his arms around my neck and violently ripped the tie from my hair. The freed strands fell loose only to have Josh's lithe fingers immediately start carding through them while he continued to devour my mouth like he was starving. His insistent touch drove me wild. I was borderline moonstruck with the need to have him.

I made a sound low in my throat, somewhere between a growl and a groan, when he tightened his hold on my hair and yanked my head back. He abandoned my mouth to nip and suck at my neck. A shudder ran through me at the overwhelming urge to do the same to him.

Teeth. No teeth. Do not fucking bite him.

The wolf inside didn't want to listen to reason. It wanted to claim Joshua Hart in every way possible. I shoved the impulse as far down as it would go. There were plenty of other ways to claim Josh. I dug my fingers into the globes of his firm ass as I pulled him free of the wall. He came away easily, still clinging to me with what shouldn't have been a shocking amount of strength as I carried him to the ridiculous white fur rug.

We hit the floor harder than I intended, but I doubted either of us was in any state to notice a few extra bruises. I shoved the toppled couch aside to give us more room. It scraped along the ground, a sound barely audible over the raging storm and Josh's harsh breathing. His mouth and hands were everywhere, creating a sensory overload I was more than happy to drown in.

When his fingers tangled in my shirt, I hooked mine under the hem and pulled it free.

Immediately, Josh's hands were on my chest, trailing through the light layer of down. "It's all gray." The husky whisper set my skin aflame.

I wasn't sure if it was a question or a statement. Not that it mattered, I could feel the heat of his gaze as it traveled down my body, following the equally gray happy trail.

The green of his eyes all but disappeared as his pupils dilated even more. "Fuck, that's hot," he said breathlessly. No sooner than the words left his mouth than he resumed hungrily mapping my flesh, sparing no inch from his fevered touch.

I groaned, needing so much more and desperately wanting to give Josh everything his scent was demanding from me. I wrapped my hand around his leg and pulled him towards me.

He gave a light "Oof" as he fell back, but in true form, he didn't stay down.

I tugged again on the captive appendage and caught his gaze. "If you ever wanna be able to wear that shirt again, I suggest you be the one to take it off."

His lithe fingers quickly set to work undoing buttons while holding my gaze. In hardly any time at all, the fabric fell open to expose his heaving chest. Finally, I knew why he always seemed to wear long sleeves no matter how mild the weather. Pearlescent scars ran rampant across his torso and arms, some small, some large, the kind of scars one only gets from werewolves.

I reflexively tightened my fingers as I stared down at him and wondered if Josh had any idea how truly beautiful he was. I absently reached out with my free hand to touch the smooth skin, a thin layer of softness over solid steel. There was no way of knowing if it was by virtue of genetics or design, but I fucking loved it.

As my fingers wandered, his eyes lidded, and he arched off the floor as if to encourage my exploration. When my hand caught on the edge of his pants, his eyes shot open and snagged mine with a burning intensity that I was sure mine mirrored. There were so many things I wanted to do to him, but first these boots had to go. They'd tortured me long enough.

Josh's chest rose and fell rapidly as he watched my hand drift down to his boot-wrapped calf. When my fingers touched the skin-tight footwear, I instantly recognized the supple material. No wonder the knee-high boots hugged his legs like a second skin. They weren't the typical high-quality tactical gear, but real, *genuine* leather, not to mention they were probably also spelled within an inch of capacity. I shook my head at what such a novelty would have cost. Billionaire playboy indeed.

"What?" he asked when I still hadn't moved.

I chuckled, a low sound deep in my chest that earned me a small moan. I filed his response away for later. "These fucking boots."

He gave me a lopsided grin and pulled lightly on the captive leg, a less than subtle encouragement.

I tightened my grip and heard his breath catch. "I'm not done with that," I growled and slid my hand further up his leg, caressing his thigh through the thin fabric. He rewarded the teasing touch with another light moan. I dug my fingers into the impervious material, and his breath hitched again. "I'm going to have to peel these off of you."

"Less talking, more touching," he ordered, out of breath.

I smirked and took my time liberating him. First, slowly working loose the hidden zipper of each boot. Then, tugging on each heel while dipping my hand beneath the leather to caress his pant-encased calf.

Josh propped himself on his elbows to watch, but the moment my hand slid up the length of his leg, his head fell back with a loud moan. He seemed to be trying and failing to keep his breathing somewhat resembling normal. That I was the one who'd brought him to this point only made me want to torture him that much more.

By the time both boots were gone, he was writhing impatiently, but I wasn't in any hurry. I'd waited too damn long for this to rush anything. With slow, deliberate motions, I peeled him out of the skin-tight clothing, softly touching each inch of revealed flesh to a chorus of desperate moans. When at last I had him completely bare, I buried my nose in the crook of his knee and inhaled the scent pooled in the tender flesh.

Josh made a high-pitched sound suspiciously close to a whine.

"Sweet moon, it's like a damn drug," I groaned, dragging in as much of the smell as my lungs could hold. "I'm going to smell every last inch of you."

"Why... why do werewolves always have to be so weird with the... the smell thing?" he panted, obviously enjoying it despite his words.

A flush pinked his skin as I lazily dragged my gaze up his body to meet his hungry eyes. "What if I promise to lick every inch I smell?" I followed the question with a flick of my tongue on his fevered skin.

His entire leg spasmed, and his eyelids fluttered as an even deeper moan fell out of him. The sound went straight to my core and sank deep to pool hotly in my lower belly. His sounds of tortured ecstasy had already driven me so close to the edge, I wasn't sure how long I'd last. Yet I couldn't bring myself to go any faster. I took slight mercy on us and wrapped a firm hand around his erection, proudly pointing straight up from a nest of pure black.

His resulting shout filled the cabin, briefly eclipsing the intense storm. I stroked him roughly from root to tip, only pausing to smear the precum glistening at the tip around the head. I caught and held his gaze as I brought my thumb to my lips to taste his essence. Instinctively, I recognized that the initial sour notes were a by-product of whatever he'd used to hide his intoxicating scent from me.

Confident in my assessment and more determined than ever to have his true taste on my tongue, I shuffled backward beneath his assessing gaze. "I am going to devour you."

"Promises, promises," he responded with a smirk and a wicked glint in his lust-blown eyes.

So that's how it was going to be. We'd see how in control he was after I had my way with him. Smirking right back, I leaned forward and swallowed his weeping dick down to the root.

"Holy fuck!" His fingers clawed against my scalp as if he couldn't decide whether to push my head down or push me away.

When neither happened, I dragged my tongue along the underside of his shaft until I reached his swollen head. Unfortunately, the sour taste still lingered. I took him to the back of my throat again with a frustrated growl.

He made a pained noise, his fingers tightening in my hair as I swallowed around his length. "Seven hells," he gasped when I pulled up to suck on his crown. I lapped up the latest burst of precum and hummed in satisfaction. *There* was the real him—musky, with a hint of sweetness and a tang I couldn't quite place. "You're... I can't... You need... I..." His incoherent babble was absolutely everything, and I absolutely needed to stop before I came.

Regretfully, I released his cock and rocked back on my heels. His gaze tracked my every movement as I stood. For a moment, I forgot what I was doing as I looked at the living embodiment of sin. He'd been gorgeous as ever in all of my forbidden fantasies, but they paled to reality.

"I'd appreciate it if you'd stop toying with me," he said as he ran a bare foot up the inside of my leg. "Or were you planning to stand there and ogle me as you jerked off?" The image of my cum decorating his chest, marking him, *claiming* him, made me borderline feral. The sultry smile tugging at his lips said he wasn't actually opposed to either of those things.

Mustering every ounce of self-control I possessed, I took my time undoing my pants and slowly pushed them down. He didn't look at all pleased when I didn't remove my briefs as well. If I had a death wish, I might have accused him of pouting. I'd always considered myself a smart man, but then I'd also been flirting with fire since I'd first seen him swagger onto the neutral ground between the town's land and pack territory.

Naked hunger shone in his eyes as I hooked my thumbs in the elastic and he licked his lips, testing my resolve to drag this interlude out for as long as possible. I took mercy on us both and dragged the clinging briefs down until my swollen cock bounced free hard enough to smack my abdomen and leave a glistening trail.

His groan came out more a growl. "Get your fucking tail down here and fuck me already or..." He let the implied threat hang, but he wasn't fooling me. Not anymore. Not with his scent betraying how badly he wanted this. The worst he'd do was tackle me to move things along. Which actually sounded hot as fuck. Either way, he wasn't *going* anywhere.

I resumed my position on the floor, the fur from the faux rug tickling my thighs as I knelt over him. "What's the matter, Detective? Are you that desperate for me to stretch your pretty little hole?"

"Yes," he groaned, as if the confession hurt to admit.

"Good," I growled right back. "So am I."

He smirked, because of course he did, as he wrapped his hand around my length and gave it a casual stroke, causing stars to pop behind my eyes. "Then what's taking you so long?"

My chest twinged at the sultry question in a way I had no interest in exploring right now. All that mattered was that Josh was here, he was naked, and he was *very* willing. "Careful what you wish for," I purred as I reached for my abandoned pants to secure the lube I kept in my wallet. Something dangerously close to hesitation flickered in his deep green eyes.

All thoughts of taking my time went out the window to be drowned by the torrential downpour buffeting the cabin. I tore the packet of lube open, not giving a damn if I made a mess, and leaned over the detective to seal our mouths together. Despite, or perhaps because of, the doubt I'd glimpsed, he met me in a tender kiss that lacked our earlier violence.

I leisurely licked my way into his mouth at the same time I breached his entrance with a slick finger. He moaned, opening to me in every way. I lost all sense of self as I continued to kiss him and slowly worked him open. There was no telling how much time had passed when he finally broke the never-ending kiss and dropped his head back with a pained moan.

"Elijah... *Please*."

While I might not know everything there was to know about the mysterious Joshua Hart, I knew he was not a man who begged. To my surprise, I hated it. I didn't want him to beg—ever. I wanted to give him everything, fulfill any and every desire he could conjure, sexual or otherwise. *Needed* to. I'd have to dissect that later. Right now, I couldn't stand not being buried in him so deep we stopped being two people. I nuzzled the side of his neck, drunk on his scent, and whispered, "I've got you."

Josh's entire body shuddered as I pulled him onto my lap. Then he pushed himself up with one arm, slinging the other around my shoulders for leverage, before grabbing my throbbing cock and guiding it to his eager hole. He briefly tangled his fingers in my hair as he stole a fierce kiss that left me aching in all the best ways. His nails scratched along my scalp and neck as those same fingers moved to dig into my shoulder while he slowly sank down with a long drawn-out groan.

My breath caught as I tried to maintain any semblance of control and not simply slam into him. Outside, wind and rain battered the cabin much as Josh's tight channel battered at my will. I fought the urge to rut like some kind of animal, digging my fingers into his hips hard enough to bruise. A hiss slipped past my gritted teeth as he pulled me deeper.

At last, he was fully seated, his heels digging into the small of my back. My entire being became hyper-focused on the man wrapped around me. I gave a small thrust and knew I'd hit that perfect spot when a moan instantly fell from his lips. So I did it again and again, settling into a rhythm. His head fell back, exposing his throat, and he arched into the roll of my hips, meeting each thrust and completely lost to the sensation.

I faltered. I'd only ever seen one other person let go like that. A man who'd continued to haunt my dreams after only one brief, fevered exchange. It was such a contradiction to everything I knew about Josh, how he always needed to be in perfect control, that it was a wonder I'd ever suspected the two could be the same man. But they were, without a doubt. I didn't know how or why, and I didn't care. All that mattered was that he was back in my arms where he belonged.

I coasted my hands up his back and gathered him close. *I found you.* He buried his face in my chest, his warm pants stirring the hair while his nails dragged sharp lines along my shoulders. The pain was secondary. *Everything* was secondary.

I fisted a hand in the longer part of his hair and pulled his head back in order to conquer his mouth as I conquered his body. My pace continued to increase until I was slamming into his perfect body so hard I had to wrap an arm around his waist to keep him in place. I wasn't surprised he was effortlessly keeping pace with me, because Joshua Hart was *made* for me.

"I'm so close," he groaned against my buzzing lips. "Don't stop."

"Never," I growled, burying myself as deep as I could in a punishing thrust. He tightened around me almost painfully and cried out his release. I wasn't sure what pushed me over the edge, but I was right there with him.

Chapter 14

Elijah

I COULDN'T BELIEVE IT. Josh was dead to the world... and he snored. It was probably too low for a human to hear, but it was crystal clear to me and might have been the cutest thing about him. Either way, he'd conked out within seconds of collapsing on my chest after our third—or was it fifth?—round and had barely twitched since. It seemed... unlikely that a man as wound up as Josh could sleep so soundly, and yet, here he was, sprawled across my torso, legs tangled with mine, with that barely there snore.

Admittedly, I was a little glad he couldn't see me smiling like a moonstruck idiot while I trailed my fingers lightly over his skin. He was slightly cool to the touch, which reminded me of the weather he'd nearly gotten himself killed in the day before. The insane man was more stubborn than a honey badger.

I traced a finger along one of his many silvery scars. Distantly, I wondered if he kept them hidden because he was self-conscious about them or because they were simply too identifying. Even the most violent members of my pack didn't have half as many as he did, and some of his looked near fatal.

I knew Josh was good at his job, but this was another level. He could *and had* killed my kind. Oddly, that didn't alarm me. Quite the opposite, I was impressed. Josh was a survivor. If ever I'd met a human that could be called an Alpha, it was him. There was an intriguing observation. I'd never considered I might be attracted to Alpha-types. I certainly hadn't been in the past.

I flattened my hands on his back to bring more warmth to his chilled flesh. He gave a light moan, still asleep, and nuzzled into my chest. My heart thumped and melted at the honest reaction. He could be the most infuriating man when he was awake, but right now he was gloriously relaxed.

This might be my favorite version of Joshua Hart yet.

A single note rang in my ear, and I quickly dismissed the incoming call. It was probably Conrad wanting to know what the hell was going on and if the detective had found anything condemning. My mood soured somewhat at the harsh reminder of reality. *That* Alpha certainly didn't appeal to me, but my obligations to the pack and the frustrating lycan hadn't disappeared while we'd been stormed-in.

I let out a sigh and began the arduous process of slipping out from under Josh. He mumbled in protest, but remained firmly asleep.

Joshua

The warmth I'd been indulgently enjoying seemed to have gotten up and walked off.

I blinked open my eyes to discover that it was exactly what had happened. While I would have preferred my fingers to be embedded in the soft down of Elijah's chest hair rather than the fake fur of the preposterous rug, I was confident he hadn't actually left. First, because he simply didn't seem like the kind of person to sneak out the morning after. Then, of course, there was the fact that he'd wrapped his jacket around me to stave off the encroaching chill. Elijah Bennett was a veritable Victorian gentleman.

I took an indulgent moment to burrow into the dissipating warmth before stretching the rest of the way awake. Aches and sores immediately made themselves known. I hummed with deep-rooted satisfaction and pulled the jacket tighter before standing.

A glance around revealed that, except for a few righted items, the room was a total disaster. I didn't bother repressing my smug grin. We'd certainly made a mess of things. The detective in me despaired that we'd destroyed any potential evidence, but the exceptionally satisfied part couldn't have cared less. Besides, there were better rooms in the cabin to ferret out clues than the living room.

My skin pebbled as I padded to freshen up as much as possible, scooping up scattered and miraculously whole clothing along the way. In the modest bathroom, I was unsurprised to find two toothbrushes along with a host of other personal items that clearly pointed to regular use by the same people. Since the cabin hadn't been listed for rent in quite some time, assuming the occupants were Tommy and Tina wasn't far-fetched, an impression further solidified when I found a hairbrush with curly blond hair and shorter gray hair.

I fought the lure of reminiscing about my surprising evening as I did up the last of my buttons and pulled my sleeves straight to hide the faint bruises mottling my skin. That some of those bruises had come from a far more pleasurable venue than the earlier fight brought another smile to my lips. The temptation to while away what little time I had on my own reliving my night with Elijah grew. To stave it off, I splashed icy water on my face, then raked some through my hair before moving to inspect the bedroom. There, I found yet more signs of a couple regularly meeting. Not that I could fault the pair. The cabin was an ideal place for illicit lovers to meet. It was well-appointed, private, and iconically romantic.

A shudder ran through me as I recalled my own illicit activities. Sex with Elijah sans clothing was infinitely better than with, not to mention he'd displayed a level of tenderness I hadn't expected. Whether it was my demeanor or simply the *weres* I chose to hook up with, sex was rarely anything short of outright aggressive. The undercurrent of gentleness after such violence had been unexpected and a different kind of mind-blowing. I shook my head, marveling at the many facets of Elijah Bennett, and made my way back to the living room.

After cleaning what I could of the space, I walked to where I'd discarded my weapons the night before. At first glance, they looked undisturbed, but I performed a thorough check anyway. All six poisoned blades were still safely secured in the back of my vest and intact. Unfortunately, the same couldn't be said of everything in the vest.

I fingered the hidden pocket, and sharp pieces threatened to break through the reinforced fabric. A sigh escaped me, and I transferred my attention to another hidden compartment only to confirm that the minor healing tonic I kept there for emergencies had suffered the same fate. Seemed my "injuries" would have to wait until I returned to the apartment.

I grinned wickedly as I pulled on the vest. Not that I minded the ache; it was a pleasant reminder. Maybe it would be possible to arrange another interaction with Elijah. After all, it wasn't like I could put the genie back in the bottle.

The door opened, and a gust of frigid air swirled through the room.

Elijah

The door shut with a solid smack, slicing through the chill blast that accompanied me into the cabin. I glanced up to find Josh already dressed, or mostly. His trademark vest hung open, and his firearm sat on the table. Those outrageously sexy boots, though, already hugged his legs as if made for him, which now that I knew they were genuine leather, I suspected they had been.

"Morning," he said. His sharp hunter-green eyes betrayed no emotion as they stared steadily back at me, and thanks to the stupid wind scattering his scent, that was no help either.

Please don't let things be weird. I don't want to go back to things being strained, or worse, awkward. Not after our incredible night.

I swallowed my mounting anxiety. "The other skimmer seems to be intact. I brought it up to the cabin to charge. Should only take a few minutes."

His lips twitched in what might have been the makings of a smile, but was gone too fast to be sure. "That's good." He noticeably did not mention that it was his fault the other land skimmer was wrecked. "Wanna give me a hand?" He indicated the couch.

Together we righted the rest of the furniture. When we were done, he rested against the back of the couch and fussed with his clothing, though the vest stayed open.

"How are you feeling?" I asked, still not sure where things stood between us.

His eyes twinkled mischievously. "I'm good."

I rolled my eyes and took a step closer. "You know what I mean."

Immediately, desire spiked his scent, and I couldn't help but wonder how long he'd had such a visceral reaction to my presence. He gave me a knowing smile. "I do."

My breath caught as he coasted his hand up my chest and cupped the back of my neck. Before I could react, he pulled my mouth down to his. Soft lips dragged a low groan out of me, and my hands automatically went to his waist to pull him closer. He came easily, pressing himself against me as he continued to conquer my mouth.

The last of the tension drained out of me to be replaced by a growing desire. In complete contrast to all of my trepidation, there was nothing awkward at all about being with Josh. I was actually hard-pressed to think of any previous partner I'd clicked so well with.

I glided my hands up his back and felt him smile against my mouth before he shifted them down to his ass. The same ass that had taunted me for weeks and had felt so incredible last night. I squeezed the exceptional globes and wedged my thigh between his legs.

He ground his growing arousal against me for a second before easing off. "Mm," he hummed against my lips. "Nice as it would be to continue this, we should probably start heading back." While he was right, that he'd yet to move lent zero conviction to his statement. Instead, he continued to pull languid kisses from my lips, his body arching into mine while he slid his fingers through my hair.

I smiled to myself and kissed him deeper, relishing the intoxicating scent of him curling around me, a heady mix of sex, desire, and bergamot, oddly enough. Literally, nothing about his behavior suggested he was ready to leave. Even his smell seemed to pull me closer. His tongue tangled with mine, demanding yet gentle. I didn't even try to contain my low growl or mounting need. Josh's responding groan had me ready to throw him down on the recently righted couch. Despite the clear signs that he was definitely up for that, he still pulled away.

"Seriously though. We should head back. I imagine local law enforcement is on the verge of sending out a search party by now," he said in that low, almost-laugh way he had.

I glided my hands over his sides as I leaned down to drink in more of his delicious scent. To my surprise, he angled his head to the side to give me better access. I took the invitation and sucked out a light bruise on the side of his neck while I was at it. I placed a kiss on it, then leaned back to look him in the eyes. "Speaking of law enforcement, what's going on between you and Officer Mack?"

The laugh that had been playing at the edge of his words finally slipped free. "And what do you think is going on between me and the young officer?" Even though I could distinctly hear the teasing in his voice, it didn't stop a possessive growl from bubbling up. A growl that only seemed to encourage the taunts. "Mack is certainly cute and ambitious, albeit a touch naïve, but I'm sure that could be easily remedied," he finished with a sinister grin.

"Would it kill you to give a straight answer for once?" I growled, my frustration with the evasion increasing with each passing second.

"It might." At his coy response, my grip on his sides tightened. Instantly, his playful gaze turned sharp. "Easy, Bennett. I may be able to take a pounding, but I'm still human."

I gentled my touch, but couldn't bring myself to fully pry my fingers off him. "Are you sleeping with him or not?"

He raised an eyebrow at the blunt question. "With the exception of last night, I'm not generally in the habit of sleeping with anyone."

The literal meaning of his words was painfully obvious and threatened to send me into a spiraling rage. I quickly removed my hands before I could leave less pleasant marks on his fragile skin. "Be straight," I bit out, all of my eloquence having fled.

He gave me a wicked smile, so unlike the ones he gave Mack. What had the officer ever done to warrant such pleasant expressions? "Surely you know by now that there's nothing *straight* about me." He emphasized his words by grinding suggestively against my thigh, which was still between his legs.

I quickly pulled my leg back. "You know what I mean."

Josh let out a chuckle, and I tensed, expecting another goading half-answer. "Fine. If it gets your ruff up that much, the straight truth is no." I narrowed my eyes at him and waited for the other shoe to drop. After a noticeable pause, he went on, "I am not sleeping with, having sex with, or otherwise fooling around with Officer Mack, nor do I have any intentions to do so."

I released an audible sigh of relief and combed my previously clenched fingers through my hair. Josh cocked his head to the side and gave me a considering look. "What?" I asked, dropping the impromptu ponytail I'd made.

"I wouldn't have pegged you for the jealous type. Guess I was mistaken." He shrugged as if it were irrelevant.

I opened my mouth to correct his gross misinterpretation. There hadn't been a single day of my life I'd ever been anything so crass as jealous. Not when I'd caught my first boyfriend cheating, or when my third had suggested an open relationship, and certainly not with a hookup, I didn't care how hot he was.

Except before I could utter so much as a syllable, the reality struck home. Not only was I jealous, I was *insanely* jealous, and had been since the start. It was practically burning me up inside. Every smile he'd shared with the officer, their easy banter, the undeniable camaraderie. Josh insinuating that more might have been going on had been like pouring water on a barrel of lithium. I didn't want Officer Mack, or anyone else for that matter, touching Josh, because Joshua Hart was *mine*. And with that outrageously territorial thought, the sickening truth swam to the forefront.

"This is not happening to me," I said aloud, even as I began frantically searching the recently righted room for something I knew I wouldn't find.

"Beg your pardon?" Josh asked in that totally unaffected way he had.

Anger surged white-hot through me. But even as the rage built, it dissipated. I couldn't even stay angry at him properly, not when it was my fault. I let out a defeated sigh that was dangerously close to a whimper.

No, no, no.

"How did I let this happen? I've always been so careful," I berated myself, still desperately searching.

Josh rolled his eyes and crossed his arms. "What are you looking for? The room is in better shape than we found it."

I shot him a glare even though I knew he was right. "I'm looking for the condom."

He gave a derisive snort. "Well, you're not likely to find one, because I'm pretty sure not a one was used during that marathon."

I groaned and seriously debated putting a hole in the wall. *This can't be how it ends. It just can't be.* But much as I wanted to believe he was wrong, Josh couldn't lie. "Fuck," I reiterated. "I was afraid of that."

"I'm not entirely sure what you're so worried about. It's not like you can get me pregnant. The only other concern that immediately comes to mind is disease. And *were*-virus aside, I'm negative. Thank you very much."

I grimaced at the undercurrent that I'd insulted him and finally gave up my pointless search. "Diseases aren't the only things werewolves can catch," I said somewhere between pissed beyond measure and more miserable than I'd ever been.

"Yeah, I'm not sure if it's post-sex brain or lack of caffeine, but I'm still not following."

I rounded on him, done with his cavalier attitude. "I'm fucking bonded, Josh."

He blinked, the only outward sign that my words had even registered. "Are you sure?" I glowered at him, and he frowned back. "That's... that's impos... It's..." I watched him struggle to say it was impossible, that there was simply no way it could ever happen. But he couldn't. The words he wanted would never come, because he knew they were a lie. It obviously *could* and *had* happened. "Improbable," he finally managed with a huff. "I mean, how? We barely know each other. And it was only—"

"It only takes once," I cut him off. I raked my fingers through my hair again before I fisted both hands and brought them to bear on the wall. There was a loud crack as the plaster and hidden brace suffered the blow. "Fuck," I said yet again. It seemed the only word capable of coming anywhere close to accurately describing the situation.

"Demolishing the wall won't change anything," he said coolly.

"I've always been so damn careful. Bonding has been like a moonforsaken epidemic since supernaturals and humans started mingling."

Josh considered me for a moment, then conceded, "Okay. Assuming you're right and you're bonded..." I shot him another hateful look, which he ignored. "What's the big deal? My occupation aside, I was under the impression wolves looked forward to the moony, love forever thing," he finished with a twisted smile.

Asshole thought this shit was funny. "First off, the bond doesn't necessitate love. Second, not every wolf wants it."

Josh shrugged. "Why not? On paper, at least, it seems like a good deal."

I advanced on him and poked his chest hard enough that he took a step back. Even that small contact sent a thrill through me, and I had to fight the urge to pull him in close. "Because the bond is also a death sentence."

His brow wrinkled as confusion clouded his features, and for one tiny second it was eclipsed by concern, as if my dying might actually upset him. "How?"

I shook my head, still struggling to come to terms with my new reality. "My life is now tied to yours."

"So?"

"So, *you* die, *I* die."

Silence engulfed the room as Josh and I stood staring at each other. I didn't know what else to say. I'd left off the part that I would probably give up my own life if it meant saving his. This was officially it for me. When Josh left this world, one way or another, so would I. But worse than my ruined life was the blank expression on Josh's face, like he didn't know what to do with the information I'd given him.

All I wanted was to smooth the worry line building between his brows, comfort him, and tell him I'd be okay, that *we'd* be okay—and I hated that impulse more than anything.

"We really should go," he repeated from what felt like a lifetime ago. Without another word, he picked up his firearm from the table, which he promptly strapped to his thigh. Then he walked out of the cabin. And like the good little puppy I now was, I followed him.

Chapter 15

Joshua

*S*HIT SHIT SHIT.

How could I have let this happen?

My hand shook as I dispelled the security layered around the apartment. One wrong move and I'd become collateral to the very spells I'd put in place. I clenched my jaw and fought to keep my composure. I just needed to dispel a few more layers.

Elijah is bonded.

To me.

The thoughts threatened to dissolve what little calm I still possessed. I fumbled the last lock and only a quick counter prevented my hand from being sent to another dimension. Now I just had to wait for the status report to finish running.

Fuck, how much longer is this damn thing going to take?

At last, the alarm beeped in my ear, signaling it was safe to enter. I thrust the door open, the knob cold and slick beneath my sweaty palms, and fell inside. I reflexively locked the door behind me, re-instituting the barrier wards by rote before I sank to the ground. The jarring impact of hitting the floor did absolutely nothing to detract from my whirling thoughts.

A werewolf had bonded to me. *Me,* of all people. But not just any werewolf. Elijah Bennett. Smart, sexy, irresistible Elijah Bennett.

"Fuck!" I slammed my head against the door. The sharp impact briefly eclipsed all other thoughts. If only the resulting pain could also have wiped away what I'd done.

I know better. Why couldn't I just keep my hands to myself? I know the dangers of unprotected sex with a lycan as well as Elijah does.

But I hadn't kept my hands to myself. I'd been like some touch-starved, wild animal in my pursuit to have Elijah again. And now...

My stomach rolled unpleasantly. I wasn't sure what was worse—that it had happened at all or that for one shining moment I'd actually been giddy at the news. There were certainly worse people to have bonded to you. And Elijah... Elijah was better than most people. That tiny spark of joy had been thoroughly extinguished, though, when I registered his horrified reaction. He wasn't upset—he was despondent. A death sentence, he called it.

I'd never thought about it that way. Sure, I'd leveraged the inherent aspects of the bond during hunts in the past, but I'd always viewed it as a beautiful thing the lycans had and the rest of us didn't. Imagine just *knowing* without a doubt who your soulmate was. It sounded incredible, impossible, and certainly not anything I thought I'd ever get in this world. Clearly, I'd been romanticizing it.

I cradled my head in my hands.

How could I let this happen?

The question seemed to be on a loop I couldn't break.

God, he was so mad. He couldn't get away fast enough.

The ride back to town on the shared skimmer had been the most awkward two hours of my life. I hadn't even argued when Elijah had taken the control seat, forcing me to ride behind him. It should have been a great excuse to feel the lycan's heat beneath my hands and steal small touches under the guise of holding on. But that wasn't what had happened.

Elijah had been like stone in front of me, distant and cold, despite the ambient heat radiating from him. In the end, I'd relied on my own abilities to keep my seat and kept my fingers curled around the metal frame. It hadn't been until a sudden gust of wind buffeted us that I stupidly reached out and grabbed him so I wouldn't be thrown yet again from a skimmer. He'd instantly stiffened beneath the touch, and I'd quickly pried my fingers, numb from the cold, from his warm body. If Elijah didn't want me to touch him, then I wouldn't.

I sat there in a puddle of despair, misery seeping out of every pore as I relived the memory. Every time I closed my eyes, I saw the look of defeat and anger stamped clearly on Elijah's face. I doubted I'd ever be able to unsee the anguish in his eyes, the way his gaze had become so lost. All because he'd become irrevocably tethered to me. It was my fault. If I'd just kept my distance like the professional I was supposed to be, then the whole disaster could have been avoided.

Logically, I knew I'd had no hand in the bonding. Not even the most gifted witches or oldest supernaturals claimed to understand the unique magic that pulled a lycan's soul to another and intertwined them both for better or worse. I knew all of that, but it didn't stop the guilt from spreading like acid through my chest, eating everything in its path.

I gasped, wrapping my arms around me as if they could somehow protect me from all the mistakes I'd made concerning Elijah Bennett and the rest of my life. My stomach clenched in time with my spasming diaphragm. I fought to regain control of my body with little success. My mother was right; I was a failure in all things that mattered. I couldn't even maintain dominion over myself.

Spots swam across my vision, and I realized that in my efforts to remain calm, I'd stopped breathing altogether. Needles spiked through my lungs as I dragged in air.

Pull it together. It'll be fine. Everything will be fine.

Death sentence.

Oh God, if he's upset now, he's going to be absolutely livid when he learns the truth about who I really am. The things I've done. The weres *I've killed. His pack...*

He'll be devastated.

Icy dread washed through me. I lurched to my feet, nearly face-planting back onto the floor. My legs were unsteady as I scrambled onward. My shoulder hit the wall as I careened around it. There was a crack as my knees crashed to the tile just in time to release what little contents my stomach held. The wretched sound echoed back at me, highlighting my misery.

When there was nothing left but dry heaves, I leveraged the vanity to pull myself upright. I leaned heavily on the counter for support for a moment before shuffling to the sink. One of my abused knees knocked into the lower cabinet, and I winced. The throbbing pain was second only to the one tightening around my chest.

I hung my head as I rinsed my mouth out so I wouldn't have to look at my sallow features. I didn't need the mirror to tell me I looked like death. I felt it plenty. The clear liquid was absolutely vile in my mouth, with a disturbing sweetness it shouldn't have. I spat out the bile-tainted water with enough force to splash the mirror, then repeated. My latest agonized groan fell out of me to ricochet in the porcelain bowl.

The last time I'd been this anxious about sex, I'd lost my virginity. I'd been terrified my mother would find out it was to a werewolf. Since then, I'd never been able to stay away from them for long. They were absolutely my drug of choice. I craved their heat and passion, the way a dying man craved water. It was never enough.

I clenched my fists on the veined countertop. That was until Elijah. The night of the bacchanal had been great, but it was nothing compared to our time at the cabin. Everything had been so unbelievably perfect, and the morning even more so. Right up until…

He'll never forgive me for this. If he doesn't hate me already, he will. It's just a matter of time.

I stepped away from the support and stumbled to the bedroom, where I fell gracelessly onto the mattress, unable to muster the will to strip down or pursue a much-needed healing tonic. The only upside to my current state was that I was officially too exhausted for my chest to start spasming again.

What am I going to do?

The hard truth was that Elijah was my responsibility now. He hadn't chosen to be bonded any more than he'd chosen to be born a werewolf.

But how am I supposed to do anything when he doesn't want me anywhere near him?

I rolled my head to the side. The sheets whispered softly beneath me, the only sound outside of my shallow breathing. My gaze caught on the nightstand and the request I'd received a couple of days ago. A request I'd dismissed at the time. Before I could second-guess the decision, I dialed.

The response was prompt and professional. "Detective Hart."

"Agent Smalls," I responded in kind.

"What can I do for you?" he replied.

"Williams still need an assist on that rogue in New Jersey?"

"Wasn't aware you had the time to spare." The edge of surprise was to be expected.

A beat went by as I debated the wisdom of the choice I was about to make. Elijah clearly needed space to come to terms with what had happened. An entire continent should be sufficient. "I can be there by nightfall."

"I'll inform Detective Williams." The line clicked off, and I was once again plunged back into silence with only my guilt to keep me company.

Elijah

I bolted out of a fitful sleep.

Josh was gone.

The knowledge seemed to be present in every cell of my body, in my very breath. I didn't want to think about how I knew that with such certainty.

Furious, I ripped back the covers and grabbed the nearest thing to wear, which just so happened to be what I'd been wearing the last time I'd seen him. My fingers tightened on the fabric as his true scent drifted up to twine around me. The short circuit it caused had me shoving my nose into the rumpled shirt to soak up more of the tantalizing smell. I doubted Josh would ever tell me how he obscured his natural scent so effectively, but the shit was like catnip. I already felt half-drugged with the day old-smell.

A low growl rumbled out of me. It was only like catnip *to me*. Because my dumb ass had gone and gotten itself *bonded*. To Josh. Who had just skipped town. I shoved the shirt deep into the hamper, then piled more dirty clothes on top of it. Not that it mattered. The damage was already done. Every fiber of my being was practically screaming out for the infuriating man.

I shook my head and ripped out fresh everything, then got dressed in the living room, because I couldn't bear to be in the same place as the smell still wreaking havoc on my nervous system. When I burst into the precinct, I still wasn't any calmer than I'd been when I'd woken. If anything, I was in even more of a state. Truthfully, some insane part of me—likely the bonded part—had hoped that he'd miraculously show up and the tension wrapped around my chest would go away. A quick sweep of the precinct unsurprisingly did not turn up the object of my obsession. With a low growl, I stalked up to his usual desk.

"Where is he?" I demanded of the man on the other side.

Officer Mack stuttered, his eyes wide with alarm as they darted between me and the young woman perched on Josh's desk. "He... um... he's away."

"Away where?" I growled, ignoring the familiar woman.

Officer Mack pulled his shoulders back and straightened. "Detective Hart took an assignment on the East Coast."

My stomach sank to the floor. He'd left? Just like that? Without a word, or note, or even a moonforsaken message? Rage battled with the horrible, persistent sinking sensation of abandonment. I felt like I was going to be sick. How could anyone stand being bonded? This was awful.

I staggered a step back before I could demand the young officer tell me *exactly* where Josh had gone so I could chase him down, and possibly strangle him while I was at it. Suicide by murder would certainly be an unconventional way to go.

Suddenly, the woman turned to face me. Her soft gray curls swayed around a heart-shaped face that housed equally gray eyes. She glanced back at Officer Mack and hesitantly asked, "Didn't you say he'd be back as soon as the mission was finished?"

I blinked down at her. "Kilee?" I really was in a state if I couldn't immediately recognize a member of my own damn pack. "What are you doing here?" *Please don't be in trouble*, I silently pleaded. The last thing the pack needed was another *were* in Josh's crosshairs.

Her rich, earthy complexion darkened with a blush that stained her cheeks a deep rose. Her gaze darted frantically between me and Officer Mack, who looked equally uncomfortable. "I can... I can explain, Alpha. Please don't be upset."

I nearly swallowed my tongue at her words.

Officer Mack took that moment to excuse himself. "I'm gonna get everyone some tea." He spared Kilee a quick glance. "I'll just be a few minutes."

I let out a shaky breath when he left and looked at the young *were* before me. She seemed on the verge of panic at being found out. She opened her mouth, no doubt to offer the promised explanation, and I held up a hand to forestall her. Instantly, her mouth snapped shut at the silent command.

I winced inwardly. She wasn't the first youngling to call me Alpha. Fortunately, none of them had ever done it where word could get back to Conrad, and I prayed to the moon it stayed that way. I didn't need any more reasons to be on his shit list.

"I'm not your Alpha, Kilee," I said as gently as I could.

The blood drained from her face, leaving it ashen and stricken. She clapped a hand over her mouth in a display of horror. "Oh, stars, Red. I'm so sorry. I didn't even... Sweet moon."

I patted her on the shoulder. "It's okay," I comforted her, even though it really wasn't. Unlike *some* people, though, *I* could lie.

Her shoulders instantly sagged with relief, and she offered a weak smile. "Thanks, Red."

"No problem." We both just had to hope that word didn't get back to Conrad about the slip. "So, you and Officer Mack..."

I said, changing the topic to something hopefully lighter. Pink tinged her cheeks once more. "He's a good guy," I offered, ignoring the fact that I only thought so now because it meant definitively that Officer Mack had no designs on Josh.

Her gaze drifted to where he'd disappeared a few minutes before. "Joel is really nice. Sweet, you know? Not like..."

"Not like the rest of us brutes?" I teased.

She laughed and relaxed a little more. "You're not a brute."

I rolled my eyes dramatically. That was a bold statement considering how I'd stormed in here ready to burn the place down. "I'm sure Detective Hart would disagree with you."

She gave me a devious smile. "I don't know about that."

I pointed accusingly at her. "It's not polite to gossip about your elders, young lady," I admonished while simultaneously praying that it was a rumor solely held between her and Officer Mack.

She rolled her eyes. "Pft, the elders gossip more than the pups."

I laughed because she was right and because I was desperately pretending not to be freaking out. How long would Josh be gone? Was he even coming back? What did this mean for me?

None of that line of thinking was good for keeping a composed appearance, so I dropped it. I'd obsess about it in the isolated safety of the cottage.

"How long has that been going on?" I asked, indicating whatever was between her and the officer.

She drew patterns on the dark grain of Josh's commandeered desk. "A couple of months," she admitted quietly. That certainly explained why Officer Mack had been at the bacchanal. Abruptly, her head snapped up. "You're not gonna tell, are you?"

The fear and wariness in her eyes saddened my heart. This is what the Klamath Pack had come to, sneaking behind the Alpha and Beta in order to be anywhere near the humans that lived right next door. We hadn't used to be so against intermingling with humans. That had changed with the Restructure.

"What's there to tell?" I asked with a shrug. I certainly had no room to judge who she wanted to spend time with, especially after...

Nope. Not thinking about it.

Kilee's resulting smile was bright with all the optimism of youth. "Thanks, Red." She glanced over her shoulder, and her smile widened at the sight of Officer Mack attempting to juggle three very full cups of tea. "I'll make sure he lets you know when the detective returns."

I didn't bother to tell her I wouldn't need the heads-up. Just waved goodbye to her and a disgruntled Mack. Outside, the damp air promised yet more rain. I rolled my shoulders and tried to ignore the tension that had etched itself there and wouldn't relent until Joshua Hart was back in my sight. Damn that man.

Chapter 16

Elijah

For the second time in a week, I burst into the Adler Springs precinct. The metal door clanged against the wall and rebounded. It landed with a sharp smack on my palm as I caught it in time to prevent it from slamming into me as well. All eyes swiveled to focus on my rude entrance. I couldn't have cared less about the obviously anxious officers. The only eyes that mattered were the hunter green ones lazily lifting to look at me.

The tightness in my chest eased slightly.

He's really back.

I quickly checked him over for any signs of injury. Joshua Hart may be exceptionally good at his job, but he'd been hunting a rogue lycan, and I'd seen the scars of past encounters firsthand. Once I confirmed he had no new visible marks, anger replaced my relief.

Fucker had left.

I took a few steps towards him to make sure his gaze was focused solely on me. And damn it all, if that undivided attention didn't send a thrill through me. I took the unwanted reaction and pummeled it into oblivion.

"A word," I demanded. "Now."

Josh straightened from where he'd been leaning over the desk, presumably reviewing some reports. His eyes were eerily devoid of emotion as he stared at me from across the room. You'd never know that four days ago he'd been a completely different person—soft, warm, passionate. The man before me now was unquestionably a cold, calculating detective, still sexy as hell, but completely untouchable.

A growl rolled out of me.

Several officers stepped closer. Josh wordlessly held up a hand to forestall them. They hesitated only a second before backing down. The complicit obedience reminded me of my interaction a few days ago and reaffirmed my belief that if Joshua Hart had been a werewolf, he'd be an Alpha. It was hard to deny the calm confidence rolling off him. He continued to look back at me with a level gaze that hadn't shifted once during the entire exchange and gestured for me to take my usual seat.

His nonchalance compounded with his assumption that I would just fall in line like everyone else only infuriated me more. I was not his pet to call to heel. I was my own person, had my own thoughts, and I would not be jerked around like a puppy on a leash. My muscles tightened, and a familiar twist in my stomach alerted me to how worked up I was getting. If I didn't calm down soon, I was likely to force a change. Considering how pissed I already was, I didn't see that going well for anyone in my path.

"Outside," I ground out from beneath the force of controlling the change, then promptly turned on my heel and stormed out. I didn't know what I would do if he didn't follow, but strongly suspected it would involve tearing down the entire department with my bare hands.

Joshua

I fought to keep my nerves from showing. Seeing Elijah so soon after returning from the mission was unsettling. I wasn't sure how much of Mack's recounting of Elijah's previous visit I'd believed, but looking at him now, I suspected Mack had down-played the event. Elijah wasn't mad. He was furious.

"You gonna be alright?" an officer who'd stupidly thought to intervene asked as I made my way to the door.

Rather than answer, I spared them a condescending look. They withered beneath it and immediately stepped away. It was a cheap trick. I was aware of how much every badge in the place feared me. Every badge, except for my local partner. That was one mercy: Mack wasn't here. Had he been, he likely would have followed me out, then I would have had to come up with some sort of meaningless platitude to stop him. It was a relief not to have to say that I wasn't worried or that I'd be fine, because the truth was, I *was* worried and I had absolutely no idea what waited for me beyond that door. Elijah's gaze had been nothing short of murderous.

A sigh escaped me as I stepped into the temperate afternoon, and there was no sign of the man. Hide-and-go-seek-the-werewolf rarely went in my favor. On top of which, I was at a clear disadvantage because Elijah was more familiar with the town.

I glanced around and, finding no clear sign of him, headed in the most likely direction. Despair weighed down each step. If Elijah was unwilling to talk at the precinct, then it probably had something to do with the bond. My heart gave a traitorous flutter. I viciously crushed the response. I had no right to be happy about any of this, especially while Elijah so clearly wasn't. Of course, I also had to figure out what in the seven hells *I* was going to do about this.

I shook my head and kept to the path I'd chosen. Whatever it took, I'd find a way. The consequences of not were simply too high. Elijah hadn't chosen this. If I had to be collateral, then so be it. It could serve as my karmic justice for all the horrible crimes I'd committed against the lycan community.

Suddenly, someone ripped me from the sidewalk and jerked me into an alleyway. My back collided with the aged brick almost at the same time my mouth was captured with a punishing kiss. Recognition flooded my senses, effectively drowning the instinct to lash out. I gasped into my captor even as my body went up in a pillar of flame at the searing possession.

My breathing was far from steady when Elijah finally released me. "What are you doing?" I asked calmer than I would have thought possible. Elijah pressed his body against mine, practically crushing me against the wall. I barely suppressed a groan and the urge to press back. *Not supposed to be enjoying this*, I reminded myself.

"Was pretty sure you wouldn't want your colleagues to see that." His low words slithered into my core, and I shivered.

"Suppose that's wise," I quipped, still fighting my reaction to his proximity to no avail.

He didn't take the bait, though. Instead, he speared me in place with a fierce look, anger burning like lava in his cognac eyes. "You left," he growled.

I blinked, taken aback.

That's what he's mad about?

Elijah

I'd expected Josh to push me away the second I threw him against the wall. To my infinite surprise, not only had he kissed me back, but his entire body seemed to mold to mine. Even more, though, he hadn't even tried to get away or break free, and now he was staring at me in open confusion.

"What?" His brow furrowed while his eyes darted between mine as if searching for some clue as to my real meaning. It wasn't really that hard of a concept. He'd left. That was the short of it.

"You should have told me you were leaving," I repeated.

He blinked, then opened and closed his mouth a couple of times. Finally, he said, "You seemed like you needed some space. I gave it to you."

Most of my remaining fury abated while my heart squeezed painfully in my chest. I'd been prepared for a callous response about how the bond was my problem, not his. This level of thoughtfulness was entirely in the opposite direction. I leaned forward and brushed my lips across his. He was right; I needed space. I also needed him to stop surprising me. I wasn't sure how much more I could take.

"You still could have warned me," I whispered, looking deep into his forest-colored eyes. If I looked hard enough, it was almost like running through the woods with so many shades of life racing past.

His brow drew down sharply. "You knew the second I walked through that portal, didn't you?"

"Bolted out of a dead sleep," I responded. I failed to mention that there'd been nothing remotely restful about that sleep. That he'd haunted every dream. That the sheer physical need to have him near had kept me tossing and turning for hours.

His eyes widened. "I... I didn't..."

I cut him off before he could choke himself on the truth. "You were right. I needed time. Probably still do. It just... hurts." I sighed and rested my forehead against his as my body sought comfort in his presence. I didn't even care that I was being bluntly honest. It did. It hurt so damn much when he wasn't here. "I've never needed anyone like this before."

I didn't even realize I'd said that last out loud until he asked, "How can I help?" His whisper was so soft, I was positive I hadn't heard him right.

To be sure, I leaned back and met his eye. "What?"

"How can I help?" he repeated, stronger.

I searched his face for some undercurrent of meaning. *Is he really serious?* Despite my search, all I found was sincerity. *He is. He actually wants to help.*

My body seemed to have a mind of its own as I leaned down to snare him in another kiss. The last of my tension ebbed out of me when his fingers lightly gripped the back of my neck and urged me deeper. I gladly gave it to him, simultaneously easing one ache and starting another. Maybe I'd been wrong to assume I'd be on my own with this whole bonding disaster.

Josh's mouth was soft, firm, and astonishingly eager. I leaned into him, needing more, needing all of him. It wasn't even until he gave a light groan that I realized I'd angled my body to rub against him. Stars, we were making out in an alley like a bunch of teenagers. Though at the rate we were going, it wouldn't be long until it was more. I wasn't an exhibitionist by nature, but fuck if I didn't want to take Josh right here, pedestrians be damned.

His latest moan vibrated through my chest, a clear indication that he'd be all for it. And since it didn't seem like he'd be protesting anytime soon, that left me to be the logical one. Somehow I pulled away from his captivating mouth, though my heavy breathing betrayed how worked up I was. As I stared down at his kiss-swollen lips, it was hard to resist the temptation to return to stealing his breath.

"What are you doing the rest of the day?" I hadn't meant for the question to sound so sultry, but by the way Josh's eyes dilated, it was clear the lower octave wasn't wasted on him.

"This. I mean, I finished a mission. I'm well within my rights to take the rest of the day for myself," he fumbled to add.

"Good," I rumbled, sliding my hands around his waist.

His breath caught, and I heard the hint of another moan. "Easy Bennett. I'm packing."

I shifted my leg a little higher, and his eyelids fluttered. "I know."

A short laugh burst out of him and twinkled in his eyes.

I smiled despite myself. I loved it when he laughed, not the ironic laugh he normally did, but a real one you could feel, the kind that lit him up from the inside.

"Lethal force. I'm packing lethal force," he chuckled. "Practically every weapon on me could kill you at a touch."

"Seems a bit excessive, don't you think?"

He shrugged. "Hazard of the job."

That reminded me. "You didn't get hurt, did you?"

He raised an eyebrow, his arms still draped over my shoulders. "Do you need to check?"

I didn't even hesitate. "Yes."

Joshua

My laugh cut short when Elijah forcibly dragged me away from the wall and back to the main thoroughfare. He towed me a good twenty paces before I jerked hard enough against his hold to get his attention.

Impatience filled his eyes when he looked back at me. "What?"

I cleared my throat and glanced down at where his fingers encircled my wrist.

His gaze traveled down my arm, leaving tingles in its wake, until at last it riveted on the minor contact. Thanks to my long sleeves, he wasn't actually touching skin, but as his fingers flexed with uncertainty, I found myself wanting him to trail them further down and intertwine them with mine.

Elijah stayed frozen, and I saw the struggle on his face: let go and trust I would follow, or risk me running again. Finally, he relinquished his hold.

Once free, I immediately stepped up to him. We were definitely standing too close for a professional capacity, but it was a far cry better than someone spotting the Klamath liaison dragging the Lycan Detective around like he was intent on murder.

Elijah looked at me with an expression on his face I couldn't quite place, then resumed his fast pace.

After an awkward silence, I finally spoke up. "Where are we going?"

"My place," he answered over his shoulder.

I stopped in the middle of the walkway. "Are you sure that's wise?"

He gave me yet another strange look. "I don't live on pack territory. A lot of the pack doesn't. Not enough housing. I have a house at the edge of town."

"You have a house?" I parroted in surprise.

"Well, I rent a house," he amended.

I stood there, unable to absorb what was happening. We weren't going to some cheap motel or even back to the cabin. We were going to Elijah's *house*. His private sanctum. I didn't take *anyone* to my house. Hell, I wouldn't let my own mother in if it was optional.

"Are you coming?" Elijah's words jolted me out of my thoughts.

I gave a sharp nod and resumed following him. It wasn't until he walked up to a cottage straight out of time that I stalled out again. The place looked as if it could qualify as an historic landmark.

"You own this?" I repeated in awe.

"Rent," he corrected as he took out an old-fashioned, *literal* key. "Lycans aren't allowed to own land."

The triggering statement briefly captured my attention. I could understand the legal ramifications—any property an individual lycan owned automatically belonged to their corresponding pack—but it didn't make the situation any less tragic. Humans passed down property to their progeny all the time. My family had been doing it for centuries.

I bit my tongue and shifted my gaze back to the picturesque home. Restoration and updates had clearly occurred at some point, but that didn't detract from the overall stereotypical English cottage curb appeal.

Stones of various shades pressed together seamlessly to the roof. Efficient solar shingles replaced the typical thatch, but the artificial wood style only added to the charm of the place. Exposed beams lent a pop of detail that paired well with the lighter facade. There were even flower bushes lining the walkway.

Elijah lives here?

My gaze continued to sweep the well-maintained structure in appreciation. Then a surprising thought occurred to me.

Elijah would love my house.

It wasn't a quaint cottage by any stretch of the imagination, but like this place, it boasted ancient architecture, and history obviously appealed to Elijah.

Suddenly, I was once again being dragged, this time through the front door. I didn't even have a chance to take in any of the rooms or decor as he pulled through the house, then practically threw me into what was obviously the bedroom.

"No tour?" I quipped.

"You can ogle the place later. This first." The low, husky words matched the way he pressed me into the dresser perfectly.

The heat of desire flooded through me, and I reflexively arched into him. His resulting deeper moan set my senses on fire. He gripped my sides and his warm hands roved higher as I once again found myself dominated by a primal kiss. A blade shifted in its holster, and alarm tore through my awareness.

"Still lethal," I cautioned him.

His growl vibrated through my core, turning everything in its path to jelly. "You should do something about that."

"Right," I responded enthusiastically. I pushed firmly on his chest until he took a step back, and kept up the pressure as I guided him towards the bed. When his calves bumped the frame, he sat. I quickly followed suit, straddling his lap and recapturing his mouth.

Heat pooled between our bodies, threatening to rob me of what little sanity I still had. Elijah ground against me, and a moan I'd been holding back since the alley slipped free. The sound seemed to be an invitation for him to pull me even closer, causing every inch of me to burn with the sweetest ache.

I teased the tie holding his hair in a low bun loose and buried my fingers in the silky strands. Another moan escaped me as he used his grip on my hips to rock me into him. The friction was at once incredible and completely unbearable. He relinquished his death grip on my waist to rove higher. I arched my back into the touch while refusing to give up his mouth.

The heat of his touch seared through the fabric separating us as it ventured higher and higher until there was a sharp jab in my back. My heart froze, and I went stock-still.

"What is it?" Elijah asked softly, the question causing his lips to brush against mine.

I barely repressed a shudder at the intimate contact, but my words were deadly serious. "Whatever you do, don't move." Carefully and *very* slowly, I maneuvered to look at him. His cognac eyes were calm and curious, but he didn't question the order. I swallowed my spike of fear and kept my next words equally steady. "One wrong move and you'll die."

I waited a breath for him to argue or do something reckless, but in keeping with my warning, he kept perfectly still. His only movement, the opening and closing of his eyes and the rise and fall of his chest. With deliberate motions, I reached behind my back and lightly placed my hands over his. "Packing," I reminded him. "I'm going to guide your hands. Ready?"

"Does it get you naked?" he asked back in near-perfect deadpan.

I bit my lip. "Please don't make me laugh. Even a paper cut from that blade would kill you in a matter of minutes."

"Excessive."

"Hazard."

"Why are you packing so much heat?" he asked, still emulating a stone.

I opted to forego saying that this particular "heat" I almost always packed. "Just got back from a hunt, remember?"

He let out a huff, but didn't continue arguing and allowed me to creep his fingers away from the wolfsbane-tainted daggers. I knew the moment his fingers brushed the hidden seams by the way his eyes widened. He closed his hand around the twin handles and gently coaxed out the blades. I made sure they were free of both of us before signaling for him to drop them. Lethal for werewolves could also mean lethal for humans. More than one careless detective had met their end by dismissing the danger of their own weapons.

As the daggers landed with a light thud, Elijah raised an eyebrow. "Two?"

I leaned forward, rubbing against him as I did so. "Sixteen," I breathed in his ear. His light groan was more than worth the confession.

The next few minutes found me completely lost to the sensuality of Elijah slowly disarming me—slowly mostly for his own safety, but it didn't make it any less seductive. His hands glided smoothly from my back to my sides, then to my chest and eventually my thighs. By the time we were reaching the last few sequestered in my boots, I was more than uncomfortable and struggling not to squirm.

"Josh," Elijah said, impatience dominating my name.

"Right." I pushed myself back to standing, then promptly stripped out of everything, careful not to let the discarded clothes hide the sizable pile of weapons.

Elijah's gaze swept over me with a hunger that made my insides quiver. At last his scrutiny returned to my face.

"Satisfied?"

"No," he growled just before grabbing my arm and pulling me onto the bed. I was mid-bounce when he pressed me into the mattress with a savage kiss, while his insanely warm hands coasted along my sides.

"Fuck, you're hot," I gasped. He pulled back enough to look down at me, concern still shimmering in his eyes. "Both metaphorically and physically. Just in case you had any doubts as to my sincerity. I also think you're wearing far too much clothing for what I suspect you have in mind," I added with a smirk.

His eyes darted between mine, but he didn't resume his amorous attentions. I licked my lips, becoming increasingly nervous as he continued to stare at me. Perhaps telling him how I saw him was a mistake. After all, he'd never wanted this, least of all with me.

"I–"

"You can't lie," he interrupted before I could tie my tongue in knots attempting to take back the careless comment.

"Correct. I cannot lie," I reiterated, since he seemed to need the verbal confirmation.

"Your... mission. Did you get hurt? Are any of these scars new?"

My heart felt like it was in my throat, along with my stomach and the rest of my internal organs. I reminded myself that his question—his concern—had nothing to do with me personally. He didn't care if *I* was injured. No one did. He cared how it would affect the bond, how much danger *he* might have been in. I shook my head "No," not sure I could form words that wouldn't betray how much that truth hurt.

He growled again, and I repressed a wince. "I need to hear you say it."

I swallowed thickly, but held his gaze. "I did not sustain any noteworthy or life-threatening injuries during the recent mission on the East Coast. My role was more as backup than as the primary detective. Is that sufficient?"

He closed his eyes and released a heavy breath. "While I'm relieved you evaded any life-threatening harm, you said 'noteworthy'." He reopened his eyes, but didn't move from hovering over me. "What do you qualify as *not* worth noting?"

"A paper cut." I slowly lifted my hand to show him the already healing line sliced into my thumb. Undeniable anger flared in his eyes before he tamped it down. I'd always been careless with my life, seeing as how I was the only one it remotely mattered to, and barely at that. Except it wasn't my life anymore I was risking—it was Elijah's. "I can go," I whispered, looking away from him.

"You don't need to do that. I'm sorry I killed the mood." He gently grasped my hand and placed a warm kiss over the cut.

"I'm sure we could revive it with enough conviction," I said with a smirk.

He chuckled low in his throat, and I couldn't help but squirm beneath him as the vibrations rippled through me. A reaction he definitely noticed. "You make a valid point. And there is an outrageously sexy, *naked* man in my bed. I vote we make it two." Before I could ask what the hell that was supposed to mean, he rocked back on his heels and pulled his shirt over his head. "Now where did I put that lube?" he asked with a devilish grin.

Chapter 17

Elijah

Josh's hands smacked against the wall where there should have been a headboard, while his knees sank into the plush comforter I'd neglected to remove as I pushed into his wonderfully tight ass. Our dual moans filled the room, and I ran my hands along the curve of his back, doing my damndest to ignore the myriad array of scars decorating his body. Thinking about them too hard would likely cause me to lose what little remained of my sanity, and I didn't actually want to hurt him.

I pulled almost all the way out and slammed back home hard enough that he scooted forward. I grabbed his hips, pulling him back toward me, and set a punishing pace. My body at least was officially convinced that Josh was physically here, but I still couldn't smell him, and it was driving me crazy. I needed all of him, not just what he was willing to give. That his scent, the very essence of him, was being withheld from me was infuriating.

I tightened my grip on his hips and shifted for a better angle. The moment I moved, his head dropped between his shoulders, and he let out a moan so deep I felt it where our bodies connected.

"That's it, baby, right there."

I completely lost my rhythm and nearly let him go. I'd never let *anyone* call me "baby," inside or outside of sex. I found the term juvenile and bordering on demeaning. I was a grown *were*, not some child. Josh remained oblivious to my internal diatribe over his poor choice of words. He seamlessly found the pace that I'd lost and kept going. I reflexively met his thrusts, still at odds about the "baby" business.

Pleasure rippled up Josh's back in a wave that had him shuddering. "Fuck. You feel so good, baby," he said, his voice raw and husky. As the subsequent moan fell out of him, I quickly decided that Joshua Hart could call me whatever the hell he liked as long as he kept making those sounds.

I wrapped an arm around his middle and pulled him up so he could be flush against me. It didn't seem possible to touch enough of him. My hands wandered relentlessly across his torso while I drove into him. When I at last took hold of his cock, he dropped his head back on my shoulder. His harsh panting filled my ears and drove me onward. I angled my head to capture him in a kiss and swallowed his latest moan. This was what I needed. Now if only I could smell how aroused he was instead of just hearing it.

He tangled his hand in my hair and forced me deeper, claiming my mouth just as much as I claimed his. His other hand landed on my thigh, where his nails instantly bit into my flesh. I rocked harder into him and was rewarded with a gasp as his channel tightened around me. Josh's entire body seemed to vibrate with need, totally consumed with pleasure.

His back arched as he shuddered in my grasp. I stroked him through his release without relenting. An unexpected wave of anger hit me again at realizing his spunk didn't hold his scent either. Rather than release him, I pulled him tighter against me and stole another savage kiss, punishing his body for the one thing it refused to give me.

Joshua

Elijah's fingers traveled lazily across my torso, tracing the assortment of pearlescent scars. It probably wouldn't be much longer before he started asking about them if the look on his face was any judge.

I rested my head back on the pillow and let out a contented breath. I was completely spent, and that was *with* the mild healing tonic I'd snagged from my vest in between rounds. The marathon had been completely worth it, though. All except for the part where I'd called him baby... twice.

I winced internally. It hadn't been intentional. I'd mostly been trying so damn hard *not* to say his name. An almost impossible task considering it had been like a damn chant inside of me.

Fuck. What was I going to do? I was so wrapped up in Elijah Bennett it wasn't even funny. And humans couldn't bond. So what was *my* excuse?

"I don't know how you do it," Elijah mused as he traced a particularly nasty scar from my collarbone to just beneath my left nipple.

I blinked up at him, torn from my tormented thoughts. "Come again?"

He huffed a short laugh and leaned down to place an open-mouthed kiss on my upper pec. I tried to stifle a moan, but Elijah's enhanced hearing caught it anyway. He glanced up, and

I got lost in his burning cognac gaze. If the man kept looking at me like that, my rest was going to be very short-lived.

"That's what I'm talking about. Your stamina borders on lycan."

I didn't bother containing a devilish grin. "Would have thought it'd be pretty clear by now that I rather enjoy being completely wrecked."

Elijah stiffened, his gaze hardening in an instant. Anxiety threaded through my chest. Where I'd been hoping for at least the ghost of a smile, I found myself watching his jaw tick beneath his grizzled cheek.

"What?" I asked when I couldn't take it anymore.

Something rippled through him, and he let out a tight breath. The kiss he planted on my shoulder seemed more like it was to ground him than to reassure me. "Just another side effect of the bond."

What? I considered pressing, officially worried. What on Earth could the bond do that would elicit such a reaction?

He pulled back to look down at me. "Don't ever let me know anyone else you've slept with."

I barked a laugh to hide my sudden unease at his serious tone. "Wasn't really planning to."

"I mean it, Josh. Never."

"Okay... May I ask why?"

Rather than answer, he returned to resting his full weight on me. Contrary to what I would have expected, I didn't feel trapped. It was actually comforting. My question continued to hang unanswered while I trailed my fingers down his back. When he finally spoke, I was positive the only reason I heard it was because the words vibrated in my chest.

"Because I'll kill them."

My heart thudded heavily. We lay in silence, each of us absorbing what he'd said. Elijah wasn't a murderer, but his tie to me could make him one. I tightened my grip on him protectively. There may not be much I could do where the bond was concerned, but I'd be damned if I let that happen.

"Are you seeing anyone?" he abruptly asked.

My laugh was much more genuine this time. "Is that a trick question? You literally just said—" A menacing growl joined Elijah's intense glower. "Hey. Easy. I already told you I wasn't sleeping with anyone." His glare intensified. "Okay. Okay. I haven't had sex or anything that might be construed as sex with anyone but you in three months."

He narrowed his eyes as if doubting my sincerity.

I huffed in frustration. "I can't give you the answer the way you want it. I *see* a lot of people." I searched his face as it warred with the need to believe me and crippling doubt. "Right now, it's just you. You're it," I added. I wanted so much to cup the side of his face and help him see the truth of what I was saying, but I forced my hand to stay where it was while he came to his own conclusion. I couldn't force Elijah to believe me. He had to do that all on his own.

Tension gradually seeped out of his shoulders, the knotted muscles loosening one by one as he forced himself to relax. When it seemed almost all of it was gone, he pulled away.

I stubbornly ignored the ache that sprang up as well as the desire to reach for him. He ran a hand through his iron-gray hair, obviously still frustrated. Unsure how to proceed, I waited in silence.

"I'm going to take a shower," he finally said, then rolled up from his seat and acquired clothes from the dresser, including throwing some at me, before vanishing into the ensuite.

I stayed where I was. Elijah had clearly not extended an invitation. The fact left a bitter taste in my mouth that I swallowed. Navigating the bond was already proving to be uniquely difficult.

Elijah

I clenched my hands against the wall as scalding hot water cascaded down my back. It had been a dick move not including Josh. A part of me wished he'd walk in anyway. Another... another was relieved that he'd done nothing more than quietly watch me leave, and *that* made me feel like an ass twice over.

I'd basically sexually assaulted the man, and he'd just gone with it. No rebuff. No taunting. Hell, he'd literally asked how he could help. The most protest he'd given had been when I'd nearly gotten myself killed groping him. He could have let me die... but he hadn't. He'd been concerned, of all things. Something I was still struggling to wrap my head around.

And I'd done what in return? Used him like some kind of living doll, gotten pissed when he'd called me "baby," thrown a change of clothes at him, and stormed off. All that, and still not so much as a syllable of protest.

Then there was the rude awakening of homicidal rage at the thought that he might be involved with someone else. That was definitely a conversation we should have had sooner, though I wasn't really sure when we could have had it. He *said* he wasn't with anyone, but who knew what that really meant. I desperately *needed* to believe him, except a deeper instinct said not to trust him. Man may not be able to tell an outright lie, but he could equivocate better than a Shakespearean witch.

I sighed and turned off the water. It was difficult to trust someone I couldn't smell. Without his scent to lend credence to his words, I just couldn't take them at face value. But I wanted to. I wanted to *so* badly. I just... couldn't. At this rate, the bond was going to tear me in two, and I'd be powerless to prevent it.

A growl rolled out, mostly directed at myself.

I may not control the bond, but I could control my behavior, and *that* needed some serious work. Much as I would like to blame Josh for this mess, it wasn't his fault. I should have recognized the signs sooner. Joshua Hart had dominated nearly every thought to the point of obsession since I'd first laid eyes on the man. I'd looked for any excuse to be near him, to touch him. Looking back, it was obvious.

I'd already been working well outside the bounds of a typical liaison. Catching his true scent had just been the final straw. The only person in the world who could have stopped me then would have been Josh himself. Which he hadn't. And now I was back to being an ass.

Moons of Jupiter. Get your shit together. There are plenty of weres that don't agonize over the bond. They live long, happy lives.

But could I live happily with Josh? How long would Josh even live? He had an incredibly dangerous job. It didn't matter how good he was. One mistake, one miscalculation, and he'd be dead—then so would I.

I shrugged off the troubling thoughts and into the sweats and t-shirt I'd brought with me. The prevalent steam caused the garments to stick unpleasantly. I shoved all thoughts of Josh's mortality away and exited the bathroom into an empty bedroom. Anxiety raced through me at the speed of light until I realized that Josh's clothes were still here, and probably more telling, his weapons, albeit now neatly stacked and safely off the floor.

I massaged my chest and went in search of the man who was gonna give me a heart attack. Without Josh's scent to guide me, I was walking blind. At last I found him in the study, openly perusing some papers.

As my gaze landed on him standing in nothing more remarkable than gray sweats and a white t-shirt, my heart skipped a beat. A literal fucking beat. It wasn't even the clothes, which didn't fit properly at all. We were of a height, so the pants didn't drag, but his waist was smaller than mine and they hung sinfully low. He must have scared up a smaller shirt from somewhere, because the one I'd tossed him would have dwarfed his frame. This one, however, hung just a tad loosely. The overall combination was sexy as hell and pulled at me in more ways than one.

Fuck. Why is Josh wearing my clothes so hot?

"What?"

I blinked and realized I'd been standing there like an oaf. To cover, I took a page out of his book and deflected. "I'm surprised they fit."

The corner of his mouth tweaked up in a half-smile as he looked down at the obscenely low pants. "Drawstrings can remedy many things," he said, then returned to his reading material.

"You just couldn't help snooping, could you?" I teased, stepping closer.

"I am a detective," he responded without looking up.

The urge to walk up behind him and wrap my arms around his waist, as if it would be the most natural thing in the world, threatened to overwhelm me. I could practically feel his hair brushing my cheek as I rested my head on his shoulder to read what he was reading. The low heat of his body as he leaned back against me. The sigh he would let out as I held him close.

"This is quite good."

The comment caught me off guard and shattered the fantasy that somehow any of this could ever be normal. He turned a page, and I realized exactly what he was reading. It would be the papers from the *locked* drawer.

"It's not often that I read literary speculation. I have to admit, I'm thoroughly impressed. And the name. Quite clever, really."

"I'm not sure I catch your meaning," I sidestepped.

Josh's gaze snapped up, pinning me in place with its usual intensity, and I had to remind myself to breathe. "Dr. E.

Darcy, premier authority on nineteenth and twentieth-century literature. I'm a little surprised more people haven't made the connection."

"And what connection would that be?"

"That you're the same person. Nice twist using Elizabeth Bennet's married name as your nom de plume." I opened my mouth to protest his assumption, even though he was dead on, but he wasn't finished yet. "I can't work out why you wouldn't want anyone to know it was you. Why hide? They are impressive dissertations."

I nearly swallowed my tongue at the praise and the implication that he'd viewed more than one. "How many of those have you read?"

A ghost of a smile flitted across his lips. "I've skimmed at least three, though I'm rather enjoying your dissection of *Great Expectations*." He let a beat pass before asking, "Are you going to answer the question?"

It was pointless to argue. Josh was not a stupid man. He could find the truth one way or the other, regardless of what I said. I held out my hand for the ill-gotten papers. "These were locked, you know."

He didn't deny it, but passed me the pages. "You're avoiding."

I sighed and stared down at my latest endeavor. My finger passed over the elegant script declaring the author. My mother had loved all things Jane Austen, so it had seemed only fitting that I should honor that, even if it wasn't with my name. "Because Elijah Bennett is a lycanthrope, and lycanthropes don't get published in elite journals."

"Speciesism," he hissed under his breath.

I ignored it for the time being, even though his anger mirrored mine. Once I'd dreamed of publishing under my own name, but this world was cruel and still struggling with change.

My assumptions about and subsequent treatment of Josh were testament I was equally subject to such prejudices.

"About my behavior earlier," I began.

"You don't owe me an explanation," he cut me off.

I frowned, but didn't press the point. "Fine then. Something else." He waited patiently for me to get on with it. "I think we need ground rules."

He cocked his head to the side. "What were you thinking?"

"First off, no one needs to know about this. The... bond." I nearly choked on the word. Eventually, I'd have to get over it. It wasn't going anywhere. "I'd rather keep it between us for now."

"Understandable. Will you tell your Alpha?"

I clenched my jaw so hard that I almost broke a tooth. "I am absolutely *not* telling Conrad. Will you tell your superiors?

"It's not my intention."

I bristled at the subtle hint that it might come out anyway. "That's another thing. I need you to be honest with me."

"I can't lie," he responded without expression.

"Not lying and being honest are not the same thing." Indignation radiated from him. I quickly rushed to add, "Also, I think it would be a good idea to get to know each other better. This whole thing feels like..."

"An arranged marriage?" he filled in. I was nowhere near ready to unpack that, so I avoided it like all the other things I wasn't ready to handle.

"Like I was saying, we hardly know anything about each other."

"I'm a Lycan Detective. You're a lycan. Did I miss something?"

I took a calming breath that was far from calming. "You are more than your job."

"Am I?" he countered.

"Fuck. I really hope so."

"Okay."

I gave him a curious look, momentarily thrown by the odd response. "Okay... what?"

"Okay, I'll do my best to answer your questions honestly and as straightforwardly as my situation allows. All I ask is that you understand that there are some things that I'm not at liberty to share."

"Like government secrets?" I teased, thinking back to our night at the bar.

"Something like that."

Rather than dig into the evasive answer, I agreed. "That seems fair enough."

He nodded once. "What do you want to know?"

"Why are you doing this?" It was the first question that came to mind and one that had plagued me the entire shower.

"That's a really broad question. Care to narrow it down?"

"You seem to be taking all of this really well, a hell of a lot better than me. You're being... nice. Why?"

His mouth opened and closed without any words coming out. "There are a lot of answers to that question."

"Give me *one*," I fired back, barely restraining my temper, a temper I'd never had before Josh walked into my life.

He gazed back at me with steady eyes, then gave me the last answer I expected. "Because you don't deserve cruelty."

"I don't even know what to do with that."

"Do with it what you will."

"I still don't get it. I feel like you should be mad, not whatever this is." I gestured wildly at his easy stance and unaffected attitude. "Why aren't you punishing me?"

His previously calm expression twisted into a scowl. "Contrary to opinion, I am *not* a sadist. I do not get off on hurting people. Being good at my job doesn't mean I also have to be a sociopath." He looked away, anger sharply lining his body.

Suddenly it occurred to me that Josh's life must be very lonely. *How many people have treated him like the devil come to ruin their lives?* "Josh, I—"

"What else?" he interrupted.

I dropped my hand, which seemed to have risen of its own accord. It was painful to see Josh upset, but this was a conversation that needed to happen, no matter how unpleasant it was. "Are you using me?"

His gaze snapped back to me with the burning intensity of looking into a green sun. "No."

I was a little taken aback at both the quickness and ferocity of his denial. I swallowed thickly and wished to the moon and back that I didn't feel the need to add, "Will you?"

There was a long minute during which he said nothing. Then his shoulders relaxed and his features gentled slightly. "I don't want to, but I can't promise that I never will. Promises—" His eyes went distant and his words trailed off. "I need... I should go. There is still a report that needs to be given."

"Write it here." It was a stupid thing to suggest. I already knew he'd say no. We weren't exactly having the best chat. The only time we seemed to get along was when we were both naked. And to top it all off, I'd been a moon-sized jerk most of the afternoon. But none of that mattered. I wasn't ready for him to leave. "At least stay for dinner." It sounded desperate even to my ears.

His gaze heated slightly at the suggestion. We both knew it wouldn't just be dinner. "It's a confidential report."

I expected the response, but it didn't make it any easier to hear. Even my wildly fluctuating moods didn't diminish how much I wanted to wake up with him in my arms. Something that might have been panic grew in my chest. What if he left again? What if he didn't come back this time? What if he died?

My heart nearly seized at the thought, and I only just didn't clutch my chest.

I have got to stop thinking about Josh's mortality.

"I could come back. Afterwards."

I frowned in confusion. "You would do that?"

He shrugged noncommittally. "It's not a lengthy report. And..." He hesitated before going on. "And I can make sure you can smell me when I return."

Those words were magic to my ears, and I couldn't believe he'd offered them freely. "Okay. I'll make something and be sure to save you some." Who was I kidding? I'd wait for him before taking so much as a nibble.

He gave a quiet laugh and shook his head. "Of course you cook."

Before I could respond, he stepped forward and placed his wrist against mine. His smooth skin brushing against the sensitive flesh instantly got my attention. "What are you doing?"

He looked at me, his dark green eyes steady. "Giving you my number."

"I already have it." I'd been issued it when Conrad appointed the Klamath Pack liaison. There was no way he didn't know that.

"This is my direct line. You can reach me at any time. No matter the circumstances."

My mouth went dry. "How many people have this number?" I whispered.

He blinked slowly. "Three."

There was a soft beep in my ear, signaling the transfer of data. Then the cool tips of his fingers rested against my wrist, lightly stroking where he'd given me a gift I never could have expected. The thoughtfulness was almost painful. I leaned forward, needing an outlet for the depth of feeling that threatened to overwhelm me. His lips molded gently to mine, and I wondered how long it would take for that to stop surprising me.

"You're not the person I thought you were."

A darkness passed behind Josh's eyes. "No, I'm not."

CHAPTER 18

Elijah

I EYED THE CASSEROLE I'd put together and debated for probably the thousandth time about testing the number Josh had given me. What exactly did he mean by "any circumstances"? And when he said three, how did he count that number? Was I one of them? Was he?

I dismissed the obsessive thoughts and the impulse to call him. It had only been a few hours, so there was no reason to get so worked up. The dish sat steaming before me, taunting me with its readiness. How much longer was he going to be? Would he like it?

Probably should have asked what kind of food he liked before he left.

The oven mitts landed with a resounding smack on the counter. "Good grief, I'm acting like some moonstruck idiot with his first puppy love." Of course, most people couldn't tell the difference between puppy love and the bond on the surface.

I sighed as I leaned against the refrigerator while I absently ran my thumb over my wrist where Josh's fingers had caressed it earlier.

Maybe I should call him. At least tell him that dinner is ready.

A beep in my ear signaled an incoming call. Excitement raced through me as I straightened and accepted it.

"Hey," I said the instant the call connected.

"Don't 'hey' me. Where the hell have you been?"

"Eric?" I asked, confused. "What's going on?"

"You need to get your tail to the House. That's what's going on. What have you been doing anyway? You haven't checked in for days."

Vivid images of Josh writhing beneath me flashed through my mind faster than I could stop them. "I... the detective wasn't in town."

"Alpha's pissed. I hope you have a good excuse."

"There was nothing to report," I argued.

"Well, there's plenty to report on this side."

That immediately got my attention. "What? Has something happened?"

"They found Keith... they also found Levi. He's dead, Red."

Cold washed over me. "Shit," I hissed.

"Yeah. Look, just get to the House. The place is in total upheaval."

My gaze shot to the cooling dish on the counter. Josh would have to wait. "I'm on my way."

"Good. And, uh, Red?"

"Yeah?" I asked as I covered the dish.

"Don't tell anyone I called, okay?"

A pit opened up in my stomach. One of our own was dead, and Conrad was *still* playing politics. "Of course not. I'm just coming in for an overdue update."

Eric's relieved sigh drifted through. "Okay. Yeah. Thanks. I'll see you soon."

The line cut out, and I stood with balled fists in the kitchen. Conrad's insistence on excluding me was damaging our pack. What if I could have helped prevent this? How long had he known? And what else was he keeping from me?

Joshua

I knew exactly what would await me when I responded to the encrypted message that had come in mid-conversation with Elijah. Poor timing didn't even come close. It finally felt like we were making some progress, like maybe the bond *wouldn't* be the ultimate end of everything. One step forward, two steps back. I rolled my shoulders and braced for the scathing rebuke undoubtedly coming my way.

I didn't have to wait long.

"You're late." A hologram of my mother walked out of the wall of my temporary accommodations, her face pinched and sour as usual. Hundreds of miles away from where I stood in Adler Springs, her phantom heels clicked on the floor while her dramatic robe drifted behind her as she paced the sitting room of her personal estate.

There was no point in arguing. I was, in fact, over a day late with my report, thanks to my preoccupation with the Elijah situation. "I'm here now."

"Don't get smart with me. You are there to do a job, and I want to know why it hasn't been done. You should be on to the next target already. What's the delay?" she demanded.

I clenched my jaw and had to force myself to relax it before I could speak. "I've encountered... complications."

"What sort of complications?"

The last thing I wanted was to out Elijah about the bond less than an hour after I'd agreed it was a good idea to keep quiet about it. "My pack liaison," I skirted.

My mother's fierce gaze latched onto me. Even half a continent away, and through the haze of technology, it had the power to send me right back to my childhood—

Her cruel voice ripping me apart while I lay on the ground with a broken ankle. Mercilessly ordering me to stop cowering like a scared rabbit, that I was the predator, not the prey. Leaving me to stumble twelve kilometers home in the dark, all on my own, without so much as a hydration pill. I managed, but the resulting infection required a healer of exceptional skill. A healer she refused to commission until the blood poisoning nearly reached my heart. Days of agony that could have been prevented with a single call. I'd only been ten.

—I pushed the painful memory away and focused on controlling what I could in the conversation.

"What about your liaison? The Portland pack should have been easy pickings. Don't tell me they've actually caught on to your true purpose."

It wasn't worth correcting her. They hadn't been called the Portland Pack in nearly twenty years. Seemed Conrad Mallin wasn't the only one stuck in the past.

I kept my expression neutral as I answered her questions. "As far as I can ascertain, the pack seems no more unified now than they were when we targeted them."

"So, what is the issue?"

"He..."

She rolled her eyes and turned away with an exaggerated huff. "So *that's* what it is."

"What exactly are you implying, Mother?" I asked, my voice betraying none of my fury.

"Don't play coy with me, boy. I'm well aware of your... *proclivities*." She spat out the last word as if even saying it was an affront to her senses. My lip curled up in a snarl I couldn't repress. "You're no better than your cousin. Imagine cavorting with lycanthropes. On *purpose*. Your ancestors would be appalled. Lying with an animal," she continued, heedless of the anger bunching in my shoulders. "I don't know why I ever expected anything more. Men have always been such base creatures, hardly a step above the abominations we hunt. How I could have ever—"

"He's bonded to me," I cut her off without thinking, just needing her to stop. The moment the words left my mouth, I would have done almost anything to take them back.

My mother instantly ceased her tirade and slowly turned to face me, her face piqued with interest. "Is that so?" she crooned.

Fuck. Fuck. Fuck. There has to be a way to fix this. I did not just get Elijah killed because I can't keep my fucking mouth shut.

"Perhaps this can be to our advantage," she mused aloud. She tapped a pointed, red-tipped nail lightly on her bottom lip, tinted the same shade. Both colors washed her out immensely, making her look vampiric.

I forced myself to stay quiet while she thought. The last thing I needed to do was give her any more ideas. As it was, I was hard-pressed to figure out how I was going to circumvent whatever insanity she came up with and still tell the truth.

Her sallow features alternated between clouding over in concentration and brightening in a sickening display of glee. At last, her pensive expression returned to me. "Could he assume the mantle of Alpha?"

Yes.

I bit back the honest response and scrambled to find an answer that fell within my limitations. "He's arguably too young to assume the mantle." I thought back to a prior conversation and added, "Practically a pup."

My mother's mouth puckered in a disappointed frown tinged with disgust.

I almost let out a sigh of relief. I didn't give a damn what she thought about me as long as she didn't think Elijah was a pawn she could use. That he hadn't already assumed control of the Klamath Pack astounded me to no end. The man was a born leader. His pack obviously respected him, and the current Alpha was a backward fool.

"Maybe in time then," she said softly to herself. "Though, ideally, our mission will be complete long before his ascension would be of any relevance. Still, that could have been promising." Her robe swirled around her as she spun to face me once again. "Are you sure?"

I was *sure* about a lot of things. I was sure my mother had never made a study of the werewolf bond or its unique properties. I was sure she had no clue about my taste in partners. And I was absolutely sure that I would do just about anything to keep her claws out of Elijah Bennett.

"Yes."

Elijah

At first glance, nothing seemed out of place as I approached the sprawling mid-century modern pack house. I caught a few curious eyes, but hardly anyone was outside. Perhaps that should have been my first clue. The House was always swarming with bodies, inside and out.

I pushed through the simple yet imposing wooden doors of the main entrance. A wave of sound instantly rolled out, nearly knocking me back. My gaze swept the crowd gathered. It seemed every wolf in the pack was here, including, to my dismay, Tommy. The poor kid was white as a sheet and being tended to by a woman with gray hair so dark it was nearly black.

Sabrina had turned up as well, and no one thought to tell me.

My anger surged. Wolves had gone missing, we were looking at murder charges, Levi was dead, and *still* I was being kept out? Plausible deniability only went so far. Conrad's actions bordered on self-sabotage.

A hush fell over those standing nearest to me and gradually rippled out. Before long, all eyes were on me. I squared my shoulders and stepped deeper into the crowd. They parted to let me pass, with a subtle babble of whispers flowing in my wake. The last row of people stepped aside, and I found myself face to face with the Klamath Alpha.

"The prodigal son returns." Conrad's words cut through the white noise, and silence descended once more.

"Alpha." Despite my best efforts to keep a tight rein on my temper, the honorific still came out more of a growl.

"How generous of you to grace us with your presence."

"It would have been nice to know my presence was required," I fired back.

"You shouldn't have to be *told* to be with your pack."

I winced at the scathing retort and wondered how much longer I could hold up this charade. "Maybe if you hadn't—"

"You forget yourself," Conrad cut me off. "Remember that it is only for the love of your mother, moon rest her soul, that I have not taken stronger action against you." He considered me with the same discerning eye that had helped him become Alpha so many years ago. "Your father was just like you, and we all know where that got him."

My nostrils flared, betraying my barely contained rage. The argument that my father had died protecting this pack while *he* cowered behind walls and legal writs was on the tip of my tongue. Then I caught sight of Tommy shivering on the couch, looking just this side of death.

Now was not the time to confront Conrad for all the slights he'd given me over the years. For now at least, he was free to resent me for being the spitting image of my father and the son of the love of his life. Conrad may have won the right to be Alpha, but he'd lost the only fight he'd ever cared about—the heart of Nayeli Redwood.

I fought to control my temper and took several deep breaths. Nothing seemed to work until I pictured Josh's deep green eyes, so open and sincere as he looked back at me and asked, "How can I help?" Hearing Josh's words come out of my mouth was jarring, but I held the vision of him in my mind's eye and repeated it just as he had earlier that day. "How can I help?"

Chapter 19

Joshua

Two days. Two whole fucking days and the most I'd heard from Elijah had been a message canceling our date. *Dinner*, I mentally amended. People like me didn't get dates. Date also implied that Elijah *wanted* to spend time with me as opposed to he didn't have a choice.

I grimaced and tried harder to focus my attention on the reports. Another homicide had come in. No one was really sure whose jurisdiction it fell under, though, as there wasn't much left of the body to catalog. My sinking suspicion was that it was one of the *weres* I'd infected. If that was the case, then the situation with Elijah was about to get a lot more complicated.

As if the mere thought of him was a summons, Elijah Bennett walked into the precinct, and I immediately frowned. The man was a veritable wreck. His hair hung loose, his shoulders curled inward, and there was an overall defeated stance to him. Even at this distance, I could see the haunted cast in his eyes.

What in the seven hells has he been doing?

His gaze swept across the office. I quickly looked away so he wouldn't catch me staring or, worse, see the concern on my face. At the sound of feet coming my way, I scrambled to clear the data tabs of any alarming information. Just as I thought I'd gotten them all, one flashed with a message alert from the coroner that the autopsy was done.

My eyes widened, and I reached out to dismiss the notice. No sooner had my hand neared the data tab than an exceedingly warm one placed itself on the small of my back. Burning heat seared through the thin material separating us to wrap without mercy around the base of my spine. I didn't gasp at the intimate contact through sheer force of will alone. Had it only been two days since he'd last touched me?

I quickly flipped the screen over to lock it and straightened to find Elijah standing practically on top of me. Need filled his haunted gaze, along with something I couldn't quite place. Doubt? Fear? Neither felt right, but my worry ratcheted up another notch. Whatever it was, it couldn't possibly be good.

"You've been absent," I said as evenly as possible and took a step to the side to put some distance between us. The move might have worked better if he hadn't mirrored it to maintain proximity.

"Can I speak with you?" Elijah whispered, crowding me against my desk.

I glanced over my shoulder to see Officer Mack watching us curiously. We definitely couldn't stay here. "Come with me," I said equally quietly and headed for the side door. Several turns and a flight of stairs later, we emerged in an obscure—mercifully empty—hallway. The second I stopped, Elijah ran his hands fretfully through his hair while he paced in place. "What's going on?"

"I need to ask you something."

"Okay."

He looked at me out of the corner of his eye. "I don't expect you to tell me, but I kind of really hope you do. I just... I know I can't expect anything, and—"

"Bennett, look at me."

He did so reluctantly, tension lining every muscle.

I didn't hesitate to step forward and cup the back of his neck to press my lips gently against his. I felt the anxiety drain out of him as well as the renewed heat of his hand on my lower back. Abruptly, he pressed me against the wall, laying nearly all of his weight on me. He caught my resulting gasp with an even deeper kiss. I dug my fingers into his bicep with one hand and buried my fingers in his hair with the other.

I tugged softly on the loose strands. To my surprise, he relented. "Talk to me." He sighed and rested his forehead against mine. I stole the opportunity to enjoy the intimate contact while I waited for him to find the words he needed.

"Do you really think Tommy killed Tina?" he asked, looking at me with some of the saddest eyes I'd ever seen.

I licked my lips and thought about how best to answer. Finally, I settled for the *honest* truth. I cupped the side of his face, rubbing my thumb across his grizzled cheek. "No." Doubt colored his beautiful cognac eyes. "I think he was framed." Which really put a wrench in everything I *wasn't* supposed to be doing in Adler Springs.

Surprise shone clearly on his face. "What? Really? Who?" he asked in rapid fire, each word more confused than the last.

I brushed the hair back from his face. "You know I shouldn't tell you."

He swallowed and nodded. "Is that why you were so hell-bent on going to the cabin?"

"Mm-hmm," I hummed, still playing with his tresses. I liked his hair loose. It was unbelievably soft, and I suspected his wolf-coat would be much the same. "Is this what you needed to talk to me about?" I asked, barely remembering why we were here. A "here" that wasn't exactly all that safe for what we were doing.

"Partly. Josh..." Elijah hesitated and looked away. "I know where Tommy is," he finished softly.

My hand froze, knuckle-deep in his hair. "I don't need to tell you that's obstruction." Not that it wasn't anything I hadn't already suspected.

"There's another thing." His gaze bored into mine once more, and my worry grew again. "There was another murder."

"I know. I was looking at the reports when you came in."

"Not a human murder. A lycan."

I forced my fingers to keep combing. Elijah was confiding in me about a murder I'd likely set in motion, and I didn't know what to do. Did I stop him? Did I tell him? Would it be easier to run? "That's not really my jurisdiction. Unless you suspect a human." Elijah stared intently back at me, and it clicked. "You think they're the same killer. Don't you?"

He nodded, then shuddered. "Josh, the things I saw... I don't think I've ever seen anything do that to a living creature."

"You saw him?" My confirmation was in his eyes. While his statement made it more plausible that my human victim had met their fate at the same hands as his lycan one, there was no way I was inserting myself into the pack without proper probable cause. Which was probably sitting on my desk right now.

Maybe the results were inconclusive.

I was still trying to gather my thoughts when Elijah pulled me into a tight embrace. For a second, I wasn't really sure how I was supposed to react. This was so far outside our normal scope. Kissing, I could handle. Mind-blowing sex, no problem. But a hug?

Elijah

I didn't know what possessed me to wrap Josh in my arms. All I knew was that the last two days had been utter hell, and holding him helped. The standoff with Conrad had been the tip of the iceberg. What I confronted next rocked me to my core. I squeezed Josh a little tighter, barely remembering to hold back enough not to snap him in two. If there had been a way to get away from the horror sooner, I'd have done it. For the first time, the bond had felt more like a life raft than a weight dragging me down. Suddenly, Josh's arms folded around me, and he relaxed into the embrace. The comforting feel of his hand rubbing my back nearly broke me.

I buried my face in his neck and wished to the moon that I could smell him. In a month, my world had been thrown into complete flux, and the last two days had added a layer of chaos I was not prepared to handle. I needed something to ground me, to hold me together. Maybe that was why I'd hugged the detective.

"I think a human killed Tina Carr," Josh whispered, startling me enough that I pulled back. His hands trailed along my shoulders and arms, but he mercifully maintained contact.

"What? Who would do that?" A human could *not* have committed the atrocities I'd seen. Visions of an inverted rib cage sitting several feet from its origin and fragments of bone embedded in tree trunks stained red flashed through my mind.

"Ashton Carr." Josh's pronouncement scattered the images.

Now I was really confused. "Her own husband? Sure, she'd been having an affair, but *murder*?" I questioned, not stopping to think that Josh might have something to say about my knowing Tommy and Tina had been having an affair. "But the body. We both saw the wounds."

He nodded. "Convincing werewolf bites are difficult to fake. Difficult, but not impossible."

"How can you be so sure?"

"The dental records don't match. Thanks to Dr. Swann's exceptional preservation skills, forensics could pull a complete bite."

I huffed a laugh. Of course. Every *were* since they hit the change had to register their human teeth *and* their wolf-form's. All this time we'd been hiding someone whose innocence was proven by the very system we abhorred. If I'd just had a little more faith that Josh would do his job properly, then we could've avoided at least half this mess.

Stars, more than half. If we'd turned Tommy over at the outset, then Josh and I wouldn't have spent so much time together, and we certainly wouldn't have ended up stormed-in at the cabin. Which meant we wouldn't be bonded now.

To my shock, I realized this was the first time I'd thought about *not* being bonded to Josh. And I hated it. Yes, I'd griped and complained. I'd been furious both at myself and at him. But in the end, even I had to admit there was something here. That there *could be* something here. Something worth having. Something I wanted.

Without warning, I caught Josh in another kiss and relished the way his fingers scraped on my exposed skin as if he could pull me closer. It took an active amount of restraint not to go further, to deepen the kiss and force him up the wall, to take him like the wolf inside demanded. But as much as I wanted to feel his legs wrapped around me again, this was not the place for that. Already I'd come dangerously close to exposing us in the main office, if I hadn't already.

I pulled away, licking my lips to taste him there, and noted with both pleasure and dismay that his lips weren't *too* swollen from the exchange.

He stared back at me with those forest-green eyes that had somehow become my steady rock, keeping me from going adrift. "Anything else?" he asked softly.

"Have dinner with me."

His lips twitched, and the almost-smile touched his eyes. "Are you sure? Last time…"

"I still have to return to the House, but I should be back in plenty of time to get a decent meal ready."

"If you insist," he quipped with a crooked grin.

I leaned forward, brushing my lips lightly against his. He arched into it, inviting more, and I wondered if he was even aware he was doing it. Rather than give in, I slipped a small token into his front vest pocket. If I'd thought about it beforehand, I'd have had his own made. As it was, mine would have to do.

He stared at me, his mouth parted slightly.

"I insist."

CHAPTER 20

Joshua

Elijah's house was just as unassuming and perfect as it had been the first time I'd been there. Wooden accents matching the roof adorned the white shutters. The windows hung open to catch the early evening breeze. An antique porch light sat primed to illuminate the encroaching darkness. And I was standing on the cobbled walkway lined with meticulously manicured flower beds... stalling.

I dragged my gaze away from the charming cottage to stare at the antique key in my hand. Its jagged teeth pressed almost painfully into my palm. The alloy felt authentic enough. But why was *I* holding it? No lycan had ever *voluntarily* invited me into their home, certainly not one that knew what my day job was. Not on purpose, anyway.

Except Elijah. He'd invited me... twice. But he hadn't just invited me this time; he'd given me a key. A key, which he arguably expected me to use. At his house. Where we were having dinner. Tonight. I wiped suddenly sweaty palms on my pants, nearly dropping the worrisome key. Why was I so nervous? Was it because this was a date? *Was* it a date? Maybe it wasn't, and I was just dressed like an idiot.

Damn it all. Hooking up is never this complicated.

"Traditionally, you put it in the lock."

My head shot up to see Elijah leaning against the frame of the now-open door. He was drying his hands with a kitchen towel and eyeing me with a small smile playing at the corner of his mouth. "I know that," I snapped, sounding more defensive than sharp.

His eyebrows rose, and he absently slapped the towel to rest on his shoulder. The move drew attention to the tight burgundy shirt he wore, which beautifully accented his physique and paired well with his iron-gray hair. I wished it was down instead of pulled back in his usual messy bun. Elijah's hair was gorgeous, just like the rest of him.

My gaze traveled lower to appreciate the dark trousers hugging his well-muscled legs and stopped shy of bare feet. The self-consciousness I'd been nursing eased slightly. He'd dressed casually, but a touch nicer than in our usual interactions.

Maybe my outfit isn't *totally inappropriate. Of course, Elijah could wear a paper sack and still ooze raw attraction. And that shirt... Fuck, that shirt is...*

My focus finally returned to his face, where he wore a knowing smirk. Instantly my lascivious thoughts petered out. I narrowed my eyes, silently daring him to say something. He didn't disappoint.

"You planning on standing there all night, or did you want dinner sometime this decade?"

I rolled my eyes and stomped up the remaining path, where I hesitated at the threshold. Being forcibly dragged into the house and walking inside of my own free will were very different things. I tightened my fist around the key, causing the grooves to dig deep into the meat of my hand. I had been invited. I was wanted.

Silently resolute, I took a fateful step forward and found myself once again at the complete mercy of Elijah Bennett.

Elijah

A chuckle slipped out before I could stop it. To cover, I pushed the door shut before turning to face Josh. Unsurprisingly, he wore a scowl that matched the death glare he'd given me outside when I'd caught him appreciating the view. No doubt he'd heard the small laugh I'd tried to hide. In my defense, it was a little funny. Josh was nervous. Or at least he looked nervous. He also looked like a damn treat in the faded gray sweater that was probably cashmere and the dark wash denim that I would bet good money on was authentic. Admittedly, I was surprised to see him out of his usual attire, but the effort was not wasted on me.

I know what I'm having for dessert.

"I'm late," he said flatly. Not an apology, but a statement of fact. And he was—by exactly two minutes. If that was his definition of not on time, then I was thoroughly impressed, especially because I knew for a fact that he'd arrived five minutes early. Was it creepy that I'd watched him dally on the walkway like he couldn't decide what to do? Probably, but I definitely didn't want him to know that I'd basically been staking out the front door either.

"Actually, you have perfect timing. Any sooner and I wouldn't have thought to check the deadbolt and couldn't have let you in," I teased.

He opened his mouth, no doubt to argue.

I stepped forward and captured the protest with a remarkably tame kiss. Barely more than the brushing of lips. So what if it made my heart skip and my breath catch? Either way, I pulled away before it could become more. "You look incredible, by the way," I whispered.

Surprise flashed briefly in his eyes, and the tip of his tongue darted out to taste his bottom lip. The invitation was too great to resist, and I leaned back in to steal another taste for myself. I sighed as I pulled away, still determined to actually have a proper date before I succumbed to my baser instincts. Plus, such a nice sweater didn't deserve to be shredded.

"It's a shame I can't smell you too." I hadn't meant to say it. But there was no taking it back now. All I could do was hope that the ribbing he gave me wouldn't be too harsh. Except, the taunt didn't come. His plush lips curved into a smile that reflected in his eyes. A decidedly mischievous smile that instantly made me anxious. "What?" I asked, not trusting that look in the least.

He held up a finger and looked down at the bio-clock embedded in his left wrist.

I stared on, more confused by the second as his brows rose in obvious anticipation. I let out an impatient huff just as he lowered his finger. My next inhale brought powerful aromas of rosemary and salt from the roast resting in the other room. The smell had begun dominating the house nearly an hour ago, but now a sweet earthiness and a musky scent of patchouli joined it. No, not patchouli—bergamot.

The shock must have shown on my face, because Josh's grin widened into a dazzling smile that threatened to steal the very breath I was intent on savoring. Before I even registered what I was doing, I snaked a hand out lightning-fast to grab him. He let out a muffled "Oof" at suddenly being crushed against me, but didn't pull away. His low chuckle rumbled through him as

I buried my nose in the crook of his neck and inhaled his scent like some kind of wild animal.

So much for keeping the beast at bay.

"Stars, you smell good," I moaned against his throat.

"Guess it didn't really matter what I wore," he quipped, though it sounded more like he was saying it to himself than to me.

"I disagree. You look good enough to eat," I purred in his ear, lingering long enough to feel him shudder, then I forced myself to relinquish him. *Date first*, I reminded myself. *It's bad enough we're doing all of this backwards. I can manage one moonforsaken meal with the man before tearing his clothes off.*

The concept was nice, but it was difficult to remain focused with his uninhibited scent curling through my nose and etching itself into the very fiber of my being. As I put more distance between us, he slid his hands along my arms, and I looked down to see them resting on my forearms. I'd been so distracted by the sudden appearance of his scent I hadn't even realized he'd been touching me.

Joshua

I snatched my hands back, feeling like a fool for touching Elijah, or more appropriately, for touching Elijah so familiarly. A reflexive apology rose in my throat, and I stubbornly swallowed it. We'd touched each other far more intimately before.

But not with clothes on, my subconscious viciously reminded me.

I mirrored the distance he'd put between us and took another step back. He gave me a strange look, which I studiously ignored. "Are you still good for that meal?"

Elijah's smile bordered on feral. "I'm good for a lot of things."

His words instantly brought to mind all the things I desperately hoped would be happening tonight. I turned to follow my nose towards whatever that heavenly scent was. No sooner had I spun than a sharp smack landed on my ass. I released an involuntary gasp and caught Elijah's snicker as he sauntered past.

He glanced over his shoulder as he made his way down the short hallway, and a full laugh rolled out of him. I continued to stand there, stunned at what he'd done. No werewolf in their right mind had ever had the audacity to do such a thing to me. That was a damn good way to lose a hand. And what was I going to do about it? *Not a damn thing.*

Grumbling to myself, I followed him into the kitchen. It was a small space, but just as quintessentially Elijah as the rest of the house. Blue tiles covered the counters, a relic from an age long past if I'd ever seen one, while ergonomic pots and pans hung by a legitimate rack suspended above the modest island.

Elijah walked around the division to check on the source of the delicious smell, which turned out to be a shoulder roast. While it wasn't a surprise that red meat was the main course, the complement of vegetables that sat at the ready was unexpected. As were the three glasses sitting full on the counter.

He caught my look and said as he pointed to each one, "Cabernet, water, and Fizz."

While I very much wanted the red wine, and not just because it would pair well with the meal, I opted for a safer option. This evening was going to be hard enough to navigate without adding inebriation to the mix.

He waited until I picked up the glass of Fizz before snagging the wine glass and taking a sip. I watched the red liquid disappear with envy and took a too hasty swallow of my drink. Elijah's lips twisted in restrained mirth as I fought the bubbles threatening to sud out my nose.

"Why don't you check out the living room while I get us plated?"

I graciously accepted the out and spun to investigate. The last time I'd been here, I hadn't made it past the study. Well, that wasn't true. I *had* made it to the bedroom. I smiled to myself as I wandered over to the far wall of the living room, with its impressive display of titles. Suddenly, I realized I was looking at music files. Hundreds of them. No sooner had the impressive display registered than I noticed that the sound system was already on. I just couldn't hear it.

"Do you mind?" I asked over my shoulder.

"Not at all. I turned it down so I could hear the door."

"So you *aren't* an anóteros lycanthrope, then?"

Elijah's laugh warmed me from the inside as I returned to perusing the selection. "I most definitely do not have enhanced anything."

"I'm not sure I'd say that," I offered wickedly, then turned up the music to more audible levels before he could respond. I smiled at the song playing. It was fun, upbeat, and cheesy as hell for a date night. It was also at least a century old. "At least you're consistent." I laughed, shaking my head.

"I like what I like. Now get that tight ass over here so we can eat."

I made a face, but didn't argue. My foot was all of three paces away from the dining table when the song changed. The undeniable melody of a love song sung by one of my favorite pop singers poured through the speakers. I froze and glared at Elijah. "Tell me you did not."

He laughed and set down the plates he was carrying on a formal dining table. "Oh, I definitely did."

I scowled at him and bit the inside of my cheek to keep from laughing.

"If you don't like it..." He made a gesture towards the sound system, and another of the same vein replaced the song.

My repressed humor burst free. "I can't decide whether I should hit you or laugh."

"Well, you're already laughing, so let's go with that."

Elijah

Hearing Josh laugh openly was music to my ears. And he kept doing it. With each new vintage nineteen-eighties pop song came a small chuckle as he relaxed more and more. I was just relieved that he was enjoying himself.

"So you actually cooked this? In *that* oven?" He gestured with his knife back towards the kitchen, through the wide pass-through wall.

I laughed like I had the first three times he'd asked. "Yes, it tastes better than using a self-adjusting module. Besides, imperfections are what make something special." He shifted in his seat as if I'd struck a nerve, and his gaze fell on my glass. I'd caught him looking at the wine longingly more than once. "Before you finish those last few bites, you should try it with the cab."

He eyed the proffered glass dubiously. "That's probably not—"

"One sip won't get you drunk, Josh."

"Fine," he caved. His fingertips brushed mine as he accepted the ruby liquid, and electricity raced up my arm. When his gaze flicked to mine, I knew he felt it too. Rather than comment, he held the glass to his lips.

Heat spread through me as I watched his throat bob with the swallow. A heat that only intensified when he closed his eyes and hummed appreciatively. "Good?" I probed.

"Fantastic. I really do like wine," he sighed wistfully. His eyes widened, and alarm spiked like bitter frost through his scent. He gave the glass an accusatory glare.

"Relax, it's okay. You're allowed to like things," I teased.

"Not normally."

I chose to ignore the heart-breaking statement and added, "That's kind of what this whole thing is about." I gestured around us, encompassing most of the house, the cleaned plates, and the music still playing softly in the other room.

"What do you mean?" he asked, his brows drawing down sharply.

"To get to know you better. I mean, you know practically everything there is to know about me from looking me up."

"I didn't."

"What?" I asked, taken aback.

"I didn't look you up that extensively."

I didn't bother restraining my smile. "Okay then. You still know more about me. I want to know about you. Who you are, what you like."

Josh's shoulders tensed, and he took another drink from the captive glass. "You already know about my taste in music."

"And that you can sing."

He winced. "You're not going to let that go, are you?"

"Not any time this century. So tell me, Joshua Hart, what else do you like to do?"

"Does sex count?"

I laughed harder than I'd expected. "Sex is not a hobby."

"It could be," he mumbled under his breath.

"I'm serious. What else? You must do something when you're not hunting down criminal lycans."

A shadow passed across his face, and he looked away. For a minute, I thought he wouldn't answer at all. Then he cleared his throat and set down the nearly empty wineglass. "Read. I like to read."

I was glad he wasn't looking at me and couldn't see my surprise. It didn't take a genius to know Josh was an educated man and wicked smart, but I hadn't expected this. "What sorts of files?"

He played with his utensils and glanced over at my modest collection of bound books. Most were digital reprints designed to imitate their original bindings, but a precious few were actual paper-filled books. "Not files," he said softly. "I prefer their original format. Moldy paper and all. Growing up, I had access to a library full of all sorts. They were my escape. I read them all."

There was a moon's worth of things to unpack in that. The wealth Josh was hinting at was staggering, as were the implications that his childhood had been something he'd needed to escape. Concerned about frightening him away, I opted to choose a lighter path. "Any favorites?"

The ghost of a smile flitted across his lips. "I've found Plato's Allegory of the Cave intriguing as well as Homer's Iliad. Then, of course, Jane Austen's Pride and Prejudice is a classic. Remind me, was it Mr. Darcy who was too proud or Miss Elizabeth Bennett?"

I was half a beat from educating the man on his rudimentary deconstruction when I realized he was grinning. I frowned. "You're teasing me." He shrugged and stood up from the table. Then he collected my plate and added it to his. The musky smell of him reached out like a caress that instantly addled my senses. He was already straightening when I finally had the wherewithal to say, "You don't need to do that. I can take care of it later."

Josh blinked down at me, and I fought the urge to pull him onto my lap. "You cooked. My cleaning is only fair."

"I don't have a washer." I'd stubbornly refused to buy the high-tech cleaning machine, just as I'd scorned the use of a more advanced oven. Though I *had* broken down and eventually gotten a sonic sprayer to help with hand-washing the dishes.

"That's fine," he responded without judgment or concern, then quietly took the plates into the kitchen.

I watched him push up the sleeves of the fine sweater and half-wished he'd just take it off. Josh was a vision sent from the Goddess herself. His ensemble may be more casual than his work gear, but it wasn't any looser. Toned muscles rippled beneath the thin material as he traded one dish for the next. My fingers itched to feel his firm legs beneath the soft fabric of true denim. And I loved that he'd abandoned his shoes to join me in being barefoot.

I signaled for the music to shift from the poppy beats it'd been producing to something more jazzy and subtle. As the seductive notes of a saxophone dominated the speakers, I vacated my seat to watch him work. I lazily dragged my gaze over his lean form, appreciating the way the delicate fabric hugged his body. Unable to stand not touching him for a moment longer, I stepped up behind him. To his credit, he didn't so much as flinch when I pressed myself against his back.

"I'm almost finished," he said evenly.

I placed a kiss above his collar and ran my nose up the side of his neck. Josh's hair was impressively jet black, almost like a raven's wing, and made me wonder what his lineage might be to achieve such a shade. With that lithe body and midnight hair, the man would make a beautiful wolf. I repressed the renegade thought, much to the dismay of my inner wolf, and returned my attention to appreciating the subtle warmth pressed against me.

I brushed my lips over the sensitive skin behind his ear and whispered, "There's also dessert."

Josh inhaled sharply, but otherwise didn't physically react. His scent, however, was an entirely different matter. Arousal instantly radiated from him like radio waves. I gave a low growl deep in my throat and pressed myself more firmly against him so he could see what that smell—what *he*—was doing to me.

A ripple passed through him. He quickly placed the last dish on the drying rack, then spun around. His forest-colored eyes held zero concern about basically being caged against the counter. I thought back to how easily he'd evaded my attempts to restrain him at the cabin. The only reason he'd lost was because he'd wanted to. Josh could take me easily, with or without that obscene collection of weapons he carried. I wish I knew why that was so indescribably attractive.

"There's cheesecake and chocolate," I said, though my mounting desire made the words nearly unintelligible.

He looked back at me without an ounce of fear in his eyes or in his scent, although I was basically growling at him. "What do you want?"

"I want to feel those ridiculous legs of yours wrapped around me again."

His resulting smile obliterated what little remained of my restraint. "I should be able to accommodate that."

"Cheeky bastard," I rumbled and promptly picked him up. Light shone in his eyes as he immediately wrapped his legs around me and squeezed. "Fuck, that's tight."

"You know it, baby," he quipped.

There was that baby-business again, and I didn't even fucking care, because Josh was here, with me, uninhibited and completely mine. I captured his mouth with an unrelenting kiss, which he eagerly returned. He was gasping for air by the time I released him. I spun us around to sit him on the island while I turned my attention to his neck.

He raked his fingers over my shoulders, digging through the fabric of my shirt as I drifted my hands beneath his sweater. His light moan as my fingers found cool flesh filled my ears. Suddenly, his mouth was back on mine, demanding and insistent as he pulled my lip between his teeth. Then, just as abruptly, he pulled away.

"What?" I asked, thrown by the shift.

Doubt colored his eyes a darker green, and he sank his teeth into his bottom lip. I was a heartbeat away from pulling the captured flesh free and sucking it into my mouth when he asked the last question I expected. Though given the hints he'd dropped earlier, perhaps I shouldn't have been so surprised.

"Am I allowed to like this?"

Sadness settled in my heart. His doubt was my fault, because I'd made such a big fucking deal about not wanting the bond. I caught him in a more sedate kiss. "Kind of already thought you did," I responded playfully, rubbing against his arousal for emphasis.

His gaze darkened with lust, but he held firm. "That's... I... That's not what—"

"I know what you meant." I sighed. How was I ever going to convince him I believed what was between us was worth exploring?

He licked his lips and swallowed.

I nuzzled into his neck, hating the spike of uncertainty in his scent. The one I'd put there. Definitely shouldn't have exaggerated about love not being part of the bond. It may not need to be there at the start, but it *always* followed, and I could absolutely see myself falling for Joshua Hart.

When I pulled back, he was still waiting patiently for an answer.

"Honestly, it would probably help if I knew you did."

"Are you sure?"

"At the very least, it would feel a lot less one-sided. I want you, Josh. I've wanted you since before the bond," I said as I drifted my hands higher under his sweater. The need to touch him, to reassure him, was killing me.

He sucked in a breath at the contact, but the doubt didn't leave his eyes. "You're my type," he blurted. "I mean, I already know I'm yours."

"And how do you know that?" I asked huskily as if it weren't abundantly obvious.

"Mack told me."

I chuckled and gripped his ass. He let out a hiss, and his eyelashes fluttered. "Kid is too smart for his own good."

"Agreed. I just... It only seemed fair that you know you're mine as well."

"So, what you're saying is that sex with me isn't exactly a hardship?" I teased.

"Maybe."

I ground hard against him and heard his breath catch. "Straight answer."

A devilish gleam replaced the doubt in his eyes. "No."

Chapter 21

Joshua

I STARED AT THE data tab and willed the coroner's report to be a corrupted file. They'd eventually find the original and fix it, but if I were lucky, it would take days, maybe even weeks.

There has to be a way to fix this. I never should have agreed to take this assignment. My mother can make her own messes. The world has moved on. She should too.

But I knew she wouldn't. No one in our family ever had. Hunting werewolves was in our blood. After all, we were—

"Detective Hart." Mack's voice snapped me out of my introspection. It didn't matter what my family had done in the past. I would never carry on that legacy. I would be the last to sow death in my wake.

I straightened in my chair and pushed the data tab under some loose files in yet another attempt to avoid it for just a little while longer. "What can I do for you, officer?" When he didn't answer right away, I looked up and found him staring intently. "Yes?" I prompted.

He narrowed his eyes and leaned closer. "Is something going on between you and Red?"

Years of training for volatile situations was literally the only thing that kept my face neutral or from me glancing around to see if anyone had heard. "And why would you ask such a thing?"

He glanced to the side, then walked around the desk dividing us to take Elijah's usual seat. One he wasn't in because he was at the House dealing with his own homicide case. Plus, it was the full moon tonight. One that would rise early.

"Because," he said quietly, "yesterday you let him touch you."

I blinked and thought about last night and even this morning. I'd done a hell of a lot more than let Elijah touch me. "Relevance?"

Mack's face soured. "You *never* let him touch you," he hissed. "Like, literally never. Last time he got close, I thought you were going to break his hand or maybe just tear off his arm."

"Is there a particular reason this has you concerned?" I countered.

He floundered. "Well... I... and yesterday..." He huffed in frustration. "Look, the way I see it, either you two are in cahoots or he's blackmailing you."

I raised an eyebrow. "Cahoots? Are we planning to rob a bank?"

"You know what I mean." He leaned closer and dropped his voice even further. "Sleeping together."

The cheeky response that we hadn't done much sleeping was on the tip of my tongue. In its place, I asked, "Do you know what a dangerous accusation that is?"

Mack blanched.

"Not just for me, but for him? What would happen if his pack suspected something was going on? What kind of reprisal would he face if Conrad called his loyalty into question? You said so yourself, Elijah doesn't exactly have a stellar history with the Klamath Alpha."

With each new line, more blood drained from the young officer's face.

I sat back and waited while he processed. There was literally no way I could deny the involvement without Mack assuming something. Elijah had said it perfectly: the kid was too smart for his own good.

Finally, he let out a huge breath and sagged in the chair. "If you didn't like my cousin, you could have just said so."

"I didn't say I didn't like Jason," I corrected him.

"Fine. But you don't like him the way you like—"

"Please consider where you are before you finish that sentence."

He closed his mouth with an audible snap. "You still could have said something," he grumbled, pushing up from the chair. "Are you ready to see the scene?" he asked, looking back at me.

My gaze flicked to where the discarded data tab lay. "I haven't read the report."

Mack scoffed. "You don't really need to. Not much in it. There literally weren't enough remains to come up with anything conclusive."

I barely suppressed my surprise. So far, this sounded exactly like Elijah's victim. That didn't bode well at all.

"I swear, if I never have to see a report like that again, it will be too soon," Mack added, leading the way out of the office.

When we arrived at the scene, a veritable army of forensic specialists was combing the forest floor and the surrounding area for anything the preliminary report might have overlooked. Mercifully, forensics, the pack, or nature had also removed most of the chunks of flesh. I diligently did *not* look in the direction where I'd been when I'd sent the two raven feathers flying. As

I'd suspected when I'd chosen the feathers as the delivery device, they were light enough to have already blown away or been carried off by an enterprising nest-builder.

The notification of an incoming message beeped in my ear. Half-second later it finished decrypting.

"Shit." Elijah's hiss immediately captured my full attention, then the line went dead.

I touched Mack's elbow to get his attention. "A message came in. I'm going to step away to respond."

He nodded, but understandably looked confused. What could be important enough to walk away from the crime scene? A question I also wanted the answer to.

I put significant distance between myself and potentially prying ears. As a precaution, I also activated a personal privacy shield before dialing out.

"Hello?" Elijah's voice instantly put me at ease.

"Is everything okay?" I asked, struggling to keep the worry from my voice.

"Josh... uh, about the message... that was an accident. I didn't mean to... I mean, I did. Anyway, sorry about that."

I let out a breath of relief. He was okay. He wasn't under attack. "Did you not believe it would work?" I asked.

His hesitation was an answer in itself.

"Now you know it does." When he said nothing, I asked, "Aren't you supposed to be getting ready for the change? Moon rises in two hours and thirty-six minutes."

"I am," he replied quickly. "I was waiting for some others and looking at the data. When I realized I'd opened a message by accident, I cut it off immediately." The defense was weak, and we both knew it.

I smiled to myself, imagining a man like Elijah Bennett debating whether to call like some teenager, then freaking out and hanging up when he did.

"To be honest, I'm surprised you've already listened to the message. I figured you wouldn't get around to it for a couple of hours at least," he admitted.

"It's a private, encrypted line. The messages and calls supersede any do not disturb settings."

"Oh. So when you say any circumstances you literally mean *any*."

"I'm literal about a lot of things, Bennett."

"Right, yeah, of course. I knew that."

"Was there a particular reason you were looking at the information?" I asked, curious.

There was a noticeable pause. "No..."

"Would now be a good time to point out how incredibly unfair it is that you can lie while I can not?"

Elijah's sigh poured through the connection. I could just imagine him running his hand through his hair, and I wondered if he was already naked. I quickly schooled my thoughts and dutifully wiped the renegade smile from my face. "You're right. I'm sorry. In all honesty, I was bored waiting around and wanted to hear your voice. Can anyone say 'hormonal teenager'?" he grumbled, adding a self-deprecating laugh.

"Hormonal teenager," I said without missing a beat.

His laugh was much more authentic this time. "Fine. Busted. I asked for that."

"You did."

He chuckled again, and I relaxed against a nearby wall. "You're funny, you know that?"

I snorted. "You might be the only person on the planet who thinks that."

"I think a lot of things about you, Josh."

I swallowed thickly at the sultry way he said it. Damn, this man got to me in ways that were hard to ignore. I cleared my throat. "There's a crime scene I should probably get back to."

"You're at a crime scene?" he asked in blatant surprise. "Why would you call if you were busy?"

"Maybe because someone dialed an encrypted line and left a potentially urgent message," I reminded him.

"Careful, Josh, that sounds suspiciously like you're worried about me."

"You are a mature lycan. I imagine you can take care of yourself."

"True, but I'd rather you take care of me." His tone left little doubt of his true meaning, and I nearly swallowed my tongue at the innuendo.

"Shouldn't you be turning into a wolf or something?" I hated how husky my voice sounded. *Why? Why can't I make it through a conversation with Elijah without thinking about having sex with him?*

Elijah's low chuckle suggested he knew exactly the effect he was having on me. "Something like that."

"Maybe you should do that before you spout off any more cheesy come-ons," I retorted.

"Are they still considered cheesy if they work?"

"Shut up."

Elijah

I was still laughing when the call ended. Getting Josh's ruff up was arguably just as much fun as making him writhe beneath me. That he'd called back so quickly totally blew my mind, and from a crime scene, no less.

"Hey, are you planning on changing with the rest of us, or are you waiting for literal moonrise?" Eric asked as he emerged from the foliage, every bit as naked as I was.

"Don't be a prat. Have you seen Tommy and Kale?"

"We're here!" Tommy announced as the two stepped free of the trees.

Kale shook his head at his older brother's enthusiasm. It was definitely the most energetic anyone had seen him since Tina's murder. His eyes were almost unnaturally bright in the early afternoon light.

"I'm so freaking amped for this. I don't know why, but it feels like forever since I shifted. This is gonna be great. Don't you think this is gonna be great, Kale?" Tommy's manic gaze swept the small group. "Come on, guys, perk up! It's a clear night, no storms, and a pleasant breeze. Liven up, will ya?" he demanded again before slipping back into the trees, presumably to begin his change.

Kale spared me and Eric a silent, wide-eyed look of concern. He'd always been the more sedate of the two, but Tommy's behavior was even more exaggerated than usual.

"We'll stay close," I reassured him.

Kale let out a sigh of relief and nodded before following his brother. They'd shift separately, but I imagined Kale wouldn't wander as far as he normally might have.

"Do you think it's grief-related?" Eric asked at my shoulder.

"I'm not sure, but I definitely want to keep an eye on him."

"Sure thing, boss."

I scowled and shot him a look. "Not funny."

He shrugged, backing away. "I'm just waiting for you to give the all-clear."

I sighed and shook my head. "Not happening."

"You say that now," he called back before finally disappearing to see to his change.

I loved the man. I did—he'd only been my best friend since we were five—but sometimes his prodding was less than subtle. He'd wanted me to challenge for Alpha when I'd returned to manage my father's funeral and made no secret that he was still waiting for me to have enough of Conrad's attitude. If I had things my way, that day wouldn't come. I had no desire to lead the pack, and I still hoped that Conrad would pull his head out of his ass and bring the pack into the twenty-second century. But with the onset of not one, but three murders, that hope looked more and more like a fool's dream.

I shook my head again as I prepared to shift. Eric was right. I didn't like waiting for the full moon to force the change. I preferred to get started on my own.

As my hands sank into the lush carpet of grass, Tommy's words came back to me. It did feel like forever since I was last in my wolf form. Perhaps shifting sooner would have helped me to come to terms with being bonded to Josh—my inner wolf had no problem with the bond at all. Shame the rest of me was struggling so much to get on board. Then again, was being bonded to Josh really so bad? He was intelligent, had an interesting sense of humor, not to mention attractive as hell. He was also surprisingly thoughtful, and I suspected actually sweet, *if* you could get past the cold exterior he wore like armor. Thus far, I'd actually enjoyed my time with him and looked forward to spending more.

I wonder if he'd be willing to meet up later tonight after the full moon?

Thinking of the bright white sphere sent a corresponding tingle through me as my body thrummed with anticipation. I pushed all thoughts of my bonded partner as far as they would go and focused on the shift.

Pain washed over me in a wave, followed by agonizing pops as all of my bones seemed to break. I ground my teeth to hold back an agonized cry as my back arched to accommodate shifting limbs. My arm spasmed, threatening to send me sprawling. Only years of undergoing this process kept my footing, even though control of my limbs seemed completely beyond me. My skin burned as every hair on my body lengthened into a full winter coat that wouldn't fade for at least another month.

Almost there.

I huffed a breath that misted in the rapidly cooling afternoon. Crushed bone morphed my face into an entirely different shape, hiding my grimace of pain. No matter how many times you endured the change, it never got more pleasant.

I panted heavily, dragging burning cold into my lungs, and shook the new fur out to settle more comfortably. Already the agonizing pain of the last ten minutes was being healed away, all but forgotten as I stretched tense muscles. My body practically hummed in appreciation as the light of the rising moon fell around me.

When was the last I shifted? Could it really have been the last full moon?

Suddenly, a crystal-clear song rose above the trees. My ear twitched. Hearing a howl was not unusual, especially tonight. However, the note's desperate call for help had my paws digging into the underbrush before I even registered I was moving. As abruptly as it had started, the sharp sound cut off. I picked up speed, thundering in the direction I'd last heard the cry. When I crashed through the underbrush into a small clearing, I couldn't believe my eyes.

Tommy, with his gray coat streaked with hints of brown, had fully shifted and was cornering another wolf. I quickly recognized Kale's lighter shade, as well as the panic shining in his eyes. Kale shot me a desperate look at my loud appearance, but Tommy didn't waver even the slightest in his focus on his younger brother.

It wasn't until I stepped forward to interfere that Tommy's head swiveled around to face me. His snarl made every hair on my body stand on end. The automatic reflex to appear larger when confronted did not go over well with the young wolf in the slightest.

His growl dropped another octave as he adjusted his trajectory to face me. Out of the corner of my eye, I saw Eric herd Kale out of the line of fire. Now that I knew the kid was safe, I widened my stance, sunk my head between my shoulders, and rumbled a threatening growl in response. The obvious show of aggression should have made any reasonable wolf back down. Not only was I older than Tommy, but I also had a good twenty-three kilos on the pup.

Except he didn't back down. He didn't even flinch. Instead, his growl became more savage, saliva dripping down in thick ropes. His muscles bunched as if preparing to launch. Clearly, whatever logic normally controlled Tommy was absent now.

Please, Tommy, don't do this.

I dug my claws deep into the earth as I braced myself for impact. I could take the hit, but I worried what it would take to stop Tommy. All around me, the sounds of the rest of the pack picked up. Short yips of excitement, broken twigs as others rolled and tumbled in the undergrowth. Then, cutting through it all, another sharp howl. The sound instantly snared Tommy's attention.

His head shot up, ears swiveling to pinpoint the cry of distress.

He's gonna run. No sooner did I have the thought than I knew I couldn't let that happen. If he left this clearing, there was no telling what damage he would do. The gruesome image of an inverted rib cage swam in my mind.

I deepened my growl, and Tommy's focus returned to me, that same lack of self-preservation still shining wildly in his eyes. Before I could second-guess myself, I launched forward.

His eyes widened briefly right before I slammed into him with enough force to dislodge a shoulder. Tommy turned at the last possible second, which meant that instead of his shoulder, his hip took the brunt of the hit. His right leg skittered beneath him, and he fell to the ground. Despite the agony that he must have been in, he directed yet another savage growl at me.

Instinct told me to get his throat between my jaws and force him to yield, but logic said that the Tommy I knew wasn't there. I rammed him again.

Without all four legs to support him, he collapsed into an angry heap of fur. While he struggled to get his bearings, I swiveled around and clamped teeth down on his ruff. The skin was just elastic enough for me to drag him several paces and throw him into a nearby maple. The tree shook with the force of the impact, and several leaves drifted down to surround Tommy's now still form.

I quickly padded closer. To my relief, he was still breathing, but was definitely out. My thankful sigh was fogging in front of me when Eric stepped back into the clearing.

He glanced at Tommy's prone form, then back at me. It didn't matter that we couldn't "speak" to each other in this form. His meaning was clear: *It had to be done. He'd have killed Kale.*

I tried to shake off the remaining adrenaline and growing sense of unease to little avail. Just because it had to be done didn't mean I had to like doing it.

Eric gave a dramatic shake of his head and huffed. Even without words, I'd seen him do the same in human form and knew exactly what he would have voiced if he could: *Alpha problems.*

I bared my teeth at him to no effect and turned to face the source of the second howl. Unfortunately, Eric didn't seem to have any better ideas about what might be happening there.

Fear coiled tight in my stomach. I left my childhood friend to watch Tommy and Kale. With each step towards the origin of the howl, my pace grew quicker, fueled by the certainty that I was *needed*.

I was running full out when I crashed through a copse of hibernating trees into complete chaos. Before I could even think of stopping, I skidded into another wolf. She turned to look at me with wide eyes, panic and fear rolling off her in waves. In a blink, she was shoving past me and running for all she was worth in the direction I'd just come.

I took in the large clearing where most of the pack usually began congregating after their shifts. Wolves were running and jumping everywhere, except they weren't playing—they were fleeing. I fought my way towards the center and instantly regretted the decision.

Three wolves larger than myself were struggling to pull down Keith. Blood matted nearly all of their fur, matching the bright crimson flowing freely from Keith's jaws and staining his paws. Keith threw one of the wolves to land with a pained thud against a tree, much as Tommy had done. When my packmate didn't immediately get back up, I rushed to fill his place.

Keith spun to face the latest threat, snarling so discordantly that my blood curdled.

Still, I stood my ground as others came to join. In a matter of moments, a good dozen wolves surrounded him. Some were fresh, while others sported vicious claw marks on their sides and muzzles. Just as Tommy had done, though—or rather, hadn't—he didn't back down. His eyes scanned the gathered group, frantically searching for a weak spot. Before he could pick a target, I stepped forward, separating myself from the circle. His wild gaze riveted back on me.

I bared my teeth and rolled my shoulders, emanating dominance with every fiber of my being.

Something flashed in his eyes. Understanding.

He's still in there.

I gave a short bark to signal the others. They moved as one, working as a synchronized unit to bring him down before he could react. In mere seconds, Keith lay incapacitated on the ground, firmly encased by half a dozen of his packmates. He fought the containment, but with so many holding him in place, he stood little chance of success.

The smell of fear and blood permeated the air. No one knew what had happened. One minute Keith had been fine. Then he'd been a mindless monster. Nervous glances made the rounds as the adrenaline from the fight dissipated, leaving only uncertainty in its wake.

I sagged as I finally let go of the tension in my muscles.

What I wouldn't give to hold Josh right now.

I glanced up at the full moon, now firmly overhead in a lavender sky, and wondered what in Her name could have happened. When my gaze fell back to the earth, it locked with Conrad's. In a heartbeat, all of my tension returned.

Chapter 22

Joshua

I SET THE STEAMING cup of coffee down on my desk, disheartened to see Elijah's seat empty for the second day in a row. It didn't seem like him not to show up for work, no matter if I had confided in him I believed Tommy was innocent. Even a brief message would have helped put my mind at ease. While I hadn't expected him to reach out the night of the full moon, I'd hoped. When he hadn't called by the following day either, though, that was when the worrying began in earnest. It didn't matter how many times I reminded myself that he was dealing with his own twisted politics, I couldn't shake the feeling that something was wrong, something he needed me for.

I sighed heavily as I sank into my chair and popped the lid free of my mocha. *Whatever is going on with the pack must be pretty damn important.*

"Good, you're here early."

I blinked at Officer Mack, then glanced at the clock mounted on the wall. Sure enough, I was almost an hour early. *Damn that wolf.* I straightened, my sip forgotten as I realized Mack was clutching something in his hands. "What have you got there?"

He licked his lips before handing me the folded missive.

I scanned the page quickly. "Who brought this in?" I demanded.

"Dispatch said the caller identified as Kale."

"Kale?" I echoed. "As in Kale *Grant*?"

The sad look in Mack's eyes confirmed what I didn't want to believe: Tommy's own brother had turned him in.

I crumpled the page and shot up. "So what if we know where he is? Thomas Grant didn't kill Tina Carr."

Mack's eyes widened, and his mouth fell open. "Are you sure? Have you found any evidence?"

My hand continued to crush the paper into oblivion. "I'm still working on that. I have some, but not enough. To clear him completely, there can't be even a sliver of doubt. There's too much stigma around werewolf violence. Until then..."

Mack's enthusiasm dwindled. "We still have to bring him in," he finished for me.

"We still have to bring him in," I echoed. Except it wasn't supposed to happen like this. I was going to quietly clear the kid's name and take care of the mess I'd made, with no one being the wiser. But how in the seven hells was I supposed to do that while walking bold as brass onto pack land to make an arrest?

Elijah is going to be pissed.

"You can't warn him." Mack's words eerily echoed my thoughts.

I stared at him a moment while I silently warred with myself about what to do. There had to be a way to fix this. "I know," I finally said, pushing away from my desk.

Elijah

Everything about Josh's body language said he was *not* happy to be here. I didn't need to smell him or even hear him talk to know that. It was clear from the stiffness in his shoulders to the way he kept clenching and unclenching his hands. His gaze briefly met mine as he approached the House, something no human had done in nearly a hundred and fifty years.

I wanted the tiny contact to last, but all too soon it was gone. The last couple of days hadn't been easy, and I needed him, to touch him, hear him, hell, just be near him. If I had met him at the boundary like I was supposed to, I might have gotten that. However, I didn't want to leave Tommy alone. After what had happened beneath the full moon, Conrad was out for blood, more specifically Keith's. If he had any idea how close Tommy had come to doing the same, then he'd lump them in together.

As I watched Kale lead Josh up to the main entrance, I questioned again the wisdom of what we'd done. Would Tommy be any safer with Josh? Saying that he believed the kid was innocent wasn't quite the same as saying he wouldn't hang him for the crime.

I swallowed my anxiety before it could add to the already prevalent nerves around me. No one was comfortable with Josh's presence. Except me. After the trials I'd endured over the last couple of days, the veritable eggshells I'd had to tread, I was bone-weary and wanted nothing more than to feel the comfort of his embrace. But that was something I couldn't enjoy, at least not surrounded by the curious eyes of the entire Klamath Pack.

Kale and Josh stopped short of the main door, which Conrad was currently blocking. I was a little surprised at how at ease Kale looked considering who he was escorting and where. That Josh looked like he owned the damn place, however, did not surprise me in the least. He didn't even blink at his way being blocked.

I barely repressed a smile at seeing the look of sheer outrage stamped on Conrad's face.

"What's the meaning of this?" Conrad demanded.

Josh met his anger with a level, unaffected look. I snickered to myself. *That's my man.* "I believe Thomas Grant is inside."

"And on what grounds are you coming to *our* House without a warrant?"

"As Mr. Grant has been the primary suspect in an ongoing murder investigation, it is my job to bring him in for questioning. You will note that in accordance with the Richat Treaty of 2070 § 25-3, §§ 6, I have come here accompanied by a member of the pack." Still not an ounce of inflection. Josh could have been ordering lunch rather than facing off against a man who held sway over the eighty-plus lycanthropes surrounding him.

Conrad snarled, and my hackles instantly went up. "Did Elijah Bennett tell you he was here?"

Josh's eyes widened slightly. "No, he did not."

Conrad's eyes narrowed in disbelief. "And you expect me to believe that?"

"Lycan Detectives can't lie," a voice said from above.

Conrad's gaze whipped around, as did most of the pack's, to fix on the man sitting on an upper balcony.

"Their oaths prevent it. Something to do with Fae magic," Eric added as he stood up. "Detective Hart couldn't lie even if he wanted to."

Josh shrugged and didn't respond.

Conrad's lip curled in anger, and a ripple passed through those gathered. I braced myself for the worst and focused on trying to figure out how to get to Josh before all hell broke loose. Then the front doors opened, and Tommy stepped into the sunlight.

"Thank you, Alpha, but I won't put the pack in danger any longer." Conrad looked borderline apoplectic as the young man stepped up beside him. Tommy spared him a brief glance, then promptly returned his attention to Josh. "Do you need to cuff me?"

Josh considered him. "I don't think that will be necessary. Do you?" he asked Kale, standing beside him.

Kale looked a bit like he might hurl all over Conrad's shoes, but pulled it together enough to look his brother in the eye. "No, he'll go willingly."

Josh nodded and beckoned Tommy forward. For a split second, I truly thought Conrad would try to stop them. Mercifully, he did nothing more than glare daggers at Josh's back, where ironically, I was pretty sure he was wearing several literal daggers.

Joshua

I was a little surprised that none of the pack followed us on the way back to town and doubly disappointed that Elijah wasn't waiting for us at the border. I understood now why he hadn't escorted me in and suspected it was the same reason that prevented him from being here now. Things were substantially worse in the pack than my original intel had led me to believe. Conrad's tenuous hold on the Klamath lycans seemed to be a secret only to him. With Elijah clearly leading as the next likely Alpha, Conrad rightfully felt threatened. A point driven home when he'd asked if it had been Elijah who'd subverted his authority and given up Tommy's location.

I glanced at the young man walking stoically beside me. He was unquestionably the youth I'd infected the night of the Bacchanalia. Something rancid bubbled inside of me, and it took me a minute to recognize it: shame. Guilt I was intimately familiar with, but shame was definitely a new one. Elijah was right. Tommy was a kid. He was younger than Mack and, from all accounts, an equally decent person.

My feet stopped shy of the boundary dividing the town from pack territory. Tommy looked back from the town side, confusion plain on his face.

When did I stop thinking of them as animals?

As I stared at Tommy's perplexed face, I couldn't pinpoint when the shift had happened, but I knew it was true. The lycans weren't animals. They were people. Just like Mack. Just like me. They didn't deserve the horrible hand humanity dealt them, and they certainly didn't deserve to be put down like rabid dogs merely for the crime of existing. So a few of them got out of hand. Humans were no different.

Crushing guilt joined the shame, and I had to force my feet to keep moving.

"You okay? You look a little green around the gills," Tommy said as I joined him on the other side of the line.

"Not really," I admitted.

"Oh, um..." he trailed off.

"Tommy, do you know who turned you in?"

He gave an ironic laugh, and I blinked at him in surprise. "Kale."

"Why would your brother do that?"

"Because I asked him to. I'm not... It's not safe for me to stay with the others. And this way, the pack doesn't get in trouble for harboring a criminal."

"Did Elijah put you up to this?"

Another ironic laugh. "Yeah, he said I'd be safe with you."

I growled to myself. *That wolf is going to be the death of me.*

Tommy laughed again. "He also said you're a bit like a *were* yourself." His mouth snapped shut, the mirth vacating his face. "Shit, I wasn't supposed to tell you that."

I frowned at him and kept walking. After a minute or two of silence, I said, "I know you didn't murder Tina." The statement met with dead silence. I stopped and looked back at where Tommy stood frozen on the sidewalk.

His face was a mix of heart-wrenching grief and disbelief. "You do?"

I nodded. "I'm working on getting enough evidence together to put the real culprit away."

"Wow. I mean, it's a little hard to accept, but you can't lie, right?"

"Not even if I wanted to," I said, mimicking what the *were* on the balcony said earlier. "Tommy, may I ask you a potentially very personal question?"

"I guess so. You're the detective, after all."

"Were you bonded to Tina Carr?"

Tommy didn't question how I could know about the bond or even what I already knew. What he said, however, surprised me to no end. "You're the first person to ask me that. No, I wasn't bonded to T. I loved her though. We called ourselves T-n-T because we were dynamite together." His chuckle at the fond memory dissipated, leaving him looking sadder than ever.

I placed a gentle hand on his shoulder. When he looked up, tears welled in his eyes. He quickly wiped them away. "We're almost there," I said softly.

Tommy's gaze slipped past me to focus on the precinct a few blocks down. Worry eclipsed the heartache shining wetly in his eyes. "It can hold me, right?"

"It can hold you," I reassured him. At my words, his shoulders relaxed, and he resumed his even pace beside me.

When we stopped again, this time in front of the booking desk, Mack was waiting for us along with a *were* I'd glimpsed at the House.

"Hey Tommy," Mack said. "If it's alright with you, I think Kilee and I are gonna keep you company for a while." He nodded at the young woman standing next to him, who offered a brilliant smile.

Tommy's gaze swung from Mack to Kilee, then back to me.

I offered a small smile and raised my hands. "He works here. If he wants to keep you company, then that's his business."

The watery look returned to Tommy's eyes. Then, with lycan-fast speed, he wrapped me in a tight embrace that threatened to squeeze all the air out of my lungs.

I held up a hand to ward off Mack and the three other officers who immediately moved to intervene. When I was positive that they wouldn't, I placed the same hand on Tommy's back.

"Thank you," he whispered, barely loud enough for me to hear, and squeezed just a little tighter. Suddenly, I was very glad I'd opted to forego my usual daggers.

Chapter 23

Elijah

I SENT THE MESSAGE to Josh and tried not to think about it or him again. What was happening in front of me deserved my full attention.

"You ready for this?" Eric said at my side.

"Honestly? No, it shouldn't have been such an ordeal to convince him that Keith wasn't well."

Eric nodded knowingly. He'd seen Tommy, and I'd filled him in on what had happened in the main clearing. It was clear as the moon that neither lycan had been themselves or in charge of their faculties. I flashed to that tiny moment of recognition amidst the chaos.

"I just hope Sabrina's tests yield something conclusive. Otherwise..." I trailed off, and we shared a look. Otherwise, Conrad would put Keith down without a second thought. Our pack may have been large, but that didn't make anyone expendable.

We entered the living room and found a decent spot to watch the proceedings. And we weren't alone. Our packmates occupied every available surface in pursuit of a good view. Many hung over railings, draped along stairs, and even perched a couple deep on furniture. A few of the whispers I picked up suggested that some of them were all for Conrad's brutal solution. Thankfully, though, the majority were just uncertain and wanting answers.

A noticeable shift went through all gathered as Sabrina Landon stepped to the forefront, clutching a data pad with white knuckles. She had her dark gray hair pulled back in a severe bun while her fawn skin was almost gray. It was an eerie combination that only highlighted her obvious exhaustion. Beside her, Conrad wasn't faring much better. While he still looked relatively fresh, there was a tightness around his eyes, and his face was pinched as though he'd eaten an entire bushel of sour berries. To cap it all, Nikolai kept shooting the lycan on the ground anxious glances.

Keith lay bound by silver chains imbued with magic to ensure he stayed restrained. I didn't want to think about how we had those. I also didn't want to consider how necessary they were. While he'd noticeably calmed down once he'd shifted back, it was hard to forget the atrocities he'd committed in his wolf form. Blood everywhere, fellow *weres* nearly eviscerated, the wild look in his eyes. Thankfully, someone had the wherewithal to clean him up. The last thing the pack needed was to be assaulted with scents that reminded them of the unspeakable violence.

I crossed my arms and waited. Hopefully, Sabrina's data tab could provide answers instead of more questions. Conrad nudged her, and she took a shaky breath.

"After extensive analysis, I have concluded that Keith Winters has Mein Zeike." A ripple passed through the pack. Sabrina squared her shoulders. "He's moonstruck."

Her words had the effect of kicking a hornet's nest. Anger, confusion, and questions swirled around her in a rising tornado of sound until at last Conrad's stern voice cut through the cacophony.

"That's not possible." Conrad stated, "Moon sickness has never afflicted any wolf in our pack."

Sabrina met his doubt with laudable confidence. "The results don't lie. I ran the test several times. Keith... and Tommy are both moonstruck."

"But how can that be?" Kale shouted from across the room. "He wasn't moonstruck before. I would have known." He glanced around at all the eyes riveted on him. "I would have known," he repeated adamantly.

Sabrina faltered slightly and referenced something on her data tab. "I... I don't know. The good news is that there's a treatment. Not a cure per se, but a way to mitigate the effects."

"And do you have it with you?"

I frowned at Conrad's clipped growl. This was a shock to all of us. Moon sickness was a fluke of genetics, usually passed silently down through generations. To my knowledge, no family here had ever had the condition before, not even when we were the Portland Pack. Then again, it was also possible that it had been "taken care of" before anyone knew. The troubling bit was that neither of them had ever displayed the classic signs before. Moon sickness took hold with the first change, not years later in your life. On that, Kale was absolutely right. *Someone* would have known.

After several minutes of digging through her kit and getting something ready, Sabrina held up a syringe with shaking hands. "Yes, Alpha, I brought the treatment." She placed her hand on

Keith's shoulder, and he flinched. "This is a mild dose. Just enough to help you calm down. It will be different when you're preparing for the full moon. But don't worry, I'll go through the whole regimen with you. You're going to be okay."

Keith sagged beneath her light touch and gave the barest nod. Suddenly, I wondered if anyone had actually talked to him about what had happened. If anyone had bothered to ask if he had any idea how he'd gotten this way. I filed the questions away until I could get him on his own.

With the steady hands of someone who'd done this a thousand times, Sabrina administered the treatment. She withdrew the needle and offered Keith a warm smile. Sabrina clearly had a fantastic bedside manner. Pride filled my chest at how far the girl running around with bandages and gauze had come. With any luck, she'd be able to return to her residency after this and continue making a name for herself.

Suddenly, Keith's eyes bulged, and he convulsed. Still restrained by the links of silver, he thrashed in place on the floor. Froth foamed at his mouth while Sabrina scrambled for her med bag.

"What's happening?" Nikolai demanded to know, even as he took a step farther away from Keith.

"I don't know. He seems to be having a poor reaction to the medication."

There was a collective gasp as blood began dripping from Keith's eyes and ears.

"Do something!" Conrad ordered.

"I'm trying!" Sabrina shouted back. She was a whirlwind of efficiency, but she was only one woman.

Keith spasmed once more and stilled. No one dared to breathe. Sabrina threw her life-signs reader on the ground. The resulting crack, as it slammed with enough force to break, echoed in the silent room.

"Get him out of here," Conrad said with a level of disdain that made me want to hit him in the face. Several people stepped forward to remove Keith's body from the floor. While they worked, he turned to Sabrina. "And *you*, figure out what the hell went wrong."

Sabrina nodded and followed the grisly train out of the building. As they passed by, I caught her gentle sobs and her whispered, "I don't understand. I did everything right."

Joshua

I pulled up Elijah's message, still not sure I'd read it right. Another glance, however, was no more enlightening than the first, or the second, or the third. With a shake of my head, I finished organizing my workspace for the end of the day.

The last of the files signaled its successful upload to the server. It turned out Mack's assessment of the coroner's report was on point—there was literally nothing useful or even remotely conclusive to be found in the remains aside from the confirmation that the victim was human. The body could just as likely have gone through a wood chipper.

There's a thought.

I quickly reopened the file I'd literally just closed and made a note to inquire about accessibility to major power equipment in the area, then uploaded again. Now that I'd put everything away, I only had one more stop to make before returning to my sad, lonely little apartment.

Don't be so melancholy. You're getting spoiled.

The chastisement stayed with me until I rounded the last corner to my destination. A head popped up from behind silver bars laced with magic, extending from the floor to the ceiling. The gray-brown hair was every bit as indicative of the youth's heritage as was the way his eyes yellowed when they caught the light.

Tommy straightened up from his seat. "Hey, Josh."

I raised an eyebrow at the informal greeting. There was literally only one person he could have picked that up from.

Oh, Elijah Bennett, what sort of trouble are you going to get us into?

Tommy blanched at my expression. "Shit. Sorry. Is that weird? It's weird, right? No one calls you that. Everyone around here calls you Detective Hart. It's just that Red..." He petered out as I stopped in front of his cell.

"Calls me Josh," I finished for him.

He at least had the decency to look abashed. "Yeah."

"How are you holding up?" I asked to distract him.

"Well, actually. Aside from the fact that I can't seem to stop fucking talking. I swear, I open my mouth and words just flow out. I need a moonforsaken dam or something. It's ridiculous. And... I'm doing it again." He sagged, careful not to touch the bars.

I winced inside. This was my fault. He was all over the place because of me. *I'd* done this to him. It was sheer dumb luck that he wasn't already dead. He didn't deserve that; the kid was bright, really bright. Aside from the incessant chatter and boundless energy, he'd already ripped through several works of literature. I strongly suspected that was Elijah's doing yet again. How the man could stubbornly refuse to take on the mantle of Alpha when he was so clearly acting like one was beyond me.

"So...um, confession."

I blinked and realized I'd been lost in thought. "What would that be?"

"I might have tested the bars," he admitted sheepishly.

"And how did that go?"

"In my defense, they look really flimsy," he responded quickly.

"I take it you haven't encountered spelled metal before?"

"No," he mumbled. "I thought lycans being allergic to silver was just one of those stupid myths they put in outdated fiction. But this shit burns." He eyed the bars warily. He had a point. They were deceptively thin, and for a creature used to overpowering even the strongest of things, they wouldn't have posed much of a deterrent.

I laughed. "I'm sure some lycanthropes are allergic to silver, just as some humans are, but that's not why it burns."

He cocked his head to the side in confusion.

I traced the stern line of the metal up, the magic tingling beneath the tip of my finger. "Silver holds magic better than other metals, longer too. Do you feel safe?" I asked quietly. He'd confided in me the real reason he was so worried about the cell holding him, which only tripled my guilt.

"Yeah, thanks. Ironic really, that I feel safest in jail, all things considered."

"You're not a criminal, Tommy."

He sighed and glanced behind me towards the main receiving desk. "You seem to be the only one who thinks that."

I followed his gaze, and the two officers on duty quickly averted their gazes. When I turned back to Tommy, sadness seemed to flow off him. "Don't mind them. They aren't the ones who get to decide if you're guilty or not. That's my job. As soon as I have all the evidence in order, you should be on your way again."

"And Lycan Detectives can't lie."

"Not even if I wanted to." I stared back at him, my desire to fix this mess warring with everything I'd been taught my entire life. How it had taken me nearly thirty-three years to find the will to challenge my mother's wishes astounded me. Again, I suspected Elijah had something to do with that. "I brought you something to keep you entertained."

"Yass," he hissed as he greedily reached for the latest stack of book files. "Wait, does this mean you're not staying?"

"Errands to run. Places to be. You know the drill."

"I get it. Thanks anyway," he said halfheartedly, then he looked down at the files I'd brought. "No freaking way!"

I laughed at his obvious excitement.

He settled into his arguably well-accommodated cell and eagerly opened the file. "Tina loved these books. We used to read them together." His voice warbled slightly at the end, but he kept it together.

"You might have mentioned that, which is why I had a little helper retrieve them from the cabin."

"These are... these are..." He flipped the tablet over to where Tina's message to him was laser-etched.

"I'll leave you to it." I was almost too far to hear when his thick words stopped me in my tracks.

"Thank you."

Rancid guilt boiled in my stomach. I didn't deserve the gratitude of a soul as pure as Thomas Grant's. He'd already suffered so much loss, and the years to come would only get harder. If there were any justice in this world, I'd be the one behind bars, not him.

But there wasn't. Not for lycans.

There was only me.

Doubt and indecision plagued my wandering journey to my apartment. I was running out of options. Tommy could only stay locked up for so long. I'd have to prove his innocence eventually...and then what? Set him free to potentially murder the rest of his pack? His brother? Elijah?

I shivered and finished letting myself inside. No, there had to be a better way, but first I needed to find out exactly what my mother's plans had been for that toxin.

I didn't bother getting comfortable before calling. There was literally nothing comfortable about talking to Beatrice Hart, and, even though she was likely hundreds of miles away, the daggers at my back still made me feel safer.

The moment the call connected, I threw it at the wall. In the blink of an eye, my mother's horrid features stared back at me. Her high cheekbones, sallow from near-manic obsession, the cruel glint in her brown eyes, and the sharp turn of her mouth all seemed to mock me.

"Well, well, well, isn't this a first? *You* actually calling in to report on time. Had I known that I would be graced with the pleasure of your company, I would have prepared accordingly." Her sarcasm hit its mark with flawless accuracy; she had never enjoyed my company, of that I was absolutely certain. I was and always had been a weapon for her to use on her endless crusade, nothing more.

"If I'm disturbing you, I can always give my report another time."

"Heaven's sake, Joshua, always so prickly." A crystalline goblet of something dark swam into view. Good, she was drinking; that would probably help. "Don't just stand there, you useless excuse for an heir. Report."

I ground my teeth and reminded myself that this call had a purpose. "You'll no doubt be pleased to hear that chaos has officially been sown in the pack. By my count, there are at least four dead already." She didn't need to know that two were humans.

"Excellent," she purred.

My stomach recoiled at the sound, and my lip threatened to curl. "However..." Her gaze snapped up to pin me like a hawk debating whether to eviscerate me or swallow me whole, but I held firm. She'd been the first predator to teach me never to show weakness. "The numbers might be higher if I knew exactly what I was looking for."

"Speak plainly, Joshua. You know how I hate when you dither around a point."

I clenched a fist behind my back, using the pain of nails digging into my flesh to keep me steady. "What does the toxin do exactly? What is its purpose?"

"Are you questioning my methods?" She arched an overly manicured brow.

Always.

"I am questioning what results I should be looking for. If I am to cause the maximum effect here, it would help if I knew what the intended effect was. I understand the goal, but I might reach my objective sooner if I knew how to—"

"Encourage things," she finished. "Yes, I see. Perhaps expanding your limited education would be beneficial to the cause. That toxin, as you call it, is an artificial hormone designed to induce Mein Zeke in lycanthropes."

I frowned. "What if they don't possess the genetic markers?"

"That's the beauty of it," she held up her glass, which glowed a deep ruby like blood in the light, "they don't need to. Even those tiny syringes contain enough to infect a fully developed wolf, making them instantly moonstruck. Resulting symptoms include hysteria, excessive energy, emotional instability, and, of course, ideally, murder and mayhem." Her sickening smile as she polished off the glass of wine was enough to make me want to gag. A drop of red clung to her bottom lip, beading to a heavy bulb only to be dabbed away at the last possible second.

It was a small wonder that the killing I'd witnessed in the forest had been so brutal. I'd doubled the dose to ensure the feather scheme would work. *Thank the stars I'm all out.*

"And how is your supply?"

I glanced over at the box in a grand show of appeasement and back at her, uncomfortable with how she seemed to have read my thoughts. "I've used all of it."

"Perhaps you aren't completely devoid of purpose." Something must have shown on my face because she added, "Don't look so dour. The latest batch should be even more effective. We're going heavier on the lunacy this go-around." Even as she said it, the woman looked stark-raving mad.

"Small note," I intruded on her premature celebration.

Her eyes narrowed into a withering look.

"My understanding is that moon sickness is a treatable condition."

There was nothing pleasant about her sinister smile. "Not with our formula. Wolfsbane is bad for lycans on a good day. Now even the tiniest dose of the remedy for an infected wolf is lethal."

Her dry cackle was still ringing in my ears long after the call ended. There was no hope for Tommy. Even if they figured out what was wrong, it'd kill him. Cold fell like a stone in my stomach. I spared a hateful glance at the box still hiding in the closet, proudly declaring our hateful name, then stormed out of the room.

Chapter 24

Elijah

I was scarcely a few feet inside the cottage when I stopped dead. Nothing *appeared* out of order, but something had certainly gotten my attention. I forcibly shook off the shroud of fog that had enveloped me at the House. The rest of the long evening had been anything but pleasant.

It was only when I set my key down on the entry table and took a deep breath that my brain finally caught up with the rest of me. The scent winding through my place wasn't days old. It was *fresh*. Without a second thought, I followed it to its source until I came to a screeching halt at the foot of my bed. My chest rose and fell in rapid time while my eyes struggled to believe what they were seeing—Joshua Hart. In my bed.

Movement stirred from the cocoon of blankets he'd wrapped around himself, and I held my breath. There was no way he'd actually come. That he was here now. The message I'd sent earlier in the day felt like a lifetime ago. But I never imagined he'd do it.

"Hey," he croaked. He was still trying to sit upright when I crawled up the bed to meet him. My disbelief reached new levels as the covers slipped down to reveal he was wearing the clothes I'd set aside for him over a week ago... *my* clothes. "Hey," he repeated more clearly, since I still hadn't responded.

Naturally, I said the first inane thing that came to mind. "You're here."

His mouth twisted into a frown. "Of course I am. You asked me to be." Despite the overall confidence of his words, there was a spike of doubt in his beautiful, beautiful scent.

"I know, I'm just... surprised is all," I whispered.

"Don't be."

Unable to stand it anymore, I shimmied closer, needing to touch him, to taste him. Josh was actually here, and I needed him so much. The kiss started tame; his velvety mouth molding perfectly with mine. I quickly lost my breath, though, as it became more exploratory. The blankets separating us vanished as he reacted to the rapidly intensifying contact. His fingers were shockingly warm as they traveled up my chest to pull me even closer. Meanwhile, his other hand drifted lower with a confidence that was wholly Josh. I moaned lightly into him, and my brain chose that moment to be responsible. Pulling away was harder than I could put into words, but somehow I did it anyway.

Josh's bright eyes caught the moonlight from the window. "What?"

I ran a hand along his arm and mentally debated pinching myself. This had to be a dream, except he felt real enough. "It's late, you should go back to sleep. I didn't mean to wake you."

His nails scratched along the back of my neck as his fingers tightened and his previously lust-filled gaze turned sharp. For a solid second, I was afraid he'd actually get up and storm out. Then his hand relaxed, and a staleness infiltrated his scent. "If that's what you want."

"What I..." I sat back on my heels, my confusion increasing as the stale scent intensified so much it all but eclipsed a more concerning scent. *Hurt.* Not the hurt of rejection, which had a sharp sting to it, though there were faint traces of that as well. A deeper hurt that made me think of anise and bruised fruit.

"Unless you've somehow lost your hearing in the last five seconds, you heard me," he said as he pushed the mass of blankets aside and swung his legs off the bed, simultaneously flicking on the bedside lamp. "I am here at your request and I will go at your request. I have no intention of burdening you with my presence."

A suspicion niggled at the edge of my mind. "Josh, how long have you been here?"

His shoulders tightened, and the anise-scent surged past the stale one, but he didn't look at me. "You didn't specify when you'd return."

"How long, Josh?"

"Five hours," he stated without an ounce of emotion.

My heart felt like someone was strangling it. "I'm sorry if I made you feel I didn't want you here," I said thickly. "Far from it. The last few days have been... a lot." I carefully reached for him. He didn't so much as twitch when I gently wrapped my hand around his bicep.

"My feelings rarely factor into decisions." The staleness and anise scents warped around each other as if fighting for dominance. Then it clicked. The stale scent was his attempt to hide the hurt. But scents weren't so easily manipulated as tone or expression.

I now knew three things. Josh was enduring an unbelievable amount of hurt. He'd probably die before admitting it. And most important of all—the one that set my insides on fire with the urge to protect—my mate *needed* me.

I tugged on his arm until he finally turned to face me, his eyes filled with cold resignation. "I want you here, Josh. Please stay."

He searched my face for a moment, then gave a sharp nod and slid back under the covers.

I quickly mirrored him, stripping down then joining him beneath the plethora of blankets. "I'm sorry, some of these are going to have to go," I said with a chuckle. "You weren't exaggerating when you said you get cold easily." I expected him to make his usual crack about not being *able* to exaggerate, and would have preferred it to what he said.

"If you change your mind, tell me and I'll go. It doesn't matter if I'm asleep. This is about your comfort, not mine." I was really starting to hate whoever made Josh believe he didn't matter, that his feelings, his comfort, his *joy* didn't matter.

Unable to bear his silent hurt a moment longer, I pulled him closer until I was hovering over him once more. "I never changed my mind about wanting you here. Asking you to come over tonight feels like a lifetime ago. I wasn't even sure you would, and I never would have expected you to wait up."

His gaze remained steady on me, but he didn't dispute it, confirming that I'd been an idiot for thinking I'd woken him.

"How about we try this again?" I suggested with a soft smile. When he didn't respond, I took that as my green light and leaned down to brush my lips over his. "Thank you for coming. I didn't expect to be out so late. It means a lot to me that you're here. I... I don't think I could have made it through tonight without you." Admitting that was hard, but it was worth it to see the surprise flicker in his eyes. "The last two days..." I trailed off and shook my head. Concern cut across his conflicting scents.

"Would discussing what happened help?"

"Probably." I nuzzled into his neck, determined to eliminate the persistent undercurrent of hurt coloring his normally beautiful scent. "But not now. Now, I just want to be with my mate." I closed the distance between us to press our lips together once more. He met my gentle exploration with equally sweet tastes. After a few achingly perfect kisses, I leaned back to stare into his quietly searching eyes.

"Consent is important to me, Josh. While I would never turn down an opportunity to have sex with you, I would be just as content falling asleep with you in my arms."

He lifted a tentative hand and lightly brushed my hair to the side, the gray strands sliding between his long fingers. "I'm not sleepy." Before I could debate the legitimacy of his statement as a stand-in for consent, he angled up and molded his perfect mouth against mine.

I released a soft sigh as I kissed him back and snaked a hand under his nightshirt. He broke the kiss with a muffled noise, then reached back to pull off the shirt. I took the hint for what it was, and while he worked on divesting the rest of his clothes, I secured the lube from the nightstand. Within seconds, he was kissing me fervently while his erection pressed against my abdomen.

"Easy," I whispered, peppering his lips with small kisses. "There's no rush, and I want to take my time." His breath stuttered as I moved to trail a lazy string of kisses along his jaw and onto his neck. I wanted this to be about him, his pleasure, his comfort.

I continued with the leisurely kisses while I ran my hands over his perfect body, pausing to stroke him. His frustration was palpable when I released his cock after only a few seconds. When it looked like he might say something, I sealed my mouth back over his. Once he was sufficiently diverted, I nudged his legs wider and circled his sensitive rim with a slick finger.

I swallowed his moan as I pressed steadily past the first, then the second ring of tight muscle. When my finger could slide in and out with ease, I added another, prompting his breath to catch. His groan when I curled them over his prostate lit me up inside and, even better, the conflicting scents were replaced by the smell I'd become addicted to—pure Josh.

As promised, I took my time opening him up, soaking in every tiny sound of pleasure I coaxed out of him, while alternating kissing his mouth and anywhere else I could reach. I waited until he was hovering on the edge, then removed my fingers. Again, before he could protest or demand I pick up the pace, I captured his mouth. Only when he relaxed into it and arched up seeking friction, did I pull back to lube my cock.

His pupils were blown wide, and I was grateful neither of us had thought to turn off the lamp. My night vision was impressive, but not *that* impressive, and I'd have hated to miss a second of the beauty washing over his face as I pressed into his tight hole. I sank into him with one long, steady thrust, mirroring how I had with my fingers.

After giving him a second to adjust, I pulled out until my crown caught on his flexing entrance, then just as slowly pushed back in. I maintained the agonizingly sedate pace, simultaneously torturing both of us and riding a high I'd never experienced. All the things I'd ever heard about bonded pairs drifted through my mind, but none came close to capturing the pure bliss that existed when I joined with Josh—with my mate.

"Elijah," Josh whispered, testing my resolve to keep things slow, to drag this out as long as possible. I loved it when he said my name. Loved it even more when he said it like that. Still, I moderated my rhythm, slowly building his pleasure and mine.

He pulled me down for another deep kiss, first wrapping his arms around me, then his legs. We rocked into each other, trading kisses and sharing breaths. It almost felt like I was bonding all over again, the way it should have been. Only this time, it was my choice. One I'd gladly make again and again. Being tethered to Josh wasn't a death sentence. It was the most incredible thing I'd ever experienced. If our lives ended up being shorter, so be it. It would be worth every second of this profound connection we shared.

I altered my angle and slid a fraction deeper. Josh threw his head back against the pillows with a cry while his whole body constricted around me.

"Fuck, baby. That's it. Right there," he panted as I rolled my hips just as slowly as before, despite how tightly he was squeezing me.

I altered my rhythm to incorporate a few quick thrusts between the long drags. In hardly any time, Josh was convulsing around me again, but I didn't stop, confident I could pull another earth-shattering orgasm from him before mine wouldn't be denied any longer.

Josh's fingers gripped my back and shoulders while he used his heels to drive me deeper. I sealed our lips back together and gave him everything I had. He broke the kiss right as another intense orgasm wracked his body, crying my name in a moan that had my balls tightening.

"Fuck, you feel so good around me, so warm and tight," I murmured as I rested my forehead against his and finally gave into the need to chase my release. He groaned something that might have been agreement, his channel fluttering around me. "Stroke yourself for me. I won't last much longer and I want to come with you."

Mercifully, he was already a raw nerve, and it only took a few tugs before he was spilling onto his stomach while I spilled inside him. He whispered my name over and over between panted breaths. I wasn't sure he knew what he was doing, and I didn't care. It was music to my ears. I'd taken care of my mate and I'd never felt more fulfilled.

Joshua

Now that Elijah was here, I felt like I could finally relax. Of course, the mind-altering sex didn't hurt either. Who knew Elijah was so skilled at instigating anal orgasms? Well worth the wait. Lying with the stunning man in a post-bliss haze, mapping each other's skin was definitely a superior way to end the evening.

Elijah's fingers glided across my torso, tracing each scar they found with a lightness that had me sighing contentedly. "Tell me about this," he said softly of a large one that ran jaggedly down my side.

I chuckled. "I was wondering when you'd get around to asking. Are you sure you can handle it?"

He snorted and placed a hot kiss on my ribs. "Why do you think I waited so long? Are you going to share or not?"

I moved my hand from his sculpted shoulder to brush the hair back from his face. The beautiful cognac of his eyes wasn't as clear in the lamplight, but it didn't diminish their apparent humor. "Suppose that's fair," I conceded. I shifted a little beneath him, and he settled more of his weight on me to prevent me from going anywhere. I laughed at the obvious ploy. "Okay, okay."

"Out with it."

As commanded, I let out a sigh, feeling more at peace than I had a right to be. "I got that one in a knife fight."

Elijah's deep laugh sent tingles of light fluttering inside me. "If you couldn't lie, I'd assume you made that up to sound impressive."

"If only. That was the last time I bothered bringing the bow."

"Bow," he repeated. "As in *bow-and-arrow*?"

"Technically, it was a crossbow, but I'm proficient in both."

He rolled his eyes. "Why am I not surprised you know how to use medieval weaponry?"

I was pretty positive I was smiling like an idiot and didn't care. "A sword, too, if you were curious."

"Oh, I know about the sword," he rumbled suggestively.

I laughed again. "Did you know you have all the humor of a thirteen-year-old boy?"

"Your point?" he asked with an arched brow and a face at least trying to be serious.

My smile was still in full force as I leveraged what little room he'd allowed me and stole a lazy kiss. "Just commenting."

"Mm," he hummed, pulling on my bottom lip with his teeth while he drifted his hand from the long scar to a twisted one on my lower abdomen. Its pearly sheen almost made it look like a star sitting on my hip. "And this?"

The husky question wrought havoc on my still addled senses, and it took me a beat to respond. "A bonded pair, actually." I watched his face carefully. When no reaction was forthcoming, I kept going. "They'd hacked a string of creditors and drained their accounts. They were in the midst of their getaway when I caught up with them in Savannah."

"Regular Bonnie and Clyde."

"Blaze of glory and all. Would have been nice to see the ambush coming, though," I added belatedly.

"Pretty sure that's the literal antithesis of an ambush," he teased. My latest laugh caught as he brushed his lips against the scar. He leaned back, with a playful smile gracing his lips, and lightly tapped on the faintest of my scars, which happened to be in the unmistakable pattern of an animal bite. "You know I can't *not* ask about this."

I huffed and rolled my eyes. "I sustained that when I was a child. Family hunting trip gone sideways."

"And what did you sustain it from?" Elijah crooned, causing my heart to skip for two reasons.

"A canine. I started avoiding 'family' hunting trips after that. Not long after, my father left. He never came back." It was the truth, but it flirted dangerously with the line of honesty. I vaguely recalled my father arguing that I was too young and my mother insisting I was older than she'd been. I also remembered with the vivid clarity of a fevered mind how willing my mother had been to watch me die.

"That got more dire than I expected. Tell me about the most ridiculous scar you've received in the line of duty." His smile and earnest expression helped banish the painful memory to the depths where it lived.

I recounted the stories of five more battle wounds. It was odd to talk so freely about things that most people pretended didn't exist. I'd never shared any of this with anyone before, and yet, despite their gruesome nature, I was at ease and actually having fun.

"How is it that I have all of these and you don't have so much as a scratch on you?" I finally asked. "That's gotta be unprecedented for a werewolf."

"Not true," he argued, then shuffled around until his knee was shining in the light.

If I squinted, I could barely make out a tiny white scar. "Are you sure that's not a birthmark?"

"Nope. Fell out of a tree. In case you're wondering, lycans do *not* land on their feet."

I clapped a hand over my mouth to smother a burst of laughter. "You know *weres* weren't designed for climbing, right?" I snickered.

"I do *now*. Been avoiding the blasted things for... oh, twenty years?"

I laughed again and ran my fingers through his loose locks. The silky strands were practically silver in the moonlight seeping in from the window. "And none of this bothers you?" I asked more seriously, resting my hand on one of my more recent, near-fatal wounds. Literally every part of my body was a testament to the weapon I'd been forged to be since birth. Most of the marks had resulted in one or more deaths. I couldn't tell if Elijah was willfully ignoring that aspect or if it genuinely didn't faze him.

He blinked slowly back at me. "I think you're absolutely beautiful."

My heart stuttered in my chest. Plenty of people had told me I was beautiful before, but no one had ever looked at me the way Elijah was doing right now as they said it. For the first time in my life, I felt truly seen.

"One more," he whispered, his hand moving to cover my heart as if sensing its struggle.

To buy myself time to regain control of the rampant organ, I said, "Now that one... That's gonna cost you."

"The price?" he purred, leaning forward to steal a kiss, one that I gave freely, though it was in no way helping my abused heart.

"A question in turn," I managed steadily enough.

He pulled back enough to look at me. "And what might that be?"

I caressed the side of his face, loving how the moonlight from the window reflected in his eyes. "Why didn't you finish your degree at Dartmouth?"

He instantly laughed it off. "Surely you already know that. My dad died."

"I know the reason you came back. I'm asking why you stayed," I clarified.

He shrugged, still playing at nonchalance. "Just easier, I guess."

"Should we revisit the unfairness of lying?"

He let out a huff. When he pulled a little further away, I let him go, recognizing how hard a question I was asking. "There better be one hell of a story behind that scar."

Now that I had the room to do so, I sat up, much to his obvious surprise.

"What are you doing? Are you leaving?"

Instead of answering, I looked him calmly in the eye and gently took his hand. Slowly, I glided it over my shoulder, making sure he never broke contact with my skin, until I reached the one spot I still dreamed about.

"You feel that?" I asked softly as his finger slipped into the shallow dip surrounded by firmer muscle. I didn't have to wait for his confirmation; I could see it in the slight widening of his eyes. "That's where his claw initially hooked me. It sank deep enough to scrape my spine. When I tried to yank free, he pulled back. We ended up rolling down a steep incline. The fall caused the claw to ease out enough that it skated along," I began moving his hand along the nearly invisible white line that was branded into my memory, up and over my shoulder once more, "until we landed with his full weight sitting on top of my chest. That finger there," I tapped Elijah's middle finger where it rested just above my aorta, "missed my heart by less than an inch."

"Shit," he breathed. "Didn't you have any backup?"

"I did. They assumed I was dead. But the *were* above me knew better," I pressed his hand flat on my chest, "because he could still hear my heart beating." The solid thud of my heart seemed to fill the room, dominating the sudden, eerie quiet that had descended.

"What did you do?" Elijah whispered.

"Finished counting to thirty. By then, the wolfsbane I'd nicked him with on the way down was in full effect," I finished with a wicked half-grin.

"Fuck," Elijah hissed. "Remind me never to let you tell ghost stories to the pups. That shit sounds terrifying."

I scoffed. "Who in their right mind would let a man like me anywhere near pups?"

Elijah leaned close. "I would. I don't know who you're thinking of when you say 'a man like me', but I know you're not him."

I stared at him in astonishment.

He tightened his hand around mine, though I wasn't sure when he'd taken it. "And I... I stayed because the pack needed me to. My father's death left a vacuum. He'd always been a kind of counterbalance to Conrad's brashness. And without him..."

"They needed an Alpha," I filled in. It made sense in a sad sort of way.

Elijah winced, but didn't pull away. "Please don't say that. I'm not an Alpha."

"I didn't say you were," I countered, silently hoping he wouldn't catch the nuance.

"The pack needed stability and support in a time of upheaval. I did what any *were* would have done. I put my pack first. I know what a lot of people think—hell, what a lot of the pack thinks—but I'm not the man they want me to be. I'm just not." He paused, obviously upset. He stared down at where his thumb was rubbing a warm circle on my hand, then looked back up at me. "Neither of us has to be the men the world says we are."

I swallowed hard at the promise in his words. I wanted them to be true more than anything, but there was so much devastation I'd already wrought. "What if we've already made terrible choices? Choices that can't be undone?" I asked softly.

"Make better ones," he said, sealing the statement with a kiss.

I licked my lips and tentatively kissed him back. I wanted everything Elijah promised, everything he said we could have, wanted to be the person he saw when he looked at me. But more than all of that, I just wanted to be the kind of man he deserved.

Without warning, I deepened the sensual kiss, curling my fingers in his hair and pulling him impossibly closer, even as his words ghosted out in a caress I felt all the way to my soul. "You're a better one," I whispered as his arms wrapped once more around me.

Waking up in Elijah's arms was quickly becoming one of my all-time favorite things, and that was a problem, because no matter how much I wanted it to, this could never last.

I let out a wistful sigh and ran my hand along the exceptional warmth beneath me before beginning the arduous process of extricating myself without waking him.

I was zipping my last boot when his sleepy words drifted out from the mass of covers. "Trying to sneak out on me?"

My grin slipped free as my gaze landed on his face with its raised eyebrow and rumpled hair. "What makes you think I'm doing that?"

"Oh, I don't know," he began, throwing off the covers to reveal his gloriously naked body, "maybe all the sneaking?"

I snickered at the gentle tease.

"And not so much as a kiss goodbye," he lamented. He shook his head and approached. "What's the rush, anyway? It's like crazy early." The second he was in range, he wrapped his arms around my waist and promptly began nuzzling my neck as if we were still curled up in bed.

"It is difficult enough getting here without anyone noticing. Can you imagine how much more so that would be with the entire town wide awake and bustling around? Not to mention, *someone* lives completely on the edge of town, making any comings and goings rather conspicuous, don't you think?"

"I could certainly do with more comings."

"Nice try."

"I could always move *into* town," he mumbled.

I bit my lip to keep from laughing. Early-morning Elijah was adorable and outrageously cuddly. Not to mention that morning beard, while sexy as sin, also fucking tickled. "Don't do that," I finally managed when I was sure I wouldn't do anything so humiliating as giggle. "There's not a house like this in town."

"Mm, so you *do* like my house," he teased. Okay, sleepy Elijah was also a tad insufferable.

"That's not what I said. But speaking of your charming cottage, if I'm going to keep coming here like this, then we need to have a serious conversation about your security. Or, more appropriately, the lack thereof. The antique key is quaint for sure, but woefully insufficient."

Elijah pulled back and looked at me with the brightest grin I'd seen from him yet.

"What? Are you offended about the key or just that excited about a free security system?"

His smile broadened. "Install whatever you feel is necessary."

"I will, but why are you smiling at me like that?"

"Because you're planning to keep coming here." I was on the verge of arguing that I hadn't exactly said that when he captured me with a toe-curling kiss. "And for the record, I know that's not what you said," he answered the unspoken rebuke, "but it's what you meant. So whatever you need to do to feel safe coming here, do it."

"It's not for my security." The words shot out of my mouth before I could reconsider their blunt honesty.

"Oh?" he purred.

"I have enemies, Bennett. A lot of enemies," I whispered.

"You said so yourself, I'm a fully grown, capable *were*."

"*Yeah, you are*," I responded, grinning like a damn idiot. I couldn't very well tell him why I was so worried about his safety, how even the thought of someone hurting him was enough to bring me to my knees.

"Have breakfast with me," he asked suddenly.

"I don't really do breakfast," I countered.

"Then coffee," he persisted, leaning into me.

"What part of 'leave before the whole town wakes up' did you miss?"

He chuckled and stole a kiss before stepping back, very much awake now. "And if I promise not to put anything on?" he taunted before turning to leave and presumably make his way to the kitchen.

My mouth instantly watered, and I had to swallow twice before I could speak. "That's cheating," I finally managed, the words way too husky.

He glanced over his shoulder and undoubtedly caught me staring at his ass. "Your point?" He flashed a wicked grin and winked, then resumed his brazen trek.

As my feet began moving of their own accord after him, there was no denying how completely gone I was for this man.

Chapter 25

Elijah

Josh leaned across the desk to acquire a data tab. He'd been a flurry of activity all morning, just as he'd been the last few days. Whatever he was determined to find, he must be getting close.

"You're staring," he whispered under his breath, just loud enough that I could hear.

"And that's different from any other day, how?"

He ducked his head to cover a laugh. His reaction confirmed my suspicion that he'd been acutely aware of my staring well before all of this started. Truth be told, he was almost impossible *not* to stare at; that gorgeous body was like a siren's call. I didn't care what your orientation was. Except now I was noticing a lot more than just his appearance. Like the way he chewed on his lip when he was concentrating, or how he would reflexively tense up at any sudden sound. I was also painfully aware of the tension he wore when he worked, a tension that was noticeably absent when we were alone.

I longed to work those bunched muscles loose, to get him to laugh openly like he did at the house, but there was a level of decorum we were at least *trying* to maintain. As it was, Officer Mack had already been eyeing the two of us a little too closely the better part of today... and yesterday, and the day before that. I let out a sigh and tied my hair back to keep my hands busy.

"If you're that bored, I'm sure there's some filing that could use your attention," Josh deadpanned without so much as blinking in my direction.

I stared at him, momentarily shocked by the unexpected taunt. Then he glanced at me out of the corner of his eye. Where before I'd only ever seen that unaffected look he'd perfected, now I saw the light mischief hiding in the green depths. I couldn't help but wonder if that had always been there, and I'd just been too blind in my assumption of who he was. Because one thing was for certain, Joshua Hart was absolutely not the man I thought he was. The heart I'd believed to be frozen solid was alive and beating with a warmth to rival the sun.

He hadn't been forthcoming in the kind things he'd done for Tommy, like having Mack and Kilee keep him company or keeping him well stocked in reading materials, but it didn't change the fact that he'd gone out of his way to make sure the kid was looked after. He hated waking up alone. And he genuinely liked helping, even if it was something as mundane as the dishes. No, Josh was an entirely different person than the front he presented to the world, and with each passing day he drew me deeper and deeper into his orbit.

Now if only I could convince him that my feelings weren't just the bond, we might actually get somewhere.

"You're doing it again," he mumbled.

"Sorry, just trying to decide when you started needing Mack to do your dirty work for you," I responded loud enough for the curious officer to hear.

Josh's jaw dropped for a split second before he regained his composure.

I smiled innocently back at him.

"I'm more than capable of fighting my own battles," Josh responded, ice practically dripping from his words.

"Prove it," I challenged.

He pushed back from the desk and spun the chair to keep me in his sights. "You know what? There might be a way you can be useful after all."

My mind instantly supplied several ways we could be *very* useful, none of which involved staying here. Or clothes.

"Save your work, Mack. We're leaving," Josh ordered as he pushed up from his seat in one fluid motion.

"What?" the young officer and I asked at the same time.

"You heard me. What do you say, Bennett? Ready to be more productive than a paperweight?" I growled at the barb, and he snickered.

"Um..." Mack began, practically racing around the desk, "is he allowed to help in an investigation?"

"One would certainly hope he'd be willing to help clear the name of one of his own. Especially since the Pack liaison's primary purpose is to ensure that none of the pack are wrongly accused or denied justice. Also, from what I know, there's technically no rule against it."

"Wait," I said, joining them as they made their way towards the exit. Neither did, not that I was surprised. It wasn't until we were outside once again that I could finish my thought. "Denied justice," I repeated. "You say that like packs can request a Lycan Detective for their own defense." Both of them stared back at me. "Can we really do that?"

Josh's small smile touched his eyes, and I had to remind myself that we were standing in the middle of the precinct parking radial with close to a thousand busy bodies within sight. "At its base level, the oath of a Lycan Detective is to ensure equal justice between two species: lycanthrope and Homo sapiens. It is only when both are involved that a Lycan Detective has jurisdiction. While historically my position has been utilized by human factions, there has never been any distinction that states only humans can employ those same services."

Understanding dawned in Officer Mack's eyes as I struggled not to fall any harder for the man standing in front of me.

"That's why you're trying so hard to clear Tommy's name," I whispered.

He gave a small nod. "It's my job. Now, you want to see about helping or not?"

"What do you need me to do?"

Instead of answering, Josh turned to Mack. "Let's go back to the original scene."

"What? Why?" Officer Mack asked.

"Because Bennett here is going to sniff out some clues for us." Josh squeezed my shoulder, and the familiar move momentarily banished my confusion. When he removed his hand, I almost reached back out to capture it with my own. Mack's stern gaze was literally the only thing that prevented me.

Joshua

I was out of my damn mind. Having Elijah *help* with the investigation? The first thing that came to mind was "conflict of interest". Except it *wasn't* a conflict. We were officially on the same side. Tommy was innocent, and I was going to put Ashton Carr behind bars where he belonged. Plus, I doubted I could have borne Elijah's intense gaze following my every move another minute. How the hell did couples actually work together?

I shook off my doubt and approached the edge of the scene where Tina Carr's body was discovered. Someone had magically removed the stain of red from the ground, and a different collection of debris surrounded the bulk trash receptacle on the corner, but the scene was still fresh in my mind.

"I don't mean to be negative, but how is this supposed to work?" Mack asked while casting a sidelong look at Elijah, who shrugged.

"You," I pointed at Elijah and crooked a finger for him to come over.

He raised an eyebrow that was a hair too suggestive given the present company. "I'm not a dog," he grumbled.

"But you are a canine with a superior nose," I countered.

He gave the relatively untouched crime scene a dubious look. "Any evidence from her murder would be long gone by now. I already told you, I'm not an Anóteros."

I frowned at the slip. That was not a conversation of which the all too eager officer was aware. "I'm not looking for old leads, I'm looking for new ones."

"Still not following."

I diligently did not roll my eyes. The stubborn ass wolf was smarter than this. I took a deep breath to calm myself. If I were right, this could be exactly what we needed. "Murderers often return to the scene of the crime."

Elijah scoffed. "Are criminals really that dumb?"

"Yes," I responded flatly. "Can you pick out the scent we're looking for or not?"

Elijah glared at me. "There's nothing wrong with my nose."

I crossed my arms. "And while you're at it, a timeframe would be appreciated."

"Moon curse you, I'm not an—"

"Anóteros. So you said. I'm not asking you to narrow it down to the minute. A few hours or even days should suffice."

He huffed, nostrils flaring with irritation. "I may not be a Howell, but I can track a weasel as well as any lycan."

"Good. Now quit stalling and get to it."

For a second it looked like he was going to advance on me, even Mack tensed. Of course it'd be a total toss-up what he'd do to me once he was in range, smack me for being an insolent twat or ravage me with a kiss to remind me of the hold he had over me. Mercifully, he rethought approaching and turned instead towards the scene.

"Oh, and don't touch anything. You'll contaminate the evidence."

He instantly stiffened. I smiled to myself as I watched him force every muscle in his shoulders to relax. He wasn't the only one who enjoyed getting someone's tail bunched.

Elijah

Work-Josh was not my favorite Josh. Admittedly, I enjoyed the banter, but I could live without the snide comments.

"No touching," Josh reminded for the umpteenth time from his post fifteen feet away.

I gritted my teeth and withdrew my hand from where I'd been about to move the large trash positioned for pickup in order to search behind a collection of wooden boards propped behind it. "That's it," I growled.

Josh raised two perfectly unaffected eyebrows at my outburst and didn't so much as flinch when I stalked up to him.

"How in the moon's name do you expect me to find anything when you keep distracting me every five minutes?"

"Well."

The simple response was infuriating. "Are you goading me on purpose, or are you this obnoxious with all your partners?" I fired back. His lips twitched in a repressed smile, and I realized the double entendre. I narrowed my eyes at him and held my ground.

"I'm merely endeavoring to make sure you don't overthink your quest. In my experience, lycans tend to find the most valuable information when they aren't actively seeking it."

I opened my mouth to argue with the millions of flaws in his logic when he held out a pair of forensic gloves.

"Here. If you insist on touching everything, you can wear these."

My growl was openly hostile as I snatched them out of his hand.

Mack's voice was barely audible as I stalked away. "If you're wanting him to help, you could try being nice."

"I could. But where's the fun in that?" Josh's cavalier response had the no doubt desired effect of forcing all my fur the wrong way.

The gloves snapped into place, and I winced. Rubbing my wrist, I began touching literally everything he'd told me for the last half hour not to.

"I think you missed one." Josh's words floated out, highlighting just how childishly I was behaving.

Absolutely insufferable, unbearable, infuriatingly...

My internal tirade trailed off. Behind the boards and other oversized scraps also left for pickup, a scent flared to life. Sharp baking spices mingled with spent tobacco in a sour stench I instantly recognized as belonging to Ashton Carr. It would seem Josh and I were both right: things needed to be moved, and I would catch the scent when I wasn't looking for it. A truth compounded by the fact that now that the scent was curling in my nose, I could clearly tell where else it had been. Everywhere.

I turned to tell Josh what I had discovered, but found he was already standing at attention and ready for action.

He hastened over. "When?" His positivity that I'd found exactly what we'd been looking for was impressive.

"I'd say as recently as yesterday. He must have rested against the wall here for a good while, because that's where I caught it. He was smoking something too," I added.

Josh casually squatted down to inspect the ground. My eyes saw nothing, but clearly he was better trained because he reached out with tweezers and plucked the remnants of a joint amidst other refuse. When he straightened back up, he met my eyes. "This probably won't be pleasant, but would you mind?" He held out the nearly unrecognizable firestick far enough away to allow me to choose.

This is for Tommy.

I leaned forward and sniffed the wretched thing. The hairs in my nose curled in revulsion, and I coughed, stepping away to fresher air. "That's definitely his. Fuck, that thing is foul."

Josh nodded, betraying no emotion, despite the obvious victory. He promptly deposited the evidence into a secure container that seemed to manifest out of nowhere, then pocketed it. "This needs to be analyzed. Mack, how fast is the turnaround on your preternatural forensics?"

"Preter-what forensics?"

Josh's sigh was *almost* silent. "I'll call my contact in Portland and see if we can speed things up. Tommy shouldn't have to sit in that cell any longer than necessary."

It was on the tip of my tongue to tell him "that cell" had probably saved his life. Keith's horrible demise still plagued my dreams. Josh had asked more than once when I'd started awake if I wanted to discuss what had happened while I was at the House. Telling him would undoubtedly alleviate the memory, but it could also bring up a whole host of other complications with the pack, especially since I was sure Keith was responsible for the murder in town as well.

Rather than let that particular genie out, I swallowed down the words and focused on what we were doing next. Josh was skimpy with the details, which, while understandable, was frustrating. Still, we'd found something. Something that only Josh had thought of. The man was damn good at his job. A familiar brightness burned in my chest—pride.

Mack was already in the hover car, and Josh was turning to join him when I reached out and grabbed his wrist.

"Bennett," he hissed, but didn't pull away. Instead, he angled his body to block the view of the contact.

"You're absolutely brilliant," I whispered.

He blinked in mild surprise. "Thanks."

"Have a drink with me tonight." I could see the doubt in his eyes. "To celebrate Tommy's imminent release," I added to sweeten the offer.

He looked away, and his tongue flicked out to taste his bottom lip, like it always did when he was uncertain.

"Please. Just us."

His gaze met mine again, and it showed a trust I had no idea how I'd earned. "Okay."

I squeezed his wrist gently. "I'll pick up some cognac and see you at home."

"Home."

It was too late to take back the words, and I didn't want to. They felt right. I ached to kiss him, but that wasn't really an option, so I released his captive wrist and settled for counting down the minutes until I got to touch him again.

Chapter 26

Joshua

MY HEAD POPPED FREE of the cotton shirt, and my gaze fell on the full glass of amber liquid. Elijah had poured the cognac nearly half an hour ago, and I hadn't so much as sipped it.

What am I thinking? Is drinking with Elijah really the smartest thing?

I let out a huff, angry at my indecision, and stalked over to the tumbler. In one fluid motion, I tossed back the contents and brought it to bear on the dresser with a sharp smack.

"You okay?"

I squashed the reflex to jump, then glanced at where the sexiest man I'd ever had the privilege of spending time with and who currently was in complete possession of my heart was leaning against the doorjamb. "How long have you been there?" I side-stepped.

His lustful gaze dragged its way down my body, then back up, sparking a wave of heat in its wake. "Obviously not long enough." His crooked smile stayed firmly in place as his gaze shifted to the tumbler. "Your glass is empty."

"It is."

"Would you like another?"

"Yes," I responded without pause.

His gaze softened, and he stepped forward to grab my glass. "Allow me," he purred, effectively liquefying my insides. It wasn't until he'd left again that I realized what I'd agreed to. Damn the honesty that popped out of me anytime he was near.

Shaking my head and silently scolding myself for my utter lack of control in all things concerning Elijah, I ventured out of the bedroom to join him in the living room. There, my fresh glass of Cognac on the rocks sat innocuously on the coffee table. Elijah's gaze tracked me as I moved around the low, rectangular table to take a seat on the couch. I sat far enough away to maintain at least a semblance of distance between us, though I wasn't exactly sure why. I'd be much happier curled up in his lap.

Like I'd been the other night when we'd watched that movie.

It had been a wonderfully mundane evening. For an entire three hours, I'd been able to pretend that we were normal. He wasn't a *were*, and I wasn't a killer. We'd just been two men who took pleasure in each other's company, enjoying an evening together. I'd fallen asleep in his arms and woken up in his bed still safely cocooned in his embrace. It'd been perfect.

But that's not reality. One day he'll find out the truth, and we'll wake from this dream.

I squeezed my glass and took a sip.

"You seem really tense tonight. Is everything alright? I would have expected you to be more pleased with today's turn of events. We're supposed to be celebrating, remember?"

"Tommy should be with his pack, not in jail. The sooner I can make that happen—"

"And it will. I believe in you. You found that evidence today, and I'm positive you'll find everything else you need to free him. But you're acting like you're the reason he's in jail."

"I am." I went to take another drink and thought better of it.

"Okay, fine, you *technically* arrested him, but you're not the one who framed him. That's all on Ashton Carr," Elijah said, seeking to reassure me. A reassurance I didn't deserve.

I took that sip. The brandy burned its way down to settle hotly in my stomach. "That forensics team will take days to give me what I need."

"Days? What exactly did you request?"

I smiled slightly at my glass. "A complete time reconstruct of the last five weeks."

Elijah choked on his mixed drink. "That's not standard police procedure."

"I'm not standard police."

"Why not order one sooner?" Elijah asked after taking another drink to clear his throat.

"DNA must be tied to the scene, and it can only recreate that strand's presence. The victim and anyone else who might have been there won't be visible, but it will hopefully be enough to reconstruct the scene."

"The drawbacks of magic," he chuckled, polishing off the last of his drink. "Another?" he asked, reaching for mine.

I handed it back again without considering what an epically bad idea getting drunk with him might be. As he left the room to refresh the drinks, I stood. To distract myself and hopefully him, I said, "By the way, I finished installing the security system."

Elijah skidded back into view, shock plainly written on his face, and I smiled. "How the hell did you manage that?"

"Someone gave me a key," I responded cheekily as I shoved my hands into the fleece-lined pockets of my sweats.

"But... when? When could you possibly have had the time?"

"Don't worry about it. However, if you could read this?" I held out a piece of paper at eye level.

Elijah squinted for a moment before reading the handwritten words aloud. "Atlas, play the playlist Vintage." His eyes widened as what he was saying sank in. There was a soft beep, and the system began playing one of my favorite collections of music.

"What do you think?" I asked, suddenly nervous.

"You installed Atlas? *Atlas*? The premier AI home automation and security system. You installed the most expensive system on the market... in *my* cottage."

"Technically, it's an extension of *my* Atlas system, but now it's programmed to recognize your commands."

"Atlas," he repeated in awe. "Josh, that still would have cost a fortune. I can't... Why would you... It's too much."

"You said I could install whatever I needed."

"I did, but... moons of Jupiter, I don't even have words for this. Just how much money *do* you have?"

"Does it matter?" I asked, trepidation seeping in. What if I'd over-stepped? Atlas was leagues ahead of any common security system, and this version surpassed what was available on the public market. "I can remove it if you're not comfortable."

"No," he said quickly.

"Are you sure?" I asked.

"I'm sure. You caught me off guard, that's all. I don't know why I'm surprised, considering you have a library full of actual books."

I rubbed my arm to stave off the encroaching chill. "I could get you some of those, too."

He finally cracked a smile, and I let out the breath I'd been holding. He stepped forward and glided a hand over the arm

I'd been attempting to warm unsuccessfully. Heat suffused the appendage, and I sighed in appreciation. "You don't have to spend all your money on me." He leaned forward and brushed his lips softly against mine. "But I won't ever say no to books."

I laughed, feeling more at ease, a feat only he ever seemed capable of achieving. "So, you're not upset?"

"Like I said, just surprised. Here," he said as he handed me my latest drink.

I quickly did a mental count of how many this made. It wasn't like I was lightweight by any stretch, but drinking with a lycan could be deceptively dangerous, drinking with Elijah more so.

"Cheers," he said, clinking his glass to mine.

"Cheers," I repeated and mirrored his move, swallowing the contents in one go.

Elijah

I was still struggling to wrap my head around the fact that of all the systems in the world, Josh had installed the single most advanced system money could buy. Even the base model was worth my entire college education, and given what I knew about Josh, I seriously doubted it was the base model. I knew Josh had money, but this was a whole other universe, and I had no idea where it all came from. There was no way a Lycan Detective's salary was *that* good. For everything I learned about Josh, two more mysteries emerged.

Who are you, Joshua Hart?

Given that Josh had already had four doubles, now seemed as good a time as any to find out. After refreshing the glasses once more, we resumed our seats on the couch. It bothered me that he was keeping a cushion's worth of distance between us, but it seemed best not to press the issue given what I was about to ask. Except I never got the chance.

"Are you sure you're not bothered, baby?" he asked, taking a strong swallow and deliberately placing his tumbler on the coffee table. I couldn't hold my smile. Him calling me baby was a good sign he was relaxing. At the very least, a sign that the alcohol was taking effect.

"Not at all. I am curious about one thing," I began, opting to take a different track and hopefully lead him into answering the heavier questions.

"Oh? And what might that be?" he asked, with a mischievous gleam in his eye. Our endeavors to get to know each other better were a special kind of fun that I was sure had no place in traditional games of twenty questions.

"This 'baby' business..."

Josh's scent instantly took on an edge of wariness. "Yeah..."

"What's that about?" I was determined to hold the course even though his response made me anxious. To calm my nerves, I took a sip of my Old Fashioned. The smoky sweetness did the trick, and I settled back to wait him out.

Josh's gaze darted in every direction but mine. His own brandy-neat sat abandoned, beads of condensation sliding down the sides. There was a part of me that felt guilty for conning Josh into drinking and then asking him questions—a very *small* part.

He cleared his throat and reached for the drink, then seemed to think better of it. "I... I'm not entirely certain."

Josh-speak for I have an idea, but don't want to say. I checked a frustrated huff. Losing patience with his evasive way of speaking now would pretty much eliminate the chance of getting anything else out of him later. Still, it warranted some digging.

Before I could figure out how to push further though, he added, "I'm also not sure if I can stop. Does it bother you?" His neutral expression suggested my response didn't really matter to him, but the hint of anxiety swirling through his scent gave away the truth. My heart melted. His constant consideration of my feelings displayed a level of thoughtfulness I suspected he didn't give most people. And that he expressed *any* level of concern for me was something I marveled at daily.

His sharp scent of nerves intensified, and I realized I'd taken too long to answer. An oversight I quickly remedied. "At first, but I think I'm starting to like it." Surprise emanated off him, and I hid my smile behind another drink.

Reassured, he reached for his neglected glass and took a sizable swallow. "Really?" he asked when he set the glass back down, apparently not fully convinced.

I chuckled and placed my drink next to his, then turned to look at him. He tried to duck away, but I caught his chin with my finger and gently encouraged him to look at me. His gaze locked on mine, and none of the uncertainty I could smell was present in those green depths. Josh had a poker face that could put cold stone to shame. It was both baffling and disconcerting to see the neutral expression given how his scent was a whirlwind of doubt.

Every fiber of my being wanted to take that anxiety away, to comfort my mate. I brushed my thumb across his plump lips and loved how they parted slightly for me. "As long as you keep making the sounds that you do, you can call me whatever you want, moonbeam." Confusion flashed in his eyes. "What?" I asked, debating whether to taste the cognac on his lips.

"I'm not sure if I've ever heard that term used in that context."

"Term? What ter—" I closed my eyes as the realization of what I'd called him sank in. *Son of a badger.*

He shifted beside me, but not enough to break our contact. "What does it mean?"

"I cannot believe I actually said that." I gave a defeated sigh and pulled away, snagging my drink on the way. Josh, however, held perfectly still.

"You don't have to tell me." All the anxiety I'd been combating was nowhere to be found. Josh's eyes were bright and curious... and patient.

"No. It's too late now, and I'll probably end up saying it again, anyway." I rolled the cool glass between my hands. "It's... it's something my father used to call my mother." *And what does it mean that I used it for Josh?*

The corner of Josh's mouth twitched, and nothing more. But I didn't need the smile to grace his lips when it shone so clearly in his eyes. I couldn't believe it. He actually liked it. It was silly and sickeningly sweet, and arguably worse than "baby" as far as endearments went, and he actually liked it.

He was reaching for his drink once more when I asked, "Josh, what's the longest relationship you've ever been in?"

The wariness I'd caught earlier returned with a vengeance. It was so sharp, I almost wrinkled my nose at the abrupt shift. "That's a—"

"Broad question," I finished. He flashed me a look. "See? I'm learning. Let me clarify. Longest *romantic* relationship. And for the record, I am qualifying this as a romantic relationship. But you can also include sexual encounters if you like." I suddenly had a very strong suspicion that he would *need* to.

He withdrew his hand and seemed to shrink in on himself. "I... I think I'm gonna go to the restroom." He got up, and I quickly put down my drink in order to pull him to me. He stubbornly remained rigid even as I wrapped my arms around his chest and forced him to lean against me.

"There's no judgment here. Everyone is different. I just want to know. I promise I won't go into some kind of possessive rage," I chuckled as I placed a kiss on the back of his neck. It took several more, along with some nuzzling, before he finally relaxed a bit.

He was close enough that I actually heard him swallow before he said, "Four months. Though I'm dubious whether it even qualifies as a relationship."

Joshua

I cringed inside at the admission. It definitely hadn't been a "real" relationship, or at least not one that normal people would qualify as a relationship. We'd hooked up all of three times in that span. Work had been hell at the time, and seeing the same person had just been easier than going out and finding someone new. I didn't know the guy's last name, nor had he even been a *were*. Desperate times and all that.

My sigh wasn't as quiet as I'd hoped and prompted Elijah to nuzzle the back of my neck again. I tried valiantly to rein in my self consciousness which he undoubtedly could smell. "What about you?" I asked, almost positive I would regret the question.

"Four years," he whispered, tickling the short hairs at the base of my skull.

I shivered at the sensation even as my heart sank. Four *years*? Even my first handler hadn't lasted that long.

"Josh, look at me."

I stubbornly refused to. I had no desire to see the pity in his eyes, the knowledge that I was so much... *less*. When his hold loosened, I pulled away, eager to retreat to some semblance of safety. I was already standing when his words called me back.

"Please, Josh. Sit down."

The soft plea stabbed at my heart. I wanted to do as he asked. I *wanted* to give him everything. But there was so much about me he couldn't know. My hand tightened into a fist that was suddenly engulfed in heat. I looked down to find that Elijah was leaning forward and holding it. Reflexively, I unclenched my hand, and he immediately twined our fingers together, grounding me in the here and now, in the *us*. The intimacy of it brought a sob to my lips that I fought to hold back.

Elijah Bennett was systematically breaking down every wall I'd spent the last twenty-five years of my life erecting, and I was powerless to stop him. Moreover, I didn't want to. If there could be only one person in this entire world who knew the real me, I wanted it to be Elijah.

He tugged gently on my captive hand, and I folded back onto the couch. He passed me my drink before settling back with his own. I stared at our laced fingers. It felt so right, and I knew there'd never been anyone in my life who'd made me feel the way the lycan at my side did. Elijah was special. He always had been.

"Hey," he whispered.

I turned to look at him. His eyes were soft with understanding I didn't deserve.

If he only knew the horrible things I've done, he wouldn't look at me like that. One day he will, and then this, *whatever this is that's growing between us, won't be there anymore.*

I tightened my fingers around his as if they could stave off the inevitable.

"We're figuring this out together, remember?" He searched my face before closing the distance between us and molding his mouth to mine. The kiss was tame and sweet, and made my chest hurt all the more. "I'm right here, moonbeam, and I'm not going anywhere," he whispered against my lips.

I kissed him deeper, stopping only long enough to relieve us of our drinks. When I returned, desire hooded his gaze. I straddled him in the corner of the couch, and he maneuvered so we wouldn't tumble off the side. He returned my eager kiss, slowly exploring my mouth while he cradled the back of my neck. It never ceased to amaze me how gentle he could be. His other hand drifted down my back to slip beneath my borrowed shirt.

Looser clothing had always been a hazard I avoided, but I lived for the way Elijah looked at me when I wore his clothes. I moaned into him as his fingers made five pools of heat on my comparably cooler skin. At the sound, he bucked up into me, and I let out a deeper moan. "Baby, you have no idea what you do to me."

"Then you should tell me." He splayed his hand across my lower back and forced me to grind against him. I gasped and attacked his mouth with a ferocity that frightened me, tightening my fingers in his hair as we continued to grind against each other. "Tell me, moonbeam," he repeated even lower as he nibbled his way across my jaw to suck on my neck.

To my infinite shame, I whimpered. I desperately wanted to tell him the truth, but I couldn't. I just couldn't. It wasn't fair to him. *None* of this was fair to him. And I was already set to burn in the ninth circle of hell.

"Josh," he moaned against my neck right before I felt the graze of teeth. My breath hitched. I wasn't afraid he'd bite me; part of me even wanted him to, just so we could get it out of the way. His nails scratched into my back as he shifted his thigh and thrust up hard. Electricity crackled through my body. "Fine," he whispered in my ear right before sucking the lobe between his teeth. "If you can't tell me, then show me."

Every cell vibrated as if he'd strummed a chord. His tongue delved back into my mouth while he used his hands to mercilessly grind my hips against him. Pleasure spiraled higher and higher to the point of pain as sensation after sensation overcame me. I didn't need him to be inside me. I just needed *him*, for as long as he'd have me.

"Elijah!" I cried out as I came, fully clothed. His fingers dug into the globes of my ass as he followed not a second later. I panted into his chest, where I'd collapsed like an overcooked noodle, and the sob I'd been holding back slipped free. Thankfully, it was muffled and hopefully unidentifiable.

How much more would Elijah hate me when the truth came out if he knew I was hopelessly in love with him?

Chapter 27

Elijah

I LIGHTLY COMBED MY fingers through Josh's hair. He mumbled in his sleep and burrowed deeper into my shoulder. Stars, this man was something else. I still didn't know what had come over him last night, or if I even wanted an answer to my question anymore.

Does it really matter who else he is?

A deeper part of me worried that the secrets he kept were capable of tearing us apart, the same part that feared if I tried to tell him how I was starting to feel, he'd pull away. I definitely didn't want that, especially not when it felt like we were really getting each other. More than the sex, I enjoyed spending *time* with Josh. He had a dry sense of humor, we shared several interests, and sometimes when he looked at me it seemed like something else was there. Of course, that last could have been the wishful dreaming of a wolf wanting his bonded partner to actually feel the same way.

I sighed and placed a light kiss on the top of his head.

There has to be a way to convince him it's not just the bond. Fuck, why did I have to make such a big deal?

A sudden brush of lips on my chest brought me out of my troubling thoughts. I glanced down to find Josh's beautiful green eyes gazing at me past dark lashes. I traced the side of his face with my knuckle as I simply stared at him.

"What?" he asked softly.

"Have I told you how much your eyes look like the forest?" He blinked, but didn't respond. "They really do. Sometimes I wonder if I look hard enough if I can actually see the different trees," I whispered.

He shifted in my arms and looked away. "Tad poetic for first thing in the morning, don't you think?"

"You've seen the essays I write."

"So you're suggesting it's par for the course?" He chuckled. The easy sound was a beautiful thing to hear first thing in the morning. "Still arguably too early for such things."

"Speaking of early, I'm amazed you're still here."

He instantly stiffened. "Is that a problem?"

"No," I responded with a smile. "Usually by now you've tried to sneak away without my noticing."

"It's my day off," he mumbled as he stretched languidly beside me.

I rolled us so that he lay beneath me. "You won't hear me complaining," I said, gliding my hand down his side.

His eyes lidded as my touch brought warmth to his cooler skin. "Mm," he hummed.

"Like that, eh?"

"Yes," he moaned, arching off the bed.

The sound was too delicious to ignore. I leaned down and captured his mouth and his groan when my hand found its destination. He tangled his fingers tightly in my hair, urging the kiss deeper even as the rest of his body came to life.

I lived for how out of breath he already was. "It's almost as if you like my hair or something," I teased while I lazily stroked his length.

"Or something," he quipped right back. He gasped as my teeth grazed his jaw on my way to his ear.

"Honesty, Josh," I whispered, my lips brushing the shell of his ear as I tightened my grip on the next stroke.

His body jolted as if I'd given him an electric shock, and he yanked my head back. There was a wildness in his eyes that spoke of pure animal need. "I fucking love your hair," he growled, then promptly conquered my mouth with a savage kiss, his teeth pulling at my bottom lip as his nails dug deep into my flesh.

My brain completely short-circuited. It was a turn of phrase, nothing more, but fuck if it didn't damn near undo me to hear the word "love" come out of his mouth.

He bucked into me, grounding me back in the moment. "Elijah," he moaned when I released him to pursue a different prize.

I growled more than groaned into his neck. There was no way I could have ever prepared for the effect Josh saying my actual name would have on me. When I was relatively sure that I wouldn't come undone just from looking at him, I shimmied further down.

A flush ran up Josh's torso while his chest rose and fell in heavy breaths. The green of his eyes was all but gone, swallowed whole by his pupils, and his hands sought to touch whatever part of me they could reach. His breath caught as I lifted his leg to place a kiss on his inner thigh. He said something, his head rolling back, but the words were an unintelligible garbled mess.

"What was that?" I asked, still lavishing attention on the captive appendage.

The wildness I'd seen earlier seemed to have taken complete control over him. "I want you."

The husky confession wrapped itself around me twofold, and I moaned. "That might be the hottest thing anyone has ever said to me."

He tried to scoff, but was too far gone to be believable. "I seriously doubt that's the first time anyone has said that to you."

I tugged him closer, and his eyes fluttered in anticipation. "True. But it's the first time I could really believe it." His mouth opened, and I claimed it at the same time I claimed the rest of him. Thanks to another full night of intense lovemaking, he was plenty capable of taking me without added prep.

The pending argument dissolved into a deep groan that reached through my core and sent the bond roaring to life. No, not the bond, *me*. The two weren't separate. The bond hadn't made any of this happen. I'd fallen for Joshua Hart, because I was *always* going to fall for Joshua Hart.

Joshua

"What's going through that head of yours?" Elijah's soft words came from somewhere above me, but I kept my gaze fixed on the white ceiling.

I'm in love with you.

My heart squeezed painfully. People who had done the things I had didn't get happiness, didn't get love. I closed my eyes and fought the tide of emotion threatening to drown me. Elijah deserved so much better than me, but thanks to the bond, he would never have it. I'd been content with my life before coming to Adler Springs, not happy by any stretch of the imagination, but content enough. I knew what my place in this world was and knew how it would inevitably end. I'd never had any delusions about that. But now it wasn't just my life I was ruining. It was Elijah's.

He moved, and a rush of cold slipped along my body, only to be banished once more by his touch. "Talk to me, moonbeam. Tell me what you're thinking."

"I don't deserve you." The unfiltered honesty flew out, and a renegade sob threatened to follow. I quickly turned away before he could see any more evidence of my emotional turmoil.

"Hey." I ignored the plea and bit the inside of my cheek, hoping the flare of pain would stave off the pending breakdown. "Josh," he tried again, more forcefully.

"We've missed breakfast," I pushed out.

"First, there's this fancy thing called brunch. Second, stop trying to dodge me."

When Elijah caged me between his arms, I didn't know what scents he might be picking up or even if my face was in any way resembling neutral. Inside, I was a riot of conflicting emotions. I wanted to tell him everything, including the horrible truth. I'd take whatever punishment he saw fit, if only it meant I wasn't lying to him anymore. My mouth opened to do exactly that when he spoke.

"Deserve or not, you have me. That won't ever change. However..." Doubt rippled across his face. He dropped my gaze and swallowed hard. "Humans aren't beholden to the bond. You've been great with all of this, you really have. But... it would be cruel to expect you to honor something simply because I have to."

I blinked at him and sat up straighter. "What are you saying?"

He took a deep breath and let it out slowly before finally meeting my gaze again. "I'm saying if you want to see other people, you can. Just... just don't let me know, okay?"

"What?" I hissed. "No. I wouldn't do that to you." Elijah looked taken aback by my adamant refusal. I pushed away from him and started scrambling out of bed, too angry to hold still.

"Josh."

"No. How could you even suggest such a thing? I'm not a *total* monster. I do have *some* morals." I yanked on the nearest pants I could find.

"Josh, please stop. I didn't mean to offend you. I just thought..."

"Well, you must have thought wrong. If you don't want me here, then just fucking say so," I snapped.

There was a loud sound of sheets ruffling, and Elijah's obscene warmth enveloped me from behind. "Please, moonbeam, stop. It's not that I don't want you here. I do. I want you here all the time. You're literally the only reason I've even made it through the last week."

"Is that you talking, or the bond?" I asked, my heart splintering under the stress.

His hold loosened, and I stepped away. When I turned around, he looked as if I'd slapped him. "Me, Josh. I'm the one who wants you here."

I stared back at him, still fighting my anger. It was times like this that I wished other people were as beholden to the truth as I was. "I can't trust that."

An echoing anger sparked in his eyes. "I don't give a new moon what you trust. When I say I want you here, it's because I do. Fuck the bond, Josh. Me," he practically shouted.

I let out a huff, not sure what to say to that, and turned to leave. Almost instantly, his hand encircled my arm and pulled me back. I didn't bother trying to break free.

"Maybe, if we could be somewhere beyond this house, I could show you that," he persisted.

"And where would we go, Elijah? I've been to more places than I can name offhand. I'm a government agent. I'm identifiable."

"You could wear a disguise," he suggested.

There was no way he could have known how much that would hurt. I dropped my gaze, officially no longer angry. "Is that what you want?" I whispered because, at the end of the day, I'd do whatever it took to make him happy.

He released my arm, and suddenly both of his hands were on my face, forcing me to look at him. "You're right, that's not what I want. I want to be with *you*, not a cheap imitation. We'll just have to get more creative with dates here. One way or another, I will prove to you—"

My eyes widened as a message marked urgent popped up in my periphery.

"What? What is it?"

"I... I don't know. Give me a minute?" He nodded, but looked uncertain. I leaned forward and brushed his lips with a kiss. "Just a minute, baby. I'll be right back." He dropped his hands, and I stepped into the bathroom, closing the door behind me. The moment I shut the door, I played the recorded audio.

> *Detective Hart, your expertise is urgently requested on assignment. Suspect Twenty-Nine-Thirteen has been located. Detective Sasha Cartwright is no longer in play. Respond immediately.*

I dialed through the coded message and was instantly connected. "Detective Joshua Hart, reporting."

"Detective Hart, your prompt response is appreciated. How soon can you be in Raleigh?" the cold, professional voice asked.

I glanced at my bio-clock and did some quick mental math. "Depending on portal allocation, two hours."

"Portals will be cleared. A specialist will be sent to your local residence."

"No," I nearly shouted in sudden panic.

"Is there somewhere more preferable?"

"The neutral territory for the Klamath pack. I can get to it with less speculation, and the area should be clear."

"Understood."

The call ended, and I sagged against the counter.

There was a light rap on the door. "Is everything okay?"

Son of a moon-bitten Howler. How the fuck am I going to tell Elijah?

Elijah

"I'm going with you," I repeated, taking out a duffel.

"What part of 'serial killer' are you missing?" Josh argued. He'd stepped into the bathroom to answer a call, and when he'd emerged, he'd already bathed, looking like he'd scrubbed every inch of himself practically raw.

"I won't sit here while you're in danger, Josh. I can't. Not again."

"This is not a debate. You're the Klamath liaison, not the North Carolina liaison. How would we explain your presence?"

"I don't give a damn. Tell them I'm nosy. Tell them I'm paranoid. Tell them whatever the fuck you have to, but I'm going."

"Damn it, Elijah. Do you know the position you're putting me in? The risk of exposure? Not to mention the fact that I'll be taking on a known lycan serial killer who has been evading capture for close to five years. My life will be in danger."

I stopped shoving random things into the bag and walked around the bed to stand in front of him. He was panting from the force of having an argument we both knew he didn't have time for. I'd heard him say two hours. They'd expect him sooner than that, and the neutral territory would take at least thirty minutes to get to.

I cupped the side of his face, and he instantly leaned into the contact, his eyes silently pleading with me to give it up. "Don't you see? That's why I have to go. I can't sit here for days and wonder if you're okay. And if you... if you die, the bond severing is not how I want to find out. Please, Josh. You don't have time to argue. We'll figure this out."

"Fine. I'll figure out something."

I released him and turned to resume packing.

"But.."

My hands instantly stilled as I lifted my gaze once more to meet his.

He looked defeated, but also incredibly determined. "But you have to do as I say. We are walking into a hostile situation. We will not be the only ones there. And above it all, no matter what happens, you cannot interfere. Do you understand?"

"Yes." I'd agree to pretty much anything if it meant he'd let me go with him.

Josh shook his head. "I mean it, Elijah. No cheeky comments. No subtle grazes. No staring. Nothing. And if you interfere in any way with the hunt, you will be arrested, prosecuted without trial, and likely tossed into a deep, dark place that no one will ever think to look for you. Can you handle that?"

There was no way to hide the fear that undoubtedly blossomed on my face as Josh listed each thing. That didn't stop me from nodding. "I won't interfere. And I won't do anything that could potentially put your life in danger."

Josh's shoulders sagged, and I wondered how much of that he found remotely reassuring. He dropped his head back and began massaging his temples with his fingers. "This is not a good idea." Finally, he took a deep breath and straightened up. "There are things I need to pick up for the mission. I'll meet you at the neutral ground in half an hour."

"Josh." I surged towards him and captured him with a kiss, likely the last one we would get for days. "Don't leave without me."

He squeezed my hands, which had somehow made it back to his face. "I won't."

Chapter 28

Joshua

The receiving agent's eyes widened in apparent surprise as we cleared the pop-up portal.

"Not a damn word," I growled at Agent O'Hara.

Despite being several years my senior, he wisely averted his gaze and kept his mouth shut. However, that didn't prevent other curious eyes from drifting in our direction. The makeshift base of operations was bustling with activity, and I doubted there was a single soul that hadn't noticed the extra body in tow.

Fuck. I knew this was a bad idea.

A distinct pop accompanied a shift in air pressure, signaling the closing of the tear we'd used to cross hundreds of miles in the blink of an eye. The medic rushed past us to provide support to the witch who brought us here. Agent Sheena Warner's travelling skills were exceptional, but such a long distance on short notice took a toll.

I watched the on-duty medic escort Agent Sheena away, then glanced back to find Elijah trying so hard not to stare at everything he might as well be gaping. At least he wasn't staring at me... for now.

I should have locked him up with Tommy.

"What's with the luggage?" Agent O'Hara asked, noting the duffels we'd brought.

I returned my focus to where it belonged. "I was already working a case in Oregon when the call came in. Is Detective Cartwright out for good?" I asked to divert him.

"Yeah. This bloke's nasty. Got the drop on her when her firearm jammed."

I shook my head. That was exactly the reason I refused to rely on the damn things. An agent should have a veritable arsenal of weapons at their disposal for that exact situation. "Anything else I should know?"

"Starling wants to see you. She's pissed about this whole thing. Apparently, Sash broke protocol."

A violent sneeze ripped through the air behind me. I barely checked my groan. We hadn't even made it five minutes without Elijah drawing attention to himself. "Get me a medkit."

O'Hara looked from me to where Elijah was rubbing his nose. "Who is he again?"

I rolled my eyes. "Patrick O'Hara, Elijah Bennett, Klamath Pack Liaison. Bennett, Agent O'Hara. Now are you going to get the medkit, or do I need to ask again?"

O'Hara paled slightly, but impressively maintained his composure. It took him less than a minute to find and pass me a discreet black bag, then make himself scarce.

As I dug through the kit, Elijah asked quietly, "Is everyone here afraid of you?"

"Mostly." I pulled out a hermetically sealed tube.

He raised an intrigued eyebrow. "And who isn't?"

"Director Starling." I nodded over my shoulder at where a petite woman dressed in a sharp black suit was supervising a crew of agents. "Don't let her size fool you. She was one of the first Lycan Detectives to survive the oath-taking. She's fierce, qualified, and has a reputation for not taking shit."

"Sounds like someone else I know," he teased.

I shot him a glare. "I'm going to break this under your nose. Breathe deep."

He eyed the tube dubiously. "What's it for?"

"The smell that's making you sneeze is burned ozone. Agent Warner tore a hole in reality."

Panic lit his eyes. "Is that safe? What about radiation? Or the fabric of reality?"

I leveled a look at him. "You wanted to come. Now breathe." The tube snapped easily, and its contents vaporized.

Elijah stared unblinkingly at me as he breathed in the concoction. The medicine immediately set to work, and he let out a sigh of relief. "Thanks. That was unpleasant."

I shook my head and disposed of the used container, then deposited the med kit on the corner of someone's temporary desk. "Stand over there and try not to talk to anyone. Don't touch anything, either."

He ceased his perusal of the area to look at me. "Am I the only lycan here?"

"No, so mind your manners and stay out of trouble. They may be pack wolves, but they will not hesitate to take action against you."

"Yes, sir," Elijah rumbled, sarcasm practically dripping off the words.

I let out a sigh and used the excuse of walking past him to whisper in his ear. "Please, baby." I wanted to say more, to explain that I understood how hard this was, but I didn't dare. Lycans weren't the only things with above-average hearing.

His huff was all the confirmation I had as I stalked across the space to meet Director Starling for my debrief. With each step, the mantle of Lycan Detective Joshua Hart settled back into place, and I struggled to figure out when I had dropped it.

"Detective Hart, I see you have joined us... with company." There was nothing warm or hospitable in Director Starling's greeting. "Your companion was neither mentioned nor approved. Care to explain yourself?"

I feigned inspecting my weaponry. "Bennett is the Klamath Pack liaison."

"That still doesn't explain his presence or why you saw fit to bring him here without prior clearance."

I dropped the pretense and looked straight into Director Starling's slate-blue eyes. She may have been almost a foot shorter than me, but the woman did not lack presence. "The urgency of the call left little room for following protocol. He is concerned about what could transpire in my absence. If I don't return to Adler Springs, the culprit will likely evade justice."

"Your reports suggest you do not believe the lycan in custody is responsible."

"I know he's not."

Starling let out a barely audible sigh and returned her attention to the reports she'd been perusing when I approached. "Even with the damn oaths, we face skepticism."

I nodded, familiar with the frustration. "Will you send him back?"

"No, I don't think I will. Don't give me that look, Detective Hart. If you didn't want him here, then you should have tried harder to stop him. Besides," the corner of her mouth curled in a half-smile, "even I can appreciate the irony of you having a tail."

My face fell into a frown to hide my shock. Of course, everyone here would think it was hilarious that the most notorious anti-lycan person in the agency was stuck with a furry stalker. *Damn you, Elijah.* "I'm sure there's something I can do to curb the rumors. Perhaps kill the killer?" I gestured at the accumulation of data.

"Perhaps. Though you should know there are at least three bets running on what the situation is."

I desperately wanted to ask what the lead suspicions were to explain his presence. "He wouldn't take no for an answer. I didn't trust him not to do something reckless in my absence."

"Like break out the suspect?"

More like find a way to follow me across the country. "At least if he's here, I know where he is."

She sniffed. "It's been a while since you've had a liaison that was so dedicated to their position."

"You have no idea," I said before I could rethink the logic of such a response.

"Are you losing your edge, Detective?"

"Suppose we'll find out tomorrow." I picked up the nearest data tab, which happened to be a detailed terrain map.

Elijah

What am I doing here? Why did Josh let me come?

I struggled to keep my panic at bay. Over the last two days, I'd learned exactly who Josh had been called in to take care of and what had happened to his predecessor. It was one thing to be told he might die. It was another to *know* that someone else already had. Brutally, without mercy, and with barely enough left to identify the body.

Goddess, give me strength. I think I'm gonna be sick.

To top it all off, the most contact I'd had with Josh had been when our eyes had met this morning. The gaze had lasted a hair longer than was probably appropriate, then he'd been back to business. Logically, I knew he needed to be focused and couldn't afford distractions, but it didn't stop me from hoping for something more.

I should have kissed him longer. What if that's the last time I ever get to touch him? What if he dies today? What if—

"First time at a hunt?"

My obsessively morbid thoughts blasted apart, and I sent up a silent prayer that my face was a mask of neutrality as I turned to confront the source.

The owner of the peculiar statement laughed good-naturedly and extended a gloved hand. "No need to look so glum. Name's Remus, and I promise I'm not here to arrest you."

I eyed the guy for a moment before accepting the proffered hand. He wore full tactical gear, including a very sizable ballistic weapon strapped to his back, but he smiled pleasantly, and most surprisingly, he was a lycan. "Elijah Bennett."

"So how'd you do it?"

"Do what?" I asked, confused as ever. Josh had warned me that there were other lycans here. He'd failed to mention they were part of the perimeter team.

"How'd you get the hard ass to let you come?"

"I didn't take no for an answer."

He nodded in appreciation. "You must have a real pair on you."

I made a noncommittal noise and returned my attention to where Josh was getting ready for the "hunt" as my new companion put it.

We stood in silence for a few minutes when Remus looked at me out of the corner of his eye and said, "He's really incredible to watch work, almost like living art."

I glanced at the soldier, curious about where he was planning to go with this. "You've seen him work before?"

"Oh yeah. A few times. Of course, it also doesn't hurt that he's nice to look at. Definitely the prettiest man I've ever seen."

Rage sprang up, and I had to force the wolf to back down. "You and he…" I trailed off, unable to finish the question.

He laughed. "Oh, *stars*, no. I just know beauty when I see it. Shame he's such a damn stick in the mud."

The tension in my shoulders eased slightly. I knew better than to correct his assumption that Josh was incapable of fun, but it didn't stop my gaze from seeking him out again. He was doing what looked to be his fiftieth weapons check.

Let it be enough.

"I'll be damned."

"What?" I asked, tearing my gaze away from Josh.

"You're bonded."

Cold slithered down my spine. "What are you talking about?"

"You and the detective," he clarified, perfectly at ease with the bomb he'd dropped.

"That's ridiculous. I'm the liaison, that's all," I argued.

He scoffed. "You can drop the act. No one can hear us." He tapped on a tiny blue light shining on his armored vest. "Silencer. Turned it on when I came over. Everyone in the unit has one to make sure we don't give away our positions and ruin the mission."

I swallowed thickly and stole another glance at Josh. He was talking with the director-woman again as well as a few others who were pointing at maps. "How—" My voice cracked, and I had to try again. "How did you know?"

Remus gave me a sympathetic look. "My sister's bonded. To a selkie, if you can believe it. The family was *not* happy about that. Anyway, she looks at her partner the same way."

"And how is that?"

"Like she hung the damn moon."

"Does, uh... does anyone else know?" I asked, terrified of the answer. *Josh is going to be furious.*

Remus scoffed again, his face twisting into a dismissive smirk. "This pack of skirt-chasers? They aren't interested in anything that they can't blow up or pour into a glass. Also, fairly sure I'm the only one with a bonded wolf in my family."

"Oh."

"I'm not gonna tell anyone if that's what you're worried about. Though it sucks that Kitty won the pot and won't be able to claim it."

"The pot? Are y'all betting on why I'm here?" I was more worried than relieved by his weird assurance.

"We're military. We bet on *everything*. But that's not the pot I'm talking about." I must have made a face, because he laughed again and added, "No one has ever seen Detective Hart with anyone, like ever. Kitty held out that he was just too damn pretty not to be gay. He is gay, right?"

I smiled, somehow at ease with the overly chatty agent. "To use his own words, there is nothing straight about him."

Remus erupted into a loud laugh that immediately had me looking around to see who'd noticed. Surprisingly, no one. There were a few glances in our direction, but nothing overly curious.

"Ah, man, that's great," he said, sobering. "You gotta admit, it's pretty ironic that he of all people bonded with a lycan."

I rolled my shoulders. "Can I ask you a personal question? About your sister?"

"Sure thing."

"Actually, it's about her partner," I clarified.

"Okay, shoot."

"Selkies can't bond, can they? It's just lycans, right?" I couldn't believe I was asking a veritable stranger this. Then again, he'd already guessed, and he clearly knew more about it than I did.

"Selkies? No, they have their own version, and I hear demons have something sort of like it, but it's not quite the same as the *knowing* that we have."

"If her partner can't complete the bond…"

"I think I see where you're going with this, and the short answer is, I've never seen two people more in love."

I scrubbed my face. "Sorry, I don't know why I'm talking to you about this. It's just that he might die today, and it's like we didn't even have a chance to figure it out."

"It's cool. To be fair, I may have provoked you and then guessed. And as far as the dying-thing, in all my years, I've literally *never* seen anyone as good as Detective Joshua Hart. Did you know he actually signed up for the Lycan Detective program before they figured out that whole oath business? It's like he was born for this."

"What? I thought the program wasn't that old."

"In the grand scheme of things, it's not. But that man over there put his name on the list when people were still dying from the oaths."

"*Still* dying?" I echoed in disbelief.

"Oh yeah, he's been in specialized training since he was old enough to enlist. Only other person I know who volunteered is Director Starling." Remus placed a warm hand on my shoulder. "Your man is gonna be just fine."

"Thanks."

"No problem. But, just in case, you know you're not allowed to interfere, right?"

I chuckled. "Yeah, Josh was surprisingly explicit about what would happen if I did."

"Josh," Remus repeated in whispered awe. "And what exactly did he say?"

"There may have been mention of a deep, dark hole, where no one will ever think to look for me," I responded.

"Sounds about right. But if you prefer, there's always friendly fire." Remus pointed at the gun slung across his shoulder and gave me a smug grin.

"Did you just offer to shoot me?" Despite the oddity of the suggestion, I was actually tempted. If Josh died today, a bullet would definitely be preferable to a slow, painful death.

"No, I offered to *accidentally* shoot you. Come on, you're bonded to the freakin' meanest Lycan Detective the government has ever spit out. You should know the importance of words." He finished the serious statement with a smile.

I smiled back, unsure of what else to do. He had a point. Words were important. I'd always known Josh couldn't lie, but how many things had he told me and I'd missed because I wasn't paying attention to his careful word choice?

"One more question for you."

I turned a dazed look to Remus, wondering what he could possibly want to know now.

"What's your profession?"

"I have a doctorate in literature and write essays. Why?"

"Damn," he hissed, smacking his palm with a fist. "That's another pot I lost."

I shook my head. "You guys really will bet on anything." He shrugged. "My turn. What are the leading bets why he let me tag along?" I asked, not entirely sure how I would feel about the answers.

Remus held up a hand and ticked off three fingers. "Blackmail, suspect, mole."

"Those are all terrible. A mole? Really?" I asked, affronted. "Which one was yours?"

"I put in that the only way Detective Hart would ever let a lycan tail him like this was if you were a suspect and a flight risk."

Truthfully, it still sounded awful, but at least it was better than blackmail or being a turncoat. "Let's go with that, then."

"How do you mean?"

"I still need a believable cover for why I'm here. Claim the pot and make sure everyone knows."

"They'll want to confirm with the detective," Remus countered.

"Do you really think he'll answer?" I fired back.

Remus let out a low whistle. "You're spending too much time with him. You're doing that creepy blank face he does. But fair point."

Chapter 29

Joshua

I switched on the silencer attached to my vest and walked into the tree line. More than anything, I wanted to look back at Elijah, but it was a risk neither of us could afford. My mother had spies everywhere, and I was under no illusion that the Agency was evading her reach. The look I'd stolen this morning would be the only one I'd get until this was over.

He'll be fine. It's me I should be worried about.

Even with magically silent footfalls, I proceeded with caution. Heat signatures had Suspect Twenty-Nine-Thirteen in the heart of Uwharrie National Forest, but that was another five kilometers yet. Trees closed in around me, the thick evergreen canopy blanketing the ground in shadow. I stepped carefully around a patch of dry leaves and stuck close to the massive trunks. The spell that masked the sound of my passage only extended so far. One misstep and the entire forest would know I was here.

I forced all thoughts of Elijah from my mind and centered my focus on the hunt. My entire life had trained me for these types of situations. Except now I had something to live for. I couldn't be reckless and take the chances I normally would. Every attack would have to be precise. I wasn't sure how thorough the bond was. Would Elijah know if I got hurt or only if I died? Either way, I couldn't risk the chance that he'd come barreling in here to save me. Which meant I had to take down one of the most violent and elusive lycans in history without getting so much as a scratch on me.

No problem.

My foot slid on a damp patch, and I caught myself on a trunk. The dry bark scraped along my side with an awful sound that I prayed only I could hear. I let out a slow breath and peered around the massive pine. A shadow of movement caught my eye, and I froze. Without sound or smell, I was invisible to all but actual sight.

A hulking form lurched free of the undergrowth. At first, all I could make out was a blob of darkness, then it shuffled closer to a ray of light. The sun shone on a blond coat matted with blood and dirt.

Found you.

I leaned a little further out to get a better estimate of his size. Stats on a data tab never compared to the real thing, and he already looked larger than what the reports had stated. Upon closer inspection, the misconception was due to his dragging a deer nearly twice his size. Sixteen ivory points shone wickedly in the light, a sharp contrast to the deer's red coat.

My mouth went dry. Red deer weren't common in this area. Which made the impressive buck dying between the massive jaws not just any deer—it was a *hart*. Suspect Twenty-Nine-Thirteen was as cunning as he was cruel. That animal wasn't a meal. It was a message.

He knows I'm here.

He finished pulling the stag free of the underbrush and dropped it with a muffled thud onto the padded earth below, then surveyed the surrounding area.

I quickly ducked back behind the trunk, but not before I caught a glimmer of life from the poor beast at his feet. There was no question. He'd been expecting me. Had I been compromised? Or had he rightly assumed that after killing Sasha Cartwright, I'd be called in? Either way, none of the options were good.

I was still focusing on regulating my breathing and heart rate when a loud snap echoed through the trees, followed by a spine-chilling bellow. My heart slowed as I inched around to get a look, then stopped altogether.

Suspect Twenty-Nine-Thirteen had broken one of the buck's legs and now had his jaws wrapped around its neck once again. Ice swam through my veins as my gaze locked with the chilling blue eyes of the *were* staring right at me. Without so much as a blink, he tightened his hold, and the head went limp. Blood poured freely from between eerily clean teeth. He dropped the lifeless corpse to the ground, where it lay forgotten, its purpose served.

My fingers were already brushing the hilt of a poisoned blade when a ripple passed over his body. I took a hesitant step back, keeping him in my sight. The ripple grew until it looked as if his skin were boiling. I watched in horror as his body shifted from purely canine to some monstrosity in between. With practiced movements, I slipped two daggers free and set them loose in quick succession.

He dodged both with alarming ease despite his body being warped and twisted beyond recognition. His toothy grin was the stuff of nightmares. A sickening crack of bones turned my stomach as his legs and arms lengthened. Skin ripped and fur fell to the floor, leaving a wake of spotty patches. With a heave of strength, he pushed his tortured form up from the ground.

I sent another blade spinning across the distance.

At the last second, he lurched into a bipedal stance, and the dagger missed its mark by a hair's breadth. The disconcerting ripples stopped, and he flexed muscles distorted by the half-change. His grin was a grotesque mockery with too many teeth in a face that had no place in nature.

A nauseating cold settled in my stomach. None of the reports had covered this. No wonder Detective Cartwright had failed. Suspect Twenty-Nine-Thirteen was a fucking anóteros.

"Shit," I hissed and spun away. Of course, he couldn't be an anóteros with a superior sense of smell or hearing. No, he would have to be an allagí with the ability to control his shift.

The faint whistle of something slicing through the air was the only warning I had. I lurched to the side, and one of my own daggers embedded itself in the trunk before me. It was still vibrating when I ripped it free in an explosion of bark and ran.

Elijah

Josh came tearing out of the forest like a bat out of hell.

Instinctively, I lurched forward only to have a solid grip tighten around my shoulder. "Aren't you going to do anything?" I asked under my breath, not that I needed to while the silencer was on.

Remus shook his head. "Like I told you earlier, this is his show. We are the last line only."

"But—"

The crashing of branches cut my argument short. I swiveled back to find Josh squaring off with a lycan that seemed to be stuck in the middle of his shift. I'd heard of *weres* that could hold that twisted form, but never seen it. Certainly, no one in my pack had ever possessed the rare gene, and I couldn't imagine why anyone would want to. It looked horribly painful.

I tore my gaze away from the hulking beast and focused on Josh. Despite his heavy breathing, only the tension in his shoulders betrayed his anxiety. He flexed his hands loosely at his sides. That's when I realized all of his firearms were missing. All three holsters were empty, and the visually apparent daggers were gone.

Defenseless. Josh is defenseless.

I tried to break loose, but Remus's grip tightened. Panic seized my heart as the twisted lycan advanced. I couldn't do it. It had been a mistake coming here. I couldn't simply stand by while he died. I had to save him.

"Easy, buddy." Remus's calm voice whispered past the roaring in my ears. "He's not done yet."

Sure enough, while I'd been panicking, Josh had manifested two more daggers. The twisted lycan leered at the feeble defense and leapt forward. Josh ducked and slid beneath the monstrosity, stabbing a dagger into the creature's ankle before emerging unharmed behind it. The lycan let out a roar that sent birds erupting from the trees in an echoing cacophony. Josh rolled out of reach as a long, clawed hand landed where his torso had been only moments before. The talons dug deep and came free with a spray of dirt.

I could practically feel the rage-filled growl as the lycan spun to confront Josh again. The memory of Josh's terrifying ghost story swam to the forefront.

Thirty seconds. He only has to stay out of reach for thirty more seconds.

Unfortunately, the twisted *were* had no intention of letting the attack go unpunished. With a savage growl, he charged. I prayed Josh would move, run, anything, but Joshua Hart had never backed down from a lycan and it didn't look like he was about to start now. The lycan pulled up short, angling to the side at the last moment and raking his razor-sharp claws through the air.

With the ease of a dancer, Josh spun inside the attack and sank another dagger into the *were*'s thigh. Josh's elbow sank into his gut, cutting short his howl of pain. Momentarily out of breath, the lycan was powerless to prevent Josh from slipping free of the close quarters. By the time he recovered, Josh already had two more daggers at the ready.

The lycan pulled the dagger free of his leg, and a ripple passed over him. Patches of fur grew and disappeared, and the wound stopped bleeding.

My eyes widened with sickening understanding. Somehow the monstrosity had enough control to access the life-saving healing that only manifested during the change. And judging by how tight Josh's stance had become, he'd just come to the same conclusion.

"Fuck," Remus hissed beside me.

Josh sprinted toward the lycan.

Remus's arms wrapped around my chest like a vice.

"No!"

My shout went unheard. It was pointless. Josh couldn't hear me, not while I was standing so close to Remus. I struggled against his hold again with little hope of success. Fear strangled my heart, and I stopped breathing altogether as the distance between them closed. Somewhere along the way, Josh's daggers had vanished again, meaning there was nothing between him and certain death.

Ten meters.
Five meters.
Three.

The lycan grinned in anticipation, glistening ropes of saliva dripping from a misshapen jaw. His blue eyes glittered malevolently in the afternoon light while the love of my life raced towards his ultimate death. The lycan leaned forward, claws prepared to eviscerate the man I'd never expected to fall for, the man who'd completely changed my life in all the best ways, and the man who would never know what he really meant to me.

Between one step and the next, Josh left the ground, gaining just enough air to evade the lethal talons. He sailed over the lycan's shoulder, narrowly evading the lethal reach. But where was he going to go? The tree behind the lycan meant that even if Josh made it clear, he'd end up hitting the trunk.

I gasped in shock as he snagged a low-hanging branch and used its elasticity to reroute his trajectory. In the blink of an eye, he was speeding back towards his opponent, feet first. The lycan turned with supernatural speed, mutated hands ready to grab Josh out of the air, but he wasn't fast enough.

Josh's feet landed with a crack dead center of the lycan's barrel chest. The force of the blow sent them both crashing to the ground. Josh followed the momentum and landed perched on the beast's chest with a snarl. When he pulled his hands back, there were two daggers blossoming out of the *were*'s chest.

It wasn't until he stepped free that I let out the breath I'd been holding. I'd never seen anything like it. Not only had Josh survived, but there wasn't a scratch on him. Relief, pride, and desire swept through me in a heated rush. I'd never been a violent person myself, but, fuck if that wasn't the hottest thing I'd ever seen in my life.

"Fuck. I think I popped a boner," Remus echoed my thoughts aloud.

A low warning growl rolled out of me. "That's my mate you're talking about, and you'd do well to remember it."

Remus held up both hands in surrender, his affable demeanor suddenly serious. "Easy, Alpha. I meant no harm. Just saying, I haven't seen a fight that impressive in years. Pretty sure half the unit got one."

"I'm not an Alpha," I growled, my hackles still firmly up despite his obvious attempt to roll over.

He raised an eyebrow. "You sure about that?"

Chapter 30

Joshua

I WIPED A HAND over my face and stared at the digital account of what had transpired earlier today. The page and a half report failed to capture the terror I'd faced in those woods. But no one wanted to know how I'd been baited or how I'd nearly lost every weapon, including the three firearms—none of which had been fired. They would eventually, but not right now. Right now, they wanted to know that the serial killer referred to as Suspect Twenty-Nine-Thirteen, who had been plaguing the East Coast for five years, was finally dead.

"Good work, Detective."

I glanced up at Director Starling. That was high praise coming from her.

She rested her hand on the desk I'd commandeered while she skimmed the meager report. "This will suffice for now. I expect the complete account by the end of the week."

"Understood, Director." I straightened up from my chair. The rejuvenation potion had done wonders for my fatigue, but I wouldn't feel completely right until I knew Elijah was okay. He'd been suspiciously absent after the hunt.

"Go home, get some rest. An agent escorted the Klamath liaison to the hotel. Apparently, there is some concern that he's a flight risk?"

I repressed a wince. There was no telling what rumors had circulated about why Elijah was here. "I'll pick him up on my way out." The director gave a dismissive wave, and I was free to leave.

The car ride to the hotel I'd set Elijah up at took longer than I cared for, but I hadn't been willing to station him any closer. At long last, we pulled up in front of the five-star accommodations that were well outside a government budget. Story held it was owned by one of the original Shadows, though I doubted there was a way to ascertain the rumor's validity.

The agent driving me let out a low whistle and put the hover-car in park. "Want me to wait?"

I stared at the gold-decorated facade, drenched in history. The building was stunning, with a careful eye towards preservation. I planned to at least spend the night, assuming Elijah could stomach looking at me after what he'd witnessed today. The hotel lost some of its appeal as I considered the reception that likely awaited me.

"No." I slammed the door shut behind me, cutting off the agent's response.

The lobby was just as elaborately appointed as the exterior. Normally, I would have devoted time to appreciating the elegant architecture, the exquisite attention to detail, and the breathtaking landscapes in their gilded frames. Tonight, I spared them hardly a glance.

The heels of my boots tapped softly on the marble floor as I made my way to the glass elevators. The ride up was smooth and swift, with only the change of scenery to denote any movement. Seconds later, the doors opened with a release of air, and I stepped out into the carpeted hallway. My gaze instantly fell on the soldier stationed outside our room.

At least the flight risk story is believable.

He snapped to attention when I approached. "Detective Hart."

"At ease, Remus. I take it you were assigned to Bennett?"

"Volunteered," he corrected.

"Did he give you any trouble?"

"I didn't have to shoot him if that's what you're asking." It definitely was not, but it was a comfort. "Great show today, by the way. I don't think I've ever seen you walk away from a hunt without *any* injuries." He cocked his head back at the door. "I'd say your guy has a newfound respect for you."

Fear coiled in my belly. I could stare down the scariest lycan to breathe oxygen in fifty years, but I was afraid of what waited for me on the other side of that door. "I'll take it from here."

"Sure thing." Remus tipped his chin and walked the way I'd come. He stopped at the elevator and looked back.

"What?"

"He's a good guy," he said as he stepped inside and let the doors close.

I let out a breath. The encounter may have been brief, but I felt like I'd run a marathon for the second time that day. Thankfully, it seemed the belief that Elijah was a suspect had caught on enough to warrant a guard.

The scanner was cool against my palm. Once it beeped, I twisted the handle and stepped inside, unsure of what I might find.

Elijah jumped up from his chair and walked over. "About time."

The door shut with a soft snick. "Hey." I tugged at my vest and restlessly smoothed the fabric. "Look, about what you saw today."

"Stop talking."

I gasped as he claimed me with a searing kiss that reached all the way to my toes and reflexively wrapped my arms around his neck as he pulled me tighter. I arched into him, more than willing to give him whatever he needed from me. And he took it. He took it all. Despite the multitude of passionate kisses we'd shared over the last several weeks, I'd never felt more owned.

"I'm confused," I panted when he finally relented.

"About what?" His purr of a growl vibrated against my throat, and I couldn't help but moan. The sound only seemed to encourage him, and he started nibbling along my neck.

"About what? You watched me kill one of your kind today."

"I know. You were incredible. I've never seen anything like it. Just when I thought it wasn't possible to want you anymore." Another growl accompanied his breathy addition as he ground our hips together.

My senses threatened to abandon me. "What?"

"I knew you were good, but shit, Josh," he said, gliding his hands over my hips.

"Is this the bond talking?" It had to be the bond. Right? There was no way Elijah was *impressed*. Or even more ridiculous—turned on.

He pulled back slightly. "No. It's not the bond."

"I don't believe you."

He cupped the side of my face and brushed his thumb along my cheek. Patience and something I was afraid to name filled his cognac eyes. "Oh, moonbeam, how to get you to see?" He placed a tender kiss on my lips. "The way you handled yourself today... I don't know of any lycan that could do what you did." He slid his hands down my arms. "And without a scratch," he added in what sounded strangely like pride.

I shuddered. "But you—"

"Have been attracted to others for similar reasons. Though none of them could hold a candle to what you did today."

My brain had to be malfunctioning. There was no way that smart, sophisticated, *pacifist* Elijah was telling me he was secretly into bruisers. "I killed someone today."

"Correction. You *survived* today. You can keep arguing all you like. It won't change the fact that you are, hands down, the most incredible man or *were* I've ever met. And watching you fucking own that situation might be the sexiest thing I've ever seen."

I chewed on my bottom lip, uncertain how much I should take him at his word. He could lie, true, but why would he? Was it even remotely possible that he could actually want me for... *me*? "Do you really mean that?"

Elijah

The uncertainty in Josh's eyes stabbed at my heart. I stole another kiss. "Yes. lycans are no strangers to violence. It's part of being in the pack. Hell, it's practically in the definition of being a *were*. Deaths may be uncommon, but they're not unheard of. Besides, I'm not the only lycan thoroughly impressed by what you did today."

"Remus. That hardly—"

"It counts plenty. He said watching you was like watching living art. I'm inclined to agree. You're an artist, Josh. A beautiful, deadly, sinfully attractive artist."

This time when I kissed Josh, his mouth along with the rest of his body molded to mine. Hopefully, that meant he believed what I was telling him, because it was true. Surprised as I was, the more Josh displayed Alpha tendencies, the more interested I became.

"How much longer until your scent comes back?"

He looked over my shoulder at his wrist. "An hour and a half if I don't refresh."

"Good." I pulled away, leaving Josh looking put out. "That should be plenty of time."

"Time? Time for what?"

I grabbed his hand and pulled him into the bedroom. He came willingly, but kept a wary eye on me. "Time for a quickie, and then I have a surprise for you."

"Quickie? Surprise? What surprise?"

"It wouldn't be a surprise if I told you, now would it?"

"Surprises aren't typically a good thing in my line of work," he argued.

I tugged him closer to the bed. "Do you trust me?"

He stared at me for a long moment. "Yes."

I could have howled with joy for that one simple word. Instead, I tugged him into me and wrapped him in another embrace, claiming his mouth once more.

"Mm," he mumbled and pushed away. "Still armed." He grabbed my hands and shifted them down to his ass. "That should be relatively safe."

I squeezed the firm globes and loved how his eyes lit up. "There is literally nothing safe about this ass."

He chuckled, and the last of his tension vanished. His hands made quick work of his vest, and it fell to the floor, taking with it the death it carried. "Elijah, I need to tell you something."

"We're kind of pressed for time, moonbeam." My pulse quickened as Josh continued to strip down to nothing before me.

"It's kind of important."

"Could you have told me yesterday? Or a week ago? Could you tell me tomorrow?" I fired off, following his lead.

His jaw worked as he no doubt struggled to find an answer to get his way. "Yes," he finally ground out.

"Then tell me tomorrow."

He let out a wordless growl and tackled me. The plush mattress sank beneath our combined weight. Much as I wanted to take my time, I wanted Josh to have his surprise more. I groaned as he nipped at my sensitizing skin and pulled his mouth back to mine. His returning kiss was every bit as eager as the body pressing into me. I shimmied up the mattress to reach the supplies I'd gotten for us while Josh's fevered touch sought to claim every inch of me.

"I'll take that," he said, snatching the bottle out of my hand. My breath caught as he speared me with a wicked look. I wanted him to look at me like that forever. He took advantage of my distraction to wrap a slicked hand around me. His eyes sparkled with satisfaction as I rolled into his firm grasp. "That's it, baby."

I let out a deep groan. This was *not* going to be a quickie if he was gonna start in on that baby-business in that husky voice. "Come here, you." I wrapped a hand around the back of his neck and brought his lips back within reach. He moaned into me, but his strokes didn't relent. "You're terrible," I gasped, rolling us so he was beneath me.

"Try gifted," he teased with a confident stroke that nearly had me finishing right there.

I snatched the discarded bottle back and sought his hole.

Josh's eyes lidded, and his hand faltered. He arched off the bed as I pressed against his prostate. "Elijah," he moaned.

I tossed the bottle clear and pulled him further down the bed. I positioned my cock at his entrance, then leaned over and tangled our hands together above his head while I steadily pushed deeper into his welcoming heat. Our tongues met in a slow, exploratory kiss that was so unlike the one we'd shared a month ago.

The words "I love you" were already on my lips, then Josh wrapped his legs around me and I forgot about everything else.

Joshua

I plucked at the plum-colored shirt Elijah had somehow acquired for me.

He glanced over from where he was straightening his own heather-gray tee. "What's the matter? Does it not fit?"

"No. It fits fine."

"Then you don't like it."

"What? No. I..." I smoothed the soft fabric. "I like it."

Elijah snorted and walked over. "Then what is it, moonbeam?"

I swear, I forgot how to think whenever he called me that. His cognac eyes shone brightly, waiting for my response. He looked incredible in his dark-wash denim, which was on the grayer side than mine, but no less fitted. "How did you get all of this? *When* did you get all of this?"

Doubt flashed in his eyes. "I had help."

"Elijah..."

"I swear I didn't tell him about the bond. He guessed."

"*Who* guessed?" I asked, then immediately answered my own question. "Remus. Fuck." I turned away, my mind already spinning with ways to mitigate the fallout that was undoubtedly coming our way.

"Hey, no. It's going to be okay. He won't tell anyone." Elijah tried to pull me close.

I shrugged him off. "Why didn't you say something sooner? How am I supposed to get ahead of this now?"

"We were a little busy," he responded with a cheeky grin.

"Damn it, Elijah. We can't be positive he won't tell anyone. That whole damn unit... Did you know they were placing bets on why you were here?"

"Yes."

I stopped pacing. "What?"

Elijah's warm hands encased my shoulders, and he met my gaze. "I'm the one who told him to go with the suspect theory. He even made a big show of getting me back to the room and how he was going to have to babysit until the nice detective could take control of his wayward charge."

I narrowed my eyes. "That's not what he said."

"Okay, he called you prickly and some other less savory words. The point is, he helped us, Josh. *Us*. He won't tell. I know he won't." There was something else in Elijah's eyes besides blind faith, an unshakeable confidence. Only one thing could give him the assurance that a request, or an order, would be followed—Alpha charisma.

He'd denied it at every turn, but there was no doubt in my mind that Elijah had been born to be an Alpha. I swallowed. It was no longer a matter of if. It was a matter of when. Suddenly, I was really glad I hadn't told him the truth earlier. If Elijah knew what I had done when he ascended, it could prevent him from ascending altogether.

"Are we good?" He squeezed my shoulders.

I nodded, not trusting words.

"Then I have an important question for you."

My gaze darted up from where I'd been memorizing the stitching of his shirt.

"Is there a back way out of this place?"

Chapter 31

Elijah

So telling Josh about Remus could have gone better. Now I worried he wouldn't be able to relax enough again to actually have fun tonight, and I desperately wanted him to have fun.

The "Employees Only" access door closed without a sound, and we stepped into an abandoned alley.

"Why does it not surprise me you know the full layout of this place?" I asked to lighten the mood.

"I'm a man of many talents," he responded absently, more absorbed with hiding the evidence of our passage.

I laughed to myself. He sounded so much like he had when we first met, all sharp edges and better things to do. I waited patiently while he brought the security cameras back online.

"Are you going to tell me where we're going now?"

"No."

We kept our distance from each other while we made our way down the street. I would have preferred our fingers to be laced, but if pretending we were strangers meant he would follow, then I'd do it.

His steps slowed as we approached the massive portal hub in the heart of Raleigh. "Elijah."

I turned on my heel to look at him, but didn't stop walking. "Trust me, moonbeam."

He cast a dubious look at the mass of people behind me, then quickened his pace.

I spun back around and wove my way through the milling throng, not worried that Josh might lose me. At last, I saw the right sign and veered off to the side. By the time I stopped and pulled up the data, Josh was by my side.

He cocked his head, confusion plain on his face. "Nebraska?"

"Ever been to Malcolm?" I held my wrist up to the reader so it could access the coordinates.

"I'm not even sure where that is besides obviously in Nebraska."

The portal swirled to life in a dazzling display of blues and purples. "It's outside of Lincoln. But we're not there to wander the streets." Before he could find some way to nix this entire scheme, I grabbed his wrist and led us through.

The world flashed brilliant white, and static raised every hair on my body. Then we were clear, and the portal was gone. I blinked away colored spots to find we were in a small room that frankly looked like a storage closet. The door immediately before us had a large sign that read: *Please vacate. Portal entries are staggered at five-minute intervals.*

"Come on." I tugged Josh forward, and he pulled back.

"Elijah, please tell me where we are." He glanced down at his bio-clock, something he'd been doing more frequently the closer we'd gotten to our destination.

Finally, I understood the source of his anxiety. His potion was due to run out any minute. I stepped up to him and cupped the side of his face with my free hand. "It's okay, moonbeam. I've got you."

Doubt and fear shone in his eyes. Joshua Hart could take down a serial killer with ice in his veins, but the mere thought of leaving the shadows had him looking more vulnerable than I'd ever seen him.

I placed a soft kiss on his lips and gently guided us back towards the door. "Trust me."

Joshua

I took a deep breath and let Elijah take the lead. Trust didn't come naturally to me, but I could do this for him.

We wandered down a long, black-lit hallway with only the occasional person to see us pass. I squeezed Elijah's hand. At some point he'd laced our fingers, a comfort I welcomed. He glanced back at me, his excitement evident, and I offered a wan smile in return. He rolled his eyes and pushed open the last door separating us from whatever the big surprise was.

A wave of sound rolled out. Music pulsed like a heartbeat, thrumming through the floors and even the door at my back. There wasn't a meter to spare in the warehouse packed nearly to the rafters with gyrating bodies.

Every cell in my body went on high alert. Where were the exits? Who was here? What were the threats? How many people could identify me?

I dragged Elijah to the side, far away from the door. People were everywhere, though none seemed fazed in the least when I pushed past them. Brightly colored lights whirled around the room, everything from faerie globes to old-fashioned disco balls.

My heart hammered in my chest as I checked my bio-clock. Only one thing registered: *Out of time.*

I pulled in breath after breath while I scanned the crowd of unknown faces, all of which could see my real one. Suddenly, Elijah loomed in front of me, obscuring the room. He pressed his body against mine, though I wasn't sure if it was to help ground me or hide that I was clearly freaking out.

"What's wrong?" he asked, concern bright in his eyes. "Is it an issue with crowds?"

"Yes," I gasped. "I mean... I just..." My gaze darted past him to the sea of faces.

"Josh, have you never been to a club?"

I dug my fingers into his arms as I tried and failed to control my panic. "I have. I just... I've never..." I had to stop and try again. "I've never done it as *me*."

Understanding lit his eyes. "No one knows you're here. It's a pop-up rave. They only released the location about two hours ago.

I blinked. "How did *you* know about it?"

He smiled and stroked my cheek. "I called up a contact from my days at Dartmouth. She helps create these events. They're exclusive with an insane amount of security in place to protect the patrons."

Despite his explanation, I still couldn't wrap my head around it. I was completely exposed... but I was safe? "Why?"

"I told you. I want to take you out. You said it wasn't possible. So I found a way." He snagged two glowing shots from a passing tray and held one out to me. "What do you say?"

I stared at the concoction that seemed alive. My hand shook slightly as I accepted it. We shared a look, then drained our glasses. The shot was like sparklers going down and tasted like nostalgia.

Elijah's mouth twisted in a grimace. "I forget how funny those are going down."

I shook my head and couldn't help but laugh. Magic shots were always weird.

"Watch this." He took my empty cup and flipped it over to stack on top of his. The moment the two rims met, the glasses morphed into an iridescent bubble that floated up to drift over the crowd.

I smiled, watching it go, then turned my gaze back to Elijah. "Now what?"

"Dance with me."

I smiled harder at the man who'd done the impossible. "Okay."

Elijah

It took a little while and a couple more of those weird-ass shots, but Josh finally relaxed. Literally nothing beat the way his eyes had lit up when the post-modern songs had shifted to retro revival.

Another dancer inserted himself into Josh's orbit. Josh merely danced his way closer to me and none too subtly pressed his swaying hips into my waiting hands. "Try someone else. I'm taken," he shouted to be heard over the noise.

I gave him a playful squeeze, enjoying how the guy's mouth twisted into a disappointed frown before he left in search of a more available partner. That officially made five people Josh had sent packing without so much as a second glance. Not that I could blame them for trying. He looked incredible as always, but his carefree exuberance was acting like a beacon to anyone who got too close.

Josh laughed and turned to face me. He draped his arms over my shoulders while keeping a perfect rhythm. Turned out

Josh was also an exceptional dancer. The song changed, and he immediately began singing along.

I spun him out, and he returned without hesitation, looking like he was loving every minute. "Still can't believe you sing," I teased.

His smile was as bright as his eyes. "Loophole," he said with a wink and continued to belt out the ancient love song.

It was obvious he genuinely loved to sing, but as the night went on, I noticed he didn't sing all the songs or even all the lyrics. He was very intentional about which words he voiced. There was a distinct gravitation towards love songs about men, and any that didn't line up perfectly, he either didn't sing or altered the words. My suspicion grew as the latest hit he was crooning spoke of dark secrets and wanting to be loved. Was it possible that Josh's "loophole" had nothing to do with the oaths?

He danced against me, embracing the lyrics with each dip of his hips. I tugged him closer and inhaled his pure scent. I didn't care what excuse he needed to say how he really felt. I'd wait as long as it took. Of course, that assumed my suspicion was right. He spun around in my arms, still lost in the song.

"I love how it's like you're singing to me," I said, dipping with him.

He coasted his hands up my chest as he finished singing the latest line. "Who else would I be singing to?"

I wrapped an arm around his waist, and a laugh escaped him as I pressed his body tightly against mine. "It better just be me," I growled.

His eyes danced with merriment as he stared back at me. "Definitely just you." He reaffirmed the statement with a kiss that left my lips buzzing.

Joshua

Elijah was the perfect dance partner. He seemed to have a sixth sense of movement that kept us perfectly in sync no matter what song played. It was wonderful and beautiful, and I still couldn't believe he'd actually pulled this off. I couldn't think of a single time in my life I'd ever felt so free to be myself, and it was all thanks to Elijah.

The song slowed, and we easily fell into the new rhythm. I twined my arms around his neck and looked into his cognac-colored eyes. Just like the liquor, their amber depths warmed me from the inside out. Everything about Elijah warmed me. It was as if I'd been cold my whole life, and his touch was the heat I'd been missing.

I twirled my fingers absently in his hair as I continued to sing to him about undying love. I hadn't lied when I'd said songs were my loophole. Most people didn't think twice about the lyrics to a song, and I doubted any had considered how the Fae magic binding me applied to them. But Elijah wasn't most people, and I suspected he was close to the truth behind my "loophole". Which meant I was running out of time.

I rested my head on his shoulder and finally admitted to myself something I'd known for weeks: I cared more about this man than I'd ever cared about anybody in my life, including myself. He'd given me something no one ever had before—acceptance. It may have resulted from the bond, but it didn't change that I'd gladly spend the rest of my life trying to be worthy of a man as good as Elijah Bennett.

He would always deserve someone better than me. And he had to learn the truth eventually, both about how I felt and about the things I'd done. But not tonight. Tonight, I wanted to be lost in the arms of the man I loved. Tomorrow I'd tell him the truth, and he'd walk out of my life forever.

Part of me wondered if there was a way to earn his forgiveness and maybe someday his love in return. He'd already surprised me so many times with his thoughtfulness and caring. He understood me in ways I didn't even understand myself, and this evening was a perfect example of that.

I wanted to give him something to show how much I loved him, but there was no physical thing that could ever measure up to how Elijah made me feel. Despite all my wealth and status, there was only one thing of any real value I could ever give him—his life.

I pulled back slightly to look at him, appreciating how the smile on his lips reflected in his eyes. I stroked his cheek and met his steady gaze while I found the words I needed. Once I had them, I said without an ounce of hesitation, "I will never do anything to intentionally harm you without proper provocation."

He smiled at me as if it were some kind of joke. No doubt the words sounded odd, but they were important.

Their weight settled into my bones. When I'd taken my oaths to be a Lycan Detective, I'd been warned not to make promises lightly, not knowing just how deep the Fae magic would reach. But in that moment, I knew without a doubt that I would die to keep that promise.

The humor left his eyes, and they softened. "Josh, I want to tell you something."

"Shhh." I placed a finger over his lips. "If I have to wait until tomorrow to tell you things, then so do you."

He smiled and kissed my finger. "Okay, moonbeam."

My heart skipped a beat. I moved my finger out of the way so I could claim his mouth for myself. His lips moved against mine while his hands sent heat radiating across my back. I tightened my hold on him and deepened the kiss. It didn't bother me that we were basically making out on the dance floor. I'd kiss Elijah anywhere, forever, if he let me.

At last, the need for air won out. I dragged in a ragged breath, but didn't step away even though it felt like my body was on fire.

"You okay?" Elijah's words of concern drifted out like a caress.

I licked my lips, which still held the memory of his touch, and asked, "Can we go home?" His smile could have lit up the night sky. I was still trying to find my breath when he stole it with a wild kiss that reached deep down to the soul he so clearly owned. Coherence was a distant memory by the time he released me.

"Answer me one thing first."

"Anything," I said, and I meant it. He could ask me anything he wanted to know, and I'd tell him the honest truth.

He tipped my nose. "Did you have fun?"

Of all the things he could have asked me, I hadn't expected that one. "Yes."

"Good. Then we can go home."

Chapter 32

Elijah

"Neat trick with the portal." Josh's voice tickled my ear while his hands roamed over me.

I nearly dropped the damned key when those venturing hands dipped lower. "Josh." The admonishment did absolutely nothing to dissuade him.

He placed a hot, wet kiss on my neck that went straight to where my dick was trying to meet his fingers. "Yes?"

"I'm trying... I'm trying..." I shook my head, unable to string two coherent thoughts together with Josh's hands down my pants.

What the hell was in those shots?

"Mm," Josh hummed as his fingers wrapped around my dick. "I'd say you're succeeding."

I chuckled. "Who has the humor of a thirteen-year-old now?"

His eyes glittered maliciously in the porch light, while he leisurely stroked my captive length.

Electricity crackled through my veins. I swallowed Josh's muffled moan as I captured his mouth and pressed him into the still locked door. He arched into me as I moved on to nip along his neck. I'd never wanted anyone the way I wanted Josh. The bond burned brightly inside me, connecting me to the man before me in such a beautiful way.

"I wish you could feel it," I murmured without thinking.

"I am." He laughed.

"Not that." I pulled another sweet kiss from his lips. "The bond. Sometimes I wish you knew what it felt like to be connected to you."

Doubt immediately filled his eyes. His hand stilled. "Elijah, I…"

"Nope. Tomorrow. Tell me whatever it is tomorrow. Right now, all I want to hear from you are moans of pleasure and maybe an idea of how to open this damn door since I seem to have forgotten how to use a key."

"I can help with that." He flashed an evil grin and spun around.

I growled in his ear and pulled his ass hard against my semi-free erection. "*That* is not helping."

He shot me another wicked grin over his shoulder and shimmied. "Sure it is, baby." He placed a palm on the newly installed glass panel by the door, and a light glowed beneath it. "Atlas, open the door." There was a soft click, and then the door swung open.

"I didn't know it could do that."

"Now you do." Josh grabbed my waistband and tugged me inside. Much as it had opened, the door closed and re-locked itself.

"That's nifty."

"Mhm. Now, what do you say we move this party to the shower?" Josh stepped away.

I watched, completely mesmerized, as he peeled off the sweat-soaked shirt. It fell to the floor in a rumple of fabric. I dragged my gaze up his fantastic legs to his now bare torso. Pearly scars crisscrossed the chiseled body, earned from a lifetime of surviving. He looked fucking magical. "Damn, you're beautiful."

"Is that a yes?" He stepped out of one shoe and then the other, each move taking him further down the hall. Then his lithe fingers found the button on his jeans. Pure animal need roared to life inside me when it popped free. He took another step back and arched an eyebrow. Slowly, he slid the zipper down. "That shower won't be half as satisfying by myself."

A denied groan rolled out of me as he hooked his thumbs in the band and worked it lower. "You're killing me."

He paused, and I lifted my gaze to meet his very serious face. "What do you want, Elijah?"

I want you to believe me when I say I love you.

The words were right there. All I had to do was say them. But I'd agreed to wait, so I would. "I want you to stop being such a tease and peel those damn things off already." I loved the way his skin flushed in response.

"Maybe I need help."

I growled and advanced on him. "Like hell you do."

Eagerness edged his light laughter as I picked him up. He wrapped his obscenely long legs around my waist, pushing my already struggling pants lower, and cradled my head while he stole my groan with a fierce kiss.

"Just so you know, if we fall, it's totally your fault."

"Duly noted."

Joshua

Elijah held out an expectant hand. "Pass me a towel."

My gaze traveled shamelessly over his glistening body. The shower had been too delicious for words, with far too much soap and a surprising amount of laughter. I grinned and shook my head. "No. You won't need it for what I have in mind." I blatantly looked him over again, noting that he was already half-hard and wanting more than anything to feel the weight of him on my tongue. "Have I ever told you how much I love that stamina of yours?"

He stepped free of the shower, crowding me against the counter. "No, but you're welcome to show me."

"I can definitely do that."

My towel fell forgotten to the floor as he mashed our mouths together. Steam from the exceptionally hot shower had every surface slick to the touch, including a very wet Elijah. I moaned into him, still hungry for his touch. I didn't care that I was getting soaked all over again from the water clinging to his skin. It was worth it to be near him.

His hand left a molten path as it caressed my side from rib to thigh. He wrapped delicate fingers around the back of my leg and guided it to hook over his hip, then bent to lick the liquid pooled at my throat. I leaned back to give him more room to work.

He continued to go lower until his mouth and that wicked tongue of his circled my nipple. My breath hitched in anticipation when he lowered himself. His head dipped out of sight, and my leg slipped free of its precarious perch. I leaned forward, curious about what he might have in mind with all this buildup. I wasn't opposed to mutual blowjobs, though without a healing tonic on hand, I'd need time to recover for another round. That's when he straightened, holding the dropped towel.

My jaw dropped as he began vigorously drying off. "Who's the tease now?"

"Were you expecting something else?" The gleam in his eye suggested he knew exactly what he was doing.

I blew air through my nose, and he smiled. Then, without warning, he scooped me up and carried me into the bedroom, where he promptly threw me on the bed. I bounced once before his skin pressed against mine once more.

"Better?" he asked, the question buzzing against my lips.

"Much."

"Good." He abandoned my mouth to work along my jaw, then my neck, and onto my chest.

My breath came in ragged gulps as the heat of his touch ventured everywhere, fulfilling the promise he'd started in the bathroom. How had I ever lived without this? No experience I'd ever had came anywhere close to the sheer possession I felt at the hands of this man. The possession I *wanted* to feel.

I tangled my hand in his hair and gripped his shoulder with the other. A loud moan fell out of me as his insanely hot mouth wrapped around my length. My hips bucked mindlessly off the bed, desperate for every ounce of attention he was lavishing. I shuddered uncontrollably with the need to let go as he pulled off and placed a tender kiss on my inner thigh.

"Joshua," he groaned and nipped again at the sensitive flesh.

"No," I gasped.

He looked up, and I could have drowned in his eyes. "What?"

I struggled to find enough breath to speak. "Don't... don't call me that. Call me... Josh," I panted.

His eyebrow quirked up. "You said no one calls you that."

"You do."

He released my leg and moved higher to steal my mouth. "Tell me what you want, moonbeam."

"You. I want you."

Elijah wasted no time fulfilling the request. He'd teased me plenty in the shower, and all it took was a liberal coat of lube on his fat cock, then he drove to the hilt in one smooth thrust. "I swear the Goddess made you for me," he groaned, pulling out a few inches before slamming back home.

"Maybe she did." Maybe she'd made us for each other. He combined a rhythm of slow drags out of my eager hole followed by hard thrusts that threatened to scoot me up the mattress. I used my hold on his hair to bring his mouth to mine for a sloppy, breath-stealing kiss before dropping my head back with a loud moan. "Fuck, baby. That's it."

"You like how that feels?" He snapped his hips harder, and I grunted.

"Yes. Fuck me. Fuck me like you mean it," I growled at him. What I really wanted was for him to fuck me like he loved me. I'd made my peace that any love between us would always be one-sided, but that didn't stop my heart from aching for it.

Our bodies seemed fused together as we chased an ecstasy I knew I'd never find with anyone else. My cry rang out as we hit the pinnacle together and tumbled over in a free fall with only each other to hang onto.

Time became a meaningless drip of sand as we came down. Eventually, I rolled onto my side, and Elijah's heat curled around me. As his arm draped over my waist and pulled my back tight against his chest, I realized I'd never let him do that before. Spooning was such a simple thing, but it required a level of trust I'd never given anyone. I gave it to Elijah freely. I snuggled into him and hoped this amazing feeling could last forever, even though I knew it never could.

He found my hand and laced our fingers together. "Maybe the bond's not so bad," he whispered, nuzzling my neck.

I tightened my fingers and wished I was brave enough to dream. "Maybe."

A sudden impact on the bed lurched me into wakefulness. I peered past rumpled covers to find a pair of cognac eyes dancing with laughter.

"What are you doing?" I grumbled. Between the hunt, the rave, the ensuing bedroom athletics, and no healing tonics on hand, I was beat.

Elijah snaked his hand beneath the covers, bringing with it the warmth I savored. "I know how much you hate waking up alone."

My hum of appreciation faltered. "I didn't use to."

He scooted closer and placed a light kiss on my lips. "But you do now. Don't think I haven't noticed how ornery you are when I've gotten up before you."

Miserable werewolf.

I pulled the covers over my head and burrowed deeper. Elijah chuckled and yanked them back, blasting me with cold air. I frowned at him, and he stole another kiss.

"I know you don't really *do* breakfast, but you think you could make an exception this morning?"

"Depends."

He laughed. "On what?"

"On if you're cooking."

"And if I am?" He raised an eyebrow.

I laughed and stole a kiss of my own before slipping free of the tangled sheets. "Then I suppose I can make an exception." I took advantage of Elijah's stunned silence to pull on some clothes and saunter out of the room. If I were lucky, there was already coffee.

"Did you just admit you like my cooking?" he called after me.

I didn't bother responding, more intent on the promise of caffeination luring me like a siren's call into the kitchen. Sunlight and a fresh breeze poured through the open windows as I drank in the intoxicating aroma of roasted coffee beans.

"Should have known I'd be tossed aside for a fresh cup."

I peered over my steaming mug to appreciate the sexy man stalking towards me. The idea that a man as delicious as Elijah Bennett could be passed over was ludicrous. Certainly not with those broad shoulders, that gorgeous fawn skin, and that irresistible happy trail of gray. "Don't worry, baby. You can still make me breakfast."

He gave me a crooked grin, no doubt having caught my appraising look. "And what if I need something to whet my appetite first?"

I quickly set the half-empty cup to the side. "Oh? Feeling peckish?"

"Maybe." He growled against my neck and nipped lightly at the thin skin.

Heat rushed through me in a wave. "What did you have in mind?"

His exceptionally warm hands slipped past the loose waist of the sweats I'd pulled on. "Just a little appetizer."

Before my quip could find breath, he dropped to his knees, simultaneously pulling the sweats down enough for my cock to bounce free, and swallowed me in one go. I leaned against the counter for support and dropped my head back with a silent "O". Mornings with Elijah were definitely something I could get used to.

An irritating beep rang in my ears. I ignored the transmission. I'd listen to the message later. Elijah's hot hands slid their way up my abs while he continued to make a meal out of me. "*Fuck*," I moaned as he tugged lightly at my balls.

"I know you're not talking to me." The sharp voice sliced through my bubble of bliss.

I immediately pushed Elijah back and straightened up. "Mother."

Seven hells. How could I not recognize the encrypted line?

Elijah gave me a curious expression. I gave him an apologetic one in return and tugged the sweatpants over my now very dead erection. Of all the times for the wretched woman to call, why did it have to be now?

"Where have you been? You're three days late on your report."

"I got called in for an assignment on the East Coast."

"And what are you doing now?"

I looked at Elijah, who was quietly laughing to himself. If I'd been wearing my usual attire, I could have activated the scrambler or even the silencer to eliminate what he might overhear. As it was, our luggage wouldn't arrive until the afternoon thanks to our fancy portal stunt and my lack of foresight. "I'm busy..."

"Are you at the precinct?" she snapped.

"...No."

"Perhaps on pack territory?" The suggestion rankled with skepticism.

"No, Mother." *What I wouldn't give for the ability to lie right now.*

"Wherever you are, it sure as hell isn't your apartment."

Icy dread poured through my entire body. "You're at my apartment?"

"Yes, and I expect you to be as well." The line characteristically died without a farewell.

"She sounds pleasant." Elijah's teasing comment broke me out of my daze.

"Fuck." I wiped a hand over my face, unsurprised to find I'd broken out in a sweat. "Fuck!"

His face clouded with concern. "Whoa. It's just breakfast."

"I need... I need to leave." I knocked over the coffee cup in my frantic attempt to pull myself together. Dark liquid spread over the counter and dripped off the counter to pool on the floor. "Shit."

Elijah stepped in front of me, expressing zero concern for the brown liquid staining his pristine floor. He rested his hands solidly on my arms. "Easy, moonbeam. It's okay."

I shook my head. He was more wrong than he could possibly imagine. "No, it's not." How had I run out of time so quickly? "I have to go." I glanced at the assortment of breakfast items littering the counter. "Maybe we can have breakfast another day?"

"Sure thing. I'll clean this up. You get changed."

"Thanks." I barely choked back a sob. It was over. All of it. This beautiful dream we'd crafted would burst like the impossible bubble it was. Before that could happen, though, I needed to tell him. He needed to know how I felt. I shouldn't have wasted so much time. Now it was practically too late. "Elijah, I..."

He looked at me with those kind cognac eyes I'd fallen in love with the first time I'd seen them. And... I couldn't do it. I couldn't hurt him anymore than I was going to. The knife I'd plunged into my own heart twisted. Unable to give voice to anything, I let it break in silence, and did the only thing I could think of: I kissed him goodbye.

CHAPTER 33

Joshua

I SCHOOLED MY FACE and adjusted the knife I'd tucked into my pant leg. Hopefully, Elijah wouldn't notice it was missing. It was a meager defense, and one I doubted I would use, but better to have it than not. I let out a final exhale and opened the door to my apartment. It came as no surprise that it was already unlocked.

There were people in this world who looked better in person. The woman before me was not one of them. She was awkwardly tall and nothing but sharp angles from her hips to her face. No one had ever made the mistake of calling this woman soft.

"Hello, Mother."

She turned away from something sitting on the edge of the bed. To my horror, it appeared she'd found that damnable box.

So much for an aversion spell.

Her features twisted into a disgusted sneer. "What are you wearing?"

I diligently did not clench my fists or fidget with the hem of the plum-colored tee. "I told you I was busy."

"And I grow weary of your excuses." She dismissed my presence with a mere wave of her hand and continued her perusal of the box's contents.

"Are you looking for something?"

"I wanted to make sure you'd been truthful about being out of the serum."

I gritted my teeth hard enough to hear them creak. "How many times do we have to go over this? I *can not* lie. No Lycan Detective can."

Her gaze lifted to spear me with furious intensity. "I will not tolerate backtalk. Is that understood?"

The argument that I was a grown, fucking man and capable of handling my business died on my tongue. "Yes, Mother."

She sniffed and closed the lid. Her fingers drifted over the bronze plate, now polished to a shine. "You are a disgrace to your ancestors. Hundreds of years our family has fought the spread of the lycan disease, and you can't manage one flea-bitten pack of mongrels. I practically spoon-feed you everything you need, and yet it's not enough. It's never enough."

"Mother, I—"

Fire blazed in her eyes as her gaze zeroed in on me. "You will speak when spoken to, you ungrateful whelp. My patience has been tried enough. You're a coward and a failure, just like your father. How I ever could have expected more is beyond me. But so help me God, you *will* finish your case *and this pack*, even if I have to aim your hand myself." She smoothed her black skirt, then plucked off an imaginary speck of dust from the folds and flicked it aside. Her composure restored, she swept a disdainful gaze over me. "Clean yourself up. You look terrible. Burn all of it."

I vibrated with barely contained rage. The knife at my ankle burned like a brand against my flesh. Despite all the training my mother received over her life, it paled compared to the lessons I'd been forced to learn.

Her heels clicked on the hardwood as she stepped toward me.

I braced myself. Would there be more scathing words or the sting of an actual slap? It wouldn't be the first time, and I didn't expect it'd be the last. Whatever it would be, I would stand my ground. Showing anything she might mistake for fear would only provoke her further.

Her eyes were cold as ice when she stopped before me. "Do not disappoint me again."

I didn't need the knife; I could strangle the bitch with my bare hands. My fingers itched with the need to do just that. If she were dead, then she wouldn't be able to make my life a living hell. Without her interference, I might actually stand a chance of a semi-normal life. A life with Elijah.

Her eyes narrowed as if sensing my thoughts. "Move."

The sickly sweet scent of my mother's perfume washed over me. I'd always hated that smell. Beatrice Harker was better experienced from a distance. Which was why I went along with her schemes rather than fight her more often than not. What was the point? She'd win in the end. She always did. Fighting her only ever made it worse.

I stepped back and turned.

She didn't even spare me a glance as she marched out of the apartment without another word. Her footsteps echoed down the vacant corridor. She bypassed the stairs and headed straight for the elevator.

I stood frozen long after I heard the doors ding. It was only when I was positive she was gone that I dared to move again. My gaze caught on the loathsome box. I stalked across the room and flung the damnable thing back into the closet where it belonged. As it crashed, I released a cry of pure animal rage.

When my vision cleared, I realized something else was sitting on the bed—a black mask. My hand shook as I picked it up. The silk was soft between my fingers. Such a simple thing to have put me in Elijah's path. Except everything about it was a lie. *I* was a lie. I fought back a sob that wouldn't be contained and crumpled to the ground.

Elijah

I knew two things for certain. First, Josh's mother had access to his encrypted line, and second, something was horribly wrong. That his mother could call him no matter the situation made perfect sense, given his line of work. What did *not* make sense was his reaction to the call. I could understand being frustrated at being interrupted or even surprised. But his scent had been neither of those things.

Fear had rolled off him in waves. If that hadn't been disconcerting enough, the cloyingly sweet smell that accompanied it had been. It was unnatural in a way that reminded me of chemicals in perfumes. By the time he'd left, the nauseating scent had dominated the kitchen.

I finished cleaning the spilled coffee and putting the food away, then returned to the bedroom. The bed was the same mess we'd left it. I crawled back beneath the covers where Josh's scent remained captive. The cleaner smells of earth and bergamot, eclipsed the rancid odor clogging my senses, and I breathed a sigh of relief. *This* was the real Josh.

Whatever was wrong was definitely bad. At first it had almost smelled like he feared his mother, but the other had quickly swallowed that scent. That, more than anything she could have possibly said, bothered me the most. It was as if my Josh was being consumed by the rancid odor.

An incoming call beeped in my ear. I'd finally had the wherewithal to assign designated notifications, so knew it wasn't Josh. Not that I expected it to be.

"Hey, Eric."

"What the hell happened to you? You sound worse than when you broke up with Carter. Or did Carter break up with you? I'm still super confused about how that went down."

I huffed a laugh despite myself. Leave it to Eric. I sat up and the comforter pooled around my waist. "You and I both know that Carter was straight, and we never dated."

A snap echoed through the connection. "*That's right*, you were put out because he wouldn't."

"Ass."

He laughed. "We all bark up the wrong tree at least once. The guy was for sure sending mixed signals. So, is that was has you sounding so glum? Bark up the wrong tree again?"

"No, definitely the right tree."

"I knew it! You *are* seeing someone. Is it serious? Why didn't you tell me? Do I know him?"

As Eric fired off questions, I could have smacked myself. "We're kind of keeping things quiet."

"Quiet? What do you mean, 'quiet'? Wait, is he a closet case? Are closet cases still a thing?"

I groaned. "He's definitely not a closet case, and no, they are not. It's just... complicated."

The line was silent.

"Eric? Are you still there?"

"What's going on, Red? We've known each other our whole lives. We don't have secrets."

He was right. It was a totally dick move not to tell him. But how hypocritical would it be if I did? It had been at my insistence that we keep the whole bond-thing to ourselves. Except this was way past that. I couldn't keep this to myself any longer. My unusual interaction with Remus during the hunt just proved how much I needed to confide in someone. Who better than my best friend?

"You're suspiciously quiet over there. It better be because you're coming up with a damn good apology for keeping me in the dark."

"How about I give it to you in person? The apology and the explanation."

Eric snorted. "Fine. Down by the spring? Rain has let up, so it should be more manageable."

The spring. The place where we always shared our secrets and schemes. It'd been where I'd told Eric I had a crush on Malcolm in fifth grade, and it was where Eric had first made the offer to be my Beta. After the influx of rain, it should also be more than loud enough to mask our conversation from any prying ears.

"That works. Thirty good for you?"

"See you there."

Eric was already sitting on a fallen log in usual attire of cargo pants and a dark Henley when I stepped into the open. He waved in greeting and stood to welcome me. "I am so kicking your ass after you spill." His smile belied the threat before he wrapped me in an embrace. "Long time no hang."

I squeezed a little harder than normal. "Yeah, sorry about that, and sorry about not filling you in."

He frowned at me when we stepped apart and crossed his arms. "Whenever you're ready."

I swallowed and went for it. "I'm bonded."

Eric's jaw dropped. "Full moon at midnight, no way. *You* fell in love?"

I shrugged. "That, too."

"Don't mince words with me. They're the same fucking thing, except the bond is like... like..." He floundered for adequate words to encompass everything the bond entailed. "Like the moonforsaken bond is what it's like. Stars, man, that's incredible. Congratulations. When did it happen? How did it happen? Wait, no. Don't answer that last one. I know how it happens. But seriously, details, details. I'm supposed to be your best fucking friend."

One thing that could always be said about Eric was that he was supportive to a fault. "To be fair, you're the first person I've actually told."

His exuberance turned to concern. "You've never wanted the bond. You've literally gone out of your way to make sure it couldn't happen. Why now? What changed?" He paused to glare at me. "What's really going on, Elijah? You were weird on the phone and you still haven't told me who you're bonded to."

"You may want to sit down." I followed my advice and got comfortable on the log he'd vacated.

He joined me, his face a mask of worry. "You're freaking me out."

"I'm freaking myself out."

"Who is it, Red? Who did you bond with?"

"Josh."

There was a notable pause, then Eric barked a laugh. "You're having a go at me." He clutched at his chest. "Damn, man, don't do that. I'm getting too old for that shit." He wiped away fake tears as he continued to laugh. "Woo, for a minute there it sounded like you said you'd bonded with Detective Hart."

I stared at him. "I did."

He blinked. "Joshua Hart? As in *Lycan Detective* Joshua Hart?"

"One and the same."

Eric launched off the log. "Are you out of your damn mind? What were you thinking? How did this happen?"

"Thought you said you didn't want to know that part?"

He glared at me. "Don't be a fucking smart ass. When did it happen? At least answer me that."

I rubbed my nose and glanced down at the forest floor. "Remember that storm last month?"

"Yeah. We lost two windows to that cell."

"That was the day I had to escort Josh onto the territory. He didn't want to go to the House, though."

"Where did he want to go?" Eric raised a reasonable question, and I found it surprising that no one had asked it earlier.

"The cabin where we found Tommy. We kind of got stormed-in."

"You've been bonded for a moonforsaken month and you're just now telling me!"

I returned my gaze to the scarce undergrowth underfoot. Spring was fighting exceptionally hard to take root this year. I kicked away several dead sticks, exposing a fresh sprig of green. "Well, at least now you know why."

Eric let out a long breath and sank down beside me. "Fuck."

"Pretty much."

Eric looked at me for a minute, then followed my lead and stared hard at the ground. It was a lot to take in. The muted sounds of the forest enveloped us. We continued to sit in relative silence until at last Eric asked, "Do you really love him?"

I couldn't fight the smile tugging at my lips. "Yeah, I really do."

He shook his head. "Damn, Red. Know if he feels the same?"

"Nope."

"Does he know about the bond?"

"Yep."

"Shit."

"Pretty much."

"So..." Eric trailed off.

I turned to look at him. "So."

"What do you like about him?"

I couldn't help but laugh. "A lot of things. He's smart, like wicked smart. Really well-read. Witty as hell. And he sings. Can you believe that?"

Eric shook his head, disbelief written across his face. "He seems kind of cold."

"He's not. Not once you get to know him. He cares, like *really* cares. He'd never admit it, of course, but he believes in fairness. He hates inequality. Which seems weird when you think about what his job is, but... I don't know. That's not all he is. You know? Not to say he's not incredible at his job. Because, fuck, man can handle himself in a fight."

"Wow, you've got it bad."

"I guess I do. I love him, Eric. I really fucking love him and I have no idea what to do about it."

"Could always start by actually telling him. I'm assuming the fact that we're having this conversation means that you haven't."

I snorted. "I was going to yesterday, but something came up. So I was going to tell him this morning. Except he bugged out before I got the chance."

"Is that why you were all weird when I called?"

"Partially, but it's more than that. His mother called... while we were occupied."

Eric snickered. "Ah, the in-laws."

I shook my head. "No, it's not that. It's not even that she interrupted us."

"So, what was it?"

"He got...weird, panicky. That's not like him. He's almost always calm. From what I gathered, she sounds like a real piece of work, but that doesn't explain his reaction."

"Maybe she's speciesist, and he knows she wouldn't approve."

I heard the unspoken addition—maybe Josh was speciesist. Was that the real reason he hadn't wanted his colleagues to know?

Is Josh ashamed of me?

Eric stared across the bubbling stream. "Conrad won't take this well."

A shot of panic obliterated my melancholy thoughts. "Conrad can't know. *No one* can know."

"But—"

"No one, Eric."

"Red, you can't keep avoiding this. You're bonded now. You have a *mate*. The next logical step is to challenge for the pack."

"I don't *want* the pack."

Eric sighed and placed a hand on my shoulder. "You can't run from this forever."

"I can try."

CHAPTER 34

Joshua

THE DESK PHONE RANG, and I forwarded it to my personal line. "Detective Hart."

"Good morning, Detective. This is Misty Starr from the Paranormal Forensics Lab in Portland. We have that reconstruct prepared. You should receive the file shortly."

"I appreciate the call. Your lab comes highly recommended."

"It's been a privilege to assist. Should you need anything, reach out."

"I'll do that."

The connection terminated, and the primary data screen beeped. I cleared my desk, propped the projector, and then opened the file. An image of the alleyway sprang to life before me. It was a backdrop only, put together from the images I'd forwarded for reference. Already, their eye for detail had me impressed.

Mack peered across his desk. "What do you have there?"

"Come, take a look." Once the young officer was settled, I waved for the file to play.

The setting remained empty for a time, then Ashton Carr walked backwards onto the scene. The firestick we'd discovered flew up from the ground to burn between his lips.

"Umm..." Mack glanced at me out of the corner of his eye.

"They work backwards from the origin of the DNA. The scene will unfold in reverse." I checked the timestamp. Elijah's estimate of the day was spot on.

Man doesn't give himself enough credit.

I spun the clock back. Ashton returned to the scene eight times. I rolled it back further until the timestamp read the morning after the murder. With a flick, the image slowed to real time. Mack and I leaned forward as Ashton re-entered the scene, looking around anxiously.

"I don't know how you do this. I'm completely lost," Mack whispered, though there was no need to be quiet as the image had no sound.

"Practice. Also..." I waited for Ash to leave the scene, then started playing the file again in reverse.

Ashton Carr hovered by a brick wall that would have been crowded with debris large enough to hide behind. The boards were noticeably absent in the reconstruction, but present in the crime scene photos. He continued to lurk in the shadows until something caught his attention. He licked his lips and tightened his hand around something. Then, with exaggerated movements, he slunk towards his target. He came to a stop, and his mouth moved. Unfortunately, who or whatever he was talking to wasn't visible in the construct. His face twisted into a snarl. Both hands clasped around the invisible object, and he lashed out.

I mentally paired each swing with a set of claw marks on Tina's body. Judging by the angle of the blow, the victim was likely prone when the fatal set was delivered. At last, the frenzied motions ceased. Rage blanketed Ash's face while his chest heaved in silent gasps.

Mack swallowed loudly beside me. "I think I'm gonna be sick."

I didn't spare him any words of comfort. The slashes weren't enough to prove he'd framed Tommy. "It's not done yet."

On cue, Ashton retreated to where he'd begun the evening and exchanged one invisible object for another. This one he considered for a long moment, then returned to where Tina's body had been found. He circled the space twice, then knelt down and began making double-handed chopping motions in the air. Judging by his face, the movement required a bit of exertion. He repeated the motion several more times in different places until he returned to his origination and retrieved the previously discarded object. He glanced around nervously, then exited the scene.

"What did I just watch?"

"Ashton Carr mauling his wife with what I would hazard to guess is an impressional." The grisly things had been outlawed for decades, though a few turned up on the black market from time to time. How Ashton Carr, of all people, got his hands on such a superior model was something I very much looked forward to asking him.

"That's... that's..."

"Grounds for a warrant." I held out a data tab with a request already drawn up. "Think you could get it expedited?"

Mack took the device with shaking hands. "His own wife. What a horrible way to die."

I arched an eyebrow. "What do you think the odds are Ashton Carr has both items still in his possession?"

He shook his head. "You did it. You actually did it."

"And I think that warrants a cup of coffee."

Mack glanced at my untouched cup of the precinct's own standard brew. "I could run over to HoT D."

I tapped the device in his hand. "I appreciate the offer, but I'd rather you get this on the books."

He nodded once and hurried off.

I stared at the empty scene of the alleyway for another minute and closed the file.

Tommy is going to be free.

Elijah

The key was halfway to the lock when I paused. I placed my hand beside the door, and a blue light shone through the glass, lighting up my palm.

"Atlas, activate security protocol Mr. Darcy."

"Security activated. Have a good day, Dr. Bennett."

I chuckled and pocketed the officially obsolete key. That would never get old. Josh might find it odd that I wanted the verbal interface, but it freaked me out to have things silently being done. I also didn't understand the need for security in the first place. However, Josh had been adamant in his message the other day that I use the system every time I entered *and* left the house. The whole thing was overkill as far as I was concerned, but if it made him happy, then I was willing to go along. Of course, it would have been a lot easier if he was also coming home, which he wasn't.

I let out a sigh and began the walk into town. It was one thing to give him space to deal with the unexpected arrival of his mother; that also gave me a chance to catch up with Eric and everything going on with the pack. It was an entirely different thing to go three days without more than a vague message flagged as *urgent* to lock the doors. Either way, I was done waiting around. He still had a job to do, and so did I.

I rounded the corner on my way to the precinct and spied the very man I was looking for walking towards me. By some miracle, he seemed not to have noticed me yet, so I took advantage of his distraction to truly appreciate what a fine specimen he was. His trademark vest and knee-high boots clung to the deep crimson button-down and trousers that might as well have been painted on. Having had the pleasure of peeling him out of said clothes, I could testify how accurate the sentiment was.

"Elijah." The surprise in his voice held what I hoped were hints of joy.

"Hey, moonbeam." His face broke into the brightest grin. I fought hard to rein in the impulse to kiss it off him. Of all the different versions of Josh I'd gotten to know, smiling, laughing Josh was my favorite.

He cleared his throat. "What brings you here?"

My lips twitched. "Someone still owes me breakfast."

His left canine sank into his bottom lip, tempting my resolve to leave him be. He seemed to think for a long moment before he freed the captive lip and offered me a more tentative smile. "I was on my way to Hair of the Dog. Care to join me?"

I checked my bio-clock. "A little late in the morning for your caffeine fix."

His smile gained strength. He stepped forward and into my bubble. "Maybe I have something to celebrate." The sultry purr wrecked my senses. This man absolutely did it for me, and if the dilation of his eyes was anything to go by, the feeling was mutual.

Stars, I hope it's mutual.

"I could be persuaded."

He arched an eyebrow and resumed his walk towards the dubiously named cafe.

We were only a couple of blocks away when a familiar scent tickled my nose. I blinked and stared at Josh's receding back, then down the side street we'd just passed. The scent was definitely coming from down there. It was faint, but I'd thought about that unusually bland smell far too much to ever mistake it.

"Is something wrong?" Josh looked back at me from several yards ahead.

"I smell something."

He rolled his eyes. "What is it with werewolves and smells?"

I didn't bother to respond. Instead, I took a few steps down the adjoining street. The scent grew stronger.

"Where are you going? Last time I checked, HoT D is that way." He pointed over his shoulder in the direction we'd been traveling.

"But I *know* that smell." I took another step. "Just give me a minute."

"Elijah..." The warning came a second too late.

I sprinted after the trail, though it took every ounce of focus I had to follow the meager scent. It wasn't a strong smell in the first place, and it was definitely a few days old. I skidded past a door, and another scent captured my attention with the force of a tidal wave.

Josh.

I quickly backpedaled and reconsidered the unassuming door.

Josh came careening around the far corner just as I opened the back entrance to the apartment complex.

"Wait!"

The shout followed me up the stairs as the intertwined scent of Josh and the masked man led me onward. All the answers I'd been seeking were here. I'd finally know once and for all.

The door lock popped free with a sharp turn, and I stepped inside without a second thought. This was absolutely the source. My nose led me through a minimal kitchenette that looked untouched and a modest living space that seemed equally neglected until at last I found myself in the bedroom. The scent was strongest here. It was also where the trail ended.

Josh's scent saturated the space. It was a wonder I'd been able to pick up the other at all. This was undoubtedly where he'd been staying. Throwing daggers lay clean and polished within easy reach of the nightstand. A handgun case sat open on the dresser. Clothes draped neatly over a chair. Nothing stood out. Nothing gave me any sort of clue why those two scents would occupy the same space.

Then my gaze fell on something dark in the closet. My feet seemed to have a will of their own as I moved toward the shadowed space. It was exactly as I remembered it. My fingers closed around the sensuous silk a second before Josh crashed into the doorway.

"Don't."

I let out a laugh. "I knew it. I fucking knew it. You *are* him." I looked back at Josh, and victory surged in my chest. "I was right."

"Elijah."

"Your secret is out, Joshua Hart." No wonder I'd been so drawn to him when we met; I'd technically already started the bonding process the night before when he'd been disguised as the masked man. His gaze darted behind me so fast I nearly missed it. I turned back to look into the closet to see what had snagged his attention.

"We were getting breakfast, remember?" Josh asked, his tone uncharacteristically strained.

"What other secrets do you have squirreled away in here?"

"Elijah, please."

My head snapped back up at the desperation in his voice. "Wait, *are* you hiding something?"

"Elijah…"

"What is it?" I searched the closet for whatever could have him in such a state, but there was only an old-fashioned box suitcase with a bronze placard. I squatted to get a better look and was immediately confused. "Whose is this?"

The color drained from Josh's face. "This isn't how I wanted you to find out."

Anger surged through me. Had he been lying about being with someone? I grabbed the suitcase and brought it over to the dresser. It smacked into the furniture hard enough to make the drawers rattle. "*Whose* is it?"

He licked his lips and then met my gaze. "Mine."

My brows snapped together, confusion replacing my anger. "This says Harker."

"I know."

Joshua

"Your last name is Hart." Elijah's voice was cold and distant.

How could I have forgotten the security spells? I never forget the security spells.

"Hart—" My voice broke, and I had to try again. "Hart is my father's last name."

He narrowed his eyes. "What is *your* last name?"

"My name is Joshua Hart. You know that." There was no reason to be evasive. It was already too late. But a desperate part of me wasn't willing to accept that this was the end.

Why didn't I tell him the truth sooner?

"Damn it, Josh. What is your *family* name?" He slammed the damnable chest down on the dresser again so hard that it popped open. Inside were all the tools of my trade, none of which were government-sanctioned.

Elijah stared into the velvet-lined box. Wolf pommeled daggers older than the United States rested in the center. Each one polished to a sheen and capable of slicing through anything in its way. Pockets filled with all manner of death lined the top, including leftover raven feathers and one empty syringe.

"My family name is Harker."

He pulled out one of the dark feathers. "Harker," he whispered. His gaze slid past the feather to stare at the daggers that haunted countless lycan stories. "You're one of *the* Harkers."

"Elijah," I stepped towards him.

In the blink of an eye, he freed one of the silver-plated daggers and had it at my throat. "How many of you are there?"

I froze. If the blade so much as broke a single layer of skin, I'd be dead in seconds... then so would Elijah. I may deserve the excruciating death the dagger would offer, but Elijah didn't.

"Answer me."

My eyes flicked down to the blade where it hovered a swallow's breadth away from death. I didn't even dare to breathe.

He let out a roar of rage and flung the dagger across the room with enough force that it embedded itself in the wall. "How many!"

"My mother and I are the last."

He staggered back. "Sweet Goddess, it's true. You really are one of them."

My heart ached at the complete look of betrayal in his eyes. "I'll tell you whatever you want to know."

"How long?"

"That's a really—"

"I don't give a new moon how broad a question it is! Answer every variation you can think of."

I swallowed hard and did exactly as he asked. "I've been trained to hunt werewolves my entire life. I arrived in Adler Springs the day of the bacchanal. And I—"

"The Bacchanal." He glanced at the mask now lying discarded on the floor. Memory played across his face, then the sting of betrayal poisoned it. "You did something to Tommy."

It wasn't a question, but I answered it anyway. "Yes."

"What did you do to him?"

"I injected him with a toxin that induces Mein Zeke, but I... I didn't know that's what it did until a few weeks ago."

"That's your excuse? You didn't *know*?" The sinister reproach slithered down my spine. "Keith is dead because of you. And Tommy... Stars, if I hadn't been bigger than Tommy, then I would have ended up just like Levi. And Zeke is fucking missing. Did you do something to him too?"

My heart constricted. I had no idea how close Elijah had come to being one of my victims. I also could only assume he was referring to the wolves I'd targeted in the woods. "Elijah, I..."

"Stop. Stop saying my name."

I recoiled. The silence became heavy, crushing me deeper into the floor with each miserable second that passed.

"Did you bond me on purpose?" The quiet question turned my blood to ice.

"That's not how—"

"I'm aware that's not how it works. But moon sickness is hereditary, and you seemed to have gotten around that. Answer the fucking question. Did you bond me on purpose? Are you using me?"

"No." I longed to say more, to offer an explanation, an excuse, anything to absolve me of my sins. But there was nothing in this world that could do that. Much as it hurt me now, I knew what I'd been doing, and I'd done it anyway.

He ran a hand through his hair, conflict written in every line of his body. His gaze landed on the open box once more.

I should have destroyed that thing long ago.

"Bennett." I stepped forward, willing to do or say whatever it took to earn his forgiveness.

Fire burned in the depths of his cognac eyes as they snapped back to me. "Don't touch me."

A pain I'd never known lanced through my chest. "Please." I barely had breath to give voice to the final desperate plea.

He spared the room another once-over, but his gaze didn't touch me again. "Don't come near me again." He lingered a moment, his gaze boring a hole through the floor, then stormed out.

It was done. Elijah knew the truth.

Now he was gone.

Forever.

Chapter 35

Elijah

I couldn't go home, not when it smelled like Josh. Not when it smelled of betrayal. There were so many more answers I needed, but first I needed to be able to breathe.

I abandoned the trek home, veering instead towards the spring I'd met Eric at only a few days ago. Was that all it had been since I'd told my lifelong friend that I was completely in love with the man I was bonded to? The man who had just plunged a dagger into the very heart he'd stolen.

My legs gave out, and I fell hard to the ground. Twigs and stones tore through my jeans to bite sharply into my knees. The pain was minimal compared to the one coursing through my chest. How could I have missed it? How could I not have known? I clenched my hand.

This whole time he's been lying to me.

But had he?

Josh chose his words carefully. He always had. How many times had he told me the truth, and I'd been too distracted to hear it? Too lost in him to realize what he *wasn't* saying?

He'd told me he wasn't the person I thought he was, had hinted at dark secrets, evaded concrete answers even when I pressed. He'd asked if it was okay to like this. At the time it had been silly and kind of sweet, but now it meant something else. Had he really been asking permission from me? And when he'd said he didn't deserve me, it had nearly broken my heart. Except now I knew the truth about who he was, *what* he was. And yet, there was still this part of me that couldn't reconcile the monster with the man I'd come to love. Still loved.

My fingers curled into the sodden earth while anger and confusion warred inside me. Suddenly, the wolf was taking control, and for a moment I hated it as much as hated the truth. The wolf had never had any hesitation about falling head over tail for Josh. How could it not have known? What good were instincts if they couldn't protect me from this unbearable heartache?

A spasm in my arm sent me crashing to the earth. Fire pricked my skin as the wolf urged a transformation in response to my distress. Every bone cracked and ached as it found somewhere else to be. But not even the excruciating pain of the change could fully eclipse the pain of learning who Josh really was, what he'd done.

He can't be that monster. He just can't be.

In my mind's eye, his eyes danced with humor while his lips curled in a seductive grin. A spike of pain shot through my chest. I curled in on myself. The cracking of my spine ricocheted disconcertingly off the nearby water. Leaves and twigs embedded themselves in my swiftly growing coat. Claws dug into soft soil as I fought an entirely different agony.

I love him.

My breath came out in a harsh gasp as the final phase of the shift finished, leaving me in a huddled mass on the forest floor, shaking from more than just exertion. I struggled to find my feet, weaker than the change had ever made me. Finally, I stood staring down at the torn earth.

I'd known Josh was a killer from the start. I'd even found it an impressive quality. But being crazy good at his job was one thing; hunting down lycans for sport was an entirely other.

Renewed fury swept through me as I pictured his face devoid of expression, not even a hint of remorse for the atrocities he'd committed. Just how many of my kind *had* he murdered over the years? A growl vibrated through my chest and frightened several birds into flight. Then I was running.

Pure rage fueled my limbs as I tore past spring growth and evergreens alike. A distant part of my mind remembered how much Josh's eyes reminded me of the forest. I shoved the memory away and pushed harder. The lingering cold burned in my lungs. Low-hanging branches whipped against my face. Not even the ones that drew blood gave me pause.

Still I ran, desperate to escape something I would never outrun. No matter how much ground I covered, the bond shone brilliant inside of me, incapable of being extinguished by anything short of death. At last, I skidded to a halt in a small clearing. My sides heaved as I struggled for breath, then I lifted my head to the sky and gave voice to the heartache.

Joshua

I forced breath after breath into my tight lungs, but it wouldn't come. Elijah was gone. He knew the truth. And I was pretty sure the only reason he hadn't stabbed me with my dagger had been because it would have killed him too.

My gaze darted over to the wolf-head pommel sticking out of the wall. Elijah had thrown it so hard I wasn't even sure I could get it out. Not that I wanted to, I'd loathed the things from the moment they'd been bequeathed to me, a moment still branded into my memory.

It was my thirteenth birthday. I hadn't been allowed to have any friends over. Not that I had any to invite. My mother made a big show of the day being particularly special, though she wouldn't tell me why. My eyes had gone wide with wonder when she'd brought out a large present. It wasn't even the fine wrapping or the size of the box that had filled me with awe. It had been the fact that I couldn't recall her giving me a gift before.

I'd carefully pulled apart the expensive trappings, equal parts excited and terrified of what might lie within. When the last slip of paper drifted to the floor, revealing the bronze plate engraved "Harker", I'd looked at her askance.

"This is who you really are," she'd said. "And it is time you came to embrace that."

My hands had shaken as I lifted the lid to reveal the twin daggers polished to a reflective sheen. Dread settled in my bones. These were the weapons of hunters; they'd been in countless stories my mother had told me over the years. Stories of death and destruction. Stories of pain.

I'd always believed them fabrications. Who would ever *want* to hurt the lycans with their incredible ability to change their shape and their beautiful wolf forms? They were creatures out of legend and so much more than human. And yet, despite that, I'd reached out to grasp the pommel. The moment my fingers had brushed the metal, cold settled over me, along with the stench of death.

"No," I hissed aloud, banishing the memory. Never again.

Without a second glance or even a thought for the security spells, I followed Elijah's lead and left the room. Whoever found the damn things could take them for all I cared. The demented blades belonged in a forgotten crypt.

The town passed in a blur on the journey to my mother. Every face was as indistinguishable as the next. There was only one face that mattered, and he'd made it very clear he never wanted to see mine again. I stumbled and caught myself on the wall. A quick glance showed that I'd finally reached my destination.

My rapid pace took me past the astounded desk clerk. I didn't need to inquire about the room number. There was only one place Beatrice Harker would be—the one and only penthouse suite. I skipped the elevator and stormed up the stairs. The strenuous climb would hopefully curb the rampant energy screaming at me to kill the bloody woman.

Air burned my lungs as I ascended to the final landing. The emergency door swung open on silent hinges only to slam shut with a clang that echoed down the hall. Not even the plush carpet could swallow the harsh sound. Stealth was officially out of the question, but the noise served a better purpose.

A nearby door opened to reveal my mother in voluminous skirts of crimson with a gold-embroidered bodice to match. Society would call her appearance timeless and eclectic. I knew the truth. The woman was stuck in an age long past. A woman out of time with ideals and the prejudices to match.

"Have you come to your senses?"

I growled and pushed past her into the room.

She sniffed and closed the door.

For a split second, every instinct in my body screamed at me to run, that I was trapped. I schooled the impulse as I had every other time and turned to face the woman who had made my life a living hell.

She smoothed the ridiculous folds of her extravagant skirts, her skeletal fingers creating lines in the otherwise smooth fabric. "You had best have a good explanation for your rude entrance."

"I quit."

Her head snapped up from her absent perusal of her intricate attire. "What did you say to me?"

"You heard me. I. Quit. I won't do your dirty work anymore."

She arched an overly manicured eyebrow and stepped closer. Instantly the smell of death wafted around me, the sickly scent curling unpleasantly in my nose.

My resolve shook. This endeavor was pointless. I'd never be free. Then a vision of Elijah, his eyes filled with a bottomless hurt, filled my mind. I clenched my hands at my sides and took a step back.

Surprise registered briefly in my mother's eyes. As quickly as it arrived, it vanished, and her mouth settled into a grim line. "You are a spoiled child that has never wanted for anything. This is how you repay me? You ungrateful wretch. How *dare* you spit on your ancestors this way?"

I gritted my teeth as the all too familiar degrading words washed over me. "I wanted plenty. And I paid for everything I had in blood and death." With my very soul. All for the distant hope of approval from a woman incapable of giving it.

"You will fulfill your obligation to this family or suffer the consequences."

"No."

She drew up to her full height, which rivaled my own. "You dare defy me? I, who brought you into this world? I, who let you live? A mistake I have come to regret with every miserable breath you take. You are a coward and a failure, just like your father. A dismal disappointment. I should have been rid of you when I had the chance."

"Then consider yourself liberated. I'm done. I won't kill for you anymore."

She snarled, and before I could react, her bony fingers were tightening around my throat. "It would have been cheaper to have you both killed at the same time."

The force of her words hit me like a physical blow. My chest became hollow, only for despair to fill the void. My father wasn't a coward. He'd fought for me and lost. Now she was going to kill me, just like she'd killed him. Water filled my vision as a sharp scent of chemicals stung my eyes.

"Coward. Weakling." Her grip tightened as she slammed my head repeatedly into the wall she'd pushed me against.

Black spots exploded in my vision. My lungs screamed for oxygen while my fingers scrabbled uselessly against her hold. Powerless. I was powerless. Just as I had always been.

"You're going to watch me destroy these creatures you find so dear. One by one they'll all die, torn apart by their own tooth and claw. And there won't be a damn thing you can do to stop it."

Elijah.

Images of his cocky grin and easy way of being assaulted my mind. Memories of his tender touch, the passionate way he spoke about his work, his laugh that could disperse even the darkest of clouds. He'd die to protect his pack.

He'll die.

I stopped pulling against her hand. Without the resistance, the full force of her assault slammed into my abused windpipe. The world went dark. Then I was bringing my arm down on hers. It made impact, and the pressure vanished.

Air flooded into my deprived lungs in a painful rush. I gasped and staggered out of her reach.

Her hands hung like talons by her side, her face a mask of fury and shock. "I'll see you dead," she hissed.

I gently massaged my throat. "You're welcome to try. My training far outstrips your own. You made sure of that."

Her lip curled in blatant hatred.

I took another step back and away from the door. A mental inventory of the weapons on me flashed through my mind, coming up nearly empty. There were two daggers nestled in the back of my vest and the firearm securely fastened to my thigh. Any movement toward either would be instantly recognized.

She flicked her wrist, and I darted to the side, narrowly evading a tiny dart she'd hidden in her sleeve. She screeched a sound of pure rage and twisted around to obtain a more substantial weapon.

I took the opening and raced past her. The door shut behind me just in time to be met with a solid thunk of something hitting it from the other side. I stepped away and looked down to see a dagger protruding through the barrier, dangerously close to where my heart had been. The point gleamed wicked sharp in the light and was undoubtedly poisoned. I didn't hesitate to race for the stairs. Another dagger embedded itself in the wall by my head. I kept going, my feet pounding down the steps.

Whatever it took, I had to warn Elijah.

CHAPTER 36

Elijah

WEARINESS SEEMED ETCHED INTO my bones. After hours of running, my body was exhausted, but it didn't come close to the heaviness in my heart. Eric and some others showing up fully transformed had just been the icing on an already miserable day. I couldn't even pretend I didn't know why they were there. They'd come because I'd called. Any wolf within ten miles would have heard my grief crying over the trees.

There's no way Conrad won't hear about that.

I disarmed the security and entered the house.

How much worse can this day get?

I ran a hand through my hair. The tie, along with the rest of my clothes, had not survived the sudden shift. Thankfully, I'd been able to find something passable at the House before venturing back towards town. The last thing I needed was to add an arrest for public indecency to my already shit day. A drink was definitely in order. Or even better, the entire bottle, maybe two.

The hall opened onto the living room. At the familiar sight of dark hair poking over the sofa, my feet froze and my heart skipped a beat.

Josh surged up from his seat and spun to face me. His hair stuck up in a disheveled mess, his clothes were far from pristine, and dark circles shadowed his eyes. Then my gaze dropped to his throat where purple bruises that were well on their way to turning black mottled his fair skin.

Worry shot through me. It hadn't even been a whole day since I'd seen him last. What the hell had happened? Were there other injuries I couldn't see? How severely was he hurt?

I stubbornly shoved the impulse to care for him, to protect him, far away. Josh didn't need my protection. A growl rolled out of me. "I told you I didn't want to see you."

"I know. I can leave after I talk to you."

"I don't want to hear anything you have to say."

"Elijah, just listen—"

"Don't call me that," I snapped. It hurt too much. It reminded me of midnight whispers that I'd deluded myself into believing hinted at love. What a fool I'd been. I turned away from his stricken face and fought to regain my composure. "Get out."

"Listen first. I'm trying to warn you."

I barked a laugh. "Warn me about what? That you're a killer who hunts lycans for sport? Or that I could wake up with a dagger between my ribs?"

"No. Yes. She..."

"There's nothing you can say to make this better. You lied to me. Maybe not outright, but you intentionally hid the truth."

A loud thump came from behind me. It probably wasn't smart to have my back to Josh, but I couldn't bring myself to look at him either. It hurt too damn much. That soft, dark hair, those lips that gave such sweet kisses, eyes that held the forest. I growled again, this time at myself.

"Were you ever going to tell me the truth, or were you just going to let me keep believing that this might actually work?" Silence met the question. I tightened my hands into fists. "Answer me! You owe me that much at least."

Still nothing. Furious, I spun around and gasped.

Josh knelt on the floor, his fingers clawing at his throat. The coffee table lay knocked askew. Streaks of red where his nails had scratched the flesh added to the purple that now extended past the ugly bruises to dip below his collar.

"Josh!"

He looked up at the shout. His lips moved, but no sound came out. Panic filled his bulging eyes.

I raced to his side and pulled him into my arms. Now that he was closer, I could hear him gasping for air. "What is it? What's wrong?"

"Warn... warn..." His face turned a deeper shade of purple.

I was painfully aware of the bond connecting us. It twisted and warped, pulled too tight until it became this terrible thrum of darkness, discoloring the light. I shook with the force of it and struggled to make sense of what was happening. Suddenly I knew, the same way I'd known I'd bonded to him. Whatever Josh was trying to say was literally killing him.

"Stop talking. Josh! Breathe!"

He shook his head. "Warn you... she... the pack..." Desperation shone in his eyes as he used the last of what little breath he'd stolen to get the words out. Then I saw it. He knew he was dying. And he believed whatever he was trying to tell me was worth his life.

I growled and shook him. "Oh, no, you don't. You die, I die, remember?"

Already, I feared it was too late. His skin was clammy to the touch beneath the layer of sweat. His eyes struggled to stay focused. Shaking wracked his body, and still the bastard was trying to talk.

I was mad, yes. I was torn and heartbroken, but I didn't want him to die. Not even because it would kill me. I didn't want him to die because I loved him too much to let him go. "Are you trying to hurt me?" I didn't expect it to work. It was a last-ditch effort based on a promise I didn't understand.

To my shock, air rushed into his lungs in a ragged gasp. First one, then another, and another. He coughed and continued to fill his lungs. Finally, he pushed away to look at me. His eyes were still bloodshot from the lack of oxygen, and his color was only just returning to normal. "I have to—"

I clapped a hand over his mouth to stop the words. His skin was slimy to the touch as if he were sweating out some kind of toxin. My jaw twitched as I glared back at him.

His eyes begged me to let him go, to finish trying to speak.

I shook my head, and tears fell freely from the corners of his eyes. "No. Whatever you're trying to tell me, stop. You're killing yourself."

More tears slipped free.

"Let's try this again. I'm going to ask you questions and you're going to answer them. Is that understood? If at any point you try to say something and your throat closes up again, you will stop talking *immediately*. Nod if you understand."

He gave a small nod, and I slowly peeled my hand away. His mouth instantly opened.

"You will answer *only* the questions I ask."

His mouth snapped shut.

"Do you need water?"

"No." The word was barely more than a rasp.

I rolled my eyes and rocked back on my heels. "Do you *want* water?"

His gaze flitted away from me to land on the ground.

I stood and wiped the filmy residue from his skin on my borrowed pants. I'd be burning them for sure. "Answer," I demanded.

"Yes," he croaked, still not meeting my gaze.

With a sigh, I retreated to the kitchen. There I poured a hefty shot for my frazzled nerves and retrieved the reluctantly requested water. The liquor burned its way to my belly, but offered none of the solace I sought. When I returned, Josh was still huddled on the floor. "Get up."

He shrank in on himself.

I let out a frustrated huff. "On the couch. Now."

Without a word of argument, he pushed himself to unsteady legs and stumbled to a seat on the couch, where he accepted the water with shaky hands. For a second, I was afraid he wouldn't be able to hold it, but he managed to take it without spilling any. He grimaced as he took a tentative swallow.

The cushion sank beneath me as I took a seat beside him, my gaze glued to the gruesome marks encircling his throat. "Who did this to you?"

He stiffened as my fingers approached his neck and remained staring straight ahead.

I dropped my hand and sighed. "Where did you go after I left?"

He took another careful sip. "To see my mother."

The ragged state of his voice raked on my already raw nerves. He needed rest, not an interrogation, but I needed answers. "Why?"

He stared into his glass. "To quit."

"I take that it didn't go well."

He flinched when the tips of my fingers brushed the sensitive skin beside his Adam's apple.

His mother *did this to him?*

"What did she tell you?"

His mouth opened, and not a sound emerged. He closed it and shifted in his seat. When he opened his mouth again, I wasn't prepared at all for what came out. "She killed my father."

Despite how angry and hurt I was, my heart still broke for him. "And now she wants to hurt the pack? Probably with whatever you used on Tommy and Keith," I hazarded a guess.

His gaze snapped to mine, then darted away again. He gave a sharp nod and took another drink.

My head flopped back on the couch. "Fuck."

While my mind spun with this latest horrible news, he sat in perfect silence like a stone, careful not to cross the invisible line separating us. When I finally stood, he followed suit, placing his empty glass on the table. I grabbed it and took it to the kitchen, needing an outlet for my restless energy. He'd almost made it to the door in the five seconds it had taken me to put the glass in the sink.

"Where do you think you're going?"

Confusion flashed across his face. "You said you didn't want me here."

My heart twisted. I did want him here. I'd always want him here, but I didn't know how to look at him anymore without seeing a killer—without seeing a *Harker*. "I want you where I can keep an eye on you. And I *don't* want you anywhere that woman can try to finish what she started. I'm selfish about my life that way." It was a cruel thing to say, but it was also the only thing I could think of that he wouldn't argue with.

Josh paled, the blood draining from his face only highlighted how grisly the marks were in contrast.

The wolf inside snarled. Given half a chance, I'd kill her myself for touching him. Her own son. The woman didn't have a right to call herself a mother, let alone continue living.

Once again I shoved the instinct to protect my mate deep as it would go. "Follow me." I turned on my heel, fully expecting him to follow, and led him to the guest bedroom. I pointed at the bathroom on the other side of the hall. "First things first, you're going to get cleaned up. I have no desire to smell whatever you're exuding when your scent returns. I'm going to get you a change of clothes and fresh towels. Everything else should already be in there."

Joshua

Elijah walked out of the bedroom, leaving me alone. I still couldn't wrap my head around it. He wanted me to *stay*? On some level, it made sense in the "keep your enemies close" capacity, but it obviously wasn't easy for him. That much was painfully apparent in the way he looked at me... or didn't.

I glanced around the guest room. It was one of the few spaces I hadn't been in, and it definitely didn't appear used. My swallow caught painfully in my throat, a physical reminder of how truly awful this day had become.

She killed my father. She tried to kill me.

There had never been any love lost between the two of us, but like a child, I'd hoped that maybe someday I could at least attain some level of acceptance, maybe even pride. The truth that she'd been ready to have me killed was a bitter pill to swallow.

I wandered into the bathroom in a daze and began removing my weapons. The firearm joined the only two daggers I had on my person. My fingers closed around a tiny vial tucked snugly into one of my many hidden pockets.

I pulled it out and stared at the potion designed to hide my scent. The backup had become necessary when I started staying the night with Elijah. The meager supply was only a stopgap to get me from here to the apartment. At best, the contents would last a few hours. Considering I was now basically under house arrest, that was going to be a problem; my scent gave away too much, especially around Elijah.

If I parse it out and am careful with my activity, I might be able to stretch it longer.

Footsteps sounded in the hall. I quickly stuffed the potion into a small drawer beneath some hand towels.

"Clothes are on the bed. These should be enough for now." Elijah placed a pair of folded towels beside my pathetic assortment of weapons, but didn't leave. He continued to stand there, his gaze like a hot poker boring into my heart.

Am I supposed to strip and bathe beneath his watchful eye? Is this how little he trusts me now?

"Hand it over."

The sudden demand startled me, as did how completely devoid of emotion his voice sounded. Uncertain, I reached for the daggers.

"I don't want your weapons. Hand over the potion."

Trepidation shot through me. Not that. Anything but that.

He shook his hand impatiently. "Now. I'm done with the lies and half-truths. While you're here, I won't abide hiding. I know you have a backup. Now hand it over."

I pulled open the drawer and took out the potion, then placed it in his expectant hand. Before I could plead my case, he unstoppered the vial and poured the contents down the sink. My heart sank as the precious liquid disappeared.

"Is there anything else that could obscure or alter your scent?"

"Not with me."

"Good. Now, the healing tonic."

My fingers trembled as I pulled out a similar vial and held it out. I'd intended to save it for an emergency.

He crossed his arms without taking it. "You're going to drink as much of that as it takes to heal your neck."

I licked my lips. The bruises were uncomfortable, but they were no more than I deserved.

"Did I stutter?"

The stopper came free with a pop. I raised the vial to my lips and drank. The cool liquid sparkled in my throat. I stopped at a quarter and lowered the bottle.

"More."

"It's enough."

"I can still see the bruises. More," he insisted.

I swallowed another quarter.

"Better. Put your clothes outside the door. I'm going to put them through the wash before what is likely to be a terrible smell suffocates this house." He spared the weapons on the counter a glance and left.

Chapter 37

Elijah

A week passed with Josh basically staying locked in the house. I wasn't sure how he accomplished that with an active investigation, but all things considered—including his homicidal maniac of a mother—I also wasn't about to bring it up. He occasionally ventured out of the guest room I'd tossed him in, but he always returned. That was seven days of seeing him walk around in a stupor. Seven days of smelling him struggle to control his responses. Seven days listening to him fight with unseen demons as he slept. Seven days of not touching him, even though he was right there.

And it was killing me.

I rested my head against the wall and stared at the guest door. Every single night it had been closed, and every single night I'd found myself outside it. The door wasn't locked. I knew, because I'd tried it... every night. He wasn't keeping me out, just keeping himself away.

None of how I was feeling made sense. I knew who Josh was now, *what* he was. The wolf inside, however, refused to accept the truth. The Josh we'd bonded to wasn't that man. He was more.

I dug the heels of my palms into my eyes. Josh was too many things, and I couldn't get them to mesh together. How could I still love a man who'd done the things he had? How could I still want to protect him? Care for him?

The imprint of fingers around his neck flashed before my eyes. I bit back a growl. The moment I'd seen them, everything else had fallen away. All I'd wanted was to hold him and take the pain away. Then I remembered the wolf-head daggers nestled in their creepy box lined with velvet the color of blood. There wasn't a lycan alive who couldn't recognize those. Just as fast as it had vanished, the betrayal came rushing back.

Then... then he'd almost died. I clenched my hands into fists on my knees. Josh had been willing to sacrifice his own life to warn me about what his wretched mother was going to do. A bitter part of me wanted to call it short-sighted. If he died, so would I, but a larger part of me recognized the attempt as selfless. He hadn't been trying to save me—he'd been trying to save the entire pack, or at least what was left of it.

I sighed and dropped my hands to the ground. There just weren't simple answers where Joshua Hart was concerned. I adjusted my seat in search of a more comfortable position on the floor. After six nights of this, though, there really wasn't one. My hand slipped on the hardwood and brushed against something hiding in the small gap beneath the door.

I frowned as my fingers registered the terrycloth of a towel. When pulling it out didn't work, I tried pushing it through. It stuck for a moment, then came free on the other side. Instantly, a bitter draft of air carrying a host of smells rushed through the small gap. My heart constricted sharply in my chest, and I gasped at the intense sorrow and hurt choking Josh's scent.

An overwhelming sense of selfishness threatened to break me right there. In less than twenty-four hours, Josh had lost everything. He'd learned his father was murdered. His own mother had tried to kill him. His mother, whom I was certain had been controlling him his entire life. He had nothing. And he'd still risked his life to warn me.

"I'm such a fucking asshole," I groaned to myself.

I pushed up from the floor and slowly opened the door. The towel he'd obviously tucked into the gap slid free. It took a moment for my eyes to adjust to the near-pitch black. When they did, my guilty heart sank further. A cracked window let in the last cold snap of the season and made the room bitterly frigid. Candles that he must have filched from other parts of the house littered the chest of drawers, along with a pile of spent matches beside them. They were dark now, but it all came together to paint a terrible picture. Robbed of the only means to keep his scent masked, Josh had sought other ways to keep his pain to himself.

The bed sank beneath my weight as I sat on the edge. Josh lay huddled and shaking beneath the sole comforter the room offered. If the window had been closed, it would have been enough. I brushed the hair back from his face. It was too dark to tell, but I was positive that in the light red would rim his eyes.

His shivering ceased as the warmth of my touch suffused his nearly frozen skin. He released a deep sigh, then blinked his eyes open. In a heartbeat, he was as far away from me as the bed would allow, his back firmly pressed against the wall. His gaze darted past me toward the open door.

"I tried to keep it to myself."

His words broke my heart. He'd chosen to suffer in silence—alone—in an attempt not to hurt me anymore than he already had. The situation may have been twisted beyond repair, but that didn't make it right. The bond undoubtedly meant that Josh was my soulmate. It also meant that I was his.

I brushed a thumb across his cheek. "I know." He sat perfectly still as I stared at him. I cupped the side of his face and slowly brought my lips to rest on his. A small spark of what I could only describe as hope flared in his scent. I curled my hand around the back of his neck and deepened the kiss. I needed him, would never stop needing him. Every inch of me craved his touch. I felt empty and untethered without it. Our tongues tangled, and I moaned into him, desperate for more.

Josh pulled away with wet lips and looked at me askance. "Are you sure this is what you want?"

"Yes." I leaned forward to recapture his mouth and paused. "Is this what you want?" He hesitated, then nodded. I closed the distance, stopping shy of his lips. "Words, Josh. Say it."

"Yes." He paused, and I could sense his hesitation before he said, "I want this. I want you."

His words filled a hole inside me and ignited something I'd been trying my damnedest to ignore this past week. I pressed my lips firmly against his while my hands sought more of him to touch. I curled my fingers beneath the hem of his nightshirt and gently removed it, then tossed mine aside as well.

A groan slipped free when Josh's fingers curled in my hair. I pulled him tight against me, craving the skin-to-skin I'd been denying myself. The heat of my body quickly banished the cold plaguing his.

"Elijah." His whispered moan settled deep into my core. It didn't matter how mad or conflicted I was, Josh was my whole fucking world and that would never change.

Joshua

Coming undone in Elijah's arms wasn't something I'd ever thought I'd get to do again. Nor was lying in his bed with him curled around me. The warmth of his touch may have been something I'd come to need, but it couldn't last. He'd wake up and remember who I was, then I'd have to watch the regret fill his eyes.

Better to leave now.

I slipped free of the sheets and pulled on my sweats. It would be a cold march to the freezing guest room, but I'd survive. I always survived.

"What do you think you're doing?"

My hand stilled on the door handle. "Going back to my room."

Elijah's aggravated huff drifted out of the darkness. "This *is* your room, and *this* is your bed. Now get back in it."

I hesitated. He said that now, but would it hold come morning? The night had been surprising and tender, but that didn't make it a reconciliation. Forgiveness for the things I'd done didn't happen overnight.

"And you can ditch the pants."

My hands trembled as I did what he asked. The moment I was beneath the sheets, his arm encircled my waist and he pulled me tight against him. "Are you sure?"

He nuzzled against my neck, and I shivered. "I already told you yes." We lay in silence for a few heartbeats until he sighed heavily. "You're not going to go back to sleep now, are you?"

I didn't have an answer for that. Anxiety coursed relentlessly through my veins, robbing me of the little rest I'd stolen. I didn't deserve this peace or this comfort. "How can you ever forgive me?"

He squeezed me tighter. "I don't know. But I'm going to have to figure it out because I can't live without you. I *won't* live without you."

"I could stay away. You don't have to do... this."

Elijah sighed again and brushed a kiss on the back of my neck. "Do you know what happens to bonded werewolves that are kept apart?"

"No."

"They still die, Josh. Not quickly or violently, but slowly and painfully. They lose the will to live."

My heart thudded hard in my chest. No matter what I did, I would always be the end of Elijah. "I didn't know."

"Not many people do." He ran a warm hand along my arm before wrapping it once more around me. "I miss you. And no, that's not because of the bond. I miss *you*. I miss your laugh and your smile. Your dry humor and quick wit."

"Elijah."

"Let me finish. I miss the way you let go and the small ways you touch me that I don't think you realize you're even doing. It hurts me to see you in pain, and while I don't know how or if I'll ever be able to move past the things you've done, I want to, because I want all of that back."

Every fiber of my being wanted to believe this was more than the bond talking.

He placed another kiss on my neck, then my shoulder, and finally my ear. "I need to know if you want that too, because I can't be the only one fighting for this." He snuggled into me, his nose buried in the crook of my neck. "Don't say anything now. Sleep on it. We'll talk in the morning."

I lay perfectly still, even further away from sleep than when I'd tried to slip out. As Elijah slowly relaxed into slumber, my resolve returned. Whatever it took, I would atone for my crimes. I would become the man Elijah deserved.

Elijah

When I awoke, the bed was empty. I rolled over and groaned.

Why did I say all of that?

Because you're in love with him and can't let him go.

I shouldn't have pushed, I continued to argue with myself as I pulled on pants and wandered into the morning.

My feet shuffled along, then stopped at the edge of the kitchen. I blinked in surprise at the image of Josh leaning against the counter, nursing a cup of coffee. Stupidly, I looked towards the guest room and back at him. "You're still here."

He shrugged and gestured at two full mugs sitting on the counter. "I made you tea and coffee. I wasn't sure which you would prefer this morning."

I approached the cups and stared into them. He'd prepared both exactly the way I liked.

"They're not poisoned, if that's what you're wondering."

My gaze snapped up. "If I were worried about you killing me, I'd have taken your weapons. Not that it would matter. You don't need daggers or poisons to kill me."

Surprise flashed across his face, and the hint of a smile twitched at the corner of his mouth. "I wondered about that."

I grabbed a mug without looking and took a sip. The tea was absolutely perfect. "You weren't in bed this morning."

Anxiety hedged his scent as he set his cup down. "I had trouble sleeping. I didn't want to wake you."

I snorted and took another large sip. "A lot on your mind?"

"You could say that."

"I did say that. And I asked you a question."

He winced. "Yes. I had a lot to think about and even..."

"Even what?"

The pause in anyone else wouldn't have been noticeable. On him, it spoke volumes. "Even being warm, it was difficult to find sleep."

I finished the last of the tea and switched it for the coffee. It seemed that was as close as I was going to get to Josh admitting he found comfort in my presence. "I owe you an apology."

"You don't owe me anything. Not after—"

"Would you let me speak?"

His mouth snapped shut, and he plucked his coffee back off the counter with an expression that bordered on petulant.

"I wasn't the only one who had an incredibly shitty day."

He opened his mouth to protest, and I held up a hand to forestall him. His mouth pinched in frustration, and he blindly refilled his cup.

When I was sure he wouldn't try to interrupt again, I continued. "Yes, I learned some... less than pleasant things about you, but you also learned some pretty awful things about your family. Not to mention your mother tried to kill you." Even after last night, I still couldn't seem to shake the image of purple fingers imprinted on his neck.

"Call it karma."

I set the cup down hard enough that coffee sloshed over the brim. "Having your mother nearly strangle you to death is *not* karma. On top of which, I'm almost positive she's been manipulating you your whole life."

Josh rolled his eyes. "If saying that makes you feel better, then go ahead, but no amount of manipulation will ever excuse the things I've done."

Just as I feared, he couldn't see it and wouldn't accept that not all of his actions had been his own. "I don't mean the standard completely-destroy-your-childhood-and-raise-you-to-be-a-mindless-killer." He flinched and looked down. "I mean, magic. Spells."

His head snapped up. "Why would you think that?"

"Because of the way you smelled."

"Seven hells. Werewolves and smells."

"So help me, if you don't stop interrupting, I'm going to sit on you until you hear everything I have to say."

He snorted a laugh, then seemed to realize what he'd done and quickly squashed the humor.

I let out a heavy sigh and walked around the island separating us. He refused to meet my gaze, but I didn't let that stop me from continuing. "When your mother called you that day, your scent took on a weird smell, almost like decay, but sweeter. That same smell was on your clothes after you showed up here. I may have fibbed a little. I didn't put them in the wash right away. I waited. Sure enough, the same cloying stench clung to them. Have you never smelled it?"

Josh's face was as pale as I'd ever seen it. "I have."

"When?"

"I just... I always associated it with my mother. Maybe I assumed it was a perfume?" He didn't sound too sure of that.

"You're telling me you've always smelled death around your mother?" It was almost too heinous to believe. Now I was even more glad I'd swapped the soap in the guest bathroom with the anti-hex soap I'd ordered from the high-end apothecary in Portland.

He nodded. "For as long as I can remember. Definitely since my dad... my dad..." Josh's face turned an alarming shade of green, and he lurched over to the sink where he promptly lost all of his morning coffee. The hiss of water hitting the basin nearly obscured Josh's continued retching.

I rubbed his back as he viscerally came to terms with this latest level of horror. Finally, he rinsed his mouth and straightened up. My hand fell away as he stepped out of reach.

He dropped his head back to stare at the ceiling. "That still doesn't... it doesn't... Compulsion spells only work if the recipient would still do whatever they're being compelled to do. It doesn't change the fact that I'm the one who killed all those lycans, the one who hurt Tommy."

I shook my head. How was I supposed to forgive Josh when he couldn't even forgive himself? "She used you, Josh. You were a child, you didn't know any better."

"I haven't been a child for a long time. What's your reasoning for that? I get you'd like an easy excuse for why I've done the things I have, but face it, *I* did them."

I ground my teeth together. Fine, he wanted a different approach, so be it. He wasn't the only one who'd spent too much time thinking. "How many have you saved?"

"What?"

"How many lycans have you saved? I know how many, legally at least, you've killed. I want to know how many you've saved."

He turned away from me. "What makes you think I know that number?"

I grabbed his arm and forced him to look at me. "Because I know *you*. How many *weres* have you spared? *Weres* like Tommy, like Leah and Nemo? Lycans wrongly accused of crimes because of prejudice."

"Nine hundred and seventy-eight."

"Damn." It was all I could say. His kill count was outrageous, but that number put it to shame.

Josh shook me off. "That still doesn't change the ones I didn't save. I've still killed more lycans than any other member of my family."

The man was stubborn to a fault. "You've also saved nine hundred and seventy-eight more than anyone else in your family." He huffed again, but didn't argue. "And we're going to push that over a thousand, because you're going to save the Klamath pack."

"And how am I supposed to do that? I can't even tell you what she's planning without dying."

"Then don't. Tell me what *you* would do."

Josh blinked once, and then his mouth curved into a smile. "You're fucking brilliant."

Chapter 38

Joshua

"You don't have to listen to this," I repeated for probably the hundredth time.

Elijah shook his head and took another shot of whiskey. If werewolves didn't have such a high metabolism, I would have been worried. As it was, the man had certainly earned a few hard shots. "No, keep going. I want to know what we're up against."

I stared at him for another long moment before returning to the plan. Sketches and data tabs covered the dining room table. Finding a way for me to warn him without saying exactly what my mother had planned was tricky, but if being unable to tell a lie for the last thirteen years had taught me anything, it was how to sidestep boundaries.

"When I spoke with her about the toxin, she mentioned they were developing a stronger version. The night I infected Keith and…"

"Levi." Elijah winced and eyed the half-empty bottle.

On the one hand, I hated putting him through this. On the other hand, it felt so good to finally be completely honest with him. It wasn't easy by any stretch. I still had moments where I instinctively altered responses, but we were making it work. And if I was being honest with myself, that gave me hope.

"Right, Levi. They turned on each other almost immediately. And you say that on the night of the full moon it was worse?" I couldn't imagine anything worse than watching a fully grown lycanthrope tear apart one of his packmates in a matter of minutes.

"The full moon heightens whatever we're feeling. That's part of what makes moon sickness so dangerous. Tommy went from depressed to hyper to willing to kill his own brother in the span of an hour. Now who's to say if Kale didn't do or say something to set him off? The point stands that it doesn't take much. You've said yourself how Tommy's emotional state seems to be all over the place."

I nodded, recalling his flood of words and inability to hold still. "And you still can't find Zeke? Was that his name?"

Elijah shook his head. "We found him, but he was talking gibberish. I think most of the pack that saw him assumed he was just on a bad trip. Conrad sent him home to sleep it off, and no one has found him since."

"It was likely shock. He witnessed the whole thing, but I didn't infect him. He ran."

"Is that why you didn't shoot him too?" A current of anger ran beneath the words. This was another one of those hard-truth moments.

I met his gaze as levelly as I could. "I didn't shoot him because I didn't need to. The goal was to sow chaos. His running into the heart of pack territory with the infected Keith hot on his trail, in theory, would have accomplished that."

A muscle in Elijah's jaw ticked.

"You should also know that I used twice the dose on Keith and Levi."

"Why?"

"My mother thought that using raven feathers as a delivery method was stupid and wouldn't work. I was determined to prove her wrong."

Elijah stared at me for a long moment. "She's a terrible person, Josh."

I looked away only to have his fingers curl around my chin and turn my face back to him.

"And I cannot believe I'm saying this, but the raven feathers were inspired. I was part of the team that was sent to survey the scene. We would have noticed syringes. Even in all that blood, they would have stood out."

I bit my lip to stop the smile that wanted to dominate my face. Finding a unique way to deliver a toxin that resulted in two deaths was not something to be proud of, yet hearing the accolade was still nice. No one ever commended me for my work. Not my mother, who apparently loathed my very existence since day one. And not my colleagues, who were likely too afraid to say anything. That was except for one.

"You never told me what you talked to Remus about or how he guessed."

Elijah pointedly looked away. "He, uh, has a sister who's bonded to a selkie. Said he recognized the look."

My brow furrowed. "You have a look?" How had I not noticed a look?

"Aren't we supposed to be working on a plan of attack? You're deviating."

"Fine. Don't tell me," I grumbled. I may have been in the doghouse, but it still wasn't fair that *I* had to answer all of his questions and he didn't have to answer any of mine.

Elijah made an aggravated noise deep in his throat and shifted to face me. "He said I look at you like you hung the damn moon. Are you happy? Now can we please get back to how on Earth we're going to stop your psychotic mother from killing my entire pack?"

I blinked, taken aback, and then refocused my attention on the table where I had laid out the few weapons I'd come here with.

Do I look at Elijah that way?

I shook off the thought and poked at the firearm. Mercifully, it was loaded, but I would have felt more comfortable with at least a dozen more blades. "The rest of my gear is at the apartment."

"No, you're not going anywhere near that place."

"Excuse me?"

"You heard me. There is no way I'm letting you go back there. What if your mother is waiting?"

"I can handle myself."

"Look, the soap you've been using for the last week and a half may be helping to purge you of whatever spell your mother put on you, but I don't trust that she doesn't have access to another dose."

"You're being—"

"Unreasonable? Go ahead, say it. You and I both know you won't be able to. She's been dosing you with compulsion for nearly twenty-five years, and from what you've told me, she regularly ups the hits. You're not going to that apartment. End of story."

"But my weapons..."

"Those daggers belong at the bottom of the ocean or, better yet, in hell along with your mother."

I huffed in frustration. "Then what do you expect me to use? I've trained my whole life to use daggers. I almost feel naked without them. And for the record, I wasn't talking about *those* daggers. The only time I've ever used those detestable things has been in closed training with my mother." I snatched a datatab off the table and pulled up a lunar calendar.

Tension tightened in the room until at last Elijah broke the silence. "You really don't enjoy killing lycans."

"I told you before, I don't have to like my work to be good at it."

Elijah's warm hand coasted over the top of my thigh. I glanced over the data tab, my anger abating. His gaze met mine. "I just... I need to hear you say it."

My hand ventured down to rest on his. "I don't take pleasure in killing werewolves. I never have."

He squeezed my leg lightly, then withdrew his hand. "When do you think she'll attack?"

I spun the tablet around and pointed at a day. "If it were me, I'd do it then."

"That's the full moon."

"Exactly. You mentioned your pack prefers to start the shift before moonrise. A handful of infected wolves could destroy the rest of the pack mid-change if they timed the attack right. Maximum effect, minimal effort."

Elijah's complexion took on a gray cast. "I need to warn the others."

"I could be wrong."

"But you're probably not."

Elijah

I could not believe I was doing this. I would much rather have been with Josh and Officer Mack arresting Ashton Carr. What I wouldn't give to see the look on that prick's face as Josh slammed a pair of ionic cuffs on him. Alas, the safety of my mate took precedence over seeing slime like Carr get his just deserts. If Josh thought he needed more daggers, then I would get them.

Caution tempered my desire to run in and out as fast as possible. Josh had mentioned protective spells on the door to keep out nosy neighbors and other potential threats. Frankly, it was a miracle I hadn't died the first time I was here. He'd also mentioned he hadn't reactivated them when he'd left, but that didn't mean someone else hadn't.

I tossed my key at the door and immediately felt like an idiot as it bounced back unaffected. Naturally, a security system that recognized biological lifeforms wouldn't give a new moon about an antique key. I took a deep breath and reached for the handle. My fingers curled around the knob, and nothing happened. I let out the breath I'd been holding and stepped inside.

Everything was exactly as it had been before. Even the dagger I'd thrown was still stuck pommel-deep in the wall. I wiped a suddenly sweaty hand on my jeans and walked over to the box. The lid sat open just as it had been when I left, the remaining dagger glinting wickedly in the faint light.

I growled at it and kept looking. It didn't take a genius to put together that Josh kept only things he associated with his family's demented mission in that box. The daggers he wanted were ones he'd had specially made for his actual job.

I looked around the room for likely hiding places. Then it occurred to me. Josh wasn't ashamed of these daggers and wouldn't have felt the need to hide them. He would have put them somewhere that mattered, somewhere easily accessible.

I walked over to the nightstand and pulled the drawer open. There weren't any daggers, but there was a thin band of fabric. Curious, I pulled it out. The moment my fingers touched the material, I recognized what it was—my hairband from the night we'd been stormed-in.

"Sly bugger pocketed it."

I shook my head in amazement and used the tie to pull my hair back, then resumed my search. Under the bed yielded the same results. The closet bore no fruit either. That left the dresser and the rest of the apartment. I didn't for one second believe he would have put his daggers as far away as another room. The second drawer in the chest proved to be the right one.

I pulled out a slim box sealed with a bio-lock. The man certainly liked his tech. Unlike the monstrosity sitting on top of the dresser, this box was elegant in its simplicity. No frills, expensive wood, or pretentious engraving. Just sleek metal that could probably withstand a nuclear fallout. Prize in hand, I checked the time. If I hurried, I might still make it to see Ashton Carr finally get what was coming to him.

Joshua

Tommy had to sit in jail for five extra days all because of me and one insignificant signature. Of course, I could have caught the mistake earlier if my entire life hadn't fallen to pieces in less time than it took water to boil. Being under house arrest and "working from home" hadn't helped either.

"It was an honest mistake." Mack's continued attempts at consolation were becoming irritating. Tommy needed to be free and far away from here before the full moon.

"I'm not generally in the habit of making mistakes." Unless, of course, you counted the unexplained and unsanctioned deaths of fifty-plus lycanthropes.

"All that matters is that we've got him dead to rights. Look at it this way. All that extra time let Tommy catch up on some reading."

"So he's been doing okay? You've been checking on him?"

Mack gave me a stupid grin. "Admit it, you like the kid."

"I'm responsible for him."

"Yeah, but not even *nice* cops are as considerate as you've been with Tommy."

"Are you ready to arrest Ashton Carr, or are you going to continue prattling off inane questions? Perhaps the response was terser than the situation warranted, but I couldn't help it. Thanks to my stubborn insistence, Elijah was on a mission to retrieve my daggers, a mission he'd casually announced before sauntering out the door this morning. I wouldn't be at ease until he was back in my sight, safe and unharmed.

As if reading my mind, Mack asked, "You sure you don't want to wait for Red? I thought for sure he'd want to see this."

On cue, the door to the precinct flung open, and Elijah dashed inside. "Did I miss it? Am I too late?"

I smiled as relief flooded through me. "We were just about to head out."

Mack coughed beside me, and I turned to look at him. He less than discreetly pointed towards his mouth as his gaze flicked over to Elijah.

Well, fuck. Guess that answers that question. The whole precinct is probably wondering why I'm smiling like a damn idiot now.

Sure enough, a quick glance around revealed several curious faces. I sighed and rolled my eyes.

To hell with it.

I walked up to Elijah, heedless of the gossip that would undoubtedly sprout. "Were you able to find them?"

Elijah's grin broadened. "I was. Though I was tempted to burn the whole place to the ground."

"What are you talking about? Burn what to the ground?" Mack asked, popping up beside me.

"My apartment. Elijah was retrieving something for me. Come on, we have a man to arrest."

"But he didn't actually burn it to the ground, right?" Elijah winked at him and fell in step beside me. "But you didn't, right? Because that would be arson," Mack insisted.

I looked at Elijah out of the corner of my eye, and he leaned close enough to whisper in my ear, "Someone smells relieved."

"Shut up, or I'll make you sit this out. Believe it or not, I don't actually need an excuse to lock you up with Tommy."

He snorted. The back of his hand brushed mine, sending a jolt of electricity through me. His snicker wasn't soft enough for Mack not to hear.

"What's so funny? Please tell me you didn't commit arson, Red."

Elijah turned to address the young officer. "I solemnly swear that I did not commit arson...today."

I glanced over my shoulder in time to see Mack's pole-axed expression and laughed.

The door vibrated beneath my third knock. The local patrol verified that Carr was definitely still home, and his reluctance to answer was making me anxious. I counted to ten and lifted my hand to knock again.

The door ripped open to reveal a disheveled and unshaven Ashton Carr. "What do you want?"

I quirked an eyebrow at his attitude. "Won't you invite us into your home?"

He sneered back at me, sparing Elijah an especially loathing look. "I don't think I will. I've already let you, and that...mongrel, in already. You got your info. Now fuck off."

If he thought insulting Elijah or blatantly airing his speciesism was a good idea, he was mistaken. A dagger was in my hand with barely a muscle twitch.

Mack and Elijah both surged forward as I brought the tip to bear beneath his weak chin. Luckily for Carr, I'd cleaned the wolfsbane off days ago.

"Here's the thing. I don't actually need your permission. Just goes to show what asking nicely accomplishes."

"You can't just barge in here."

"Can't we? Mack, show him the warrant."

"W-warrant?" Carr swallowed hard, a poor choice considering how close the blade was to his skin. A thin rivulet of red streaked down his neck to disappear beneath his twisted collar.

"That's right. We have a warrant to search the premises."

"W-what do you expect to find? I already gave you all of Tina's files."

"Yes, Mr. Carr, and while those files led to a rather eventful evening, I believe your cooperation was a pathetic attempt at a red-herring."

His eyes widened. "What's a red herring?"

"A red herring, Mr. Carr, is when you intentionally mislead someone by providing false clues. Now you're going to apologize to my partner for your bigotry and step aside." In one swift move, I cleaned and re-sleeved the dagger.

His hand shot up to his neck, which had suffered no real damage short of his own stupidity, and glared at me. "I'll see your license revoked."

I smiled. "I'd like to see you try. Apology, Mr. Carr. This day can go much worse, I assure you."

Finally, he growled something that might have been an apology and moved out of the way.

I stepped inside, quickly followed by Mack and Elijah, as well as a host of other uniformed officers.

A warm hand on my lower back steered me to the side. "You didn't have to do that," Elijah whispered in my ear.

I turned and cupped the side of his face. "But I wanted to." I dropped my hand before anyone could note the intimate contact and fished out a sealed container. "Do you think you can find the weapons he used?"

Elijah looked from me to the blood sample. After a moment of hesitation, he took it and unscrewed the cap. He set off on his search, and I rejoined Mack.

"Are you going to try telling me there's nothing going on between you two again?"

I took in his challenging expression and laughed. "No, I won't. You're a talented detective, Joel Mack, and I have thoroughly enjoyed working with you."

His challenge melted into surprise. "Thank you. I've enjoyed working with you too. But nothing says we can't stay in touch just because the case is over. I mean, we're friends, right?"

I stared at his outstretched hand, then smiled and clasped it with my own. "Friends."

"Found them!"

We both looked up at Elijah's shout. A moment later, he rounded the corner holding a homemade set of talons attached to a pole, the illegal impressional, and most important of all, he was wearing gloves.

I turned to face a shell-shocked Carr. "Aston Carr, you're under arrest for the murder of Tina Carr and for the framing of Thomas Grant. Officer Mack will read you your rights."

"You can't do this to me!" Carr screeched in fury.

Two officers restrained him while Mack continued to cite his rights. The ionic cuffs glowed eerily in the gloom.

"That beast was fucking my wife. They both deserved it." Spittle flew from his lips as he continued to rage. "Animals, the lot of you!"

HART'S BETRAYAL

Elijah stepped forward, heedless of Carr's fury. "Next time, use bleach."

Ashton Carr let out a mindless roar which was promptly cut short as the resident witch on the force slammed him on the chest with a hard hit of sedation. His entire body went limp, and only the two officers already holding him prevented him from crashing to the ground.

"Was that entirely necessary?" Mack asked the witch.

"Probably not, but would you have done any differently?" I answered for her.

Chapter 39

Elijah

Eric shot Josh another hateful glare as he walked past. Maybe it had been a mistake telling him what was really going on. He'd fluctuated between blatant disbelief and loathing looks, not to mention firing barbs at Josh every chance he got. And it was getting ridiculous.

I grabbed Eric's arm before he could get too far and forced him to look at me. "You need to stop."

His anger set his brown eyes ablaze. "Stop? How can you say that to me? He's a moonforsaken *Harker*. He hunts guys like us just for existing. And it's wrong that I'm not okay with that? How are *you* okay with that?"

"When did I ever say I was okay with any of this? I'm a fucking mess right now, but we have bigger problems. Like I don't know stopping his psychotic mother from trying to murder the entire pack. And for the record, while you're on your high horse, he almost died trying to warn us."

"You should have let him."

"You did *not* just say that to me."

Eric's rage deflated, and he sighed heavily. "Shit. Sorry, man. This whole thing is just so... *fucked*."

"You think I don't know that? I'm howling with you, brother, I am." My mind flashed to the run and subsequent howl I'd inspired when I'd discovered the truth about Josh. Eric had led the group that had found me and had refused to leave my side the entire day. He was a great friend that way, but right then, I could have used a lot less of the angry on-my-behalf bit. "Besides, you're forgetting it's his psychotic mother who's the root of all of this. She's been magically manipulating him since his father died. A father *she* had killed. He's had a harder life than either of us can fathom. So ease the fuck up."

Eric rolled his shoulders and looked away. "It still doesn't change the fact that he's the one who struck the blow. It doesn't change *who* he is."

I huffed in frustration. "Now you sound like him. I get it. This is hard. Don't you think I know how fucking hard this is? But it's not exactly like I can walk away."

Eric speared me with a look. "And if you could?"

I hesitated. Even if I *could* walk away, if there was no bond holding me, I doubted I would. I was just too deep for the man.

"That's what I thought." Eric pulled his arm free and resumed his stalk out of the clearing to check on the others.

I ran both hands through my hair and looked over at Josh. It was easy to blame the bond for everything—why I was here, why I wanted so desperately to forgive him even if I had no clue where to start—but deep down, I knew it was more than that. I knew Josh, the *real* Josh, the one I was positive no one knew, maybe not even him. And *that* man did not hunt lycans for sport or out of some age-old grudge fed by centuries of hatred. *That* was the man I was hopelessly in love with, with his warm laugh and eyes that glowed, his silly quirks and enough compassion to move mountains. That was the *real* Josh. It had to be. Because if it wasn't, I had no idea how I would ever forgive him. For the things he'd done to lycans. For the things he'd done to my pack.

As if sensing my thoughts, he turned to look at me. Things were undoubtedly strained between us despite the peculiar truce we'd established. Of course, it didn't help that I believed he was *still* hiding something from me. He'd stayed true to his word and answered every question I'd asked, but either I wasn't asking the right questions or he really didn't want me to know, because the hint of a secret was still there in the sad way he looked at me. The way he was looking now.

Assuming we all survived this, we'd have to have a serious conversation about his being more forthcoming with information without my having to pry it out of him. Whatever he was withholding, it couldn't possibly be more earth-shattering than learning he was a mythical werewolf hunter.

I took a step towards him, and he immediately averted his gaze. Tension lined his shoulders, and every instinct inside of me was screaming to do something about it, to protect my mate at all costs. It was already abundantly obvious that I couldn't stay away even when I tried. The hardest truth to accept was that I didn't *want* to stay away. I wanted to take his pain and comfort him over the renewed loss of his father, to help him grieve the mother who had used him like a puppet. He may have despised her, but she was the last family he had. And I hated seeing him hurt. I hated it more that he was doing it all alone.

Moon, help me, I still love him so much.

One way or another, I'd find a way to forgive him because I couldn't live without him, and didn't want to. But first, we had to see tomorrow.

We could die today.

I shook my head. No, we would survive. We had to. There were still things I needed to say to him.

Eric stomped back into the clearing. How many times had the two of us been here? It was where we always met and where I'd changed ever since my dad's passing.

"How was the call? Is everyone all right?" It was a sad excuse for a peace offering, but it was all I had.

"Everyone is fine. But I had to talk to Conrad. He's super pissed."

No surprise there. He hadn't taken the news well that the entire pack couldn't shift like normal. It had gotten even worse when Josh had essentially ordered the entire pack to remain sequestered in the secondary warehouse. The one further into pack territory than the one we'd used for the Bacchanal... one that Josh wasn't supposed to know about.

"He can be mad all he likes, as long as he keeps the others far away." I worried he'd do something brash. That was exactly Conrad's MO. In the end, it took Josh threatening to arrest him for obstruction to make him tuck his tail and concede.

"He'll make you pay for this." Eric shook his head, though I doubted it was in sympathy.

"I don't care what he does to me." We both knew there was quite a bit Conrad could do to me. Though most likely, he'd banish me. It would certainly solve most of his problems, and he wouldn't even have to get his hands dirty. Exile might normally have been a horrible death sentence for a pack wolf, but he didn't know about the bond. I could survive banishment as long as I had Josh. Josh was my pack.

Eric scowled, his frustration with my obstinacy growing. "You know how to stop all of this. You don't have to keep taking his shit. If you would just challenge for Alpha..."

Josh's head snapped around. It was something he'd hinted at wanting to know more than once. I'd given him the same flat reasonings as I'd given Eric over the years.

"I'm not having this conversation *again*. Not here. Not now. We have much bigger problems than Conrad being a dick at the moment."

Eric snarled back as we stood toe to toe. For a second, it seemed like Josh might interfere, but then he calmly resumed his weapons check as if my best friend wasn't openly baring his teeth at me. We stayed locked in the standoff until Eric finally huffed and went back to glaring at my mate.

This is fucking ridiculous.

"How do you even know this is going to work?" Eric's challenge lashed across the clearing.

Josh straightened after checking the daggers in his boots. There was no telling how many he had on him. I assumed all of them. "I don't."

"Then why are we out here? Why *here*? This could all be for nothing."

Josh stared back blankly. "It could be."

I barely didn't growl. Josh's unflappable stoicism was not helping. This was a solid plan built on what he knew about his mother and his own twisted training. "But if it's not?"

Eric spun on me. "Then he's risking your life. And for what? A crazy vendetta with his mother?"

Josh bristled, his anger spiking through his scent like thorns while his eyes flashed dangerously. "*I* am supposed to be the bait, *not* Elijah. If I thought for even half a second that the stubborn man wouldn't fucking follow me out here, I'd insist that he shelter with the rest of you. I tried to prevent him from coming." He gestured wildly in my direction. "You see how well that went."

And he had tried. He'd done everything short of begging me to drive far away and change in another forest. But as with the hunt in North Carolina, there was no way I was letting him do this without me.

"Of course he came. Poor fool is fucking bonded to you."

Something flickered across Josh's face, gone before I could place it, but he didn't look surprised at what Eric had said. "Some things are out of my control."

Eric took an angry step towards him. "Oh yeah? Was it out of your control when you fucked him in the first place?"

The scent I'd come to recognize as guilt mixed with shame slammed through Josh's scent with the force of a tidal wave. At first, it had started off oddly sweet, and I'd feared that all our efforts to liberate him from his mother's control were for naught. But as the days had gone by with him locked in the house, the smell had soured like fermenting apples, until now it was the sharp scent of vinegar burning my nose and stinging my eyes. And there was no way Eric didn't smell it too.

"Enough." My firm demand, laced with Alpha influence, echoed off the trees. "Go change." I hated to do it, but we didn't have time for this. The cords in Eric's neck bulged, and his body shook as he fought the order. He struggled for a solid minute before finally caving. "He's trying to help. Back off."

Eric's sharp glare cut to me. "He's going to get you killed."

My gaze swept over Josh, who seemed determined not to let Eric's words get to him. If his scent was any judge, he was failing miserably. Truth be told, I wasn't worried about Josh getting me killed. I was much more worried about Josh getting himself killed. A moot distinction as far as Eric would be concerned, since my life was irrevocably tied to his.

"Worry about yourself. Don't let *anything* hit you," I reiterated for what felt like the hundredth time.

Eric scoffed and rolled his eyes. He was one of the fastest members of the pack and sneaky to boot, but his lack of concern was troubling.

"Don't be flippant. I don't care if it's a moonforsaken feather. Nothing." Josh winced, but I kept going. "I promise you, whatever stuff this lady is packing is going to make what happened to Keith look like child's play."

Eric paled slightly. "G-got it."

While I was relieved that he was finally taking this more seriously, I didn't like frightening my friend. "Go on. You should get changed. Moonrise will be here before you know it."

He nodded and turned to leave, but not before shooting Josh another hateful glare.

I let it pass. We'd already wasted too much time. When I was positive he was far enough away, I approached Josh. "Moonrise is less than an hour away."

Josh nodded and continued to fiddle with his weapons. "He's right."

"Stop it."

"If I hadn't come here, if I hadn't... You wouldn't be in this mess."

"And I wouldn't have met you."

"Difficult to categorize that as a positive given the current situation." His dry dissemination got my hackles up.

"We've talked about this. We'll work on mending things when this is over." *When you're safe.*

"I... I know." His hands stalled in their ceaseless movement. "There's something I should probably tell you. Just in case."

I grabbed his shoulders and forced him to look at me. The same sadness that had haunted his eyes for weeks looked back at me. "Don't you dare talk to me like you're planning on dying."

"Elijah—"

"No. You die, I die, remember? Do you want me to die?"

He swallowed hard and shook his head.

"Words."

"No." The word came out more of a croak, but it still settled me. I'd been too scared to ask before, but it was such a relief to hear him actually say it.

I pulled him into a tight embrace, mindful of the weapons adorning his body.

He buried his head in my neck and squeezed back just as hard. The sour scent of guilt was completely gone now, replaced with something infinitely worse—fear.

I placed a kiss on the side of his head, and his death grip loosened.

I have to tell him. I can't wait any longer.

"Josh, I—"

The crash of undergrowth cut me short. In the blink of an eye, Josh was three paces away, a dagger in each hand. Another loud crash echoed through the small space, followed by a crack. There was a breath of silence, then a blast of gray fur erupted from the treeline.

Josh tensed, but didn't take aim.

The wolf was almost on top of us before I finally recognized Eric. His feet pounded into the earth as he closed the distance in record time. At the last possible second, he altered course and veered back into the forest. He brushed so close he stirred the air in front of me. My heart thudded heavily in my chest. I chanced a glance at Josh, possibly the last one I would ever get.

This was it.

CHAPTER 40

Joshua

THE SLIGHT WHISTLE GAVE it away. I didn't think, just reacted. In one step, my hands collided with Elijah's chest. He stumbled back from the force of the shove, tripped over an exposed root, and went crashing to the ground. The arrow sped through the area he'd been occupying not a heartbeat before. It lodged deep in a trunk, thrumming to stillness as I rounded to face the threat.

The snap of a branch was all the warning I had before yet another gray-shape barreled out of the forest. Unlike when Eric had burst out of the foliage, this one didn't alter course. I let out a curse as a hundred kilograms of pure muscle slammed me into the ground. The daggers in my hands went flying as the force of the fully grown lycan landed on top of me. I immediately brought both hands up to fend off a mouthful of razor-sharp teeth.

The wolf snarled, its serrated teeth on full display. I pushed up, and his jaws snapped at empty air. Undeterred, he bore down even more of his weight and tried again. I struggled to breathe beneath the pressure and his ferocious determination to sink his teeth into my neck. I pressed a forearm into his throat while I continued to fend off a muzzle full of razor-sharp points.

A vicious growl filled the clearing we'd chosen as our last stand. The *were* above me didn't even flinch at the impending threat. Suddenly, his eyes widened, and he lifted slightly. He fought to keep his hold on me, jaws snapping uselessly at nothing.

The weight shift wasn't much, but it was enough. I scrambled out from underneath the lycan in time to see Elijah rip free an arrow covered with wicked barbs from the wolf's side.

The wolf howled in pain and turned to snap at Elijah.

I lurched forward and sank a fresh dagger into a paw the size of my face, then rolled away.

The wolf's head whipped back around at the unexpected assault. I danced out of range, and his teeth clacked together on nothing. Furious, he made to pursue me, only to be pulled backward by the dagger pinning him to the ground. He instantly began gnawing at the slim handle. The metal bit into his gums with each desperate attempt to dislodge it, yet he kept trying.

While he was distracted, I moved to Elijah's side and snatched the arrow from his grasp. I plunged the wicked arrowhead into the nearest tree as hard as I could. Bark cracked at the point of impact. I snapped the head off and tossed the useless shaft aside.

"What the hell?" Elijah asked gruffly.

"It's tainted. He's already infected."

"How is that possible? Everyone is safe." Elijah's eyes went wide with recognition. "Mother of the moon, it's Zeke."

"I thought everyone was accounted for."

He shook his head, still staring at the wolf whose mouth was now painted red. "No one's been able to find him for weeks."

"Fuck." So much for the plan. Whoever Zeke was, all I could hope was that he didn't know where the others were. "We need to reevaluate." A rogue wolf, already infected on top of confronting my mother, was more risk than I'd accounted for. What if she had more?

"No time."

My focus snapped back to the wolf, where it should have been the whole time.

He spat the dagger aside and turned to face us, heedless of the gaping hole in his paw or the gashes lining his muzzle.

Another faint whistle tickled my ear. I pushed Elijah and darted to the side. The arrow embedded itself in a trunk that lined up perfectly with where we'd been standing. Before I could assess the trajectory and determine exactly who the target had been, the wolf lunged again—this time at Elijah.

Damn it.

Loose twigs threatened my balance as I skidded over the ground. A dagger streaked across the distance as I pulled two more and slammed bodily into the wolf's side. The three blades were barely more than a nuisance, but the momentum was enough to knock him off course.

A screech of rage echoed through the trees, and the splinter of another arrow hitting bark cracked through the noise. A quick glance showed the arrow had met a destination nowhere near either of us. I shifted my gaze to look back through the trees and glimpsed a whirl of crimson fending off a gray blur. The wolf surged beneath me, and I released my hold on the daggers. All thoughts of my mother and Eric fled as I focused my attention on the wolf actively trying to kill us.

I set loose four more daggers in quick succession as I retreated.

He dodged two, but the rest met their mark with a thud and an angry snap of teeth. One remained sprouting from his shoulder, while the other fell loose with a shake of his coat.

To my dismay, none of the six daggers seemed to have any effect. Blood poured freely from each wound, clumping fur as it streaked down his hulking form. Twigs and leaves crunched beneath his feet as he dug his claws into the earth and lowered his head between his shoulders. His enraged growl dominated all other sounds, a promise of death in his too-bright eyes.

I took a careful step back, simultaneously palming two more daggers.

His eyes followed my movements, and his growl lowered an octave.

Elijah stepped up beside me, claws at the ready. "How much longer?"

My heart sank at the question. "They're not poisoned."

The statement brought with it an eerie moment of stillness. Then everything shattered.

Voicing his own growl of challenge, Elijah launched himself at the *were*. At the last second, he skidded to the side, much as Eric had done earlier. The expert move narrowly evaded his quick death.

The wolf spun to keep him in sight.

Elijah rushed him again, and the two collided with enough force to break bones. Elijah's claws sank deep, the talons slicing through fur to the muscle beneath.

The wolf released a howl of pain.

Before Elijah could pull free, though, the wolf rolled, taking Elijah down with him. The wolf's action tore Elijah's claws free from his chest, leaving ten more gaping holes for blood to gush out of. Mindless of the blood loss, the wolf pounced on his disoriented attacker.

Elijah gasped as the air was forcibly expelled from his lungs. He struggled to get a hold of the slippery fur and shove the wolf off. Despite the accumulation of grievous wounds, the wolf still wasn't slowing, nor did he show signs of doing so soon. Then the wolf stepped back. Elijah remained on the ground, still too out of it to realize the impending threat.

My heart froze in my chest at the realization of what was about to happen. Elijah was defenseless. He'd never get his bearings in time.

What have I done? He's not a fighter. I never should have allowed him to come.

My feet were already moving before I had the conscious thought to interfere. A frenzy of daggers preceded me as I closed the distance as fast as possible. Some met their mark; others didn't. Twigs crunched beneath me as I fell into a slide.

Elijah let out a grunt when I collided with him just as the wolf lunged.

I gritted past a shout as teeth sank into my right arm, which had taken the place of Elijah's throat. Pain raced like fire through every nerve ending. The dagger I'd planned to sink into his neck met only ruff.

He bit down harder and scraped bone.

My scream finally tore free as he used the captive appendage to toss me to the side. I rolled with the throw and stumbled back to my feet, for once grateful for the obscenely thorough training I'd received over the years. My right arm throbbed and hung uselessly at my side. I shoved the mind-fogging pain aside and pulled another dagger free with my left hand.

Once again, Elijah staggered up beside me, miraculously unscathed. "Are you out of your mind?"

"We don't know if he's contagious."

"That's not—"

I shot him a look and immediately returned my attention to the wolf already bearing down on us.

His body trembled as he squared off scarcely three meters away. Blood pooled in a crimson pond beneath him. Even an allagí anóteros should have been feeling those wounds, but he took a step as if they were nothing more than flea bites. In a burst of speed that should have been impossible, he surged forward.

I snarled and tightened my grip on the cool metal in my hand. A second too late, I realized he wasn't aiming for me at all.

The shoulder of my injured arm slammed into Elijah, once more forcing him clear just in time for the wolf to hit me instead. The world dissolved into a blur of teeth, fur, and pain. Blinding agony eclipsed everything. Claws raked down my side, piercing the protective clothing as if it were paper. My arm screamed in pain as I tried in vain to use it to stave off more teeth from finding a home in my flesh. Saliva dripped down in sticky ropes that made it harder to hold him at bay. His growl vibrated through my entire being like an earthquake, shaking me to the core.

I growled back and finally pulled free my last remaining dagger. It plunged without resistance into the beast above me. Hot blood spilled past my fingers, making the handle slick. The blade sank deeper, sliding between the junction of head and neck. My hold slipped. In a surge of strength, I slammed the dagger home with the flat of my palm.

The wolf shuddered once and collapsed to the side.

I gasped for air, dragging pained bursts of oxygen into my crushed chest, then used the dead body to pull myself up.

"Josh."

I held up a hand to stop him from advancing. "I just need to catch my breath."

He offered a shaky smile. "You did it."

I smiled back at him, relieved to see him unharmed. "We did it."

"You're bleeding."

I barked a laugh. The adrenaline rushing through my system and roaring in my ears was keeping the pain at bay... for now. That wouldn't last, and there was still danger in the woods.

"We should get out of here. Regroup."

I nodded in agreement and took a surprisingly steady step forward. Inexplicable pain blossomed in my torso. My breath caught in a ragged gasp. Elijah's cry rang in my ears. I looked down at the arrow protruding from my chest. The barbed points glistened wetly with blood and an oily substance that was undoubtedly the toxin. I mindlessly took another step towards Elijah and crumpled to the ground.

"No!"

A numbing cold spread from the point of impact. I blinked up to see a fuzzy Elijah hovering over me. I tried to reach for him, but my arm wouldn't listen. Was I lying on top of it?

"Josh."

"Where's Mother?"

"Shh, don't talk." He pulled his shirt off and bunched it around the shaft.

Smart not to take the arrow out. So smart. "Elijah."

He shook his head and pressed against the wound. I felt a peculiar pressure, but that was all.

"Elijah."

"Eric is dealing with her. Now stop talking."

If only I could, but there was still so much I needed to say. "I'm sorry. I never meant to hurt you." I coughed, and wetness coated my lips. I wasn't sure how much of what I was saying was actually coming out, but I had to keep trying. I wanted him to know before it was too late. "Didn't want it to end this way.

"No. You're going to be fine. You were bitten. You'll turn, then you'll heal. You're going to be okay."

I managed the barest shake of my head. "No."

The stubborn man continued to argue. "I know not everyone does, but you will. You'll turn, Josh. The change can save you."

If only that were true.

My hand flopped against his arm, and he looked at me. Desperation swam in his beautiful cognac eyes, clear to me despite the haze that dominated everything else. Those eyes had stolen my heart long before I knew there'd been a heart to steal. "I *can't*. I'm so sorry. Should have told you."

"What are you talking about? I know being a werewolf wasn't at the top of your list, but..."

"Im-mune."

Horror spread across his face. "The bite from when you were a kid. It wasn't a canine. It was a werewolf."

"Wolves *are* canines."

"It's not true."

I coughed wetly. "Can't. Lie."

"Josh, please, just hang on. We'll get help. You can still make it."

I wanted so much to believe him, but more than that I wanted to hold him, to feel his touch one last time. Except my hand wouldn't obey. Already my fingertips were completely numb. "Sorry for everything. Sorry it was me. You don't deserve this."

"Stop. Talking," he demanded, his voice thick.

I tried to move my hand again. This time he took it, his strong fingers wrapping around mine, but not even his incredible heat could warm me now. Everything was so cold. Air rattled in my lungs as I fought for enough breath to say what I'd wanted to tell him forever. What I should have told him every day.

He squeezed my hand tighter, an absent pressure that barely registered. "Please stop talking."

I fought to keep my eyes open. "I love you. So... sorry."

Darkness closed around me, and with it, an even deeper cold that seeped all the way to my bones. All sense of feeling washed away as I fell into its endless depths. The only pain left, the one I carried in my heart.

I love you.

Chapter 41

Elijah

Josh looked up at me with green eyes the color of a summer forest and said two words that destroyed my world. "I can't." The fight, the dead body lying not five meters away, the continued danger that hovered around us—all of it fell away.

"What do you mean?" I asked, unable to mask the strain in my voice. I applied more pressure to the wound, but blood continued to seep past the shirt bunched around the arrow sticking straight up from his chest.

"Im-mune."

"No, you'll turn..." A sob stuck in my throat. "The lycanthropy gene can save you. It just needs time. You have to hang on. You have to..." My words trailed off as his words finally struck home. A memory surfaced, one I suddenly wished to the moon and back that I didn't have. "You said it was a family hunt. Your family hunts werewolves. The bite from when you were a kid. It wasn't a canine. It was a werewolf. And... and you didn't turn." I choked on the truth even as bile threatened to crawl up my throat.

"Wolves *are* canines."

"It's not true. You're lying." Even as I said it, I knew it wasn't possible.

"Can't... lie."

"Damn you, Joshua Hart! Why didn't you say anything? You could have told me. It wouldn't have mattered," I sobbed. None of it mattered now. It was too late. He was dying in my arms, and no werewolf bite could save him. "Please hang on. We can get help. You can still make it. I need you to make it."

His fingers dug weakly into my arm. "Sorry... everything. My fault..."

"Stop. Talking. Save your strength. I haven't given up on you yet, and I don't plan to start now."

His hand fluttered against my arm again.

I took hold of it and squeezed. There was no warmth in him, as if all the heat in his body was leeching out through the mortal wound in his chest. "Please stop talking."

His fingers wrapped weakly around mine. The sadness in his eyes was almost too much to bear, but I couldn't look away. His breath rattled, and drops of blood flecked his lips. "I love you. So... sorry." His eyes fluttered, then closed.

I stared down at him, my heart broken, my soul devastated.

"I love you... so... sorry..."

"No!" My howl split the air. This couldn't be it; couldn't be how it ended. "Josh, please, wake up." I released his hand and shook his shoulders, but his eyes stayed firmly closed. The bond that connected us, once beautiful and bright, darkened and cracked. "No, no, no, no, no. You can't die. You can't! You die, I die. Please, Josh, you have to hang on. I don't want to live without you." The words tore a hole in my chest. Words

I should have told him months ago, words I should have said every day. "Please," I begged, while the tether that bound our two souls together continued to fracture.

I reached for the fraying connection deep inside and held onto it for all I was worth. Josh's chest shuddered with a sudden, labored breath. I held on tighter. "I'm not ready to let you go."

Another breath.

"Hang on." My grip shifted from his shoulders to slip carefully beneath him, mindful of the wicked barbs connected to the arrow discolored with crimson and poison. I tried to stand, and my leg buckled. We both crashed back to the ground. He let out a pained cough that painted his lips even more red. A sob escaped me. "I'm sorry. It's gonna be okay. I've got you."

The crash of undergrowth ripped my gaze away from Josh's pallid features. Eric burst through the trees, still naked from his change back to human form, clutching a pair of pants in his hand. "I heard you call. What hap—" His words trailed off as he caught sight of Josh practically torn to ribbons and an arrow sticking out of his chest like he was some kind of human pincushion. "Oh, shit."

"Where is she?" The last thing I wanted to dwell on was the whereabouts of Beatrice Harker, but she was a danger, as the arrow clearly established.

Eric tore his gaze away from my dying mate. "She... she's gone. Chased her to the north side and lost her. Pocket portal, by the smell."

So she was still out there somewhere. I wasn't violent by nature, but at that moment I wished to the moon and back that Eric had killed her. My hair fell loose in a gray sheet around my face as I shook the morbid thought free. "Give me a hand."

"Red..."

The sympathy in his voice had me automatically tightening my grip on Josh's still form and the bond that somehow hadn't severed. "He's not dead yet." My words were so thick they were barely intelligible.

"I know you want that to be true, but there's no way—"

I shot him a glare, and his words stopped dead. "Are you going to stand there and argue, or are you going to help me save him?"

Eric's hover truck was still technically moving when I vaulted out of the back and lowered the gate. The vehicle lurched to a stop, and I cursed as Josh's prone body slid along the bed. We'd broken the head and fletching off the arrow before loading him, but the remaining shaft still tugged violently on his already shredded torso. The smear of blood coating the metal stood as a testament to how ineffective my attempts to stop the bleeding had been.

Eric hopped out of the driver's side and raced around to help me lift Josh. He glanced at Josh's nearly bloodless face, but wisely kept his mouth shut.

I grunted as Josh's deadweight settled once again in my arms. *Not dead. Not yet. There's still time.* "Run ahead," I said through gritted teeth.

Eric didn't hesitate.

I struggled to walk without overly jostling Josh's body. Blood matted my chest, some dried, some fresh, in some kind of demented shirt to replace the one I'd foregone to stop the bleeding. It lay matted and soaked around the point of impact, serving as a painful reminder of how much blood Josh had already lost.

The crisp, purified air barely registered as I walked through a burst of decontamination. The hospital was a flurry of activity.

Thankfully, Eric had already snagged someone and was leading them over.

"Please, he needs a healer."

The doctor placed a hand an inch above his heart. "It's still beating."

I sagged with relief to hear the confirmation out loud and missed whatever they shouted to the surrounding people. Before I knew it, someone gently took Josh from my grasp, and he hovered horizontally in the air. Someone else began taking his vitals. They appeared in a hologram above him for all to see as they called out stats. He floated down an adjoining corridor, and I moved to follow.

"You can't go back there, sir." The nurse who stood before me was easily half my size, but stood her ground.

"Yes, I can."

"No, you can't. We'll take care of him, but first I need to ask you some questions."

My gaze ripped away from where Josh was about to disappear behind double white doors. "What? I don't have time for this. Let me pass."

"Did you bite him?"

My stomach lurched.

"Sir, I'm going to need you to answer the question. Did you bite him?"

I gestured wildly at the doors sealing shut. "He has an arrow in his chest, and you want to know if I bit him?"

"If you cannot maintain your temper, I will be forced to call the authorities. That bite on his arm didn't get there by accident, which leaves two options—it was on purpose or it wasn't. You two could have easily gotten into an argument and things escalated." The gaze she raked over my blood-covered body made it clear what she believed had happened. "Or it was an intentional turning, in which case I'm going to need to see the requisite licenses. So, I'll ask again, did you bite him?"

I glanced around. Already, hospital security was closing in around us, loosening electroshock weapons and pouches of sleeping dust. "This is ridiculous." The fragile bond faltered in my chest, and my attention riveted back on the doors. "No." There were only a few yards between me and the doors when hands closed around my arms and pulled me to a halt.

"Sir, the local authorities have been called. You will be escorted to a holding room until they arrive."

I fought their hold, desperate to get to Josh. More cracks appeared in the bond, and I tightened my grip on the ephemeral connection. "You have to let me go. You don't understand. Eric!" I searched the waiting area for my best friend and whatever help he could offer. When it landed on him, already fighting off four security personnel, I realized what a vain hope it was.

Eric's savage growl as he pulled against his captors sent other patients fleeing to the far corners of the waiting room. The bond dimmed even further. Hopelessness spread through my chest.

It wasn't enough. We're too late. And I never even told him I—

The white doors whisked open, and a young doctor came running out. "Let him go," she panted.

The security's hold on me tightened. "He's a danger and a disruption, Doctor. ASPD has already been called."

"I don't care what you think he is. He's the only thing keeping that man alive." Everyone looked at each other askance, but the doctor grabbed my forearm and yanked me after her. The doors whisked open once again, and I immediately caught sight of Josh.

The flurry of activity around him grudgingly gave way as the doctor barked at them to let me through.

I ignored all of their curious and judging eyes as I staggered back to his side. "I'm right here. You're going to be okay. Just hold on a little longer." The bond strengthened infinitesimally, and the readout showed his heart flutter.

"What do you think you're doing?"

I looked up to see another doctor approaching swiftly. To my surprise, she wasn't talking to me.

"They're bonded. We didn't even get the patient twenty yards before his life signs began to fail," the original doctor stated, shoulders back and head high.

"This is not the time for your outrageous theories, Dr. Lyons."

"And we don't have time to argue, Dr. Florence. Unless you want to explain to the CoS *and* the UFH why we let a Lycan Detective die on our watch."

Dr. Florence's mouth thinned into a line.

I held my breath, waiting to see what would happen. The microseconds slipped by like tiny eternities.

At last, she turned to the staff that had hooked Josh up to an IV drip and a blood bag while they argued. "Put him in the plague ward and call the healer."

"Healer Constance is already on her way," a nurse responded quickly as Josh's hovering form drifted along once more at a rapid pace I easily kept up with.

Dr. Florence shook her head. "No, we need a healer from the Valens school. Where is Lucas?"

On cue, a man in a pale green doctor's coat with the universal symbol of a healer emblazoned on his chest, stitched in white to denote his school of training. "Right here."

The team abruptly turned right, and I fell back against the wall to get out of the way. Everyone filed into a large room lined with glass, except for Dr. Lyons. She held out a hand to prevent me from following, and the door closed behind them.

"Wait." I pressed against the glass, and magic rippled across the surface.

"They need room to work. Healer Lucas is the best healer on the West Coast. Detective Hart is in excellent hands."

I flashed her a concerned look. "How do you know who he is?"

"All patients are scanned upon admission. Detective Hart has a rather impressive medical policy. I'm surprised you didn't know. Why didn't you tell them you are his bonded partner when you came in?"

I snorted. "Would it have changed anything? He's human. I'm lycan."

She nodded in sad understanding and stepped up to gaze through the glass to watch with me.

I glanced at the demure woman with her bob of brown hair and almond-colored eyes. "Why aren't you in there?"

"I'm technically here in a different capacity."

The glass rippled in rainbow hues as I flattened my hand against it. On the other side, they pulled the remaining arrow shaft free and laid Josh to rest on a bed. "What capacity is that?"

"My specialty lies in lycanthrope medicine. Many of my views are considered controversial and not widely accepted or utilized in modern practice. I'm working to change that."

It was obvious she was trying to distract me from what was going on in the other room. I welcomed anything that kept my thoughts from spiraling around the fear that had taken root the moment the arrow had sprouted through his chest. Bitch had shot him in the back. Who did that? And his own mother, no less.

I glanced down at her. "You're not a lycan."

"No, I'm not."

"So, why?"

Her brown eyes fixed on me. "Because if his bio-chip had registered him as anyone other than who he is, he'd be dead in that lobby right now."

I swallowed at the truth in her words. "That's how you knew about the bond."

She nodded.

Suddenly, there was a flurry of activity in the other room. The door flew open, and Dr. Florence's shout rang through the hall. "Everyone out. Now!" The bodies that had filed in so professionally earlier, now flooded out of the room in a panicked rush.

"What's going on?" My gaze immediately went back to the room.

Josh convulsed and spasmed, his body arching off the small bed, drenched in red.

"You can't leave him." I pushed past two nurses before someone finally got a decent hold on me. "No. Let me in there. You can't let him die."

A hand rested on my arm, and I looked down into Dr. Lyons' calm eyes. "He's not dying. He's turning."

"But... he can't." I looked into the room.

Josh's body continued to convulse into horrid shapes until he fell off the far side of the bed. We waited with bated breath, with nothing but his tortured cries to give us any clue what was going on inside. Then the sounds stopped.

Time slipped by in eerie silence. A soft scrape of claws reached my ears, followed by a hollow ring of metal hitting metal. Without warning, a black shape launched itself over the bed and collided with the glass. The magic strained in colored bursts to meet the ferocity of the attack. Again and again, the black shape struck the spelled surface to get to the people on the other side. Teeth scored the barrier as he refused to admit defeat, mindless in his pursuit to get to the people cowering on the other side.

Dr. Florence stepped forward and smashed a button next to the door.

Mists of white filled the room with a persistent hiss. The large wolf stepped back, snapping at the insubstantial smoke when it got too close. He looked at the glass, his lips pulled back from viciously sharp teeth in an open snarl. Our gazes met, and the snarl deepened. Then he staggered to the side and fell in a heap.

My fingers curled on the glass, and I rested my head against the cool surface. He didn't even recognize me.

"Josh." My whisper was the only sound to be heard in the shocked hall.

About the Author

Sam Bolanos (she/they) is a genderqueer author and founder of Chaotic Neutral Press LLC. They believe in love, equality, and the Oxford comma. When not playing with her three dogs or spending time with her incredible husband, she's probably agonizing over edits or escaping into her latest fantasy.

Newsletter: subscribe
Website: sbolanos.com
Facebook: @sbolanos
reader group: Sam's Sunbeams
Instagram: @sbolanosbooks
TikTok: @sbolanosbooks

www.ingramcontent.com/pod-product-compliance
Lightning Source LLC
LaVergne TN
LVHW040035080526
838202LV00045B/3352